*"I've see*
*you look at m*

"Moira, wanting a man won't send you to hell. It's no sin to have the same feelings and needs that the good Lord gave Adam and Eve."

"Those temptations were the devil's serpent whispering in their ears," she protested even as her body relaxed against his, and she allowed him to slip his arms around her. "Are you the devil, Josiah Chee?"

He smiled. "I'm a man. Plain and simple." Then he lightly brushed his mouth across hers.

Holding her breath at this first kiss of her life, she shut her eyes, and her hands tightened.... In betrayal of her staunch morals, she felt her body come awake, impulsively lift into his, tingle with awareness of every hollow and plane of his form.

"Again," she whispered to him. "Again, Josiah ..."

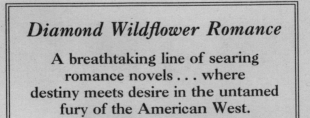

*Diamond Wildflower Romance*

A breathtaking line of searing
romance novels ... where
destiny meets desire in the untamed
fury of the American West.

*Diamond Books by Catherine Palmer*

**GUNMAN'S LADY**
**RENEGADE FLAME**

# RENEGADE FLAME

## CATHERINE PALMER

DIAMOND BOOKS, NEW YORK

This book is a Diamond original edition,
and has never been previously published.

RENEGADE FLAME

A Diamond Book / published by arrangement with
the author

PRINTING HISTORY
Diamond edition / October 1993

All rights reserved.
Copyright © 1993 by Catherine Palmer.
This book may not be reproduced in whole or in part,
by mimeograph or any other means, without permission.
For information address: The Berkley Publishing Group,
200 Madison Avenue, New York, NY 10016.

ISBN: 1-55773-952-8

Diamond Books are published by The Berkley Publishing Group,
200 Madison Avenue, New York, NY 10016.
DIAMOND and the "D" design
are trademarks belonging to Charter Communications, Inc.

PRINTED IN THE UNITED STATES OF AMERICA

10  9  8  7  6  5  4  3  2  1

For Norma and Perry Maples,
whose unconditional love
and constant support
have helped teach me the true meaning of family

# Acknowledgments

No book is the product of one mind or one person's effort alone. Among those who merit my constant gratitude, admiration, and love are:

Tim Palmer, my husband of sixteen years, who has lived with and weighed every word on every page along with me.

Judith Stern, my beautiful editor, who graciously nurtures, emends, and goes to battle for my writing at every step from concept to publication.

Patricia Teal, my super agent, the most optimistic, cheerful, and empathetic woman I know.

My warm and enthusiastic readers, who write to me, call me, laugh and cry with me. Without you, my books would have no life. I love to hear from you! Please send your letters to Catherine Palmer, Publicity Department, The Berkley Publishing Group, 200 Madison Avenue, New York, NY 10016.

# Chapter
## 1

*Lincoln County, New Mexico Territory, 1887*

Moira O'Casey's freshly laundered sheets snapped like whips in the dry breeze that raced down from the Sacramento Mountains. As she stood in the parched, dusty side yard of the adobe ranch house, Moira surveyed the sheets with satisfaction. Spotless, they gleamed as white as the caliche crust on the arid ground.

Of course, no one in the big house cared that Moira scrubbed the laundry in lye soap until her knuckles were nearly raw to the bone. Innis Grady, consumed with his cattle and lands, never acknowledged that his ward mended, washed, starched, and ironed from sunup until sundown every single Monday of the year. Such labor was expected of her.

Moira didn't mind. She loved good hard work better than anything. The toil of running the Grady homestead kept her mind from wandering where it shouldn't. It kept her hands busy with fine, decent women's work—the duties she would have performed as a wife and mother had she been destined for that lot in life. She wasn't, however, and that was fine, too.

1

But as she stood watching her laundry billow, Moira decided it wouldn't hurt her guardian to take note of the extra things she did for him and his son, Scully. Not once in the thirteen years since Moira and her sister had come to live at Fianna had Innis remarked on the fancy embroidered shams that she slipped onto his pillows every laundry day. He had not mentioned the new braided hearthrug that lay under his feet as he sat by the fire and smoked his pipe in the evenings. For that matter, Innis had not said a single word about the carefully pieced quilt that now hung drying on the line. This past winter Moira had designed and stitched the coverlet in the pattern known as drunkard's path. Apt, she had thought.

"Sure and you'll stare at the sheets until they march down from the line by themselves!" The voice behind her scattered the silence of the afternoon.

Swinging around, Moira gave a breathless chuckle at the sight of the scrawny young man who was sauntering toward her across the brittle grass. "Wirra! You've scared my hair curly!" she exclaimed. "What is it with you now, Scully, sneaking up on me like an Apache warrior bent on mischief?"

"I'm no Indian, Moira," Scully said, "and I'll warrant your hair's been as red and curly as a new flame since the day you were born."

"My hair is *auburn*," Moira clarified. "Like cinnamon. Yours is carrot red." Smiling, she bent over the willow laundry basket to lift out her small cloth pouch of clothespins. "So what brings your nose out of your paint pots and into the fresh air this afternoon, Scully? Sure the real world can't be more interesting than that fine young lady on the easel in your bedroom."

The youth hung his head for a moment. "If the truth be known, Moira, her fingers look like great fat sausages. I can't paint them right no matter how hard I try." He lifted his eyes. "Besides, the mail hack's just come up from Badger, and Papa's fair scalded over some letter

he's had. You should hear him blustering about the
house like a banshee. I'd take my time with the laundry,
if I were you."

Straightening, Moira pulled the wooden pins from the
nearest sheet and slipped them into her pouch. "What is
it, then? Some bad news?"

"Aye, it is. That half brother of his, you know?"

"The sheepherder?"

"Don't call him that to his face or you might find
yourself in ballyhooly with him. Call him a shepherd,
and he'll like you better when he comes."

"No, but is the man coming *here*, then? To Fianna?"

"Aye, by wagon down from Fort Stanton sometime
today or tomorrow. And from the sound of it, he's half
dead."

Moira paused in the midst of folding a dry sheet. "Half
dead?"

"He was working at the copper mines in Butte,
Montana, and got himself nearly killed. They sent
him to the fort to go under the doctor's knife. But
now Grandma Sheena's packing him off here to Fianna
to get well."

Rolling the sheet against her stomach, Moira regarded
the distant plain with its few scrawny cattle and patches
of yellowed grass. The last thing Innis Grady needed
now was a visit from one of his half-breed sheepherding
relatives. The past two winters at Fianna had been so
severe that Innis's cattle had died in droves. The stock on
the neighboring ranches had suffered, too, including the
cattle Moira had inherited from her father. Innis and his
cowpunchers tended both herds, and in former years the
Irishman had earned large profits. Times had changed.
Weak, emaciated, maimed, and frostbitten, the cattle had
been unable to survive the prolonged cold. This spring
the punchers were finding hundreds of them dead, piled
in the ditches and lying beside the thawing streams.

To make matters worse, the summer of 1887 was
shaping into the hottest season anyone in the New

Mexico Territory could remember. The new spring grass had barely sprouted before it began to shrivel and wither. The usually gushing Rio Peñasco had slowed to a damp trickle, and even the wells were low. The few cattle Innis had left bawled pitiably day and night, so that Moira couldn't sleep without burying her head under her pillow.

"Why is your grandma sending him here?" she demanded of Scully. "Why Fianna? If the spalpeen's well enough to ride a wagon, why can't he stay at his mother's house? The Mexican settlement on the Berrendo is closer to the doctor at Fort Stanton than we are."

"Too much trouble about those parts. Sure Grandma Sheena's safety is yet another reason Papa's worried. Some of the devils who fought in Lincoln Town's five-day war have been threatening the families who live on the Berrendo. Grandma doesn't think her house is a good haven for a bed-sick man to be healing in. She's written Papa a letter begging him to take his brother in."

"*Half* brother," Moira cut in. "It's the same mother they share, not the same father."

"What difference does it make? Papa can't refuse his own mother's request, now, can he?"

"No, of course not." She dumped the bedding in her basket and jerked the pins from the next sheet on the line. It would never do to criticize Innis's mother in front of Scully. Sheena was the boy's grandmother, after all, a strong woman and a devout Irish Catholic. But to think that after her first husband's death she would abandon the Irish community in the Peñasco River valley to marry a poor man of mixed heritage—half Apache and half Mexican. And a sheepherder at that!

"You'll be tending him, Moira," Scully said. "I hope you know that. It's the woman's place to care for the sick and dying."

She shot him a reproachful glance, only to find that his green eyes were as merry as ever. "Oh, get on back to your sausage-fingered lady, then!" she said, snapping him with a damp dish towel. "You and your father are quite a pair, the both of you, when it comes to women. It's no wonder to me that the ladies wouldn't abide Innis Grady's courting."

"Whisht! Speak of the devil, and he will appear." Scully jabbed a thumb in the direction of the house and the stocky, red-faced Irishman approaching like a steam locomotive from hell.

"Moira!" Innis bellowed, his cheeks scarlet beneath crisp red muttonchop whiskers. "Leave the washin' and get your backside into the house. There's work to be done!"

"God save you, Innis Grady," Moira said, greeting him in a calm voice.

"And God save you kindly." Grinding his teeth, the little bullock of a man glared at the sheets on the line as if they were somehow at fault for this newest catastrophe. "You'll pardon my ballyraggin', Moira, but I've a headache twice the size of Lincoln County."

"It's no wonder," Moira said, screwing up her courage to confront him about the situation that had been bothering her for weeks. "You were up till all hours last night drinking your blazing whiskey."

"By japers, young lady, what business is it of yours how I spend my nights?"

"It's my business because the more you drink the less you're able to keep a clear eye on the land and the cattle—my father's as well as your own. You've let the herds eat the grass down to nubbins, Innis, and if my father hadn't left such a fine, sturdy breed—"

"None of your blather about cattle now, Moira O'Casey. To tell God's truth, what you know about the cow business would fit in the pocket of that apron you're wearing!"

"I know some things. I know you overstocked the range without thinking about the future. I know the cattle are dying and the land is turning into a desert for lack of care. I know that the only remedy you've found for your troubles is in a whiskey bottle. I swear you'd drink Lough Sheelin dry if it weren't in Ireland, so you would. Whiskey may be sweet to the taste, but it's bitter to pay for it."

Innis's face turned purple. "No more of your holy blatherumskite, girl! You sound just like Deirdre, so you do. That wife of mine—"

"God rest her soul," Moira inserted.

"Aye, Deirdre was pious enough to be an angel, so the damned cherubs stole her away from me! And you're just as blazing holy."

"I'm sorry you lost your wife. Sure Deirdre was the joy of my young life, too, before she died. And I'm sorry the winters have been a trial, Innis. But you can't drink your troubles away."

"Who're you to tell me what to do? You're *nobody*, that's who you are! And I'll drink if I please."

"The devil bless you, Innis!" Moira exploded, losing the battle to control her temper. "What will it take to make you see that you can't go drinking every night and keep these two ranches going at the same time? I trusted you with my legacy, Innis. You've claimed all of the profits for yourself, and I haven't said a word about it because up till now you've kept the land thriving. I know it takes money to do that. But I won't see my father's dream withered away! I'll give the ranch to another man first."

"The hell you will!" Innis roared. "Deirdre and I took you in when you had no home, you little strap. I've been a father to you more years than Griffith O'Casey ever was, and that land is *mine* now. Mine, you hear?"

Moira stared into her guardian's cruel, unyielding green eyes. She tried to swallow the lump in her throat, the knotted fear of him. "It'll not be your land if you don't keep it alive, Innis Grady," she returned. "I'll take, it away from you, so I will."

"And I'll knock the priest's share out of you if you don't shut your gob—"

"Enough ballyhooly between the two of you," Scully cut in. "Look, there's a wagon just now by the gate at the end of the yard. I'll hold you it's him. That renegade."

All three turned to study the high-sided, rickety cart coming along the rutted track toward the big house. A small gray burro strained to pull the wagon up the low hill. On the board sat an old Mexican man who seemed content to allow the burro to set its own slow pace. When he spotted the three beside the clothesline, the man lifted his battered hat and gave a slow wave.

"Have you ever met your half brother, Papa?" Scully asked as they watched the cart roll up to the house.

"Once. Him and his four damned mixed-breed brothers. He was about your age, Scully, and a tall gawk of an eighteen-year-old at that. He was skinny and dirty, and he hardly spoke a civil word to me. Being a sheepherder and the son of a sheepherder, the scoundrel wore a sheepskin coat and leather chaps stained with windmill grease and blood from his work at marking his papa's woollies. He carried no weapon—nothing but a wooden crook, a sling, and a whip. I'd wager he couldn't shoot a pistol to save his life. He's called Josiah, of all things, and if truth be known, I couldn't tell there was a drop of Irish blood in him." Innis snorted in disgust. "Aye, Scully, I've seen your uncle, that I have. Once. And I know enough to say I don't like him, and I don't want him in my house."

Shoving his beefy hands into his pockets, he started across the grass. Scully glanced at Moira before following his father. She shrugged, picked up her laundry basket, and headed after the two men.

Innis had built his adobe house facing away from the Sacramento Mountains and toward the vast, empty plains that made up his holdings. The house, plastered in a burnt orange stucco, sprawled atop a low hillside. It was a maze of small rooms and hallways that wound here and there with little sense of order. The only wood the structure could boast was a plank floor, a ceiling beamed with heavy vigas, and a number of white-painted window frames. A deep porch spanned the front of the house. With a narrow shingled roof overhead, a dogtrot behind the main building protected the open pathway to the separate structure that housed the kitchen and storeroom. Well lit and equipped with a fireplace for cooking, the kitchen was Moira's domain.

The rest of the house and Fianna itself were dominated by Innis. He called his range "the cattle ranch of the Grady dynasty." Of course, Scully was Innis's only heir and, in Moira's opinion, not likely to start his own dynasty any time in the near future.

As she strode toward the wagon to view this latest intrusion into her orderly life, she watched Scully and his father marching a few paces ahead, their bright red heads at an even height. What a pair! The father a greedy, ballyragging Irishman who was more wicked and spiteful than any rattlesnake, the son a lovable sheela who would rather paint pictures and gaze at the sky than get his hands dirty helping his father.

Things had been better—much better—when Erinn had lived on the cattle ranch, too. With her rebellious younger sister by her side, Moira had found Innis not quite so intimidating and the loneliness of the vast plains not quite so intense. But Innis had sealed Erinn's future in return for a handsome profit. With a trade of cattle for a bride, Innis had married Erinn off to the wealthy Seamus Sullivan. He lived on the Pecos River, a full two days' wagon ride from Fianna, and the sisters never spoke except through letters.

So Moira had a pair of Irish galoots to look after all by herself—and now this ailing stranger nobody wanted. The devil's blessings to the lot of them!

"*Sí*," the old Mexican was acknowledging as Moira approached the wagon. "He was alive when they put him in at Fort Stanton. But I don't know now . . . maybe not."

"You didn't check on him now and again while you drove, Pedro?" Innis demanded as he stared into the wagon bed. "Almost a week on the trail and no food or medicine?"

"Señor, they pay me to drive the wagon, not to be the doctor. Besides, he had water. See the bucket there."

"I think he's dead," Scully announced. "He looks dead to me."

Moira clutched her laundry basket against her waist and peered between the slats in the side of the wagon. On a dark wool blanket, unshaded from the blistering sun, lay the limp bulk of an enormous man. Beneath the natural bronze of his skin, a pallor as white as death had crept over him. The dirty bandage around his stomach was bloodstained, dark, and dancing with flies. His fingers curved loosely around the coil of a braided whip, but when the burro gave a shake of its head, the whip slid to the bed of the cart. Arms slack, head lolling away from her, the man showed no sign of life.

Swallowing, Moira realized this was the first actual dead person she had ever seen. When her parents burned to death in a fire at the home of friends thirteen years before, neither she nor Erinn had been allowed to look at their charred bodies. A part of her had wanted to see them, to know that they really were dead and not just away at the neighboring farm for a short visit. But the sight of death now made her thankful that she had been spared.

"I'll pay you to help me bury him," Innis said to Pedro. "We'll roll him in a blanket, lay him under the cottonwoods by the river, and bid good riddance to him and all sheepherders."

"Speaking ill of the dead again, Innis?" Moira chided him lightly. "And won't you build him a coffin or see that he's given last rites? He should have a priest at the very least."

"In this sun he won't last till I build a coffin and fetch a priest. Just look above you now."

Overhead in the cloudless sky, the black wedges of buzzards circled lazily. With a shiver, Moira looked down at the poor dead man again. "He'll have my wedding trunk for a coffin," she announced suddenly. "We may have to push and shove him a bit, but he'll fit. I'll clear it of my things while you dig the grave."

"You'd put a stranger to rest in your wedding trunk, Moira?" Scully asked.

"With the vow I made to your mother to look after you and your father all my life, Scully, I'll not be needing a wedding trunk. And besides, this man's no stranger. He's your uncle Josiah, the son of your own grandma. He's an Irishman—at least partway he is. And for that he deserves the best we can give." She set her laundry basket on the ground and removed one of her clean white sheets. "Slide him out, now, Innis, and we'll drape him in this. We'll lay him out on the table in the front hall as is right and proper, and if there's no time for a wake, at least we'll drink him a toast, God rest his soul."

"Better do what she says, señor," Innis told Pedro, "or she'll ballyrag the devil out of us, she will."

Moira stood at the side of the wagon while the Mexican crawled in and began to shove the man's shoulders.

"Pull his feet now, Scully," Innis ordered as he attempted to haul the deadweight out by dragging the man at the knees. "By herrings, he's a big whacker of a fellow. Must weigh nigh onto two hundred pounds. I suppose I disremembered him right in some ways."

More ways than one, Moira thought as she gazed at the man's thighs, each as thick as a large aspen trunk, and a grand rock slab of manly chest sliding slowly out of the wagon. This Josiah was no skinny, dirty boy, but a great mountain of a devil. Even when slack in death, his bare shoulders were bunched with muscle, and his upper arms were nearly as big around as Moira's waist.

As he came off the wagon bed, one of his arms flopped to the ground, and his fingers dangled in the dirt. Spying a chance to help, Moira bent and gingerly took his thumb between her fingertips. It didn't feel as cold and stiff as she had expected, but all the same, she didn't like to touch a dead body longer than necessary. While the Mexican attempted to get under the shoulders to support the torso for the trip into the house, Moira settled the hand on the man's bare chest.

"Take hold of him in the middle, Moira," Innis commanded. "He's as awkward and heavy as a dead horse."

"He's mortal weighty, so he is," Scully puffed as they started for the front door.

Abandoning the sheet she had planned to use as a shroud, Moira quickly assessed the task at hand. One look at the bloody bandage around the man's middle and she decided she didn't want to clutch him there, even though he wouldn't feel the pain. Then her eyes traveled down to his hips and his tight, beltless jeans.

"By all the goats in Kerry, girl, take ahold of him before we drop the blackguard in the dust!" Innis shouted.

Jumping to attention, Moira threw her arms around the man's great bare chest. Though her hands didn't half meet around the other side of him, she dug her fingers into his big, warm back and tried her best to support some of his weight.

Like a slow-moving train, the four inched their way toward the house under the burden of the man. At the first porch step, Moira laid her head against his chest and heaved upward with her shoulder.

*Beautiful woman.* The words formed in a groaned sigh deep inside Josiah.

Moira's head shot up. "Glory be to God," she gasped as she stared into a pair of eyes the color of oak. "He's alive!"

With that news, the train derailed. Scully let go of the feet he was toting and ran for the house as if the devil were after him. Innis slung down the long legs. Pedro dropped the man's head like a hot potato, and Moira crashed to the ground on top of him, her arms around his chest and her hands buried under two hundred pounds of living flesh.

"Aii-yee!" Pedro cried, hopping around at a safe distance while Moira fought to free her arms. "*El vive! El vive!*"

"Scully! Innis!" As Moira jerked at her own trapped hands, she realized that the stranger's arms had slipped around her back. "Somebody help me!"

"Please . . . I hurt," Josiah whispered.

"What?" Moira lifted her head and gazed into his face. At the sight of his pain-filled brown eyes, the panic went out of her in a breath. "Now then," she murmured, "it's all right. You're in God's pocket here with us, sir. Rest easy." At her soothing words, his eyelids dropped shut, and she felt the gentle rise and fall of his bare chest against her breast.

Turning, she gave Innis the evilest eye she could manage. "The lot of you," she snapped, "have nearly killed this poor devil twice over with your shenanigans! Now pick him up and take him to the back room before he stops off the very blood in my arms."

Like a group of cowed schoolboys, the three men hurried back to their posts and, with great effort, hauled their burden up the steps and into the house. Moira rushed ahead, her heart hammering against her rib cage as she ran down the long, cool hallway.

Had he said she was beautiful? No, he couldn't have. The man was half dead. But she had heard him say *something*; she knew she had. *Was* she beautiful? Of course not. Erinn was the cooleen, the fair-haired angel of the pair of O'Casey sisters. Moira had always been known as a rumple-headed, gangly chicken.

Besides, the man hadn't actually seen her anyway, had he? Well, his eyes *had* been open, Moira thought as she jerked back the quilts and sheets on the bed in the spare room. Of course, he was probably having visions. He might have been seeing angels, as close to death as he was. Oh, but he *did* have elegant fine eyes—deepset, fathomless brown pools. How those eyes had looked into her face!

"You want him on the bed, Moira?" Innis bellowed as he tramped into the room. "He'll dirty your sheets, so he will. He's bleeding still, and he's cruel dusty from the long ride."

"I've clean sheets by the cupboardful, in case you hadn't noticed, Innis Grady," she shot back, still a little angry. "Of course, put him on the bed."

As the men heaved Josiah up onto the feather mattress, he gave a deep groan, and his face contorted in pain. "No," he murmured, "no, no . . ."

"Out with the lot of you," Moira ordered. "Scully, hang a kettle of water over the fire to boil, and then fetch in the rest of my laundry. Aye, Innis, Scully can take the sheets off the line. Sure and it won't kill him to do a bit of woman's work now and again."

"You'll turn him into a blazing sheela—"

"*Off*, the two of you! You're cats of a kind, both standing there gawking with your gobs hanging open wide enough to catch flies!"

Flapping her apron at them, she chased them out of the room, shut the door, and hurried to the windows. In a moment she had pushed back the curtains so the room filled with sunlight.

"A merry pair of patthas they are," she murmured to herself as she lifted the sashes to let in a drift of fresh air, "spoiled rotten and expecting me to do everything for them. If I weren't such a good Christian woman, I'd set them straight on a thing or two, I would. I'd saddle a horse and ride clear down the trail to Roswell, that's what I'd do! I'd spend some of that money Innis has been hoarding for himself. I'd buy myself a . . . a stove. A grand nickel-trimmed stove with a teapot warmer. Sure he'd have kinks over that one, so he would, and serve him right."

She swung around to find Josiah's brown eyes regarding her. As sudden as a rainstorm in the desert, her hands went damp, and her breath hung in her breast. "Why then, you're awake again, are you?" she asked quickly to cover her discomfort. "We thought you were dead. Innis almost had you buried under the old cottonwood tree."

"With your wedding trunk for my coffin," Josiah said in a low voice.

"You heard that, did you?" She approached him slowly, wondering if he had heard, too, the cruel insensitivity in his half brother's words. "Well, it's a good big trunk. Just the size for a giant like yourself. Now, you'd best get some sleep, sir. Sure you're as white as a soulth."

His eyes never left her face as she moved to stand by the foot of the bed. "A soulth?"

"A ghost, of course. If you don't know what a soulth is, you're not much of an Irishman, are you then?"

His dark eyes regarded her. "I'm a man. Plain and simple."

Glancing inadvertently at the breadth of his naked chest, Moira felt her cheeks flame suddenly pink and hot. "A man, aye, but you'll be wanting whiskey to numb the pain of that wound in your belly so you can sleep. I'll fetch the bottle for you now."

"Wait," he called, stopping her with a lifted hand. "Where's my *látigo*?"

"Which?"

"My blacksnake. My whip."

"Oh . . . we left your whip in Pedro's wagon. I'll claim it before he goes." She turned to leave, but his voice halted her again.

"You're not much of an American if you don't know what a *látigo* is, are you, then?" he asked.

She looked back to find him smiling at her through the pain etched on his face. The expression softened the chiseled angles and planes of his features and slightly crinkled the skin at the corners of his eyes.

"I'm a woman," she said. "Plain and simple."

"And beautiful."

She grabbed the doorknob. "I'll fetch the whiskey."

Before he could say another word, she swung out of the room and fairly ran down the hall, her heart thumping an Irish clog dance all the way.

"I'll not wash him!" Scully protested vehemently. "A man washing another man—it's not right."

"And you would have *me* wash him, then?" Moira poured the steaming water into a wooden basin. "He's *your* uncle!"

"Clean him up, Moira," Innis ordered from inside the pantry. "You don't have to look at his privates to scrub the dirt off him."

He emerged with a bottle of whiskey and lifted it to his lips. Moira let out a sigh of exasperation. "Did you bring in my sheets, Scully?"

"No, he didn't," Innis answered in his son's place, "and I'll make you smell hell if you mention such a thing again. On Deirdre's deathbed you took a vow to tend to Scully and me. You told my wife you'd be good for the woman's work around here as long as you lived. Now, blast your soul, you'll do the laundry and the cookin' and the cleanin' and whatever else I tell you to do to keep the house goin' while I take care of the man's work. And that's managing these two ranches!"

"If I took care of the house as well as you've taken care of the land, Innis Grady, the roof would be falling down around your head!" Moira snapped back without thinking.

"Shut your smush, you impudent streel!" Innis came for her with the back of his hand, but Moira scampered around the kitchen table.

"Glory be to God, Innis, don't start beating on me again! I'm sorry for what I said. Truly I am."

"You're a clart and I rue the day I ever took you and your wicked sister in, that I do! Now get into the house and clean up that devil so we can pack him on his way before I throttle you and him, too!"

Before Innis could make good on his threats, Moira hurried out of the kitchen and through the dogtrot to the house. She was thankful to have escaped her guardian's temper. So many times in the past thirteen years she had provoked the man, pushed him too far, and with his swift and brutal punishments he'd made her pay the price for her sins. It was wrong of her to speak so boldly to Innis, who had taken her and Erinn in at such a desperate time in their young lives. She owed her guardian so much. But what a sherral he could be!

Scully was right behind her as Moira strode into the house. She had half a mind to dump the basin of hot water right over the lad's head. Giving Josiah a bath was the last thing—the very last thing—she wanted to do!

"Sure I've never seen you so wrought, Moira," Scully said as he caught up with her. He followed close at her side while she marched down the hall. "You were sharp as a ciotog with Papa just now."

"Aye, and I'll be sharp with you, too, Scully. Here I am a bare twenty-one years old, and I might as well be mother to the pair of you! They say bad luck comes in threes, and now I know I've had my fair share. First my parents die, the both of them, then I'm sent to Fianna to look after you two galoots, and finally Erinn is wedded off so that I'm left alone here with nothing but brown grass and dirty sheets to call my own!"

"Ah, Moira, it's not been so bad here, now, has it?"

"That it has, young Scully." She paused at the chest that sat at the end of the hall, lifted the heavy wooden lid, and took out a set of clean, folded white towels. Tucking them under her arm, she gazed down at the basin of steaming water.

"No," she recanted softly, "in truth, it's not been bad here at Fianna. Your father's provided for me, for the most part. You're a bold daltheen, Scully, but you're dear to me all the same, so you are. I'm not a bit sorry about my work. All I've ever wanted is a house of my own and a family to . . . to look after. Sure it's a good enough life, and I've no right to ballyrag."

"All the same, you think there might be more for you."

Moira lifted her head. "What can you mean by that, Scully?"

"I know you, Moira. You're like my mother. For all your blatherumskite, you're soft. . . . You're tender inside. You want more than just a house; you want a home. You want more than a man who treats you worse than he does his punchers; you want a husband. You want love."

"Scully—the idea!"

"Aye, Moira. You'd be married and having babies if you hadn't made that vow to my mother. You'd leave Fianna if you didn't fear that Papa would come after you. You know he'll never let you go, because then he'd lose Griffith O'Casey's land and cattle. But if you could get away, you would."

"Scully, you've been listening to fairies, so you have. I'm a good Christian woman, born in Ireland and reared to know my place in this world. I'll not be listening to your blarney."

"What I say is not blarney, Moira, and . . . and . . ." Suddenly blushing crimson, he shoved his hands deep into his pockets. "And if ever you see your way to marry me, I'll take you away from Fianna—to Paris, where I'll study painting and . . . and you can do anything you like!"

"Scully!" Moira gasped, but the boy—all gangly legs and elbows and bright red hair—was fleeing down the hall.

With a chuckle mingled with disbelief, Moira adjusted the basin of hot water on her hip. "Oh, Scully, God bless you, I don't want to be a wife," she whispered. "Not yours or anybody's."

As she placed her hand on the doorknob, Moira considered this new dilemma Scully had laid at her feet. She'd had no idea he was harboring foolish romantic thoughts about her. *Love*? Surely he couldn't be serious, not with her being three years older and a good two inches taller, a level-headed, common woman well settled into the lone life of a spinster, and Scully being a dreaming artist with grand thoughts of Paris. How could she gently reject the boy? How could she make him understand that it would take a saint of a man to be better than no man at all in her life?

In the past few years several unmarried Irishmen in the valley and a few ardent cowpunchers had tried to court Moira, drawn by the lure of the O'Casey land. Innis had run them all off with his rifle. Not that Moira truly minded. Before Deirdre Grady died, she had taught her young ward to be godly and righteous, and she had asked Moira to make a vow that a good Christian could never dishonor.

So the vow stood: Moira would give Innis charge over the O'Casey land, cattle, and profits until his dying day, after which it would pass to Scully. And in return for the security of food and shelter, Moira would tend to the two Grady men. She would be dutiful, hardworking, and as pure as a nun—and not a man alive could make her break that vow.

Comforted by these settling thoughts, Moira turned the doorknob and went into the spare room to give Josiah a bath.

# Chapter
## 2

Inside the spare room all was silent save the labored breathing of the sleeping man. Moira stood at the side of the bed and studied this Josiah-the-sheepherder for a long while. She didn't want to wake him, peaceful as he looked. She certainly didn't want to wash him, though he needed a bath in the worst way. Most of all, she didn't want him gazing at her with those brown eyes and saying strange, unexpected things that put her off balance.

The late afternoon sun had slipped below the horizon, bathing the room and the man in an orange glow. Moira knew she had to shut the windows, or the mosquitoes would make a feast of the poor devil. She set her basin and towels on a small table by the bed and went across the room. After lowering the sashes, she drew the heavy curtains to block the last of the light.

Time for lamps. Back across the room she went, feeling her way by the furniture—a rocking chair here, a bedpost there. She drew her matchbox from her apron pocket and struck a match against the iron bedstead. The moment it burst into flame, the man's face emerged from

19

the darkness. Those great deep-set brown eyes, bright with fever, stared up at her.

"Glory be to God, I thought you were asleep," she whispered. With shaking fingers, she lit the wick and replaced the glass globe on the lamp. "You've got the eyes of a shee, so you have." She glanced at him and saw that his expression hadn't changed. "A shee is one of the Good People, the fairies, in case you don't know."

"I know about the shee. My mother was a Lachlan from county Cork."

His voice was deep, lower in pitch than she remembered. Though he claimed to have Irish blood, his words bore not a trace of a lilt.

"And a good thing your mother is from the old sod," she said, "or you wouldn't be welcome in Innis Grady's house."

"Unless I misunderstood my brother's words this afternoon, I'm *not* welcome here."

Moira dipped a towel in the hot water and wrung it out. The man might be burning up with fever, but his speech was sensible enough to let her know that he was thinking with a clear mind. "I'm sorry you heard Innis," she said. "Forgive him, if you can. You must understand that your brother has been carrying a heavy load lately— two huge ranches and cattle dying in droves. The past winters have been fair evil. Now this hot summer, the devil bless it, is sure to ruin him unless we have rain soon."

"You make excuses for my brother."

She shrugged. "I tell the truth." Lifting her chin, she met the man's brown gaze. "It's time you were washed and patched up. Did the doctor send any medicine with you?"

"I had a bag. There's a bottle in it."

"Ah, yes, this elegant piece of luggage." She held up a battered, travel-worn leather satchel—the only thing the poor sheepherder could call his own. The bag was so light that Moira couldn't be sure it held even a change of clothing. "I fetched it from the wagon along with your whip."

"You found my *látigo*?" He lifted his head, his eyes intense.

"Aye, now lie down, or you'll be resting in the clay before your time."

"Where is it?"

"It's here, on the floor." When he refused to lean back against his pillow, she put her palm on his chest and gave him a gentle push.

Instantly his hand covered hers. "Give it to me. Give me the blacksnake." She tried to take her hand away, but he squeezed it, drawing her closer. "I need it."

"Sure you'll be riding about whipping horses tonight, sir, you with your middle covered in blood and your legs as weak as a newborn colt's. Now then, don't break my arm! Here's your *látigo*." She tossed the coiled rawhide whip onto the bed and jerked her hand out of his grasp. "Blast your soul, but you're strong for a man with one foot in his grave."

He grabbed the whip, then shut his eyes, breathing hard. "I have to get out of here. Fisher's coming. Searching . . . Gotta leave . . ."

"We're so bad, are we, then? All right, let me wash you and change that bandage of yours so you can heal up and be on your way. Don't fight me, will you? I don't have the time for it."

Swallowing her discomfort at being alone with a stranger, Moira pulled back the sheet and quilts that covered him. At once she realized that she hadn't imagined the height of the man or his uncommon size. Thank heaven his eyes were closed, she thought as she laid the warm, damp rag on his bare shoulder and drew it gently down his long arm. His skin was a deep color, as though years in the hot sun had bronzed and gilded him.

She dipped the towel into the water again and wrung it out. Taking his hand, she covered the blunt-nailed fingers with the cloth and carefully circled them one by one. His was a good hand, she decided, callused with hard toil, the fine seams of skin embedded with the soil of long labor, as a man's hands should be. Maybe this Josiah was no more than the son of a sheepherder, and a miner by trade, but he was clearly a hard worker.

Rinsing the towel once again, Moira thought about the times she had washed her own body in such a way. How strange to be tending to a man instead. Where she was softness, curves, and gentle hollows, he was solid planes of muscle and sinew. Where her skin was velvety like a new rose petal, his was as taut and supple as tightly stretched leather. Where her bones were thin and delicate, his were large and heavy. Where her arms were strong but feminine, his were corded with thick tendons and laced with ropy veins.

She laid the towel across his chest and began to rub back and forth across the great bare expanse. Innis Grady had a bear's pelt of thick red curly hair on his chest, but his brother's torso was as smooth as polished wood, his two flat brown nipples boldly exposed on mounds of hard, solid flesh. She tried to avoid touching them, but when the end of the towel brushed across one, she watched it tighten into a tiny hard seed.

Moistening her dry lips, Moira kept her eyes steadfastly on her labor. The thing to do in such a situation, she decided, was to talk. If she blathered, neither of them would give heed to the untoward task she had been ordered to perform.

"I trust you'll eat beef stew," she commented as she circled the bed to tend his other arm. "You being a sheepherder's son and all, I suppose I should offer mutton, but Innis won't abide the stuff on his table, so there we are the poorer for it."

"My father is a *shepherd*," he said.

"So he is. Forgive me." She glanced at him, but his eyes were still closed. Thank God. "It's beef stew we'll eat for dinner tonight," she went on, "and Innis and Scully will be after me in a minute to put it on the fire. Never have you heard such ballyragging as those two can give when they're hungry."

"You're my brother's wife?"

Moira lifted her head in surprise. "Innis's wife—God forbid!"

He was looking at her. "The boy's?"

"Of course not. Innis is my guardian. I look after him and Scully."

"Who are you, then? What's your name?"

She dipped the towel in the water longer than was necessary. "I'm Moira O'Casey . . . and you're Josiah, they tell me."

"Josiah Chee."

"You're father's an Indian, so they say."

"Half. Apache and Mexican. Does it matter to you the way it does to everyone else?"

She began to examine the bandage wrapped around his waist. "I don't care a whit what you are, as long as you'll eat my beef stew and get well enough to go back where you came from." Unwilling to meet his eyes, she began to pick apart the soiled white dressing. "What sort of mining engine did this to you, Josiah Chee? It looks as if you got your middle tangled in a chopping machine."

When he didn't answer, she glanced up, only to find that he'd shut his eyes again. Moira had tended to birthing cows and flyblown calves. She'd nursed a horse that had been nipped by wolves; she'd tended a dog that had done battle with a bobcat. She took care of the minor ailments of all the punchers on the range, and she usually didn't think a thing of mopping up blood. But at the sight of Josiah's bare stomach, she shuddered in horror. A crisscross pattern of stitched wounds, each one red and angry-looking, some still seeping blood, ran across his abdomen.

"Holy saints!" she whispered. "What did this to you?"

"Who," he answered, his voice slightly slurred. "Not what."

She looked down at the mangled mass again and this time saw the wound for what it was. "A shotgun," she said softly. "A shotgun did this!"

It was what folks in the territory called a gutshot, and Moira knew this was the worst kind of wound a man could have. It was a wonder the poor devil was still alive. "Why?" she whispered. "What did you do to deserve this?"

Without answering, he clenched his jaw and swallowed against the obvious pain. Then he spoke. "Will you clean it for me . . . Moira?"

"Of course I shall. Just stay calm while I find your medicine." In a panic for fear that he'd die on her right then and there, Moira rooted around in his satchel until her fingers closed on a bottle. She pulled it out and quickly began to douse the wound with the stuff. Though his body went rigid and his fist tightened on the coil of his *látigo*, he didn't make a sound while she carefully worked over the expanse of torn flesh.

Who would have shot this man? And why? He didn't even own a gun! He only had his silly shepherd's whip— not much good against a shotgun, was it? Innis had said Josiah didn't know how to shoot. What had he done to make someone angry enough to try to kill him?

Should she tell Innis? Of course she should! But then Innis would surely send Josiah away. What if the man who shot him was looking for him even now, planning to finish him off? What if it wasn't a man who had pulled the trigger, but a woman?

Sure he was good to look at, this Josiah Chee. It had been a surprise to Moira to see that instead of the dark hair that his father's bloodline suggested—or red hair, as his mother's implied—Josiah had thick, straight dark gold hair, almost brown but gilded to a honeyed blond by the sun. Any woman would take a second look at such a man. He was fine and strong, and a hard worker, too, and his face was good. Wonderful, his face was, with a straight nose and strong lips and those brown, brown eyes.

Perhaps a woman was behind the devastating injury. Moira wouldn't have put it past some bold *oanshagh* to work her wiles on a man like this Josiah Chee. No doubt in the mining camps there were plenty of loose women who made their living by the lace of their petticoats. With most of the town of Butte filled with Irishmen from county Cork, there'd be rivers of whiskey and a rash of flaring tempers to go along with the liquor. A strong mix of drink, women, and Irishmen was sure to bring trouble one way or another—as Moira knew from firsthand experience.

"How much buckshot did the doctor take out of you at Fort Stanton?" she asked Josiah.

"I don't know," he murmured. "I was unconscious most of the time. They thought I'd die."

"If you've survived the surgeon's knife and Pedro's wagon ride, I suppose you'll live. The good Lord must have grand work for you to do in this life. When you're fit, you'll have to go to church and ask Him what it is."

"I know what I'm supposed to do."

She lifted her eyes from the clean bandage she was wrapping. "Do you, now? And what might that be?"

"Listen to me." He put one hand over hers, stopping her busy fingers in the midst of their tucking and tying. "When I was a boy, my mother taught me to read. I read every book I could get my hands on. Those stories made me want to become something different, not just a poor *pastor* with a single flock. I decided to be a great man— rich, famous, important. I left the ways of my fathers when I went to work in the copper mines."

His voice was ragged, but Moira had no trouble making sense of his words as he went on speaking. "I got some of the things I was after. But what I learned there in Montana was much more important. Stripping the soil, cutting away the heart of the earth, carving a slash of destruction—it is wrong. I have to turn back to the path."

Unable to escape the intensity in the wounded man's eyes, Moira sat on the edge of his bed. "Tell me about this path," she said softly.

"My father's people—Apaches and Mexicans—we work *with* the land. There's respect, unity. It's a marriage of equals."

Moira gave a brief laugh. "Marriage! You've got that wrong, Mister Josiah Chee. Marriage is an arrangement between master and servant, so it is. There are no equals in that."

"No," he said, gripping her hand, his eyes lit with fever. "It's give-and-take for the good of each. In a strong marriage, the husband and wife both profit. And that's how it should be with the land. I've got to go back to that. I've been violating the earth . . . but it's time for me to court her again. I want to mold her with my bare hands. I want to caress and stroke her—"

"You've fair lost your mind with that gunshot wound," Moira said, jumping off the bed and pulling her hand from his grasp. "I've never heard such blarney in all my days. No man I've ever met treats a woman like that, and no rancher thinks of his land as a wife to be coddled and spoiled. He puts out his cattle, they eat the grass, and then he sends them off to market, and if he's lucky he might have a spare dollar or two to buy his wife a length of cloth so she can sew britches for his sons. It's a battle, so it is. The rancher against the land, each fighting to bring the other down."

"No," he whispered, his voice husky, "you're wrong, Moira. I'm going to rebuild the dream. And that's why my life was spared. I'll make that marriage, and it's going to bear fruit. One day my fathers' lands—the Sacramentos, mountains of the Holy Sacrament—will be rich with orchards and fields of alfalfa. Cattle will graze the hillsides, and sheep heavy with wool—"

"Sheep? Don't even say that word around me! Sheep are the devil's scourge on the land, so they are. They eat the grass down to its roots. Cattle can't live where sheep have grazed."

"No, Moira." He was shaking his head.

"Aye, Josiah! What do you think the prophet Ezekiel says in the Good Book? 'Woe be to shepherds. . . . Seemeth it a small thing unto you to have eaten up the good pasture, but ye must tread down with your feet the residue of your pastures? And to have drunk of the deep waters, but ye must foul the residue with your feet?' "

"Moira, listen to me—"

"Sheep eat everything in front of them and kill everything behind them. If you start talking of raising sheep in the Sacramentos, your brother will kick you out on your grug. You're barely alive as it is, and as full of blatherumskite as googeen. Sure if Innis sends you packing, you'll die for good, and the buzzards will pick your bones." She stuffed her hands into the pockets of her apron and took a deep breath. "Now then, I'll bring your stew, so I will, and you'll get yourself well and leave us in peace, Josiah Chee. Here at Fianna, we don't need your talk of sheep and sacraments and Apache ancestors. And we don't need your foolish dreams."

She set her shoulders and turned toward the door. But as she stepped into the hallway, she heard him speaking softly behind her.

"Everyone needs dreams, Moira," he was saying, "everyone . . . even you."

Images and sounds came and went like flames flickering in an open window. Always there was the blast of the shotgun in Josiah's ears. The roar, the shattering pain, the blackness. People hovered over him—miners, Paddy, a doctor, soldiers in clean uniforms. *A woman?* Yes. She floated in and out of his sight like an angel, gently touching, bathing, wrapping, slipping a cup between his lips.

There was the jerk of a train, the rhythmic chugging. Sometimes the sound of that train came from far away, and sometimes from inside his brain. And then the jarring wagon jolted him awake, and he sensed sunshine beating down on his face and sweat stinging his eyes. The sound of flies came to him, a low buzzing that hung around his head and kept him from sleeping as he wanted to sleep—a forever slide into blissful, eternal unconsciousness.

Amid the echo of the gun and the hum of the flies there floated a voice. That woman's voice. It drifted in and out. Sometimes the voice was so clear that Josiah was sure he recognized the woman who was speaking. She was soft and clean and swathed in the auburn glow of her hair. Her blue eyes haunted him, and he tried his best to keep his own eyes open so he could look into hers and find the healing they promised.

Her voice held a familiar lilt like his mother's, but the woman's words were smoother, younger, filled with the music of unexpressed laughter. Sometimes she spoke to him, and he knew her name. *Moira.* They talked together, and from the distance of his pain he heard his own speech making perfect sense. He carried on conversations with her, and he seemed to know exactly what he was saying.

In fact, when the woman was nearby, he talked more than he ever had in his life. Though he was usually silent, reluctant to reveal his innermost thoughts, Josiah could now hear himself rambling on and on, stating as fact thoughts that weren't fully formed, ideas he hadn't quite formulated. But he couldn't seem to make himself be quiet. Something about the woman—the way she smiled and laughed and touched his body so gently—loosened his tongue.

She was beautiful. Her face, pale and milky, held a softness that belied the inner strength of her character. Blue eyes, as deeply hued as morning glories, sparkled with laughter as easily as they flashed in anger or glittered with determination. Her hair, tightly swept back, seemed determined to drift free of pins and ribbons. Auburn curls, as shiny as polished cedar, danced around her forehead and neck. It was all he could do to keep from reaching out to her, touching that cloud of hair.

The scents that wafted into the room with this woman made Josiah long for her presence when she was away. First, and always, came the perfume of lavender. The sweet, slightly tart, rich fragrance clung to her skin, her hands, her hair. When she worked over him, he drifted in the scent that floated around her.

Mingled with the lavender that was the emblem of the woman came the other aromas—clean sheets fresh with sunshine and starch and soap; stew rich in potatoes, tender beef, and black pepper; honeyed beeswax coating the floor; pungent ammonia on the windowpanes; sweet roses in one corner of the room; and the grass-scented breeze drifting through open windows.

And always, always, there was the smell of medicine in the small, cool room. Day and night the woman touched his skin, dabbing his wounds, wrapping him in clean white bandages, tucking the cloth against his skin. There was a drink—greasewood tea, she called it. She made him gulp it by the gallon. "It'll save your life when nothing else can," she always said in her gentle voice.

And there was the bright, fermented redolence of whiskey. She kept the bottle by his bed and the cup at the ready. He had come to relish the feel of her arm slipping under his neck to cradle his head as he parted his lips to drink the warm liquor. When the pain was too great, she was always there, always ready to numb his anguish.

Then he would lie back in the bed and watch the woman, this Moira with the auburn hair, and he would float in the fragrance of lavender until his eyes drifted shut and sleep took him.

*    *    *

"If you'd stop drownin' him in my good booze, he might come to his senses and get the hell off my land." Innis stared at the sleeping giant who had occupied his spare room for two weeks. "He's no frainey, Moira, not with those big arms and a chest as broad as a barn. Let's slap him out of this drunk and get him into the sunshine, what do you say?"

"Slap him? You'll do nothing of the kind, you great glunter. I haven't spent day and night piecing him back together only to have you knock him out again."

"Sure it's been no great harm to you to take care of him. You've treated him like a sweet colleen, so you have, always bringing him the best of the dinner and jumping up in the night at his slightest groan."

"The way you throw sheep's eyes at him," Scully added, "anyone would think he'd turned your heart, Moira."

"Glory be to God," she snapped back, "I've only done what you expected of me, the two of you. I've put him back on the baker's list, and if you want to send him packing now, it'll do me no harm. One less chore to muck up my day."

She grabbed the tray that held Josiah's empty soup bowl and marched out of the room. *Let them drag him out of bed and heave him onto a horse,* she fumed as she made her way out the back door to the kitchen. These past two weeks had been exhausting.

It wasn't so much the extra work of tending Josiah that had tired her. Rather, she had come to enjoy preparing special dishes she thought he might find delectable. She viewed his healing wounds with great satisfaction each time she changed his bandages. She didn't even mind bathing him now—in fact, she felt almost comfortable at the sight of his great bare chest and strapping arms.

The tasks of washing and combing his hair and shaving his jaw every morning didn't seem like chores at all. If truth be known, Moira could hardly wait to put the

breakfast dishes away so she could heat the water
for Josiah's bath and shave. She liked the way his
skin felt and the way it smelled. The very thought
of taking his face in her hands and stroking it with
the sleek razor sent a shiver of anticipation through
her stomach each night before she went to sleep, and
she had grown used to his overwhelming presence in
her dreams.

All this Moira could accept about the stranger who
had invaded her comfortable world at Fianna. What she
could not come to terms with were his words. Josiah
Chee didn't speak to her the way Innis did. He didn't
order her about and treat her like a half-witted child who
didn't know her left hand from her right. When Josiah
spoke, he said things that haunted her.

Phrases he had uttered in his ramblings ran through
her mind on an unstoppable track. "You're beautiful,
Moira," he had murmured more than once. She had
almost come to expect the words.

"Let me touch your hair, Moira," he had whispered
once in the middle of the night. She hadn't let him, of
course, but the thought of his hands on her hair mesmerized her.

"I'm drunk on the scent of you," he had told her softly
one day when she was bathing him.

"It's lavender," she had returned, and she had held
her wrist to his nose before she realized how bold and
forward that might seem.

"I want to take you with me, Moira," he had told
her one night in the midst of a fever. "You're beautiful,
Moira. . . . Oh, Moira, just sit here beside me on the bed
and let me watch you. Moira . . . let me touch your hair,
Moira."

Well, he was drunk, and that was all there was to it.
She had kept him intoxicated on purpose. From the time
he had started in about wanting to reclaim his father's
lands for the sheep and make a marriage of respect
and unity, Moira had known that listening to this man

would be dangerous. The things he said weren't right and proper. Not at all.

From the kitchen window now she watched Innis and Scully haul Josiah out into the side yard. He dwarfed them both, his long arms hanging over their shoulders and his steps sluggish in the dirt. In the sunshine, his hair seemed lighter—almost golden, and as straight as wheat. They hadn't bothered to dress him, so his broad back was bare and brown between their white homespun shirts.

As Moira guessed, it wasn't long before Innis and Scully gave up trying to walk Josiah around and eased him down onto a bench under the tree that held one end of her clothesline. Scully leaned against the trunk, huffing and puffing as though he'd just done the hardest labor of his life—which he probably had. Innis settled on the bench and began to speak to Josiah, his stubby little hands moving this way and that as he talked.

What was he saying? She stood on tiptoe, as if that might somehow help her to hear. Would Innis order Josiah away now? Would he send him home to their Irish mother who lived in the Mexican settlement on the Berrendo River? Would Moira ever see Josiah Chee again? No, of course she wouldn't. And it didn't matter.

She rolled up her sleeves and began to peel potatoes. Life had been good enough before Josiah came to Fianna, and it would be good again. There would be sheets to wash and bread to bake and floors to scrub. Innis would snort and grumble and drink too much. Scully would carry on with his paintings in the back room. The youth had never again mentioned the addled notion of marrying her, and she was hoping he'd forgotten it. Her routine could return to normal.

If normal was so wonderful, though, why had a huge lump swelled up in the middle of her throat? Moira swallowed and blinked through the mist in her eyes at the half-peeled potato on the table. Taking care of a sick, raving, half-dead man was no treat. She should be happy as a lark to bid him farewell. She sniffed and rubbed the back of her wrist across her damp cheek.

She was just a little lonely, that was all. If Erinn still lived at Fianna, things wouldn't look so dull. She just missed her sister, Moira told herself. If only she could see Erinn again, walk hand in hand with her through the pasture to the river, laugh and giggle over some silliness, and share the labor of the house, life wouldn't seem so hard. Shutting her eyes, Moira whispered a quick prayer: "Dear God, please send Erinn . . . or someone . . . to fill up the empty spaces inside me."

Though she could be a devil with her little deceits and trickeries, Erinn had always been fun. But Josiah certainly wasn't fun. Not at all. What could be fun about changing bloody bandages day and night? It was true Moira jumped out of bed at his least little groan. No wonder she felt as tired as a mother tending a newborn child. In fact, she was so exhausted she felt she could drop off to sleep this very moment, while standing in the kitchen peeling potatoes.

Lifting the corner of her apron, Moira dabbed at the persistent tears she couldn't seem to blink away. It wasn't as though she didn't have plenty to do every day of the week. There was washing and ironing, cooking, cleaning, mending, sewing, polishing, scrubbing, tending the kitchen garden, not to mention the little extras she chose to do for Innis and Scully.

She'd bake a big pie for them today, so she would. There was a handful of old apples in the cellar beneath the kitchen, just enough for a fine pie. She'd flavor it with cinnamon and sugar and a dash of nutmeg. Moira sniffed again. Everyone said her pies were the best in the valley, and if Josiah took one bite he'd . . . But a woman didn't bake pies to get compliments, did she? Innis always ate every crumb on his plate, which was testament enough to her good cooking . . . so if Josiah was gone by suppertime, it wouldn't matter in the least. . . .

Moira pulled her handkerchief from her apron pocket and blew her nose. No doubt it was as bright red and shiny as a new cherry, and if Innis saw her swollen eyes . . .

"Moira?"

Sucking in her breath, she swung around. Josiah Chee stood in the doorway of the kitchen, one shoulder leaning against the wood frame.

"God save you," she whispered in greeting.

"Moira, you're crying."

"It's . . . it's just . . . onions," she lied, backing up against the table to block his view of the sack of potatoes. "I've been peeling onions."

He nodded. "You work hard here at my brother's place."

"There's a lot to be done." She wadded the handkerchief into a ball and stuffed it into the pocket of her apron. Oh, why did Josiah have to see her now, with her eyes rimmed in red and her nose fat and drippy? She must look like a fishwife, while he looked absolutely wonderful.

He was much taller than she'd realized after seeing him in bed all those days. His presence seemed to fill up the kitchen, dwarfing the fireplace and the cupboards and her pine table. He had hooked one hand on the pocket of his britches, and the strain pulled the fabric tight against his thighs. She glanced away.

"So, you're up and about," she said, fiddling absently with the paring knife. "I suppose you'll be on your way soon."

"Tomorrow."

"Tomorrow . . . Well, your mother will be glad to see you looking fit."

"She'll have you to thank for my health."

"I only did what was expected of me."

"I didn't expect it of you."

"Well, Innis did, and he's the one I have to please."

"You did more than please *me*, Moira." He walked slowly toward her, wanting to make her understand how much she'd come to mean to him. "I don't believe I'd be alive today if you hadn't cared for me."

"Sure you're a big whacker of a fellow and strong as an ox. All you needed was bed rest and some greasewood tea." She grasped the edge of the table behind her and squeezed it as he approached. Why her heart was thumping fair out of her chest she couldn't imagine, but she knew that the closer he got, the more she felt the urge to bolt like a young calf in the presence of a wolf.

"I want to thank you," he said. He stopped and put his palm on the table beside her, resting his weight on the hand. "I may have said or done certain things. . . . I don't really remember everything."

"No, it's all right. I kept you half potted most of the time anyway, especially when you were groaning so much. I knew you weren't in your right mind."

"But some of the things I said, Moira—"

"Really, it's all right. I knew you were raving."

"I meant some of the things I said. I want you to understand that." How could he make her see that she was so unlike the coarse mining-camp women he had known? She was different, too, from the girls he'd grown up with in the Mexican village and even from the few fine society ladies he'd met. Moira accepted him as a man. She might not take to his dreams of stocking sheep, but that was what he planned to *do*, not who he *was*. She didn't throw his skin color in his face. She never snubbed or ridiculed him for his ancestry. For the first time in his life, he'd met a woman who took him at face value, and she was a good woman—strong, beautiful, and honest.

"You're gentle, Moira," he said, trying to show her that she'd touched him as no one else ever had. "You're kind and faithful, and if you weren't promised in marriage to Scully—"

"Scully! Holy saints, who told you that?"

"He did."

"That sherral! I never agreed to such a thing. The very idea." Moira crossed her arms and glared out the window. She could feel the heat in her cheeks, and she knew they must be as red as her nose. Scully and Innis were still talking under the big tree, the pair of them huddled together. "Did your brother say anything about this cock-and-bull story of Scully's?"

"He seemed to know about the arrangement. But Innis was more interested in making sure that I'm fit enough to head out."

Moira clamped her mouth shut. The two men, father and son, had lifted their red heads and were staring in the direction of the road. Cats of a kind, she thought. So this was Innis's new plan—to marry her off to Scully now that the boy was grown. That way Innis could permanently secure the O'Casey ranch as his own and make it a part of the great Grady legacy. But if Innis's plot was mercenary, Scully's agreement to it was surely based on his besotted notion of carrying Moira off to Paris and living a romantic life as an artist.

"I'm not going to marry Scully," she announced, giving Josiah a sharp look. "Don't think I am, and don't spread the word down the valley. You'll keep your mouth closed about such a chuckleheaded idea, do you twig me? I've chosen to be a lone woman, and lone I'll be until my dying day."

"You don't want a husband, Moira?" Josiah asked. "A family?"

"No. I don't." As she said the words, she felt the lump in her throat knot more tightly. "Now be gone with you Mister Josiah Chee. I've work to do."

"Peeling *onions*?" He glanced down at the table, then raised his head, his mouth lifting into a slight smile.

"They're potatoes, so they are, and what of it?"

"You were crying because I'm leaving, weren't you?"

She stared into his brown eyes. "You'd better get back to your bed, Josiah Chee," she whispered. "You're drunk yet, so you are."

"I haven't had a drop of Innis's whiskey since last night. For that matter, a good part of the time my head's been as clear as a bell when you've come into my room with your lavender scent and your soft hands. Moira, you didn't *have* to shave me every morning. No one ordered you to wash and comb my hair the way you did. You tended me out of the goodness of your heart. And there were times . . . times when I would have sworn you were an angel in my room . . . times when I was sure you were sitting in the darkness watching over me and wanting . . . wanting . . ."

"Wanting what?" she whispered, her lips dry and her breath ragged in her breast.

"Wanting to touch me the way I wanted to touch you, Moira." He lifted his hand to her hair, but as his fingers found the end of a curl, the kitchen door burst open.

"It's Erinn, Moira!" Scully shouted, barging into the kitchen. "Erinn's come up the valley for a visit. Her wagon's on the road just now! Come on—I'll race you hotfoot to the house!" A moment later the youth scampered away, his boots churning up dust.

Moira turned to Josiah. "Erinn's my sister," she said. "God has delivered her to me, just as I prayed."

But as she hurried out of the kitchen, Moira turned her eyes heavenward. Erinn had been sent. And now Josiah would leave.

# Chapter
## 3

"* Céad míla fáilte!*" Moira called, waving as she ran toward the wagon.

"And a hundred thousand welcomes to you!" At the sight of her older sister, Erinn pulled hard on the leather reins. When the horses had stopped, she lifted her skirts and fairly flew to the ground. "God save you, Moira!"

"God save you kindly!" The sisters threw their arms about each other's necks, kissing cheeks and dancing in excited circles. "Oh, I've missed you so, Erinn! What brings you to Fianna—and where's Seamus?"

Erinn glanced at the road for an instant. "Seamus is at the ranch, so he is." Then she laughed. "I've come for a visit. Now let me look at you!" Erinn held Moira at arm's length and studied her sister. "Sure you're thin and pale as a rawney but bright-eyed as ever. Eyes still as blue as the whole sky, but sunk in your face so they are, and red-rimmed at that. Has Innis been working you too hard, Moira?"

"As ever."

"Oh, Innis!" Erinn turned to the older man with a mock scowl. "Isn't Moira to have a moment's joy in life? You'll work her into the ground, so you will. And there's young Scully. Still a sheela painting grand pictures, are you?"

"I've taken your old room for a studio, Erinn," Scully said with a lift to his chin. "And I've made plans to study art in Paris, so I have."

"Good for you, Scully!" Erinn chuckled and rumpled his damp red hair. "Oh, it's fine to see the lot of you— and the old house at Fianna. Faith, how I've missed this place. You'll never know how blessed you are to have such a home."

Sensing the wave of sadness that had suddenly swept over her younger sister, Moira slipped her arm around Erinn's shoulders. "Time has healed your memories. You were glad enough to be leaving Fianna when Seamus offered for you, Erinn. Come into the house now and let me pour you some cold lemonade. You didn't drive all this way alone, did you? What was Seamus thinking, sending you off on your own in this wild country?"

"I'm safe now. That's all that matters, Moira. I'm safe with you again here at Fianna." Erinn paused at the foot of the steps, and Moira heard her sister's breath catch. "Who is *that*?"

At the end of the long, shadowed *portal* of the adobe house stood Josiah Chee. His massive chest and bare arms were silhouetted against the sunlight. As he walked toward them, he emerged from the cool darkness to reveal a mane of tawny hair framing a face that might have been cast in the finest bronze.

"It's Josiah Chee," Moira said softly. "Innis's half brother."

"God save you, Mister Chee." Erinn dipped her head in greeting, and for the first time in her life Moira saw her sister through different eyes—Josiah's eyes.

A stunning beauty, Erinn had a small porcelain nose and a pair of dimples that deepened in her pink cheeks when she smiled. Her neck was silken and as creamy as new milk, her hands as delicate as a child's. The rolls of thick hair on her head gleamed like beaten gold, and when she straightened, her breasts beneath the low-cut bodice of her dress seemed to strut out like a pair of proud peacocks.

In fact, Moira had to admit the two sisters couldn't have been more different. Where the elder was tall and angular, the younger was short and curvy. When loose from its pins, Moira's hair was a tangle of auburn curls while Erinn's fell as straight as a golden sheet. Moira felt fulfilled doing good hard work and was prone to musing on deep thoughts, but Erinn escaped as many chores as possible, and she didn't have a religious bone in her body. She had perfected the telling of white lies to a fine art, and she was so able to charm her victims that they were completely disarmed and forgiving.

Moira tried to swallow the lump of envy she had never felt until this moment. "Josiah, this is my sister, Erinn. She's come up from the Sullivan place on the lower Peñasco." She gave Erinn a kindly smile, but her willful tongue wagged on, uncontrolled. "Erinn's married, you see," she added. "Seamus Sullivan is her husband, so he is."

"Good afternoon, Mrs. Sullivan." Josiah made as if to lift his hat, then realized he wasn't wearing one. He grinned instead, and his smile fairly lit up the afternoon. "You've come a long way alone."

"Aye, and so have you, sir." Erinn's voice was light. Moira could have sworn she was flirting. "I understood you to live near the Berrendo with Innis's mother."

"The doctor sent Josiah down from Fort Stanton," Scully explained, cutting in. "He got injured in a mine in Butte where he was working. We've been looking after him for two weeks."

"Wounded? God save you, sir. So, you're a copper miner, then, Josiah Chee?"

Josiah glanced from Erinn to Moira. The look on her face told him she had not informed Innis and Scully that his injury was caused by a shotgun rather than by mining equipment. Neither of the Irishmen would know that an enemy had tried to take Josiah's life—and that the same enemy was probably searching Lincoln County for him even now. Moira had kept this information from them; she had protected him from his brother even as she fought to save his life.

"I was a miner in Montana for three years," he answered the fair-haired younger sister. "And it's Moira who has taken care of me the two weeks."

"Oh?" Erinn arched one eyebrow at her sister. "He looks as good as new, Moira. I'm certain Innis is pleased to have his brother healthy and here in God's pocket at Fianna."

"By japers, you'll talk the rivers dry, Erinn," Innis snapped. "Get inside, gligeen, and sit your backside down. Moira, serve us up some cold lemonade before we perish in the heat."

"Aye, Innis," Moira said, grateful for something to do. She hurried through the house to the kitchen.

The cellar was cool and dark. The few lemons left from last summer had shrunk and withered, but Moira knew that with effort they would make a full pitcher of lemonade. After filling her apron from the bucket, she settled for a moment on a stool, her lap full of lemons.

Though she needed to think, there wasn't time. She should be squeezing lemons and adding cold water and sugar to the pitcher. She should be piling napkins, a tablecloth, and glasses on a tray. She should be slicing cake and setting out dishes.

Oh, but how Erinn had looked at Josiah! He had looked at Erinn, too. Moira grabbed two lemons and held them tight. What difference did it make if they looked at each other? Even if they found each other attractive, why should it matter to Moira? Erinn was married to Seamus Sullivan, the richest Irishman in the valley. Josiah would be leaving Fianna tomorrow. Besides, Moira knew she held no claim to those deep-set brown eyes.

She jumped up from the stool, climbed the ladder into

the kitchen, and began to work. Never, never had she been this flustered over a man! Halving lemons with a butcher knife, she watched the pale juice dribble onto the cutting board. Anyone would think she was a regular googeen over him—studying his every move, thinking about him day and night, allowing bold thoughts to slip into her mind where they didn't belong. After wedging a lemon into the hinged wooden squeezer, she used her pent-up energy to crush the fruit until its juice ran into the porcelain cup beneath. But the things he had said to her in this very kitchen only minutes ago! Had he meant them? Did he really think she was beautiful and kind and good?

"If you weren't promised in marriage to Scully . . ." Josiah had said those very words, and they had slid down her bones like warm honey. But she wasn't promised to Scully. What would Josiah do about it? Was he serious about her, or was he just a bold shoneen who chased every petticoat in sight? Even if he meant what he had told her, she'd gone on and on about how happy she was being a lone woman. And she *was* happy. Wasn't she?

Moira dumped the strained lemon seeds into the pail of potato peelings by the kitchen door. Sugar, sugar, would there be enough sugar? Hurrying, she plunged the dipper into the sugar bin. What if Josiah left Fianna before she had a chance to say good-bye?

It shouldn't matter. God had sent Erinn to fill his place in the house. *Erinn.* Moira poured a jug of cold water over the sweetened juice and gave it a stir. Erinn was her best friend, her bosom companion, her sister. They shared everything! Didn't Erinn know better than to behave like a whipster around Josiah? Didn't she see that Moira had cared for him, that Moira had tended him, that Moira . . .

*Moira what*? What *did* she feel for Josiah? She slammed the pitcher onto a tray and thunked five glasses beside it. Nothing, that was what. She felt the way any good-hearted woman would feel about a sick person she had nursed back to health. She felt glad to see him up and about, and pleased that he would be on his way again soon.

No, she didn't want him to go! Not at all.

Hurrying through the dogtrot, Moira glanced into the sitting room. Erinn sat on the settee, her blue skirts spread out over the velvet cushion and her golden hair glinting in the sunlight that streamed through an open window. She looked like an angel from heaven, so she did. Josiah stood by the fireplace, one arm on the mantel and his eyes pinned to Erinn's face.

Sick at heart, Moira crossed the hall into the dining room. As she laid out the tablecloth, napkins, and glasses, she eavesdropped on the conversation next door.

"There's a good killeen of artists I could study under in Paris," Scully was saying to Erinn. "It's done, you twig me? I've read in the newspapers that people from the East sail to the Continent all the time to learn about painting. There are galleries in New York and Philadelphia and Boston just looking for new talent."

"God bless you, Scully, I do believe you mean this!" Erinn said with a laugh. Moira had never noticed that her sister's chuckle held such a tinkling note.

"He'll be a millionaire before we know it, *mor-yah*," Innis snorted. "People will be grubbing to hand over their life savings for his fat-fingered ladies."

"Innis, let him be!" Erinn protested. "Sure Scully has a good measure of talent."

"Enough to fill up a thimble and no more. He'll take over this ranch, blast his soul, and he'll see that the Grady line has a fine future and a home along the Peñasco for years to come."

"Papa, you know I—"

"Lemonade," Moira cut in before the conversation could take an unpleasant turn. She could sense Innis's growing black mood, and she didn't want Scully to provoke him in any way. Since his mother died, Moira had been the buffer between father and son. "There's poppyseed cake, too. Baked fresh this morning."

"Moira is the only one I can count on around here," Innis grumbled as the company rose and made for the dining room. "She's steady as a rock, and good thing, or I'd be flat on my face with my braddach sheela of a son to look out for."

As the others settled around the table, Moira began pouring the lemonade. Just what she wanted to be, she thought, a *rock*.

"Where's Josiah?" she asked the moment she realized he wasn't in the room.

"He's fetching a shirt," Innis said. "What did I tell you, Erinn? See how your sister watches over the pattha? He barely whimpers, and she's there beside him in a flash. She's always in his room, opening his curtains, closing his curtains, opening his curtains—"

"Glory be to God, you're jealous!" Erinn chided. "I never thought I'd see the day when Innis Grady would be chittering about Moira. Maybe you ought to marry her and be tended to as well as your brother has been these past two weeks."

"Erinn!" Moira gasped.

"Quit your ballyraggin', Erinn," Innis snapped. "You're as full of blatherumskite as anyone I know. I'm only put out because Moira's filled Josiah full of my whiskey day after day as though it was this damned lemonade. She's torn up half the sheets in the house making bandages for him. She's always trotting in and out of his room with thick slices of pie or steamin' cups of tea when it's not even teatime."

"I owe Moira my life," Josiah said from the doorway. Everyone turned to watch him walk across the room. Though his pace was slow, he moved with the natural grace of a cat. His big shoulders strained the seams of the clean white shirt he had put on, and his boots were heavy on the pine floor.

Moira noticed at once that the coiled leather *látigo* he

had been so concerned over now hung by a thong from the belt loop of his denim trousers. She knew that the traditional gear of a sheepman included a wooden crook, a sling, and a whip, and that these were used only for the control and defense of the flocks, never as offensive weapons. Yet Josiah wore his whip against the side of his thigh, much as cowpunchers wore their holstered six-shooters. All the same, Moira couldn't imagine what good a length of braided cowhide could really do, other than speed up the gait of a horse. His blacksnake certainly hadn't protected him from that shotgun blast.

"Without the whiskey, the greasewood tea, and the bandages," he was saying as he seated himself in the empty chair between Erinn and Scully, "I wouldn't have survived. I thank her, and I thank you, too, Innis, for putting me up."

"It was no great shakes," Innis said. "If it isn't one calamity or inconvenience at Fianna, it's another. We're used to it by now, aren't we, Moira?"

Nodding, she kept her eyes on her cake. "Aye, Innis. So we are." Why couldn't she look at Josiah? For two weeks she'd bathed and shaved the man; suddenly she couldn't bring herself to meet his eyes. How foolish, how silly she must look with her cheeks bright red and her eyes downcast.

"I trust you'll take a letter from me to Mother when you go," Innis was saying to Josiah. "She'll want to know how we're getting on here. Maybe she'd like Scully to come for a visit. God knows she hasn't seen the boy since he was but a crowl and his mother had just died."

"I'm sure she'll want to see him," Josiah answered, thinking of his mother and how her green eyes were so like Scully's in shape, depth, and coloring. "He's her only grandchild, so she talks about him a lot."

"Does she, then?" Scully asked, brightening. "Maybe I'll just ride up with you, Josiah. I'd like to see my Grandma Sheena."

"Not this time, Scully," Josiah replied. "There's trouble along the Berrendo."

"What sort of trouble?" Erinn asked.

"Some years back, after the worst of Lincoln Town's troubles were over, there was a camp of my people living on the North Spring River near Roswell. Some of them were *ricos*—rich sheepmen."

"Sheep, bah," Innis muttered under his breath. "There's the root of the trouble right there."

Josiah glanced at Moira, but she was concentrating on cutting her piece of cake into tiny squares and then pushing them around her plate. He wondered if this family, like the one he grew up in, was accustomed to lively dinner talk. They sure were a sullen bunch.

"These Mexicans began to dig a ditch in hopes of irrigating the valley," he continued, deciding it couldn't hurt to try and strike up a conversation, "but they were forced to abandon it before it was finished. Ten of the families joined my father's settlement on the Berrendo. The camp was growing, and everyone was doing well until a band of outlaws, still in the Territory after Lincoln's five-day battle, attacked our settlement and stole everything, even the women's *mantóns*."

"You were growing sheep, that's why," Innis snapped.

"Maybe so. Or maybe they attacked us because we're Mexicans." Josiah studied the stocky red-faced man who was his half brother. He wondered whether Innis's dislike of him stemmed more from Josiah's Mexican-Indian heritage or from the sheep his father ran. "The outlaws warned us to get out of the area or they'd come back and kill us. My father and the others suspected that the desperadoes were members of the Horrell gang, who had murdered Mexicans up and down the Pecos Valley a few years before. Most of the families in the settlement fled. My parents chose to stay on, but there's a bitterness in the community toward gringos. Some have even whispered of massacring every white man in Roswell."

"Great ghosts!" Innis exploded. "You'll not go there, Scully. And what of my mother's safety? Sure she's as pale as new snow, and she's Irish through and through. Is her life safe in the hands of these Mexican black-guards?"

"My father's a strong man," Josiah stated simply. "And Mother is a strong woman. He protects her, and she keeps her eyes open."

"Gabriel Chee is a damned half-breed sheepherder with nothing better than a whip to guard her!"

"My father is the son of an Apache warrior, and he's braver than any man I know," Josiah returned, struggling to tame his temper. "I have four brothers at home, too, who'd give their lives to protect my mother. She's safe from outlaws who might come along. In spite of the fear and hatred of gringos in the Mexican village, my mother's been accepted by the people there. The color of her skin and country of her birth make no difference to them. She won the women over with her kindness, and my father has become a leader of the men."

"But he's a heathen, by japers! An Apache! A Mexican, too. If there ever was a combination that promised treachery, idleness, trickery, filth—"

"Innis!" Moira admonished, unable to control herself. "You'll guard your tongue now, sir, so you will! Josiah's father is the man your mother chose to wed. You disgrace her by speaking ill of him."

"And you shut your smush!" Innis snarled, turning his wrath on her. "What do you know about anything? My mother made the greatest mistake of her life when she let herself be seduced by that half-breed. Apaches are killers, murderers. They'll sell their very souls for a swig of whiskey, so they will. And Mexicans—never have I seen a more dirty, scrabbling, lazy killeen of lice—"

"The devil take you, Innis! You'll not talk like that in this house, you won't. It's Scully's grandmother and your own mother you dishonor with such words. What do you know about those people anyway? You've never been to the Berrendo to your mother's home, and you've not—"

"None of your slack jaw now, you strap!" His face flushing crimson, he pushed up from the table, upsetting the pitcher of lemonade as he lunged at Moira. Faster than a flash of lightning, he swung at her with the back of his hand. She ducked, and he missed by a hair. Her forehead glanced off the edge of the table. She slid to the floor, her arms vainly shielding her head.

He stumbled over fallen chairs trying to get at her. "I'll not have a woman's hysterics in this house!"

"Innis, no!" Erinn shrieked. "Moira, run!" Knocking her chair to one side, she lifted her skirts and fled.

Scully muttered, "Not this again," then grabbed his plate of cake and vanished.

"Sure you'll be praisin' the nesters in a minute," Innis shouted at Moira over the scramble of the others leaving the table, "and the sheepherders, too, so you will. And always onto me about my drinkin'!"

"Innis, don't hit me!" Moira struggled to her feet, her eyes wide and her heart as frantic as a drumbeat in battle. In some distant fog, she caught a glimpse of Josiah. He was staring at Innis, transfixed. She clutched the back of her chair as if such a barrier might protect her from her attacker. How often had they been at odds this way, and how often had she failed to placate him? "I'm only trying to talk some sense into your clotted brain, so I am," she reasoned, her voice trembling.

"You'll talk yourself into a leatherin', so you will," he hollered, his green eyes aflame with rage. "Come here now and take your medicine, throllop!" He caught her wrist and jerked her out from behind the chair.

"Please don't!" she begged. This would be no ordinary cuffing, she knew at once. Innis had been pushed too far. His face was scarlet, his cheeks puffing, his nostrils flared and white-rimmed.

"This is for your impudence," he growled. His hand

smashed across her mouth. Her lip tore across her teeth and burst open with a spray of blood. She cried out and tried to cover her face, but he pushed her against the dining room wall. He drew his fist back. She flinched and shut her eyes.

A crack exploded in her ear.

"*Aaah!*" It was Innis whose voice filled the room. Moira's eyes flew open. The Irishman lay on the floor, his right hand wrapped in the leather tip of Josiah's whip. Josiah strode across the room and stomped on Innis's wrist.

"Apologize." His voice was low, deadly.

"Let me go, demon!" Innis barked. "She deserved it, so she did. And what's more—"

"Apologize, or I'll break your wrist."

"The devil take you, boy."

Josiah jerked the butt of his whip, and Innis howled. "Tell her you're sorry. You'll never hit her again."

Innis's green eyes lifted to Moira, who stood with a hand over her mouth. She knew he wouldn't apologize— he never had.

"I'll deal with you later, clart." He glared at Josiah. "Now then, *brother*, to get myself out of this tangle, I'll apologize. And, Moira, you'd damn well better accept."

"I accept," she said quickly. "It was a sin of me to be so bold with you."

Josiah was gazing at her, his brown eyes veiled. He lifted his foot from Innis's arm and jerked loose his whip. As Josiah coiled the leather blacksnake, Innis rolled onto his knees. Then, puffing, he struggled to his feet.

"You get out of my house," he snarled, punctuating the command with a stabbing finger. "You weren't welcome to begin with, and now you've put your nose where it doesn't belong."

"I'll leave tomorrow," Josiah agreed. "At sunup."

"You'll leave now!"

"If I go now, I'll take Moira with me. I won't let a

woman come to harm at my own brother's hand, Innis. When you're calm, I'll leave."

"The sooner you leave, the quicker my temper will settle. You're the cause of all this, so you are. If you hadn't come here, I wouldn't have to be reminded of my mother's sin and her half-breed whelp. I know why she sent you here. She thinks she still has some claim to Fianna through her marriage to my father. You're her second son. She wants you to stand against me and put your stamp on half the land here, doesn't she?"

"Our mother sent me here for my own safety. She has no designs on your pitiful dry land, Innis, and neither do I. I don't need your cattle to build my fortune."

As he stared at the little bulldog of a man, Josiah realized how far apart he and his brother really were. If he'd had visions of being welcomed into this broad extended family, this clan of Irishmen his mother had spoken of so often, his dreams were nothing but an illusion. Innis Grady despised him. Worse, maybe, Innis feared him.

Josiah certainly had plans for his own future, but they didn't include stealing his brother's property. Innis had no idea that Josiah was in a financial position to ease the hard times at Fianna. Income from his mining partnership in Butte could more than restore Innis's fallen empire. If the brothers banded together, they could truly build a strong, unified ranching empire along the Peñasco. But the hatred in Innis's green eyes told Josiah there would be no peace between them.

"I'll leave at dawn," he said.

"That you will, and don't come back."

Without responding to his brother, Josiah turned to Moira. "May I speak to you?"

Her heart jumped into her throat. Fearful of disrupting the uneasy peace, she glanced at Innis, but he was already stalking off toward the kitchen, no doubt to fetch a drink. "We'll talk in the parlor," she whispered.

Josiah nodded, took her elbow, and walked her across the hall into the cool afternoon shadows of the sitting room. He could hardly believe what his own eyes had just witnessed. Still numb from the sight of a man— his own kin—slapping the spirit out of a woman, Josiah swallowed at the lump of bile in his throat.

He knew the depths to which a man could sink when greed, lust, liquor, or rage had hold of him. But to turn that evil on a woman—a woman as good and gentle as Moira O'Casey? For the first time in his life, Josiah felt the urge to use his strength, his cunning, his weapons, all he possessed, to exact a terrible permanent revenge.

Moira dabbed at her lip with a handkerchief as she stood beside a horsehair settee. She felt jittery and a little faint. In the dining room Erinn was scrambling to clean up the broken dishes. Scully was no doubt painting out his fear and frustration in his studio down the hall. Innis would be in the pantry, opening a bottle of whiskey. The family had dispersed, shattered. Moira couldn't help believing it was all her fault—the fault of her heedless tongue.

She took a breath. "Josiah, you mustn't think Innis—"

"Stop defending the man, Moira," he cut in. "How often does he beat you?"

"Oh, it's usually more of a cuff than a beating. And it's only when I ballyrag that he loses his temper. I shouldn't have run on at him so."

"No matter what you said or did, he had no right to hit you, Moira." He took her shoulders. They felt so small, so fragile, in his big hands. He heard his own voice, low and intense, almost a whisper. "The hell of it is, you were defending *me*. And I didn't do a thing to protect you until it was almost too late. I just couldn't believe it. I couldn't accept what I was seeing."

"I've always had trouble keeping my mouth shut."

"I don't believe that. You didn't tell Innis I'd been shot, and you never mentioned my plan to raise sheep. When you finally spoke up, you stood against him to defend his own mother, and he beat you until you were . . . until you were bloody."

She gazed into his dark brown eyes that so intently searched her face. "Josiah, really, I—"

"Moira, you can't stay here." His fingers tightened on her shoulders. "I'll take you to the settlement on the Berrendo, to my parents' house. You'll be safe there."

"Oh, I could never do that," she whispered. But even as she said the words she felt her heart slamming against her ribs. "Sure I made a holy vow to Scully's mother before she died. I swore I'd look after the boy and his father for the rest of my life. Deirdre was so good to me, and I loved her deeply. I would never betray her. Besides, my father made Innis Grady my guardian—"

"Guardian! The man will kill you one of these days. You need protection from your protector, Moira. Your lip is torn and swollen." He touched her mouth with his fingertip. "Who'll take care of *you* while you heal?"

She couldn't speak. His hand left her lip and moved up across her cheek to touch the bruise on her forehead. Gently, gently, he probed, brushing back her hair and stroking the soft skin. His fingers felt warm against the cool pallor of her face, and his eyes asked for answers she couldn't give.

"Come with me, Moira," he said. "I'll keep you safe."

As she looked into his face, a thousand pictures rolled in a giant wave through her thoughts. If only she *could* leave with Josiah! She would escape Innis and his beatings. She'd leave Scully to make his own way in the world. There would be a home for her—a home of her own. For one instant she dared to dream of things that as a young girl she had put away forever—a man's shirts hanging on the line, his socks in her mending basket, his plate beside hers on the table, his pillow next to hers in the bed. This man's pillow and this man's bed . . . Josiah . . .

"No." She shook her head before the images became too compelling. "I belong here at Fianna. I've promised to stay with Innis. As cruel as he can be sometimes, he has no one but me to take care of him. Scully needs looking after, too. They don't have anyone to cook or wash or sweep or make a fire."

Even as she spoke, her own words sounded hollow. Now Josiah's hands had slipped down to her shoulders again, and he drew her toward him until her skirt touched the toes of his boots. Too close, far too close.

"And Erinn," she fumbled, searching for something to keep herself distant from him. "Erinn's come for a visit. She needs me, too."

"I'm the only one who doesn't need you, Moira," he said, aware of an ache that had caught in his chest and wouldn't let go. How could he make her see that she'd come to mean more to him than just a caretaker? How could he let her know that he desired her for the woman she was? "I don't need a washerwoman and a cook. I don't *need* you, but I *want* you."

"Josiah!" She caught her breath as he pulled her hard against him. His hands cupped her head, his thumbs tilting back her jaw to force her eyes to meet his.

"Moira, listen to me. Every day in that room I watched you come and go. You were an angel to me."

"Sure I'm no angel, Josiah Chee!" She pushed against his chest, but he only held her closer. Her hands closed on the fabric of his shirt. "I'm a good Christian woman, and it's my duty to serve others, so it is. But I've a temper straight from the devil, and I can't keep a rein on my tongue. I'm stubborn as any mule. I have wayward thoughts—"

"Thoughts about me."

"No."

"Yes. I've seen the way you look at me, Moira. The way you touch me."

"I was only washing you because Innis said—"

"Moira, wanting a man won't send you to hell. It's no sin to have the same feelings and needs that the good Lord gave Adam and Eve."

"Those temptations were the devil's serpent whispering in their ears," she protested even as her body relaxed against his, and she allowed him to slip his arms around her. "Are you the devil, Josiah Chee?"

He smiled. "I'm a man. Plain and simple." Then he lightly brushed his mouth across hers.

Holding her breath at this first kiss of her life, she shut her eyes, and her hands tightened on the clumps of shirt fabric she had clutched. In betrayal of her staunch morals, she felt her body come awake, impulsively lift into his, tingle with awareness of every hollow and plane of his form.

"Again," she whispered to him. "Again, Josiah."

She heard his breath grow ragged as he caught her hard against him. "Moira," he murmured, and the word brushed against the down of her cheek. "Moira, I—"

"*Moira?*" The door to the dining room banged open, and Erinn's steps came across the hall toward the parlor. "Moira, where are you?"

Jumping backward out of Josiah's arms, Moira stared at him, guilt written in her blue eyes. "I'm here, Erinn!"

Erinn walked into the room. She spotted Josiah immediately, then took in her sister, bright pink cheeks and all, and raised her golden eyebrows. "Oh, Mister Chee, you're here, too. How good of you to tend Moira in her time of distress."

"Someone should."

"Aye, but you mustn't think badly of Innis." Erinn squinted at Moira's swollen lip as she spoke. "Ever since his wife, Deirdre, passed away, God rest her soul, Innis has had a blazing time keeping Moira and me under control. With Moira, it's her tongue that won't obey. With me, it's just . . . well, it's me. All of me. And Innis taught us that when a woman won't listen, then . . . then . . ." Erinn's lower lip began to quiver, and she quickly tucked it between her teeth and bit down hard.

"Erinn?" Moira asked softly. "What is it?"

She gave an exaggerated shrug. "You'll be leaving us tomorrow, will you, Josiah Chee?"

"I'll take Moira with me if she'll go."

Moira studied him as he stood there, his hands planted on his hips, the great coiled whip hanging at his side, its butt end loose against his thigh. He was a giant of a man, she thought, both powerful and intelligent. He was kind, too, and he clearly wanted to protect her from any harm. Though he carried no gun, he had proved himself skillful with the *látigo*. But to go with him? To leave Fianna? The very idea was unthinkable.

She took a deep breath. "Can you imagine?" she asked, turning to Erinn with a forced lightness in her voice. "*Me* on a sheep ranch? Hiding out with a bunch of woollies? Sure Innis would come after me, and a lot of good that whip would do against his six-shooter. No, I'll stay here at Fianna where I belong. Thank you kindly for your offer, Mister Chee. You're a good man, so you are." She hesitated a moment before adding, "A fine man. Plain and simple."

Before he could answer, she gave him a quick nod and fled from the room.

# Chapter
## 4

With teatime ruined, Moira made up her mind to put on the finest dinner she could manage. If only she could create an atmosphere of peace, the antagonists at Fianna might calm down and unite—might truly become *family*, as they were meant to be. Family was all Moira had ever wanted.

She and Erinn didn't mention the upsetting incident in the dining room. Instead they worked together in the stuffy kitchen to create the wonderful dinner Moira had planned—an enormous shepherd's pie topped with mounds of fluffy mashed potatoes, plus a hearty pot of baked pinto beans, a basket of corn bread, and a heavy pound cake sprinkled with cinnamon sugar.

Ignoring her throbbing lip and bruised forehead, Moira labored over the hot fire until her gingham dress was damp and her hair had curled into a thousand tiny auburn ringlets. Cheeks ruddy, she carried heavy porcelain plates and silver from the wooden dresser in the kitchen to the dining table. Erinn, as expected, gave up the cooking project when the evening grew too hot, and she wandered out to the stables. Moira decided she didn't mind, although it occurred to her that Josiah might be grooming a horse for his journey down the Peñasco the following morning.

In her nest of a kitchen, Moira felt she could relax. While she worked in the cozy niches between the dresser, the cupboard, the dry sink, and the fireplace, she could ponder matters and try to make sense of them. She knew she had made a great muddle of the whole day—publicly reprimanding Innis, causing a mess in the dining room, and then flirting with Josiah as though she were a loose woman with no morals at all.

Every time she recalled the way she had stood on tiptoe to seek another kiss from the man, she wanted to fade away into the shadows of her kitchen and perish of shame. How bold she'd been—grabbing his shirt and pressing herself against him! The merest memory of that moment sent strange aching curls through her stomach and down into her thighs. Her knees felt like quicksand, and her heart raced at such speed she was sure everyone for miles around could hear it slamming into her ribs.

As if preparing the meal were her penance for these unacceptable feelings and thoughts, Moira shifted steaming pots and pans on the grate, stirred vats of cooking beef, peeled countless potatoes, and baked enough corn bread to feed two armies.

Of course she managed to drop on the floor almost as many eggs as she was able to break into the pound cake. Her trembling hand spilled a dipperful of precious sugar across the kitchen table, and like sand, it invaded everything else she was cooking. She tripped over one of the calico farm cats and broke a jug of milk—to the cat's great delight. Worst of all, she singed the mashed potato topping on the shepherd's pie.

*That* was Josiah's fault. She kept stopping right in the middle of her cooking to dwell on the most untoward things! Why had Josiah asked her into the parlor to talk that afternoon? He knew she couldn't leave

Fianna. This was her home. Innis and Scully needed her. Didn't they?

Gingerly she touched her swollen lip. Oh, what if Josiah left Fianna and she never again knew the warmth of his kiss? What if she never again in her whole life felt the sweet surge of honey that had flowed through her veins when he'd taken her in his arms? The pressure of his mouth on hers had been so . . . so stirring . . . so aching . . . so tempting. . . .

*The beans!* As the odor of burning sauce drifted through the kitchen, Moira gasped and leapt to the handle of the kettle. The moment she grabbed it, a searing pain shot through her bare palm and up to her elbow. She jerked her hand away and buried it in the folds of her apron. Instantly she felt a row of stinging blisters rise on her palm. Water! She swung around to plunge her hand into the bucket of cold water by the door, just as Josiah walked into the kitchen.

"Moira?" His brow furrowed at the sight of her pale face.

"Josiah!" She jerked her hand from the bucket.

"I came to talk to you."

"But my beans—"

"Beans?" What was she talking about? He scowled at the wisps of smoke drifting from the pot on the fire. Beans . . . The beans were burning. He grabbed some dish towels and in two strides lifted the heavy black kettle from its hook over the fire. He set it on the wooden table, found a spoon, and gave the pot a quick stir. The thick, bubbling beans oozed around the stem of the spoon, their aroma wafting up out of the pot.

"It's okay," he said quickly. "They're not stuck to the bottom. We'll add a little water and some more pepper, and they'll taste fine."

When he raised his head, he saw that Moira was staring at him, her beautiful lips parted in surprise. As always, she seemed like a vision to him—pale and fragile, her hair wild but her blue eyes as soft as petals. She was cradling one hand, her breath coming in shallow gasps, and it was all he could do to keep from taking her in his arms and pressing her sweet mouth to his.

But no, Moira was as uncertain as a doe in an open field—a wounded doe who had learned never to trust man. Her eyes were wary of him, and he knew she would flee if he made even the slightest movement to frighten her. She was a woman, and yet she was a child. He had to go slowly with her. But there was so little time.

"Do you have pepper, Moira?" he asked.

She glanced at the grinder.

He carefully ground just enough pepper into the beans to mask the burned taste, then stirred the pot again. "Water?" he asked.

She glanced at the pail by the door.

He poured in a fair amount. She had let a lot of the liquid bubble away, and his mother had taught him that beans needed a sauce to keep them from tasting like glue. It wasn't like Moira to make a mistake in the kitchen. For two weeks he had been nourished by her savory meals, the likes of which he hadn't tasted since he was a boy at home.

"Back onto the fire with it," he said, lifting the kettle onto its hook. "Mind if I kick down some of these logs so the beans don't burn again?"

She shook her head. Her big blue eyes followed every movement he made as he stuck a boot into the fire and nudged the wood. As the burning logs shifted and crashed, their flames faded into glowing embers. The beans would simmer safely now.

"Moira," he said, straightening and turning to face her, "I'll say what I want to say straight out. I can't leave you here. I've been walking for two hours, thinking about it. I'm asking you to come with me. I'll protect you."

"From what?" she whispered. "Fianna is my home, Josiah. You know I can't leave."

"You'd stay here with Innis? With a man who beats you? Who brutalizes you?"

"Sure I should go away with you, a man I don't even know."

"You know me. You know everything about me—more than anyone does. I've said things to you, Moira. I've told you—"

"You were drunk and swooning with fever besides." She gave a careless shrug, though it was difficult to be false with him. "I hardly listened to you, Josiah. You were blathering day and night, and most of it was the purest nonsense. Sure you might as well be a stranger to me."

He slammed his palm down on the table, rattling the array of bowls. "We're no strangers, Moira. Why won't you admit that?"

Swallowing, she shook her head. Couldn't he see that she was bound to do the right thing, the moral thing? She had always obeyed, always behaved as she should.

"I'm a good Christian woman, Josiah," she whispered. "I won't leave my duties. My loyalty is to my family, no matter what you might think of them. Erinn—I'll always tend and protect my sister. The memory of my father and mother, God rest their souls—I won't taint that. Innis and Deirdre Grady—they took me in when I was but an orphan. Innis has looked out for me and for my dead father's land for thirteen years. When Deirdre was dying, I made her a vow on her deathbed. I swore I'd take care of Innis and Scully for the rest of my life. Innis may be cruel at times, but he has provided for me. The least I can do is be loyal to him. So don't tempt me, Josiah Chee. I won't go away with a stranger."

Josiah studied the staunch young woman with her chin firmly set and her blue eyes flashing with stubbornness. Lord, he wanted her. He wanted her spirit, her fire. He wanted her devotion—he wanted it turned toward him.

Most of all, though, he wanted her tenderness.

As he stood watching her reject him, Josiah made up his mind. He would win Moira O'Casey. He would waken her sleeping passion. He'd win her loyalty away from his brother until she willingly gave it to him. He would soften and mold her until she was his. Completely.

"You'll stay here with Innis, then?" he asked, turning the tables on her.

She nodded resolutely. "So I will, and gladly, too. Why shouldn't I?"

"Because Innis won't give you what I will."

"And what's that, Mister Chee—a ride across the plains on a horse that's not even yours? A house in a village where the people despise me because of the color of my skin? All you have to offer a woman is yourself—a man with enemies who would shoot him full of lead, a man whose grandest dream is to breed woollies to strip the land of what little grass is left, a man with a heritage of blood and savagery."

She gave him a defiant stare, and before he could answer, she spoke again. "Here at Fianna I have a home and food and good work to do. I'm safe, and I'm content enough. What could you possibly give me, Josiah Chee, that could be better than that?"

"This," he said. He caught her arm and drew her into his embrace.

With a gasp, she pushed her palms against his chest. "No, Josiah!"

"Yes." He gently touched her with his mouth, pressing her bruised lip and sliding his mouth back and forth across it. When he heard her breath return again, this time in quick tiny sighs, he slid his hand down her back to urge her closer.

"Josiah," she whispered. The word was suffused with longing.

He gazed down and saw that her eyes were closed as though she had been drugged by his kiss. Thick red-gold eyelashes dusted her high cheekbones. Her mouth was slightly parted, and he bent to stroke the tip of his tongue over her lower lip. She gave a startled cry, her eyes flew open, and she jerked backward.

"Moira," he said softly, "has a man ever kissed you before?"

"No." She shook her head, her blue eyes frightened. "Not like that. Never."

"Not like this?" He leaned down and kissed her again, this time stroking his tongue across the tight seam of her lips. With instinct born of innate sensuality, she opened her mouth slightly to him. He tasted the dampness of her inner lip until she leaned back in his arms to break the spell.

"No," she murmured. "Josiah, it seems like a sin."

"Why, Moira?"

"It makes me weak and drunk. Sure I'm shaking like a leaf in the wind, and my head's not right. I should be thinking about dinner and such."

"You should be thinking about how it would feel to be kissed again . . . and what it might be like to part your lips against mine . . . to let me touch you deep inside."

Before she could deny him, he lowered his head and met her uptilted mouth. This time when he caressed her lips, she opened to him with just the barest hint of willingness. When he slipped into her moistness, she caught her breath. Gently, as his kiss deepened, she allowed the tip of her tongue to touch his. At the meeting, a shower of fire burst open inside her, startling and thrilling her.

Oblivious to the kitchen, the fire, the steaming dishes, Moira knew only the clean scent of this man whose hands stroked the length of her back and whose thighs pressed hard against hers. She couldn't smell her bubbling beans or her cinnamon cake, but she could taste the thrilling essence of a man she had thought she knew all about.

How wrong she had been! *This* was Josiah—strong, compelling, demanding, gentle, bold, tender. He was a man. Not a patient in need of fresh bandages. Not a hungry stomach to fill. Not a feverish rambler. He was fully male and more dominantly masculine than any man she had ever known.

As their mouths slid together, slowly, languorously, she settled her body against his as if it were the most natural thing in the world. She drank in the smell of his cotton shirt, his bare skin, his hair.

Oh, how she wanted to touch his hair! Many times she had washed it—a perfunctory scrubbing and rinsing. Now she ached to slide her fingers into the smooth, straight strands and feel the silken warmth. Even as she thought of this, he began stroking her hair. His fingers dipped into her tight curls, brushed damp tendrils from her forehead, kneaded and loosened the bun at the nape of her neck.

"I've dreamed about your hair," he whispered.

"You kept asking to touch it . . . in the fever."

"That wasn't the fever, Moira. It was . . ." He couldn't make words come as he reveled in the thick mane of auburn waves that had tempted and entranced him from the moment he first saw her. Her hair was soft, yet coarse. It tumbled through his fingers and danced down her back. It smelled of lavender. Moira's lavender. "This hair . . ." he murmured. "Your hair."

"It's wicked hair," she said quickly. "My mother always said so. Wicked hair. It won't do as it's told. It won't behave."

He smiled. "Wicked hair on an angel?"

"Sure I'm no angel, Josiah. Just look at me now, a whipster in your arms."

"When I look at you, I don't see a whipster. I see a beautiful woman with hair that tempts me and lips I want to kiss. I see a woman who's strong and kind and honest. I see you, Moira, and I want you. And it's good."

"It's a sin, as sure as I live and breathe."

"It's good, Moira."

Oh, it *was* good. It was wonderful, dizzying, mortifying—a throbbing, dancing whirlwind of tingles that shot down her arms and into the very pit of her stomach. Her mouth felt dry, and she could hardly breathe. The tips of her breasts tightened into sharp, aching points. And there was something . . . some melting, pulsing, hungering need that started at the base of her spine and slid between her thighs where it now lurked, urgent and demanding.

"It feels good, I think," she acknowledged finally, "but I fear that something so strong . . . and so *fleshly* . . . must be from the devil."

" 'All good and perfect gifts come from above,' " Josiah quoted, summoning the verse of Scripture he had learned during long hours in the small church where his family had worshiped, " 'coming down from the Father of lights—' "

" 'With whom there is no variation, or shadow of turning,' " she finished. "But, oh, Josiah, I can't stand here in my kitchen and boldly kiss a man, the brother of my own guardian. It's as though we're married, Innis and I, without all the trappings. I've given him a promise, a vow. We have an arrangement. How can I betray him? It's not proper."

"Can you turn me away, Moira?"

She looked into his brown eyes. *No*, her heart pleaded. *No, don't turn him away.* But the voice in her head was louder. "Sure I've turned away every lone man in the Peñasco Valley and a killeen of punchers besides. I can turn you away, Josiah. I must."

Hands on her shoulders, he set her back from him and studied the expression on her face. "Moira, don't give up what feels right just because it might not look right. Don't bury your dreams under a stack of duties. You deserve more."

As she stared at him, he turned and walked toward the door. But before he stepped into the dusk, he gave

her a quick grin. "*Shepherd's* pie for dinner, Moira?"
Then he lapsed into her lilting speech. "My dear brother
will be scalded, so he will, at such a dish—*shepherd's*
pie. Glory be to God, but you're a bold daltheen, Miss
O'Casey."

As he vanished through the kitchen door, she called
after him, "It's made with *beef*, so it is!" But she didn't
think he heard.

At dinner that night the group sat quietly around the
table. Innis had drunk half a bottle of whiskey before the
meal, and the liquor had turned him brooding and silent.
Erinn attempted to engage Scully in a discussion about
his latest painting, but he only remarked on the trouble
he was still having with the lady's sausage-shaped fingers, and then he too fell silent. Next, Erinn turned to
Josiah and asked him all about Montana and the copper
mines. He answered her, but his responses were short
and to the point, and he wouldn't be drawn into subjects
he didn't want to discuss.

Moira listened to everything Josiah said, but she
couldn't bring herself to look at his face or meet his
brown eyes. She felt torn apart over the man—half of
her certain she had been right to shun him, and the other
half aching with desire for him. Just one more kiss! How
could she live the rest of her long, solitary life without
just one more kiss?

Later, as she washed dishes in the dim kitchen, she
found herself listening for Josiah's footsteps in the dogtrot. Why didn't he come to her? But then, why *would*
he come, after the way she had treated him? Where was
Josiah now? In his room? In the stables? Would he be
fit enough to leave Fianna at dawn? Would he go and
never lay eyes on her again? Of course he would. She
had set herself against him, insulted him, spurned him.
Why should he come after her yet again?

Sick with longing, she slipped through the house to
the room she had always shared with Erinn. Josiah's

room was next to hers, and beneath the door she saw a golden bar of lamplight. He was still awake. Still there. Should she go to him? Should she boldly knock on his door and enter the room where they had spent so much time together? Should she fall into his strong arms and beg for one last kiss?

*No.* Josiah Chee was the devil's temptation, and she must resist. She turned the knob on her own door and pushed it open. In the moonlight through the open window she could see her sister's small curved form on the bed. At the sound of footsteps on the wooden floor, Erinn sat up and turned toward the door.

"Moira?" she asked.

"Aye, it is."

"Oh, I'm so glad you're here at last. Sure I've been lying in the dark, trembling, just waiting for you to come."

"Trembling?" Moira sat on the edge of the mattress and took her sister's hand. The dried cornhusks in the mattress shifted and settled beneath her. Though no lamps had been lit, Moira could see that Erinn's face was pale and drawn in the moonlight. "You know you're in God's pocket here at Fianna," she said softly. "What's to tremble over, Erinn?"

"Oh, Moira, it's . . . it's Seamus." The name left her lips in a breathless whisper.

"Seamus Sullivan? Sure your husband's a fine and hard-working man, Erinn." Moira paused, considering what about the man could have upset her sister so. "He's good to you, isn't he?"

"Sometimes he is," Erinn acknowledged. Then she added in a low voice, "But more times he's not."

Moira curled her legs up onto the bed and regarded her sister for a moment in silence. Erinn's long golden hair spilled over her shoulders like a grand silk cape. Her white gown, billowy though it was, did little to hide the swell of her full, dark-tipped breasts. She was beautiful, womanly, witty, a charmer. What could possibly have gone wrong between her and Seamus?

"I'm your sister, Erinn," Moira said softly. "You must tell me the trouble—all of it."

Erinn let out a shaky breath. "I've run away."

"What? Seamus doesn't know you're here?"

"I escaped with the wagon while he was out in the pasture. But I'm afraid he'll guess I'm at Fianna, and I know he'll come after me. Moira, he . . . he's cruel to me. Sure I fear him night and day."

"But why? He's thought of as a good man, Erinn. I've never heard a hard word spoken against Seamus. He's rich enough to keep you well, and he looks all right, if you don't give his nose much credit." She paused, thinking of Erinn's sharp tongue. "You haven't ballyragged about Seamus's nose, have you?"

"Of course not, Moira. Oh . . ." Erinn slumped over and began to weep loudly.

"Whisht, little alanna. Now then, what is it? You must tell me, Erinn, before Seamus comes. I'll always take care of you, so I will. I swear it."

"Will you?" Sitting up, she squeezed Moira's hand. "Then you must take me away from him."

Moira stared at her sister. "Take you away? What can you mean, Erinn?"

"I must escape. I have to get clean away and hide. Or . . . or he might kill me."

"Erinn!" A chill prickled down Moira's spine as she clutched her sister's icy hands. "Sure you can't mean this."

"Seamus doesn't like me. He thinks I'm a terrible wife—and truly I am! I can't cook like you, Moira, or keep the laundry washed and mended and ironed. The house is so dusty a person's like to sneeze just walking in the front door. And, oh, Seamus and I, we're not a match . . . not in bed."

Moira swallowed. "You're not?"

"No." Erinn shook her head. "We're not."

Though she ached to ask more, Moira knew it wasn't her place to pry into such private matters. But to think that a man and a woman could fail to be a match in bed! She'd never heard of such a thing.

"He beats me, too," Erinn added with emphasis. "Just the way Innis beats you. Only worse."

"Sure you can't mean it. In all your letters, you never wrote me about Seamus larruping you, Erinn. Why didn't you tell me before?"

"Well . . . he's just started it, so he has. Since we've been having our troubles."

Moira brushed her hand over her eyes. "Oh, Erinn, you'll have to go back to him, don't you know? The Church won't allow you to part. It's a mortal sin, so it is. You're Seamus's wife."

"Moira, you don't understand—he'll kill me! You must help me get away. You have to hide me from him. I'm your sister, Moira. You can't abandon me!"

As Erinn dissolved into a fresh round of weeping, Moira caught her in her arms. "Now then, alanna," she soothed, "I won't let you come to harm. Haven't I always looked after you, my little colleen? Sure I'll talk to Seamus, so I will, and—"

"No!" Lifting her tear-streaked face, Erinn clung to Moira. "He won't listen. He's angry with me. You have to help me! I beg you!" She gulped and sniffled, then turned her head in the direction of the room next door. "What's that? I heard something!"

Moira listened for a moment. She could hear a faint groan, almost inaudible through the thick adobe wall, and she knew the sound all too well. "It's Josiah," she whispered. "The fever often comes over him at night, so it does. I'll have to go to him, Erinn, just to keep him quiet. If Innis wakes up and finds Josiah moaning and you blirting rivers of tears over Seamus—"

"Come back to me quickly, Moira!" Erinn tried to clutch at her sister's hands as Moira slid off the bed. "We have to make our plans."

"*Whisht!*" Moira put her finger over her lips. "I'll be back in a flash. Calm yourself, Erinn. We'll work it out, so we will. You'll see."

She drew open the door and slipped out into the dark hall. Oh, she should have known things weren't right with Erinn! She should have guessed the moment her sister rode up alone in that wagon. Seamus would never have let Erinn come all this long distance by herself. But what could have happened between them to put the fear of the devil in her?

And now Josiah was taken with the fever again, just before he was forced to ride away at dawn. The devil take that sherral Innis! Josiah probably wouldn't even make it to the Berrendo. For all his strength, he was still a wounded man and in need of rest and healing.

When she pushed open the door, she at once saw Josiah sitting on the edge of the bed. His white shirt lay on the floor, and his back glistened with sweat as he bent over, holding his head in his hands.

"Josiah!" she gasped.

"It's all right," he said, his voice husky with effort. "The fever's back."

"Where's your medicine? Shall I wrap you a new bandage?"

He lifted his head, and she could see the pain etched on his face. "The medicine won't do any good, Moira. It's something inside . . . feels like a knife twisting."

"Oh, Josiah," she whispered, rushing to kneel near him. "You must lie down again. I'll boil some grease-wood tea, shall I?"

"No." He caught her hand, the thought of the potent and foul-tasting tea making his stomach knot even tighter.

"Whiskey, then?"

"I can't drink. Not if I have to ride tomorrow. I'll need a clear head. Moira . . . I need my *látigo*."

She grabbed the coiled whip beside his bed and thrust it into his hand. Then she began to probe the familiar wounds on his hard flat stomach. "Did the doctor at Fort Stanton take out all of the pellets?" she whispered. "Maybe one's still in you."

"They're gone." He laid his hand on her head and began to sift through the strands of loose curls. "Moira—"

"You shouldn't have been up and about so much today. It was your first good day, after all. The devil bless Innis for sending you away tomorrow. You'll collapse before you get to your mother's house, so you will."

"Moira, listen to me." He tilted her chin so that she was forced to look into his eyes. "I'll be all right. But there's a chance . . . a chance I might have some trouble on the way. There's someone looking for me. . . . You know that, don't you?"

"The man who shot you. John Fisher?"

"How did you know his name?"

"You mumbled it in your fever, over and over again."

Josiah groaned. What else had he told her? Had he muttered things that could endanger her life if Fisher got hold of her? "Will you look in my bag, Moira? There's something I want you to take out. Papers."

She hauled his battered leather satchel onto her lap and dug through its contents until she discovered a small packet tied with rough twine. "This?" she asked.

Josiah took the packet. "Inside are some papers—the claims to some of my mines in Montana," he said. "John Fisher would kill me to get his hands on them. They're worth a lot, some of them. Moira, I want to leave them with you. You're the only one I can trust to keep them safe while I'm on the road."

"Leave them with *me*? Sure I don't know what to do with mining claims."

"Bury them. Then forget you ever saw them. If John Fisher comes around asking for me, swear you never saw these papers. If you hear that I didn't make it to the Berrendo, see that the packet gets to my father, Gabriel

Chee. He'll know what to do with them."

He placed the packet on her lap. Moira studied the large, sunbrowned hand that hadn't moved from atop the papers. The hand felt heavy on her thighs, and she contemplated the silent man beside her on the bed. Never mind about Erinn and Seamus. Never mind about mining claims and trips down the Peñasco. Here was Josiah Chee . . . and she was alone with him that one last time she had dreamed of.

"Things are a muddle," she said. He hadn't moved his hand, and now she boldly slipped her own much smaller hands around his. "Erinn's crying next door. Innis is drunk down the hall, and he'll be craw-sick tomorrow, sure as the devil. In his bedroom Scully is plotting to marry me and take me off to Paris. You're riding away down the river to get yourself killed. I've a packet full of mine claims to guard." She gave a short laugh. "And to think I used to worry that my sheets weren't white enough."

"I didn't plan to mess up your life, Moira," Josiah said.

"You didn't." She sat beside him for a moment, thinking what an utter lie that was. Of course he had messed up her life. Things had been tidy before. She'd known who she was and what she wanted. Now, as Scully had instinctively guessed, she ached for more. She lifted her gaze. Would it be wrong to ask?

"Josiah," she began, her heartbeat throbbing in her throat, "would you mind doing something . . . something for me? That is . . . if you're well enough."

When he didn't answer, she forced herself to look at him. That was a mistake. Everything she felt inside was mirrored in his face. Though his fever had put a sheen on his brow, he slid his hand up her shoulder and drew her hard against his naked chest. The kiss was rough, demanding, terrifying, and everything she had dreamed of. She willingly enticed him this time,

stroking his tongue with her own until she heard his
breath grow shallow.

His hands crushed her hair, loosening the knot and
sliding through the countless curls, over her shoulders
and down her back. The packet of papers dropped to
the floor unnoticed as she drew her fingertips up the
bare skin of his arms, around his neck, and into his thick
hair. Soft and malleable, his tongue teased hers, then
grew hard and thrusting. She met it stroke for stroke,
her breasts rising and falling against the damp skin of
his chest.

"Moira," he murmured, when they burst apart in need
of breath. But before she could respond, he took her
again, this time cupping her head and caressing the
inside of her mouth with deep, stirring kisses. He could
feel her weaken in his arms as her head sagged into his
hands and her body went languid against his. The pain
in his side blurred, blocked by new, stronger feelings that
surged through his loins.

"Moira, come with me—"

"Josiah, don't go—" Their words overlapped, and they
clung to one another, fighting for control, yet driven to
succumb to the powerful drive that had impelled them
to come together.

"You're everything I want," he murmured against her
neck. "Everything."

She breathed in the scent of his naked skin and allowed
her fingertips to slide across the damp muscles of his
back. She could feel his hands move down her spine,
his fingers strong and warm. He drew a path around her
waist and upward . . . upward. . . . She held her breath.

His palm crested the tip of her breast, barely touching the taut pebble of her nipple. Neither chemise nor
petticoat nor gingham tucks and ruffles could mask the
incredible fire that shot through her body. Her heart
raced, and her breasts swelled inside her dress, demanding more of him. But his hand was a tempter, barely
grazing the apex of her need, teasing her nipple upward

and outward, tighter and more aching with each brush of his fingertips across it.

Her thoughts tumbled wildly. If she felt this way with just a mere stroke of his hand, what would it be like to bare her breasts to him? How would it feel to know the sweet caress of his fingertips on her naked skin? Forbidden images suddenly appeared—his mouth on her breast, his tongue licking at her nipple, his hands cupping and lifting her. . . .

"I want you, Moira," he whispered, but his touch was still restrained. He was waiting for her, luring her but unwilling to go beyond her limits. And even as she dreamed of him, she knew what she must say. It was her only choice.

"You're everything I can't have, Josiah." She hated the words even as she said them. "I was brought up to be godly and pure, to serve and to put my needs after the needs of others. I was brought up to love the Irish and look down on all others, to love cattle and hate sheep, to honor my guardian and fulfill my promise to him." She drew back from the haven of his arms and looked into his eyes. "You would tempt me away from my home and my family and my vows. You'd lead me astray, Josiah. To tell God's truth, your kisses are like honey on my tongue . . . but they're the devil's kisses, and I must flee them sure as I flee all sin."

Before the promise in his eyes could dispel her stalwart decision, she slipped from the bed, picked up the packet of papers, and made her way to the door. "You'll look after yourself tomorrow, Josiah, won't you?" she asked. "You'll take care on the trail?"

He didn't answer, and so she was forced to shut the door while his brown eyes were still locked on her face.

# Chapter
## 5

The moment Moira stepped back into her own room, Erinn flew to her and caught her around the waist. "Swear you didn't tell Josiah about our plan to run away!" she entreated, her face buried in the folds of her sister's apron. "Sure he'll blather to Innis, and then Seamus will find us, and he'll take me back to the ranch and—"

"Now then, Erinn!" Moira grabbed her sister's shoulders and held her so they were face to face. "You sound like a banshee, so you do. Stop your keening and sit down on the bed this instant."

Shamefaced, Erinn slinked back across the room. Moira went to her side and settled on the edge of the bed. She was so tired from the day's events she could hardly think straight. Her forehead throbbed where she'd banged it on the table. Her lips burned, and she was sure the pulsing tingles weren't a result of Innis's slap. Josiah was next door to her even now, still waiting, still wanting her.

But she had to do what was right, didn't she? She couldn't just surrender to her whims and impulses.

Reared by the strictly religious Deirdre Grady from the time Moira was eight, she had learned to shun sin and to place honesty, truth, godliness, and good deeds first in her life. There was little room for pleasure and none at all for ardor in the severe code of morality Deirdre had taught her young orphaned charges. Erinn had rebelled against such strictures, but Moira had embraced them wholeheartedly. Family was more important than passion. Dreams should be set aside for reality. And at this moment Moira knew her reality was her sister.

"I didn't say a word to Josiah about you and Seamus," she told her sister. "It's none of his affair."

"No, of course it isn't," Erinn sobbed. "It's just that I was afraid he might have heard us talking and asked you about it. He seems free with you, and it's clear he likes you."

"Sure I've brought him back from the grave, so I have. Of course he likes me. Now, enough of that nonsense. Tell me what you intend to do about Seamus. You can't go hiding out at Fianna forever."

Erinn shook her head. "I expect him here by tomorrow. Or even tonight!" She lifted her swollen eyes to her sister. "If he was angry with me before, he'll be a hundred times angrier that I ran away, so he will. Oh, Moira, you must protect me from him."

"Me? Faith, he's twice as big as I am, and he's mortal good with a horse and a gun. Sure you don't expect me to stand and face him all alone, do you? If Innis can bloody my lip, what's to stop Seamus from doing worse if I try to keep him from his rightful wife?"

"That's why we must escape!" Erinn gripped Moira's arm as she spoke. "Don't you understand? We'll run away. You'll be free of Innis and his lambastings. You won't have to slave day and night here at Fianna with no pay and nothing to call your own but a pair of useless galoots who don't care whether you live or die!"

"Erinn!"

"Sure you're nothing more than a servant to the pair of them, Moira," Erinn went on, her voice impassioned. "When was the last time you had a new dress? And look at your boots. Your toes are practically coming through! You're work-worn and empty, with not a thing to hope for in this life. You don't even have Papa's lands to call your own. Innis has taken them, and he'll pass them on to Scully, so he will, and not a penny will come to us. We both know it, Moira!"

"Erinn, the devil take your tongue for such words!"

"I only speak the truth. We've nothing to look toward, neither of us. But if we run away—you from Innis and I from Seamus—we can start new lives. We'll go east! You can find work and earn your own pay. You could have a shop, so you could, with beautiful gowns for high-toned city ladies to buy. You're a fine seamstress, Moira, and never will you hear a word about your lovely stitches from Innis Grady! Why not sell your work to those who'd appreciate it? Or you could cook in an eating house. Sure you're the best baker in the Territory."

"Erinn, you're full of blather, so you are. I'm not going to run off from Fianna and cook in a dirty eating house somewhere. I don't think I would like city life at all. Here at Fianna I've room to breathe, fresh mountain air to dry my laundry, a garden of my own, a good kitchen, and a killeen of hungry mouths to feed. Why should I leave?"

"Because you deserve more! And because . . . because I *have* to get away. I need you, Moira! You're the only one I can count on to help me. It's why I've come back to Fianna, don't you see? You must take me away and help me to hide."

Moira looked at her sister in silence. She knew what Erinn proposed was rash, headstrong, impetuous—yet there was something in the notion that compelled her. To leave Innis Grady and his drinking far behind, to make a new life for herself free of the constraints she had brought with her from childhood, to become her own person, strong and independent . . . and now that she had tasted temptation, to escape from sin, too— to leave all memory of Josiah Chee and his kisses far behind her. . .

"Where would we hide?" she whispered.

"There's a place . . . a church in St. Louis, Missouri. I read an article about it in the *New Mexican*. It's a grand cathedral, so it is, with stained glass and a high altar and a bishop. The Order of the Sacred Heart has a school and a novitiate nearby in a town called Florissant. The nuns have been there almost seventy years. They would keep me safely hidden from Seamus until . . . until I could get the marriage annulled."

"Annulled!" At the profane word, Moira jumped up from the bed. "Sure you're speaking blasphemy now, Erinn! You can't dissolve your marriage just like that. The Scripture plainly says, 'What God has joined together, let not man put asunder.' And yet you'd ask me to help you commit just such a sin, Erinn?"

"I'm not asking—I'm *begging* you!" Again Erinn threw herself on her sister, clutching Moira's waist and burying her face in her sister's skirts. "If you don't, he'll kill me! And that will be a worse sin on your shoulders, so it will. Please, please Moira! Help me!"

"Oh, Erinn—"

"*Please*, Moira!"

Stroking her sister's damp hair, Moira lifted her eyes to the ceiling. If only she could see straight through it to heaven and understand what God meant by all of this! Sure she hadn't called such chaos down upon herself, had she? All her life she'd been obedient and faithful. She had gone to mass whenever it was at all possible. She said her rosary and obeyed every commandment to the best of her ability.

On the other hand, she had to admit that she had failed the good Lord rather often lately. She'd bally-ragged at Innis, a man God had put in her life to honor and respect. And though she'd kept up with her work at Fianna, she had to admit that Scully might be right about her secret dreams. How many times a day did she catch herself gazing off into the Sacramentos? Sometimes she even dared to think of bursting free of the bonds of her confining world to explore a life she'd never touched. Sometimes, before she was able to stop herself, she imagined how it would feel to ride a train or take a painting class or taste ice cream or talk on a telephone.

But her greatest sin was Josiah Chee. Moira could almost envision the saints in heaven frowning down at her. What a bold strap she'd been with him! Sure it was no surprise after all that she was faced with such troubles on this night. "Sow the wind and reap the whirlwind," the Scripture said. And what a whirlwind this was!

"Moira, if you don't go with me," Erinn was murmuring in a tear-choked voice, "I'll go by myself, so I will. I'll take the wagon and leave on my own."

"Whisht, now." Moira knelt before Erinn and embraced her trembling little body. Sin or not, Moira had no option but to shelter her sister. "I'll take care of you as I always have. Stop your crying and hear me out. We'll go away together—but not in the wagon. If Seamus comes after you, sure he'll find us straightaway in that."

"We'll take two horses. We'll ride down to Badger—"

"No," Moira said. "Seamus will be coming up the Peñasco that way. We'll go to Lincoln and Fort Stanton. Then we'll ride up to White Oaks—"

"And we'll take a stage! Look, Moira." Erinn slipped out of her sister's arms and hurried across the room to her bags. In a moment she had drawn out a small leather pouch and was holding it triumphantly before her sister. "It's gold!"

Moira rose slowly. "Erinn . . . where did you get it?"

"Sure I took it from Seamus, that devil! He kept it in a trunk, and not even locked. I didn't take it all, of course. That wouldn't have been right. But here's what I judge I'm owed for putting up with him all this time."

"Erinn, a husband doesn't *pay* his wife to stay with him."

"The devil bless you, Moira. You're such a crawthumper, always moralizing and quoting Scriptures just like Deirdre. I got nothing out of that marriage but whippings and ballyraggings. For that matter, you might as well take some of Innis's money from his pot under the tree. Sure he's going to keep all our papa's land for his own, and you've worked like a slave for him these thirteen years."

"Never!" Moira crossed her arms. "I won't steal from Innis Grady. He's been good to me all in all."

"You've a scabby lip and a bruised forehead to prove that, Moira O'Casey," Erinn chided as she buried the pouch of gold in her bag. "Now, we'll take passage on a coach from White Oaks to Las Vegas. Then we'll board the train to St. Louis. Seamus would never expect such boldness from us. He'll think we've been killed by Indians."

"And so we may be. You've cooked up a grand plan, Erinn, but there'll be a hundred things to dissuade us along the way."

"Nothing will stop me. I'm going to St. Louis, so I am, to make myself a new life."

Moira gazed at her sister. No matter what had driven Erinn to this point, in truth she was no more than a baby. She needed looking after, and Moira knew it was up to her to take care of her sister. Family must come first. It always had.

"We'll leave within the hour, so we will," Moira said. "I'll fetch two pairs of Scully's britches for us. We'll travel as boys and hide our hair under hats. We'll take one of Innis's six-shooters and a rifle."

"Oh, Moira, it's going to be a grand adventure!"

"Whisht. No more blather, Erinn. You pack a saddlebag for each of us while I fetch some provisions from the kitchen. Sure I'll meet you at the stables in fifteen minutes."

"Thank you, Moira. You're a good person, so you are."

As she left the room, Moira reflected on her sister's words. Yes, she was good. Always good. Too good.

As reliable as a rock, she was.

Innis controlled her. Scully wouldn't know how to survive without her. Erinn depended on her. Everyone needed her and counted on her . . . and used her. She felt dry and empty inside—and frightened. Would there ever come a time when she could reach out for what *she* wanted? When she could grasp her own dreams?

Glancing at the closed door of Josiah's darkened room, she listened for a moment. There was no sound. Only silence. And so she hurried on.

"By all the goats in Kerry," Innis exploded, "where's Moira?" The dawn light filtering into the dining room through the starched white curtains outlined the squat, stocky form of the little Irishman.

"She's not in the kitchen." Scully trotted into the room to face his father. "I checked. This time of day she's *always* in the kitchen."

"There's no breakfast on the table! My boots weren't polished last night. And the fire's not even built on the grate. Sure she'll get a leatherin' for this one!"

Scully glanced at the bare table. "I can't remember a morning without the smell of eggs and steak and hot coffee. More times than not there's fresh cinnamon rolls, too." He looked up. "It's cruel odd to have Moira gone, so it is. Have you talked to Erinn?"

"Erinn!" Innis snapped. "How could I talk to Erinn? She's disappeared, too. They're gone, the both of them!"

"Where's Moira?" Josiah asked as he entered the dining room.

Innis rounded on him, his green eyes red-rimmed and rheumy. "*You!* You're the cause of this, so you are! Moira's not been the same since you came here to Fianna. Now she and Erinn have vanished clear away, and we don't know where to start looking for them. Cats of a kind, so they are, and wicked as sin!"

"I've checked the kitchen," Scully informed Josiah. "Moira's always in the kitchen, so she is. But this morning the fire's not even lit."

Josiah frowned, remembering the previous night. Moira had seemed agitated when she came into his room, and he knew he hadn't helped her state of mind by kissing her. Not that she'd appeared to mind. Later he had fallen asleep to the image of himself holding her close, their bodies entwined and their hearts released from the barriers that separated them.

But he knew their sweet stolen moments disturbed Moira as much as they tempted her. Had he frightened her into running away from feelings she considered sinful? Or was her disappearance the result of Innis's beating the day before? Or had Erinn, that wily sister of hers, had something to do with her disappearance?

"I heard them whispering," he said, almost to himself. "Moira and Erinn. I fell asleep to the sound of her voice."

"Whispering?" Innis snorted. "That's nothing new. The pair of them were always having a great cuggermugger in the middle of the night. Sure they're braddach colleens, so they are. I was never gladder than the day I married off Erinn to Seamus Sullivan."

Ignoring his half brother, Josiah became aware of a sense of uneasiness prickling down his spine. He felt a sickening certainty that Moira had not run away on a lark, that something had driven the two young women from Fianna.

"I'll go check the stables," he said. "If Erinn's wagon is gone, I'll ride out after them."

"You think they might have hotfooted it?"

"You couldn't blame them for leaving. Moira was upset yesterday, Innis," Josiah reminded him. "You were wrong to beat her."

"Glory be to God, you'll blame *me* for this, will you?" Innis's red face went purple. "It's *you* who upset the streel, casting sheep's eyes at her day and night. Before you came, things were regular. Normal. Moira was rock here at Fianna. She did her work, and if she strayed, I put her in line with the back of my hand. Then you came along, and she started changing the way she cooked and staring off at the mountains and staying up half the night in your room—" He caught his breath. "Blast your soul," he whispered. "You didn't lift her petticoats, did you?"

"No. But I didn't backhand her across the face either." Josiah turned on his heel. "I'll check the stables."

As he strode through the house and out the front door, his mind reeled with patchy memories of the night before. There had been that stabbing pain in his side, and he'd been unable to ease it. But then Moira had come into his room, as she always did. This time she had melted into his arms, and his pain had diminished as their passion mounted. He had kissed her and touched her hair, then stroked the tip of her breast. Like a frightened rabbit, wanting an offered morsel but afraid to take it, she had slipped away from him.

Left alone in his room, he had listened to Moira whispering with her sister—impassioned voices, tears, soothing words. Vanity had made him imagine that Moira was weeping over him, wanting him, but afraid to take such a bold step. He'd wanted to believe that Erinn was comforting her and encouraging her so that this morning he would be able to take her away with him.

Now, in the bright early daylight, he realized what a fool he'd been. Moira had been the comforter in the night, not Erinn. It was Moira's voice from the next room that had soothed and lulled him until his pain and ardor subsided and he fell into a deep sleep.

Josiah fingered the smooth curve of his whip as he rounded the corner of the stable. The wagon would be gone, and Moira with it. He had no doubt she'd been lured away by that flighty sister of hers. Erinn must have gotten herself into some kind of trouble, and she'd cried until Moira agreed to whatever addlepated idea she'd come up with. The thought of two unarmed women jolting over rutted trails in plain sight of Indians and outlaws sent a knot into the pit of Josiah's stomach.

But when he stepped into the stable, the first thing he saw was the wagon. He stared at it for a moment, trying to readjust his thoughts to fit this new development. If the women hadn't taken the wagon, they must still be at Fianna. They must be hiding somewhere, or they'd gone for a walk in the night and been captured, or . . . He squinted into the darkness and saw the two empty stalls, the missing saddles, the missing bridles.

No. Surely not.

"Who're you?" The voice in the stable was loud and harsh, and Josiah grabbed his whip as he swung around. The moment he faced the man who had spoken, he found himself staring into the shooting end of a cocked rifle.

"I said, who're you?" the man repeated. He was tall and rawboned, blue-eyed and black-haired, and he boasted a nose like a hawk's beak.

"You'll answer that question first," Josiah shot back. "And you'll put that rifle down when you're speaking to a stranger."

The man snorted and lowered the gun. "I'm Seamus Sullivan, so I am. I've come for my wife, and if you've got her, so help me I'll—"

"I don't have Erinn. She and Moira have disappeared."

"So she *did* come to Fianna! I thought as much. Sure they're hiding out here somewhere, and the devil bless them both." He brushed past Josiah into the stable. "Erinn, get your grug into plain sight, you stag!"

Josiah studied the blustering man for a moment. "Erinn came here to get away from you?"

Seamus swung around. "And why not? Fianna's where her precious sister lives, the godly Moira who can do no wrong. Moira would do anything for Erinn, so she would—even protect the streel from her just punishment at the hand of her husband."

"Punishment?" Josiah frowned. He was beginning to think these Irish kinsmen of his had but one thing on their minds, and that was to beat their women whenever and wherever possible. "If Moira's protecting her sister, it's because Erinn needs shelter from someone who's threatening her."

"And just who are you to defend the cats?" Seamus demanded.

"I'm Josiah Chee. I'm Moira's . . ." He paused. What was he to Moira after all? Her pursuer? Her tormentor? Another needy soul sapping the spirit from her? "I'm her friend," he finished, "and no one scorns her name in my presence."

Seamus laughed, but the sound was entirely without mirth. "Her friend! Sure you're a lover to the craw-thumper, so you are. Where do the two of you hide out to do your dirty deeds? Here in the stable? Rolling in the horses' hay like Erinn and her fancy man—"

"I'm Innis Grady's brother," Josiah cut in, "and a friend to his ward. Nothing more."

Seamus clamped his mouth shut. Breathing hard, he stared at Josiah. Then he took off his hat and brushed the back of his hand across his forehead. "You'll forgive me," he said, his voice low. "It's been a long ride for me up the river, and I'm not thinking straight."

Josiah weighed the man's words. "If Erinn did you wrong, I don't know anything about it, and I don't care to. But if the women have run away, I'll be the man to go after them. Moira nursed me back to health, and I owe her my life. They won't be safe on the road alone."

Seamus nodded, and Josiah could see the man's throat working as he struggled for words. His blue eyes clouded, and he stared up at the rafters of the stable. When he finally spoke, his voice was broken. "I did right by Erinn, so help me God," he said in a low voice. "And she betrayed me. That woman has the heart of the devil himself, so she does."

The men stared at each other for a moment, a silent communion of past injustices. Josiah understood the shallowness of women like Erinn. He, too, had cared and been betrayed. He remembered the women he'd reached out to and been rejected by. In the Mexican village the lovely Rosita had scorned him for his Irish blood. In Roswell the beautiful minister's daughter had laughed in his face when he asked her to dance. No, she wouldn't stand up with a man who had Indian blood, she'd said. No, sir, not her. Long ago Josiah had learned to lend his body to a woman without handing over his soul. He'd learned to take what he wanted and to give without risk.

Only Moira O'Casey had turned his pattern upside down. Unlike the village girls on the Berrendo, Moira didn't revile him. She accepted who he was. Unlike the loose mining-town women in Butte, Moira didn't pursue him. She ran from passion. Instead of demanding, she gave. She wasn't brazen; she was godly. Where other women were hard, Moira was soft. Where they flashed wandering eyes, she was faithful almost to a fault.

Moira was a gift, wrapped and tied up in tight, careful layers. And it was Moira, and only she, who had tempted Josiah to explore. To desire with a passion that went beyond the physical. To consider, for the first time in his life, the possibility of trust.

As Josiah studied Seamus Sullivan, he recognized wounds that had cut deep. Seamus was a strong man, obviously intelligent and reportedly wealthy. With great consideration, he had chosen his woman and had committed his life and future to her, only to have that commitment thrown in his face.

"Seamus, I—" Josiah began, but he was interrupted by a sound at the stable door. Both men turned.

"Seamus?" Innis Grady stomped into the barn, followed closely by his red-haired shadow. "I saw your horse at the gate. You sent Erinn to Fianna, did you?"

"I didn't send her here." Seamus slammed his hat onto his head again, his black look returning as swiftly as it had vanished. "Sure she ran off and left me, Innis Grady, and now it seems she's taken Moira away, too."

"Left you?" Innis exploded. "The blackguard! Why would she do a damn fool thing like that?"

Seamus glanced at Josiah, as if willing him to keep secret the moment of confession that had passed between them. "Erinn was unhappy with me," Seamus stated bluntly, "and I with her. We're not a match, it's true. But I wed her, and I stood by her in faithfulness, as a husband should. Now she's gone, and she's taken her sister with her. But in faith," he swore, "if I ever get her back again, I'll make her rue the day she ever set foot off my land."

Innis crossed his arms over his barrel chest and regarded Seamus. "Erinn's your problem. Moira's mine. Moira belongs to me, and I'll have her back, so I will. Where do you think they've got to?"

"They have no kin in the Territory, and none in the States for that matter. Save Moira and Erinn, the rest of the O'Caseys are still in Ireland. I'd wager the women are riding for Las Vegas with plans to board a train to the East and from there take a ship to the old sod."

"With no money to their names?"

Seamus again gave his bitter laugh. "My dear wife stole a pouch of gold from the chest in our bedroom, so she did. They've enough to see them to Ireland twice over."

"But how could they have gone?" Scully queried. "They didn't take the wagon. See, it's there where we left it. They must still be at Fianna somewhere."

"How many horses pulled that wagon up here, Seamus?" Josiah asked.

Seamus's brow furrowed as he scanned the row of stalls. When his eyes fell on the pair of empty booths, he grimaced. "Blast their souls," he whispered, "they've stolen two of my horses as well!"

"Give me another, Innis, and I'll ride after them."

Innis regarded Josiah. "I won't be sorry to be rid of you, that's for certain. But why would you do it? What's to gain? If you think I'll pay you good money, you can dream on, boy."

Josiah considered the reasons he had for remaining in the Territory and those he had for leaving. If he stayed around, John Fisher would soon sniff him out. That could only mean trouble. But if he left and went on this wild-goose chase, his dream of claiming land and starting a sheep venture would have to be set aside that much longer. On the other hand, that dream was looking less and less bright without Moira.

"Moira gave me back my health," he said, knowing he'd made his decision the night before in Moira's embrace. "The least I can do is to keep her safe."

Innis gave a derisive snort. "What do you say, Seamus? My gallant sheepherding brother has no land to look after, as we do. Sure he's still donny after his accident in the copper mines, but he's well enough to ride after the women."

"Or *I* could go," Scully put in, without much enthusiasm.

"You'd be lost the minute you set foot off Fianna." Innis's voice was heavy with sarcasm. "You don't know the front end of a horse from the backside. Sure I've let you get away with your blazing painting long enough, boy. Moira's bucked my rule, and you will, too, if I don't put my thumb on you before it's too late. You'll get your grug on a saddle this very morning, so you will, and follow me out to the pasture to learn a man's work."

Before Scully could protest, Innis turned to Josiah. "Take that gray gelding there, and don't come back until you've got Moira in the saddle."

"Seamus, will you ride with me?" Josiah asked.

"Aye, down the Peñasco to where it joins the Pecos. But I've a spread to run, and roundup is under way. It's all I could do to come this far after Erinn. If you'll go in search of her, Josiah, I'll pay you well to bring her back to me. In the meantime we'll comb the Peñasco together while I ride for my ranch."

"I won't take your pay, Seamus," Josiah said, "but I'll find your wife. And, Innis—I want the black stallion."

Turning a deaf ear on the little man's protests, Josiah hefted a well-made saddle into his arms and strode across the stable to the horse. The stallion would be strong and healthy if the ride proved long, and it would have the strength to outrun pursuers.

As Josiah fastened the girth, he listened to Innis and Scully arguing over which of them would attempt to cook breakfast before they headed out to the pasture. It occurred to him that for all Innis's professed determination to bring Moira back to Fianna, she was little more to him than a cook and housekeeper. The realization sent a flicker of defiant anger through Josiah. Moira was so much more than Innis Grady deserved.

Not only was she a beauty, but she had a good soul as well. Josiah could count on one hand the number of women he'd met who were as kind and caring as Moira. And not one of them could match her fair skin and blue eyes and fiery auburn hair.

But Josiah knew he saw something else in Moira, something that other men must have ignored or been too blinded by her selflessness to notice: Moira O'Casey simmered with passion. Unexplored ardor bubbled just beneath the surface of her practical, righteous exterior, taunting Josiah and drawing him to her.

On the one hand, she was innocent and untouched, an angel who could slip out of his arms in a breath. On the other hand, she was fire and wit, stubborn determination, and ripe womanhood. Like a fruit on the vine, she was swollen and ready to be tasted. Josiah intended to be the man to savor the first sweet drops of her liquid heat, to explore her sultry body, to waken her to her fullness.

What would come beyond her surrender he didn't know. He couldn't think past the image of Moira's body naked in his arms. That picture was enough to propel him onto a horse and out into the heat of the New Mexico summer.

While the two Gradys walked out of the stable, still arguing, Seamus approached Josiah. He watched for a time while Josiah finished saddling the stallion. Then he cleared his throat.

"You should know," he said, "that Erinn won't be eager to return to me. The night I found her with . . . found her with one of my punchers, I swore to kill her."

Josiah glanced over his shoulder. "Do you aim to make good on that threat?"

Seamus squared his shoulders. "It would be justice."

"Where's Erinn's lover now?"

"I sent him packing—with a bullet in his grug to remember me by. But it wasn't him who betrayed me so much as her. We had a vow, you understand—husband and wife. She swore before God to keep faithful, and then . . . then . . ."

"There'll be justice for Erinn, Seamus," Josiah said, "but it may not be your place to hand it out." He set one foot in the stirrup and settled into the saddle. "If your wife swore her vow before God, leave the vengeance to Him."

"Aye," Seamus whispered.

"My father once told me there's a history of bloodshed in my veins. Violence, revenge, betrayal, treachery, hatred—those are my heritage. I can live by them, he said, and be destroyed in the process, or I can rise above them. Turning the other cheek, Seamus. That's what a *man* does."

When he looked up, he saw Scully leading Seamus's horse up from the gate. "Ho, young Scully," Josiah greeted the young man as he walked into the stable. "So your father's cooking the eggs this morning, is he?"

Scully frowned. "He doesn't believe I can do anything right. Not even fry eggs."

While Seamus mounted his horse, Josiah leaned down and clapped the boy on the shoulder. "I wager you'll be ready to take over Fianna by the time I come back with Moira. See if I'm right."

The boy gave a lopsided grin. "Maybe so. I don't suppose I'll ever get to Paris anyway."

"Sure you'll never plow a field by turning it over in your mind," Josiah said, taking on his mother's strong Irish brogue. "God save you, Scully."

With a flick of the reins, he urged the stallion out of the stable and onto the trail that led down to the Peñasco river. Seamus Sullivan joined him, and together they rode toward the gate. As their horses sped up to a canter, he could hear Scully calling out behind him.

"God save you, too, Josiah Chee!" the boy shouted. "God save you kindly."

# Chapter
## 6

A wagon journey from Fianna to Fort Stanton on the Rio Bonito usually meant a long, slow bumpy wagon ride of four or five days. On horseback, Moira and Erinn made it in two and a half. Their first night on the trail, they rode from midnight until dawn with only two brief stops to water the horses. Their trek took them up the Rio Peñasco just past the Paul ranch, where the trail divided, before the women turned north toward Casey's Mill, an important junction on the Rio Hondo.

Neither Moira nor Erinn was accustomed to long hours in the saddle, and certainly neither of them had ever before ridden astride, like a man. After only a short time they were sore and aching, their tender buttocks chafed and their thighs rubbed red.

Scully's britches hung baggy on Moira's hips and were too short in the leg, while another pair gripped Erinn's thighs as tightly as a pair of stockings. It was a good thing they were alone on the trail, Moira decided as she observed her sister kneeling to scoop a handful of water from the stream. In those denim pants, Erinn was as curvy and round as the women Scully tried to paint. The petite blonde would never pass for a boy in a hundred years, no matter that Erinn had stuffed her hair under a hat and was wearing a man's checkered shirt.

Moira, on the other hand, was tall and straight, and she didn't possess such sizable breasts. Moira had never considered herself particularly well endowed, but she hadn't ridden very long before she began to believe that if not for her supporting chemise and stiffly boned corset, her breasts would be bouncing down around her knees.

She despised the rough blue denim britches from the moment she put them on. There were seams running down her hips and over her legs, along the insides of her thighs, between the soft curves of her bottom. There were copper tacks and ridges and pockets, all in contrast to the full free fabric of her dresses. The front placket with its metal buttons pressed into her stomach and pulled up at her crotch, making the cantering ride all the more uncomfortable. In fact, that pounding tightness between her thighs kept her twitching, and made her think thoughts she was certain were more than a little sinful.

As the two horses made their way up the trail toward the crossing at the Rio Feliz, Moira tried to keep her mind off Josiah. But the harder she tried not to dwell on him, the more she found herself running over and over their stolen moments in the night. The farther behind they left Fianna, the freer of its restrictions she felt, and with that freedom came bold imaginings.

What if she had given in to her impulses that night in Josiah's arms? What if she'd allowed him to slip apart the buttons on her gingham dress and run his warm hands over the bare skin of her breasts? Oh, those delicious kisses . . .

She shut her eyes and let the horse take its own path down the trail. How would it feel to lie on a bed with Josiah? What would it be like to press her body hard against his, their tongues dancing and their hands working magic on naked flesh? How would his skin feel in the places she had never touched—the corded muscle of his legs, the flesh of his inner thighs, the unknown magic beneath the belt of his trousers?

But she had left Josiah far behind her now. Fianna was gone, and Innis Grady and Scully, too, though Moira most surely intended to return to them once she had safely sheltered poor Erinn from harm. All the same, for this time, these few precious weeks of travel, she was free! But free to do what? Now that she had her independence, Moira wasn't the least bit certain what to do with it. And she didn't feel at all confident of her ability to handle the world outside the comforting confines of Fianna.

Approaching the Rio Feliz, she and Erinn rode past the ranch that once had belonged to an Englishman named John Tunstall. This was dangerous territory, Moira knew, a land rife with tension, bloodshed, and betrayal. It was Mister Tunstall's murder, Moira had been told, that had sparked the famous five-day battle in Lincoln Town. Many of Tunstall's supporters had been killed in that battle. Even the outlaw, Billy the Kid, who had fought to avenge the Englishman's murder, had been dead for five years—shot by a man who once had been his friend.

Now John Tunstall's ranch and all his Lincoln Town properties belonged to his sworn enemy, Jimmie Dolan, who was well known as a clever, powerful man—one of the first Irish settlers in the area. In spite of reputed double dealings, he was highly regarded by many in the Irish community along the Peñasco.

After recovering from the financially disastrous skirmish in Lincoln, Jimmie Dolan had become a well-to-do merchant, cattleman, and politician. He now served as county treasurer, and it was rumored that he hoped to be elected to the territorial senate. Such was justice in New Mexico, Moira reflected.

As well liked as Jimmie Dolan might be, Moira had no desire to encounter the man, especially when she was trying to remain anonymous on the trail. Besides, Moira knew their next rest stop would be at the home of Ellen Casey and her children—unrelenting enemies of Jimmie Dolan.

Moira and Erinn crossed the nearly dry Rio Feliz without stopping at the Dolan ranch house, then continued north to Casey's Mill. The Casey family had immigrated to the territory from Ireland. They were yet another family of devout Irish Catholics, though they were no kin to the O'Caseys who lived near the Peñasco River.

The Casey family had had their share of misfortune. The father had been murdered some years before, and many of the children were sickly. Though Mister Casey had obtained a quitclaim deed on his house and gristmill when he first settled there some twenty years ago, the law considered him no more than a squatter on the land along the Feliz. Recently Jimmie Dolan had annexed the Casey land, claiming that no one had ever properly filed on it according to the Homestead Act. The Caseys were in constant litigation with their countryman, and no patriotic ties could mend a feud over land rights.

Moira and Erinn stopped to water their horses at the mill, and though they were all but strangers to the Caseys, they were invited to spend the night, as territorial hospitality demanded. Typical of homesteaders, the Caseys were a closemouthed bunch, asking few questions of the two women traveling alone. Still musing over Josiah Chee, Moira carefully observed the Caseys' large flock of sheep. They were a despicable flock of woollies, she decided finally, and no matter how persuasive Josiah's tender touch or how delicious his kisses, she would never be wooed by a sheepherder.

Her mind made up on that matter, she hauled a complaining Erinn out of the bed the following morning just before dawn, and they set off up the Hondo River with the goal of reaching Fort Stanton by night. The Caseys had given them plenty of good, nourishing food, so they stopped only occasionally to rest and water the horses.

Before reaching the little town of San Patricio, they veered north on the trail and began to ride alongside the Rio Bonito. By late afternoon they had reached Lincoln Town. Although Erinn begged to stop there for the night, Moira had heard far too many horror stories of the little one-street village to make her comfortable.

Lincoln was Billy the Kid's stomping ground, the scene of more murders than people cared to remember. Lincoln was where homes had been burned and soldiers had been called in to keep the peace. Eight years had passed since those bloody times, but Moira had no intention of spending the night in such a town.

She dragged Erinn up the mountain stream toward Fort Stanton, the outpost where, not a month before, a military surgeon had operated on Josiah Chee.

The fort had been built more than thirty years before, in 1855. It had stood against the warring Apaches, and it had been held by both Texas Confederates and Union troops during the Civil War. The late Colonel Kit Carson had commanded a garrison of New Mexico volunteers there at one time. After the native-born Mescalero Apaches were brought back from their exile in Florida, Fort Stanton became the economic support of their reservation in the White Mountains.

Erinn was thrilled when she and Moira arrived at Fort Stanton. It was a bustling place, thronged with men who recently had been employed to repair and enlarge the post. The area around the fort had been settled by ex-soldiers and their families, and thus it boasted every amenity of modern civilization. There was a mercantile with fresh vegetables and canned goods, a post office, a telegraph office, and medical facilities. In addition to the army headquarters, there were soldiers' barracks, officers' homes, and guest quarters enclosed within the fort's strong walls.

Moira used some of the money in Erinn's pouch to pay for lodging, and the two women spent a restful night in the comfort and protection of the fort. The next morning, Erinn pleaded to stay a day or two longer. Moira knew they were both on the brink of exhaustion, but she refused to consider delaying their departure. If they were to be certain of evading the villainous Seamus Sullivan, she insisted, they must leave the Territory altogether— and the sooner the better. So they mounted their weary horses and rode north for the town of White Oaks.

Moira had always longed to visit White Oaks, for the little town seemed to her the center of life in their part of the Territory. Lincoln was wild and lawless, and Roswell was no more than a Podunk cow town. But White Oaks was said to be different. It had sprung up around the discovery of gold in the Baxter Mountains, and it was a new town, in existence for only six years.

Though a boomtown, White Oaks had been settled mostly by law-abiding easterners. There might be saloons and gambling halls, but there were churches and schools, too. And there was definitely no room for violence. Billy the Kid had tried to pull some of his shenanigans in White Oaks several years back, and he had been run out of town by the local citizenry.

In White Oaks Moira and Erinn were finally forced to take a rest from their travels. The stagecoach to Las Vegas, New Mexico, would not arrive for two more days. They sold Seamus's horses at the livery stable, and Moira insisted she would reimburse him at the first opportunity. Erinn merely pursed her lips at the notion and stashed the money in her leather pouch. Then they took a room at the hotel.

On a Monday morning bright and early they planned to board the stagecoach for Corona, Vaughn, and then Las Vegas. From there they would travel on the Atchison, Topeka, and Santa Fe railway up and over the Sangre de Cristo Mountains, through Raton Pass, and into Colorado. From there they would journey eastward across the flat

Kansas prairie to Kansas City, Missouri. And then, finally, they would ride the last miles to St. Louis.

There, Moira assured herself, they would find haven in the town of Florissant. Poor Erinn could at last rest in the secure arms of the nuns who would protect her and give her the future she deserved. And Moira could return to Fianna . . . where she belonged.

Josiah Chee thought he had died and gone to hell. Riding a horse down the winding Rio Peñasco in the blistering heat with his gut aching and his body as weak as a new colt's was sheer torture. The river had cut deep chasms in the earth, and the dusty trail was forced to follow every dip and curve. Thick vegetation grew along the streambed—junipers, piñons, and weeping willows—and the two men kept a close watch for Indians or outlaws who might be waiting in ambush for travelers.

In spite of Josiah's pain, he enjoyed the sweet scent of the white and yellow wildflowers that grew along the banks. The river, clear and olive green, raced in white ripples that lapped over its gravel bed. Cattails clustered around the banks of slower-moving pools, and purple-flowered thistles carpeted the ground. By some means Josiah couldn't fathom, the tiny river managed to nourish huge cottonwood trees whose branches arched over the water and whose leaves whispered promises of better times to come. Even the poplars had leafed out, tall and green like fingers reaching into the bold blue sky.

As the riders descended the Peñasco toward the Pecos River, the land grew flatter and even more parched. Rock faces wore knobby bunches of prickly pear cactus clustered in their crags. Large mottled rattlesnakes as thick as a man's arm coiled on stone ledges. The junipers and piñons of the highlands gave way to spiked century plants, mesquite bushes, and long-armed cholla cacti. Yuccas, unwilling to bloom in the arid environment, perched on tall stems draped with dead leaves from past, lusher years. Even the vegetation bespoke the hostile landscape—devil's-head, catclaw, snakeweed, needlegrass, greasewood.

The grass was yellow, almost white, and so dry it was a wonder to Josiah that any animals could survive on it. Yet deer bolted across the plains at the first sound of intrusion. Jackrabbits scampered to safety, their long ears flat against their backs. Only when they felt danger had passed them by did they lift their dark-tipped ears once again. Prairie dogs poked their heads from tunnels to observe the passersby. Burrowing owls stared impassively as they perched at the entrances to their underground homes. Roadrunners darted across the trail, their tails stretched out behind them.

If the lack of rain had been hard on the wildlife, the insects seemed to have flourished. When Josiah and Seamus stopped to water their mounts, they had to keep a closer eye on the bugs than on any outlaws who might be sneaking up on them. Black widow spiders, fat and as glossy as ebony, spun webs to lure unsuspecting grasshoppers and cicadas to their doom. Only the crimson hourglass on each spider's abdomen gave away its hiding place. Small brown scorpions scurried from stone to stone. Lizards, invisible until startled, came to life with a quick, heart-stopping rush that resembled the slither of a snake.

For Josiah, the only solace in the long, torturous trip was Seamus Sullivan, a man he quickly came to regard as a friend. Seamus was as strong as an ox and stubborn besides. He kept a watchful eye out for the health of his traveling companion, stopping to rest when Josiah tired. Though the two men conversed about life in the Territory, Seamus gave no further details of the pain his wife had caused him. Instead he spoke of his own plans for the future—to acquire more land and better waterfronts, to build a home of stone instead of adobe, to plant fruit trees and breed cattle.

When they arrived at the Sullivan farm late that night without having found a trace of the missing women,

Seamus invited Josiah to stay a few days longer and to rest as long as he felt the need.

But Josiah demurred. "I'll head for Roswell in the morning," he said to Seamus as he eased his large frame into a cushioned bent-twig chair on the long porch of the Sullivan ranch house. "I think I'd better send a telegram to Fort Stanton."

Seamus settled in an old oak rocker and regarded the rising moon in silence for a moment. Then he passed a cheroot to his companion and lit one for himself. At last he spoke. "You don't believe the colleens came this direction down the Peñasco after all, do you?"

Josiah shook his head. It was the first acknowledgment between the men that their attempts to locate the women had been futile. "Not that I can tell. My grandfather was an Apache. Before he died, he taught me a lot of things about the ways of the Indeh. One of them was to track wild game. I can trail a deer for miles, and I know the spoor of every animal in the Territory. If I can't find an animal, it isn't around. And I didn't see a single sign of those two women."

"Sure they've outfoxed us, so they have," Seamus grunted, "and I'm not surprised. That Moira is as keen as a well-honed knife. She probably guessed we'd go searching the logical way, down the Peñasco, and so she took another trail. You suppose they went north, do you?"

Josiah took a drag on the bitter cigar and watched the smoke drift across the stars. "It makes sense. From Casey's Mill they could take any number of trails."

"East to Roswell. West to Ruidoso and Tularosa. Or they might keep going north to Fort Stanton."

"That's my bet. Moira's practical. She'll head for the railway. If they stop at Fort Stanton, there'll be a record of their stay. Someone will notice them. I'll find out."

"And then?"

"I'll try to catch up with them, but where they go from the fort is any man's guess. Los Tablos. White Oaks."

He dropped the cheroot on the wood floor and crushed it with the heel of his boot. "Where would Moira take Erinn?" he asked. "Where would they go if they wanted to escape? If they wanted to hide so well no one could find them?"

"So well *I* couldn't find them, you mean?" Seamus said, his voice low. "It's me they're running from. And I know as well as I know my own name that Erinn won't come back here."

"I hardly know your wife, but I think I understand Moira pretty well. If she's made up her mind to hide Erinn, she'll do it."

Seamus nodded. The rocking chair had slowed, and his long legs stuck out all the way to the edge of the porch. He studied them a while before speaking again. "I loved Erinn, you know. I love her still in my own way, in spite of what she did to me."

"What she did can't be excused. All the same, she's not much more than a child."

"She's woman enough to know how to hurt a man. Josiah," he asked, "have you ever loved a woman?"

The image of Moira's face filled Josiah's thoughts. He could see her bending over him, her rich auburn hair curly and thick around her head. He could see those blue eyes, soft, shining, lit with a light from somewhere deep inside her. And he could hear her voice, that gentle Irish lilt.

"Aye," he answered, unaware that he had spoken as she would, "I think I loved a woman, Seamus. But I've lost her, too."

The tall man sat forward suddenly and brushed a hand under his eye. "Ah, well, at least you didn't make the mistake of yoking yourself to her, as I did, for better or for worse, in sickness and in health. Let me tell you, boy, I took those words to heart when I said them."

Josiah studied the stars, pondering Erinn's betrayal of Seamus, wondering if he would ever know the joy of such commitment or the pain of such faithlessness.

At this point he couldn't be sure he'd ever see Moira O'Casey again. He hadn't been able to win her at Fianna. Now he'd taken the wrong path and lost her on the trail. She could be anywhere. The idea that he might never again know the pressure of her sweet lips against his sent a twisting knot into his stomach.

"I wouldn't call marriage a yoke," he answered Seamus. "You might have liked it if you'd found the right woman."

The Irishman stretched and stood. The empty rocking chair swung back and forth, a rhythmic creaking in the night. "Sure marriages are all happy, as my mother used to say," he drawled. "It's having breakfast together that causes all the trouble."

With a wry chuckle, Seamus started for the door. In the dark, Josiah smiled. "I'll be leaving at dawn," he said.

"Take two fresh horses from the stable, as well as your stallion. You'll need them all three for such a long trip." Seamus stepped through the door, and his tall frame was silhouetted by lamplight. "I hope you find your ladylove. You're a good man, Josiah Chee, and Moira O'Casey's a good woman. God save you both."

Moira had thought White Oaks was the center of civilization. But when the stagecoach pulled into Las Vegas, she could only stare out the window in awe. To the west the Sangre de Cristo Mountains rose tall and purple, their tops still dusted with the last of winter's snow. The Gallinas River ran through town, feeding both industry and agriculture. To the east stretched a plain veined with rivers—the Canadian, the Conchas, the Mora. Although nearly as dry as Fianna, the landscape breathed with mountain air, thick grass, yuccas, and cacti.

But it was the grand town itself—a town of more than five thousand residents—that stunned Moira. Las Vegas not only had more saloons, dance halls, hotels, and mercantiles than she'd ever seen, it also boasted a post office that delivered letters along the area's Star mail routes, a whining sawmill, the *Las Vegas Optic* newspaper, a bustling stagecoach station littered with trunks and parcels, and, one mile east of the central plaza, a busy railway depot on the Atchison, Topeka, and Santa Fe line.

Right in the center of the Old Town plaza stood a forty-foot windmill derrick. One of the travelers in the stagecoach, a doctor who was returning after a trip south to visit friends, told Moira and Erinn that the derrick had failed to keep water in the nearby well, but the structure had still been put to good use. Six years earlier, three outlaws had been hanged from it, their squirming bodies peppered with bullets by the vengeful mob. Later that year the derrick's platform had been used to display the corpses of four other villains who had been killed by vigilantes in a village near Las Vegas. A notice posted on the derrick had warned other thieves, thugs, fakirs, and bunco steerers that if they ventured within city limits after ten o'clock at night they would be invited to attend a grand necktie party.

The derrick gave testimony to the toughness of the pioneers who had made their homes in Las Vegas. Not only were there rowdy railroad construction crews, gamblers, and outlaws, the physician told his wide-eyed listeners, but the town was also inundated with painted ladies determined to entertain their customers for fifty cents a dance and not much more for baser pleasures.

Moira was almost ready to tell Erinn they would stay on the stagecoach and ride it all the way back to White Oaks without setting foot in such a den of miscreants when the good doctor offered the comforting news that Las Vegas also boasted many respectable, hardworking citizens. As the second largest town in New Mexico, it was booming with construction. Already there was a brewery, an iron foundry, a brick kiln, a slaughterhouse, a flour mill, and a factory that manufactured wagons and carriages. The two banks in Las Vegas held more money than did the two in Albuquerque. A modern water company supplied the town's needs, and a volunteer hook and ladder company was always ready to fight fires. Around the corner from the water company was an electric company. Horse-drawn streetcars rolled along the mile of track that linked the railroad depot to the plaza.

"What are all those wires strung on poles everywhere?" Moira asked the doctor as she peered out the stagecoach window.

"It's a telephone system," he explained. "Las Vegas has had telephones since 1879, only three years after Mister Alexander Bell took out his basic patent. We have more than one hundred eighty telephones here in town, though our Mexican population won't talk on them. They can't believe an American machine can speak Spanish."

Moira chuckled, though she didn't understand how it could either. All the same, she wanted to appear sophisticated and knowledgeable as she and Erinn made their trek into the high circles of modern civilization. But *telephones*! She had never even seen a telegraph office, much less a telephone.

"Wirra!" Erinn punched her sister in the ribs. "Did you see that shop, Moira? A hundred dresses in the window, sure as I breathe."

"Look at that lady!" Moira grabbed her sister's arm. "Have you ever seen such a gown?"

"Ohhh, it's beautiful!" Erinn leaned against Moira to watch the woman sashay into a millinery shop. "Did you see her bustle? There must have been ten yards of draped silk. Yellow with purple stripes—can you imagine?"

Moira unconsciously reached behind herself to smooth the flattened and wrinkled folds of gingham that fell over her bottom. She and Erinn had shed the denim trousers they'd taken from Scully's blanket box, but the dresses they had hastily stuffed into their saddlebags were a far cry from those on the glorious creatures strolling down the streets of Las Vegas.

"I'm going to have a dress like that," Erinn vowed, "only mine will be pink. I'll have lace frills and embroidery and tassels everywhere. Satin ribbons, too."

"Sure the nuns in Florissant will welcome such shingerleens in their novitiate!"

Erinn laughed. "Oh, Moira, it's so good to be with you again—the two of us together. Aren't you just as giddy as a goose to be away from Fianna and that sherral Innis Grady?"

"Well . . ." Moira had to admit that it did feel wonderful to be free of the man's constant orders and commands. On the other hand, she missed her linen cupboard and her sheets scented with lavender. She missed her cozy kitchen filled with the sweet fragrance of baking apple pies. She missed her garden, the green sprouts pushing up from the earth and reaching toward the blue, blue sky. And her needlework, she missed that, too. The evenings in her chair on the portal, her lap filled with crisp cotton fabric and her fingers flying back and forth.

"Innis *did* give me a home—" she began.

"*His* home," Erinn cut in. "A castle where he was lord and king over all. Sure you were his slave, Moira. For four years you've been nothing more than that devil's thrall, wearing rags, working your fingers to the bone, sweltering in the heat of that miserable kitchen. You can't deny it. But now you're free—free as a bird."

"Perhaps. It feels odd to do exactly as I please, but I suppose this is not such a bad way of life."

"If you'd ask my opinion, I'd say it's *good*."

Moira shrugged. She had to acknowledge that traveling on the trail for a week had been difficult, exhausting, and even frightening at times, but it *was* interesting to see new places and to meet people she'd never known before. Moira and Erinn had been born in Ireland, but they had come over the ocean and across the States as tiny babes. The largest town Moira could ever recall visiting was Roswell, and that only once.

As she and Erinn stepped down from the coach into the dusty street of the city, they instinctively clasped hands. "Where shall we go?" Erinn whispered, her eyes darting from store to saloon to hotel, from dandy gentlemen to scampering children to bustling women. "Shall we ride in one of those streetcars?"

"We'll *walk* to the depot. It's only a mile," Moira said quickly, giving her sister's hand a jerk to divert her attention from a bevy of ladies who were swaggering down the street, their hips swaying from side to side. Their dress bodices dipped well past the cleavage of their ample bosoms, and as they walked they cast bold glances at the men along the path.

"Have a look at those dresses, Moira!" Erinn whispered, nudging her sister's arm as they carried their heavy saddlebags toward the railway. "Red! Crimson! And purple! I'd wager that's brocade, so it is. And in this heat! Just see the paint on their faces."

It was all Moira could do not to stare in fascination along with Erinn. Never in her life had she seen women with rouged cheeks, powdery white skin, and lips that glistened in bright shades of scarlet and pink. Laughing loudly, the women fairly undulated along, and as they walked they swung large fans back and forth in the sweltering noontime air.

"I want a red dress," Erinn announced, "just like that one in the middle."

Startled, Moira turned to her. "Erinn! Sure you must be joking. Those are ladies of the night, don't you know? Fallen women. Bold straps they are, and not the sort of good, decent ladies who go to church and raise families, as we do."

Erinn arched one blond eyebrow. "Please, Moira. None of your holy blatherumskite today. You might as well face the truth. We're neither good nor decent. I've run off from my husband, and I'll have the marriage annulled. If not that, I'll be divorced, then."

"Oh, Erinn!"

"You're no better, Moira. For all your saintly talk, you've not wed yourself to a man and you're not bearing children and raising a family either, are you?"

"No, but I—"

"We're not so much more decent than those women are, now. Sure their lives might even be better than ours. They've pretty dresses and elegant shoes. They have a fine place to live, money of their own, and more than enough men—"

"Now, Erinn," Moira snapped. "You're blathering, so you are. Never would you sell your sweet body for a price to any man. You're a good Christian woman."

"And you're as blind as a bat." Erinn hitched her saddlebag higher in her arms and started down the street in the direction of the depot. "You look at the world as though you were standing behind a church's stained-glass window. You don't know what you want out of life, Moira. You don't have a clue about the pleasures the world has to offer. You don't even know who you are!"

When Moira didn't respond, Erinn called over her shoulder. "Now, come along and let's buy ourselves a pair of tickets for St. Louis. I'm ready to be rid of this blazing Territory with its dirty, smelly, work-worn men and its bone-weary women. Sheep and cows and adobe houses! Apaches and Mexicans and outlaws and punchers—the whole killeen of them be damned. We're off to the big city to take hold of life!"

Moira stared after her sister as Erinn sauntered down the street, her hips swaying as provocatively as those shameful women's did. Of course, in her limp pale blue calico dress with no bustle and the collar buttoned up to her throat, she didn't look the least bit sinful. But the things she had said!

Moira glanced around, hoping no one had heard Erinn. Surely her sister couldn't have meant those words. *Divorce*—the very idea! And the things she had accused Moira of. How awful! Could they be true?

Slowly Moira followed Erinn down the boardwalk that fronted a row of mercantiles. Was she really a slave, a bone-weary woman, as blind as a bat to true joy? All she had ever wanted was a home of her own, a warm fire, a heavy iron stove, a comfy bed, a few flowers in a garden outside the door. But would she be happier in red dresses with lace frills? In elegant shoes? Did she really need money of her own and a fine lace fan and men . . . lots of men . . . hungry men?

Shivers skittering down her back, Moira half ran into the depot. Erinn was already at the ticket window. "Two for St. Louis, please," she announced.

"It'll cost you twenty-five dollars for a round-trip ticket to Kansas City," he said, studying the young woman with a skeptical eye. "And even more to St. Louis."

"We're bound for St. Louis, so we are, but we need only one-way fare. We're not coming back, you see. When do we leave?"

"This train's just in from Lamy." The agent jabbed a thumb in the direction of the hissing locomotive and its string of passenger cars. "It leaves for Springer and Raton in fifteen minutes. But if you'd like to wait a few hours, there'll be another—"

"No, we'll take this one."

"Suit yourself. That'll be thirty dollars total."

"Thirty! Great ghosts." Clamping her mouth shut, Erinn opened her pouch, counted out the coins, and slid them across the counter. When the agent handed her the tickets, she swung around holding them up in triumph. "We're going east, Moira, to St. Lou—" Her face went rigid. "Glory be to God," she whispered. "It's *him*."

# Chapter
## 7

At her sister's words, Moira whirled around. Josiah Chee, riding an enormous ebony stallion, was leading two horses down the street toward the railway depot. A buckskin-colored hat banded in braided black leather dipped low over his brow, and his brown eyes were trained on Moira.

She moistened her lips. She should run, she thought. They were escaping, after all. She should just grab Erinn's arm and bolt down the street. Instead, she stood stock-still, as if her boots were stuck to the platform with blackstrap molasses.

"Moira." Josiah touched a gloved hand to the brim of his hat.

She had forgotten how deep his voice was. Silvery dust lightly coated his blond hair, his black vest, the thighs of his chaps. He gripped the reins to steady the restless stallion.

"God save you, Moira."

"Josiah Chee," she said softly. "God save you kindly."

She glanced at Erinn, who was staring at him with her lips parted and her fingertips at her throat. All Moira's efforts to convince herself that Josiah was unworthy of the fantasies that had been playing through her mind fled in the dominating reality of his presence. Until this moment she had thought of Josiah as handsome, gentle, and more than a little intriguing—*but*, she had told herself, he was a landless shepherd without even a gun to protect himself.

Now Moira realized that the man, healed of his wounds, was rugged, powerful, and so masculine that at the sight of him her heart bogged down in the same molasses that gummed her feet. His clothing fit him like a well-worn glove—leather boots, denim jeans, brass-buckled belt, white shirt, black vest, and that hat . . . such a hat!

Instead of a pair of six-shooters at his thighs, he carried his long, coiled *látigo*. It hung from one hip, thick and black against his rawhide chaps. The haft of the snakelike whip was hard and shaped like a leather-wrapped club. From there it grew thinner, deadlier, winding for fifteen feet until it ended in a single knotted thong. With her own eyes Moira had seen Josiah take aim and, with a sound like a pistol shot, snap the blacksnake around an enemy's wrist. She had told herself the weapon was all but useless against a gun, but now, seeing it on Josiah's hip, she felt a shiver of apprehension skitter down her spine. Her beliefs about him, about everything, were beginning to topple. The man was lethal.

He gave Erinn a quick nod. "And you, Missus Sullivan. Good day."

"Top of the morning, Mister Chee," Erinn returned breathily. "How odd to see you here in Las Vegas."

"I wouldn't call it odd. I've been tracking the pair of you for more than a week now."

"Tracking . . ." Erinn swallowed. "If you mean to return us to Fianna, Mister Chee—"

"I wanted to find you. Make sure you were safe."

Though he was speaking to Erinn, Moira realized he was looking straight at her.

"We're safe, of course," Erinn replied. "Did you think we'd be scalped or something?"

He turned to the younger woman, his eyes half-lidded. "The possibility crossed my mind. The Sacramentos and Capitans are full of Apaches, you know. Not to mention outlaws. Your husband noted that fact a time or two while we were scouring the brush around the Peñasco for you."

"Seamus was probably hoping he'd find me bald-headed with a tomahawk through my heart."

At that comment, Moira finally found her voice. "Sure we're as happy and well as fleas in a doghouse, so we are."

To her surprise, Josiah laughed out loud. "Fleas? Well, you might have picked up a few on that stagecoach you rode into town. Let me get you a room at the Exchange Hotel down on the Old Town piaza. You can wash up, and I'll buy you both a good hot meal."

Erinn tilted her chin. "The Last Supper, Mister Chee? Certainly not. We've tickets on the next train, so we have, and we'll be bound for St. Louis before the afternoon is over."

"St. Louis?" Of all the places he had thought Moira might take her sister, St. Louis was not one of them. That was a *city*. A big, modern city with every kind of vice imaginable. He himself had never been farther east than Denver, and he couldn't even picture how Moira would react to such a foreign place.

"Aye, St. Louis, and don't try to stop us." Erinn reached for Moira's hand as she spoke. "I know Seamus Sullivan must have paid you well to take me back, but I won't go. I'll pay you more myself, so I will. See, I have a pouch full of gold, and I'll give you whatever you ask if you let me go my way in peace."

"Seamus isn't paying me, and I don't want your money either—though your husband was fit to be tied when he discovered that pouch missing from his trunk."

"Then why have you come if it's not for the money?" Erinn asked.

Josiah looked at Moira. Could he tell the truth—just blurt right out that he'd been worried sick for Moira's life these past few days? Could he say that the thought of her lying dead or ravished at the hand of some outlaw had knotted his gut worse than any shotgun blast? Would she spurn him again if he admitted that he'd come after her, wanting her, determined to make her his, no matter what it took?

He studied those blue eyes and that clenched little jaw of hers. One look told him she hadn't braved the wilderness with plans to cart her little sister all the way to St. Louis only to swoon into Josiah's arms at the first avowal of devotion. Besides, she'd made it clear she didn't take to him—even though her body betrayed her words. He was a sheepman, a man she'd been taught to scorn.

"Innis Grady sent me," he said. "He wants Moira back."

Moira flushed with surprise. "Innis said that?" The little Irishman had never once given the least hint that he valued her. Since Deirdre's death, Moira had never believed she particularly mattered to anyone except Erinn.

"That's more or less what he said." Josiah didn't like the look of those bright spots of pink that had appeared on Moira's cheeks. Was there something between her and Innis that he hadn't seen before? She certainly was devoted to taking care of Innis's house. But did she actually care for the devil himself?

"My brother wants you back at Fianna," he said. "He claims you belong to him."

"There!" Erinn cried in triumph. "What did I tell you, Moira? Innis thinks you're his slave, so he does."

"And Seamus asked me to ride north, too," Josiah added. "He wants his wife back."

"*Mor-yah.* So he can strangle me till my eyes pop out

of my head." She sniffed and tossed her head.

"Whatever trouble there was between the two of you, I think Seamus wants to make things right again."

Moira leaned against her sister and cupped a hand to her ear. "Josiah wouldn't lie, Erinn. Maybe you've taught Seamus a lesson with your running away. Maybe he'll make peace with you and treat you kindly, as he should. Let's go home, shall we?"

Erinn studied the ground for a moment. Her lips pursed, she scowled at a scorpion scrambling from the shade of a rock and into a chink beneath the depot boardwalk. Then she crossed her arms over her chest and lifted her chin.

As she began to speak, the train suddenly blew a long, ear-jangling whistle that drowned out all other sound. A bevy of pigeons fluttered into the sky from the station roof. A throng of passengers hurried from the restaurant. Parents dragged children, while others scrambled to tuck food away in small baskets.

The moment the whistle died, Erinn stopped speaking and turned to Moira. It didn't matter that no words had been audible. Moira knew from the look on her sister's face what she had said.

"We'll be going to St. Louis," Moira told Josiah softly. "Please tell Innis I'll be back at Fianna by the end of summer. I must settle my sister's future."

Picking up her saddlebag, she grabbed Erinn's elbow. "Good-bye again, Josiah Chee," she said, but the train blew a second whistle, and the words died unheard.

Moira hurried Erinn up the wooden steps and onto the train. She couldn't bear to see Josiah there behind her, to know she'd left him once more! What was she thinking of? He had come after her, and not just to return her to Innis. She knew he would never willingly take her back to Fianna, not after he'd tried to persuade her to leave Innis and go away with him to the Mexican village on the Berrendo.

Taking Erinn's arm, she pulled her sister to an unoc-
cupied bench in the crowded car. Oh, she shouldn't
have gotten on the train! It was a sin to take Erinn
away from Seamus when he'd offered to make peace
between them. And Josiah was out there on the depot
platform even now, astride his great black horse, waiting
for her.

"Erinn!" she began, and grabbed her sister's arm.
"Erinn, I'm—"

The train jerked, and she and Erinn were slammed
against the bench back. Before they could right themselves, it jerked again, this time throwing them forward
off their seat. Their saddlebags tumbled to the floor in
a heap. Moira slid to her knees. Erinn flopped on top of
her, crumpling her amid a tangle of arms, legs, gingham
skirts, and the contents of the dumped saddlebags.

The train jerked a third time, and then began to
move forward. Steam hissed from the undercarriage
and clouded the air. The jolts became more rhythmic
as the engine slowly pulled away from the station. A
hail of black soot sanded the window, blew through
the opening, and peppered Moira and Erinn, who were
attempting to elbow themselves back onto their bench.

At the sound of a deep chuckle, Moira lifted her head
to see Josiah bending over her, his hand outstretched.
"May I be of assistance, Miss O'Casey?" he asked.

She gulped and sucked in a breath of hot steam.
*Josiah!* He was on the train. How could he have managed it? He'd had those three horses with him. And
where had he gotten the money for a ticket if Innis
and Seamus hadn't paid him to find her and Erinn?
Confused, coughing loudly, she took his hand and felt
his strong brown fingers close around hers as he lifted
her onto the bench.

"Help me, too, for heaven's sake!" Erinn cried, struggling to emerge from the tangle of her skirts.

"Oh, Erinn, you're covered with soot!" Turning from
Josiah, Moira reached for her sister. As she lugged the

younger woman onto the bench at her side, she tried to brush the coal dust from Erinn's rolls of golden hair.

"Sure this train is a nasty beastly creature, so it is," Erinn wailed. "Oh, my dress! Oh, Moira!"

Josiah settled on the bench opposite the two women and watched them fuss over their shabby cotton skirts as if they were made of the finest silk. It was amusing, in a way. They'd come this long distance on horseback and stagecoach, their once-porcelain skin was deeply tanned, their possessions fit into a pair of old saddlebags, all of their money was stolen, and yet a man might think they were the finest ladies in the Territory, the way they dusted off their clothes and adjusted the pins in their sooty hair.

Crossing his arms over his chest, stretching out his legs, and leaning against the back of the bench, Josiah allowed himself the luxury of studying the young lady who had drawn him all this distance. There she sat. Moira O'Casey. Seamus had referred to her as Josiah's ladylove, and for more than a week Josiah had debated with himself whether Seamus was right about his feelings for Moira. But was this dusty ragamuffin really worth the emotional energy he'd invested in her?

He let his eyes trail down Moira's body, slowly scrutinizing the object of his fantasy. The heat and humidity had tightened her hair into a mass of auburn ringlets that danced at her brow and hung in soft corkscrew curls from her temples. The collar of her dark blue gingham dress was buttoned all the way up her long neck and fastened at the top with a brass brooch that had turned green around the edges.

Her narrow shoulders were straight and proud, but the seams that joined her sleeves to her bodice had sagged, loosened, and faded. Below her tight cuffs, her slender wrists and hands were bare of gloves or fine, soft lotions—items other women insisted upon. Moira's fingers looked worn to him, hardened from washing clothes in lye soap, and slightly callused from her labors.

While Moira attempted to bring order back to her sister's hair, Josiah gave himself permission to evaluate boldly the body that had seemed so enticing just days before. Her breasts might be luscious, but how could a man tell? They were encased in her tight bodice, with its row of mismatched buttons. Layers of underthings he didn't know the names for had molded her bosom into a uniform curve like the side of a china teacup, a smooth arc that didn't give the slightest indication of fullness, supple weighty flesh, or peaked nipples.

Her small waist had been cinched with a stiff belt from which hung a leather holster and a gun that was probably too big and awkward for her to even shoot. The folds of gingham fabric covering her legs and feet were limp from repeated washings and spotted with dirt. Even her boots, barely visible as they were, had one black and one brown lace and were worn down at the heels.

He looked at her—a bedraggled, impoverished, worn-out, common woman, past the age of marrying and skinny as a rail—and he knew as well as he knew his own name that Seamus Sullivan had been right.

Moira O'Casey *was* his ladylove.

"Josiah, so you've come on the train?" She lifted her blue eyes to his, and he felt his heart lurch in his chest. "Your mother will be in kinks of worry over you, so she will."

It was like Moira to think first of everyone else, Josiah thought. She would give more weight to the feelings of a woman she'd never met than to her own. He'd never known anyone with a spirit like Moira's. She was a treasure.

She would give until she was empty and never ask for anything in return. But Josiah knew that in spite of all her generosity, there were things Moira O'Casey needed. Under that faded dress was a body that had never been touched, never been brought to life. Under the holy servitude was a fire that had been banked. It was time for

Moira to wake up—and he would be the man to kiss her into arousal.

"I'm a grown man, Moira," he answered her worries, "and my mother let me go a long time ago."

"All the same"—she shrugged—"it's a good long way back from here to the Berrendo River, so it is."

"It'll be farther when I'm in St. Louis."

"St. Louis!" Erinn exclaimed, her attention suddenly diverted from the saddlebag she was repacking. "Sure you're not thinking of going all the way to St. Louis with us, are you?"

"No, I'm not thinking about it. I'm doing it."

"Whatever for?" Moira countered, startled by the announcement. "We're well enough alone, so we are."

Josiah took in the set of her jaw and wondered if there would ever come a time when she would let him in. "I've given my word to Innis to bring you back to Fianna," he said. "Besides, you'll be better off with me to look out for you."

Moira glanced out the window at a landscape that seemed to slide past the window as if it, and not the train, were moving. So she had been wrong about Josiah after all. He did intend to return her to Innis, no matter what he had said about wanting to protect her from the man.

"Sure that elegant whip of yours will protect us so much better than this gun at my side," she remarked, striking out in her hurt.

"Now, Moira," Erinn cut in, her voice suddenly soft. "It won't be so bad to have a man along with us, will it, then? Mister Chee is strong and brave, and he'll protect us. We're no more than poor wandering slips, after all, and it's only by the grace of God that we've come as far as Las Vegas." She turned to Josiah. "You're wonderful skilled with that whip, so you are, Mister Chee, the way you took Innis to the floor when he was larruping Moira. And with your shoulders so broad and your arms so strong, I'll wager you could defeat any man who tried to attack us."

Moira nearly gasped aloud at her sister's bold words. Even now Erinn was gazing at Josiah, her eyes lazy-lidded, a coy smile on her lips. Her fingertips fluttered over a button that happened to lie directly between her peacock-proud breasts, as if at any moment she might open her bodice and show the strong, brave, broad-shouldered Josiah Chee what enticements lay beneath it.

"Josiah is a single man," Moira said, jerking Erinn's errant hand to her lap, "and we're lone women. It wouldn't be proper for him to go such a distance with us. Not at all."

Erinn arched one blond eyebrow. "Sure you think some widowed daisy-picker would take us to St. Louis on a train?"

"If we must have company, a female chaperon would be right. Not a young man, lone himself. Not Josiah."

But even as she spoke the words of protest, Moira knew her objections to Josiah didn't stem from the fact that he was not a proper chaperon. He was a problem to her, so he was. On the one hand, she didn't like the way Erinn was throwing sheep's eyes at him and talking like a whipster. Erinn was married to Seamus Sullivan, so she was, Moira told herself. For Erinn, flirting was a sin. Besides, what if Josiah responded to Erinn's overtures? Moira knew she couldn't bear to see him fall in love with her sister.

On the other hand, what if he didn't want Erinn, after all? What if he really had come all this way to look after Moira herself? How could it be right to travel alone with him, feeling the things she did for the man? Day and night to be so close to him, imagining things she shouldn't, wanting what wasn't right . . .

"Erinn, you're a married woman," Josiah was saying as Moira struggled to concentrate. "If Moira is wor-ried about what folks will think of us, *you* can be our chaperon."

Erinn looked crestfallen. "Daisy-pickers are usually

very old and ugly. And I no longer think of myself as married. I never considered my marriage to Seamus Sullivan a true union."

"So I hear."

Her eyes widened with surprise, and she sat forward, her golden brows furrowed. "What has Seamus said about me, that sherral?"

"The same thing you just told me. That you didn't hold much with your wedding vows."

Erinn gasped. "That's *not* what I said!"

"Whisht, Erinn," Moira cut in. "Here's a man taking tickets. Where did you put the ones you bought for us?"

"Hmmpf," Erinn snorted. After giving Josiah a scowl, she bent to shuffle through her saddlebag in search of the tickets.

Moira mopped her damp neck and temples with a white handkerchief. It was too hot, even with the slight stirring of breeze that drifted in through the open window. The iron train car seemed to act like her Dutch oven at Fianna, trapping heat and radiating it inward. Every now and again when the train chugged around a bend, black smoke from the engine billowed through the window, choking everyone and coating clothes, hair, and skin with a fine charcoal powder. All the same, none of the passengers was willing to shut the windows. To do so would have turned the passenger car into an inferno.

As Moira watched the conductor make his way down the swaying aisle from bench to bench, she realized what a pickle she was in. Where once her world had been a tidy place, now she was trapped in a mortal big tangle of sin. None of them behaved as they properly should—the wayward Erinn, the sensual Josiah, the angry Innis, the vengeful Seamus, and Moira herself acting bold, impudent, disobedient, willful.

Oh, what she wouldn't give for a nice big batch of newly washed linens to press! In spite of the heat, Moira would gladly have given up this wild adventure in order to be spreading a white cotton shirt across her table, sprinkling it with water, hooking the handle onto her sadiron, and running it heavily over the damp sleeve with a hiss of steam and the scent of starch wafting into her nose.

Maybe Innis did beat her too hard and too often. Perhaps she had been blind about his cruelty for too long now. It was past time to stand up to the man, wicked as he could be. But at least at Fianna she had had her own kitchen. Her own washtub. Her own cookstove. Her own cupboards.

Crossing her arms and settling back against the bench, she studied Josiah Chee, the man who had wandered through her dreams day and night since the moment she had seen him in Pedro's wagon. He was talking with the conductor, clearly discussing his failure to purchase a ticket back at the Las Vegas depot.

Josiah was indeed a fine-looking man, tall and as powerful as that great stallion he'd ridden up from Fianna, all sleek muscle and brawn and elegant strength. His brown eyes could look through walls, so they could. Certainly Moira was convinced they could see right into her heart. And his mouth . . . Faith, just the sight of his mouth stirred something to life deep inside her that made her uncomfortable and twitchy on the hard bench.

Oh, the man made a braw picture on the outside. But in truth, Josiah was nothing that a true man should be, Moira thought, reciting the litany that had comforted her after she'd left Fianna. He might be able to ride a horse, but Innis had said he didn't know how to shoot a gun, and his shepherd's whip was merely a weapon of defense. He had no friends, or surely they would have helped to defend him against John Fisher, who had shot him in the stomach. And why, after all, had Fisher wanted to shoot Josiah? An honorable man didn't make enemies of such a low breed as that.

As to providing a future for a woman and a family, Josiah had no job and he owned no land. Without land, what good was a man? Even if he had claimed an acre or two, he wouldn't know how to build a fine stone house or even a strong adobe dwelling with a shady portal and thick protective walls. Shepherds didn't do that sort of thing. Josiah would probably put up some rudely built havverick like the ones that sheepherders slept in at shearing time. There wouldn't be cupboards or a kitchen or a fine cookstove. Instead there would be an outdoor fire, a rude pallet on the dirt floor, a rusty old skillet and kettle, chipped crockery, and nothing to eat day after day but mutton, mutton, mutton!

"Round trip," Josiah was saying to the conductor as Moira finished relegating him to a status about equal to that of a screwworm. Relieved to have convinced herself that Josiah, although he might be as handsome as the devil himself, was actually a poor shooler, Moira was surprised to see him take a small pouch from the pocket of his trousers and count out enough coins to pay for the ticket. *Round trip*.

Erinn jabbed her elbow into Moira's ribs. "Have a look at that," she whispered. "We've been foxed, Moira! Josiah's an elegant shoneen, so he is. I'd wager there's enough gold coin in that pouch of his to give the man flahoolagh good fun for at least a year."

Moira watched Josiah stuff the pouch back into his pocket and bid the conductor a pleasant afternoon. Then as casually as you please, he slouched down and let his head rest on the bench back. With one hand he tugged his tan hat low on his brow to shade his eyes. He settled the other on the coiled whip at his side. And then he went to sleep.

Erinn nudged Moira again. "Don't you think he's braw?" she murmured. "In all my days I've never seen such a fine man as Josiah Chee."

Moira felt two spots of pink heat flare in her cheeks. "Whisht, Erinn! He'll hear you."

"Why then, he's gone to sleep, so he has. He's as deaf as a doorpost."

Moira gazed at the sleeping Josiah. Though she couldn't make out his eyes beneath the tilted hat, she could still see his mouth. That mouth had kissed her once, and perhaps . . . perhaps it would again. Such a thought! But her guilt couldn't erase the swift sweet tugging in the depths of her stomach. She crossed her legs. The train's sway and the tight clasp of her thighs only intensified the sensation. She liked it.

Her cheeks fairly flamed with embarrassment as she thought of her own boldness. Quickly she averted her eyes from Josiah and crossed her arms. The movement lifted her breasts inside her chemise. All of a sudden she could feel her nipples constrict into hard little cherries, as they did when she took a bath on a cold winter evening. In a flash she uncrossed her arms. The weight of her breasts pulled them down, sliding her nipples against the fabric of her chemise and sending an unbearable shiver down her back to nestle in the sweet throbbing place at the apex of her thighs—a place she'd hardly noticed before, but one that was now becoming a constant source of both pleasure and consternation.

"It wouldn't harm you to chase after him just a wee bit," Erinn was whispering.

"*Chase* him? Oh, Erinn!"

"Sure he'd make you a good enough husband, so he would. If he has a pouch of gold, what more could you want? With a man like that in her bed, any woman would be satisfied."

"Erinn, you shut your gob this minute. You'll burn in hell for such foolish talk."

"Don't be such a crawthumper, Moira. There's nothing wrong with admiring the turn of a man's shoulders or pondering the muscles of his chest." She leaned against her sister and spoke into her ear. "He's all stretched out now, long legs halfway across the aisle and eyes hidden under that hat of his. Why not have a gander at that fine lump beneath his trousers there? Have you ever seen such an elegant packet of goods?"

"Erinn O'Casey! Deirdre will be dying a second death and rolling in her grave to hear you speaking so!"

Erinn tossed back her head and chuckled. "Oh, Moira, when will you stop being such a voteen? As a matter of fact, I'm starting to think *you'll* want to join the nuns in Florissant instead of me. You'd rather go to mass than to bed with such a man as Josiah, so you would. You'd rather whisper your confession to a priest than have Josiah murmuring naughty words in your own ear. You'd prefer to take communion than put your lips on Josiah's grand, hard—"

Moira clapped her hand over Erinn's mouth. Hot as a fire in summer, Moira gasped for breath. Such sinful words! And yet she ached to hear more. What *did* a man and a woman do in bed? Erinn seemed to know plenty about such pleasures—yet how could that be? She had clearly stated that she and Seamus had made a poor match.

Erinn jerked Moira's hand away from her mouth and turned on her. "Don't you want him?" she hissed.

"He's . . . he's just a sheepherder," Moira said with a gulp, suddenly trying to remember all the comforting things with which she had convinced herself to turn away from Josiah. "All he wants out of life is a flock of woollies."

"Fine, then! If *you* don't recognize a good man, a strong man, a hungry man ranging about with his nose in the air like a randy stallion, *I* do."

Moira stared at her sister. "Erinn . . . what can you mean?"

"I mean that it's clear Josiah Chee didn't ride all these miles and board this train because he's some glunter. He claims Seamus isn't paying him, and in spite of that heavy coin pouch, I don't think he's lying. But *something* made Josiah come all this way—and him with a wound in his gut that makes him groan in the night. If it wasn't the promise of money that drew him along after us, what was it?"

Moira glanced at the man on the opposite bench. His chest rose and fell at a regular rate. "Why then, he told us he came to protect us . . . to make certain we're safe from harm along the trail."

"And you believe that? How many men do you know who would risk their lives to guard a pair of poor, land-less colleens—with no reward in the offing?"

"Josiah's an honorable man."

"He's a *man*! Men don't work for nothing, Moira. Have you been living in a hole? A man expects a reward for his labor."

"What are you saying, Erinn?"

"I'm saying that Mister Josiah Chee rode all the way from Fianna to Las Vegas with a burning wound and an empty stomach, that he spent his hard-earned miner's pay to board this train, and that he'll follow us all the way to St. Louis because he's found something he wants."

Again Moira glanced at Josiah. "What does he want, then?"

"A woman." Tilting her chin, Erinn looked trium-phantly at Moira. "He's after a fair colleen, so he is. Sure with that pocketful of coin he could have found quick satisfaction at any saloon. But at Fianna he saw the other sort of woman. Men appreciate our sort, Moira, so they do. We don't come cheap. We're not easy. We're to be prized."

As Moira watched Josiah sleeping, she wondered how she could have been so wrong about him. He hadn't seemed like the greedy, prancing sort of man Erinn had painted him out to be. But then, at Fianna he *had* been sick abed, frainey, and pale as death. Erinn certainly seemed to know what she was talking about.

"You could have him," Erinn said softly. Then she placed her shoulder against Moira's and whispered in her ear to keep the other passengers from catching the gist of her message. "You could know his pleasures, Moira. You might even entice him into marriage if you wanted.

Sure you're a pretty slip. Your hair is nice enough if you keep it brushed and pinned up. You've got good clear eyes, white teeth, and a full mouth. Your diddies are big and round, so they are, just the sort a man likes to fondle. And what's more, you're still a maiden. There's nothing drives a man like the notion of lifting a maiden's petticoats."

At the thought that she possessed the power to tempt Josiah Chee into fondling her breasts and lifting her petticoats, Moira felt a damp pulse begin to throb in the twitchy place between her thighs. She sucked in a breath and let her eyes drift boldly over Josiah's sleeping form. Sure that swell beneath his britches looked taut and tempting, even though she hardly knew what a woman might expect of an encounter with it. Thinking of his big work-hardened hands toying with her breasts and sliding up her thighs, she moistened her lower lip.

"But to let him take me without the bonds of matrimony," she began, letting out a ragged breath, "would be—"

"*Bonds* is exactly what they are," Erinn returned. "If you want to get the most out of a man's pleasures, Moira, you won't slave yourself to him with a wedding band."

"But it would be a sin."

"The devil take you, Moira! You might as well enter a convent. Marry a man and you'll lose every grain of freedom you ever had. You'll spend your days toiling over vats of lye soap and dirty linens, sweating like a pig over a rusty stewpot, mopping and sweeping, digging, hoeing, grinding, shelling, baking, scrubbing, darning—"

"But that's exactly what I like to do with my days!" Moira exploded finally. She grabbed her sister's shoulders and gave her a rough shake. "Glory be to God, Erinn, what's gotten into you? I'll never willingly give myself to Josiah Chee. I've got my pride. I won't lower myself the way you suggest—and there you have it!"

Erinn pushed Moira's hands away and curled her upper

lip. "It's not lowering yourself to want a little pleasure out of life. I've suffered enough. If you won't take what's handed you on a silver platter, then by heaven *I'll* take it."

"Take what?"

"Him." Erinn turned on the bench, crossed her arms, and stared at the object of her pursuit.

Scarcely able to breathe, Moira turned, too. As she did, she saw Josiah adjust the brim of his hat with the tip of a finger. His brown eyes were pinned to her face.

# Chapter
## 8

So that was what Moira thought of him, Josiah thought as he studied her from under the brim of his Stetson. He was beneath her. He was low—a landless, friendless sheepherding loser unworthy of being called a man.

He knew he should forget her. In a few hours the train would pull in at the Springer depot. He could hop off the car, buy himself a good horse at the livery stable, and take a leisurely trip back down the trail to the Berrendo. That would give his body time to finish healing, and it might even add some adventure to his life. He could do some gambling, a little drinking, maybe dance with a saloon girl or two. . . .

Gritting his teeth, Josiah tried to quell the sick feeling in his gut. Any other man would give his right arm to have a pouch full of gold and the freedom to spend it as he pleased. For most men, drinking, gambling, and whoring were top-notch entertainment. Why didn't those pleasures hold any appeal for him?

The reason, he knew, was sitting on the bench opposite him. Pale as one of her carefully bleached sheets, she was staring out the window. Blue eyes luminous, she seemed to be trying to hold back tears. He couldn't figure out why. Her life seemed settled enough. Stubborn as she was, she had plainly stated how she felt about the notion of hooking up with him. And he'd heard every word.

She sure was a mule-headed little beauty. Josiah knew he ought to take her at her word. He ought to hotfoot it off the train in Springer and let her find her own way to St. Louis with her overheated little sister. Then she could head back to that rooster of an Irishman she was so devoted to, and slave for him until she was old and withered and too tired to care that she'd missed the best in life.

But even as Josiah formed these thoughts, another part of his mind painted pictures, images that erased the bitterness as swiftly as it grew. *Moira.* He could see her now, her head held high on that fine long neck of hers. She had wanted him to kiss her neck that night when she came into his bedroom. He couldn't forget the way she had arched against his lips. She had come into his arms willingly, eagerly, full of hunger for nourishment she hadn't even known she needed. Moira might say she felt nothing for him, but her body betrayed her.

She wanted him. He wanted her. But was it merely lust that drove him after her like a hot-blooded stallion thundering after a prancing filly? Could a raging case of the itch be all that had prodded him to chase Moira from Innis Grady's ranch all the way to Las Vegas?

There was no doubt in Josiah's mind that he wanted to bed Moira O'Casey. He couldn't stop thinking about her lips, about her long eyelashes, about the scent of lavender that drifted wherever she went. He fairly ached to touch her hair. His body swelled and hardened at the merest thought of what might be waiting for him under all those layers of gingham and petticoats she wore.

True, Moira had given him the worst case of the all-fired, hot-blooded, rip-snorting rut he'd ever had in his life. But it wasn't only the fact that he knew she was a keg of powder just waiting to be lit that kept him beating down the brush in pursuit. There was something else about Moira. Something he couldn't quite put his finger on. It had to do with the way she smiled as she worked. The way her hands had smoothed the sheets over his chest as he lay sick in bed. The way she righteously defended her tart of a sister against the obvious truth.

For some reason he liked the fact that Moira was religious to a fault. He appreciated her fierce loyalty, even to a rat like Innis Grady. He even enjoyed the way she stubbornly clung to the values she'd been taught from childhood—a creed that said sheepherders were as low as pond scum, that full-blooded Irishmen were lords of the earth, that passion was a sin, values that put up a mile-high fence between her and him. He'd sure rather climb that fence to get to Moira than walk through an open gate into the arms of her randy little sister.

After chugging uphill at a little more than twelve miles an hour, the train made it to Springer just in time for the passengers to take a late lunch at the counters in the depot. It was so hot—a parching, dry heat—that Moira thought she might swoon. She couldn't bring herself to even look at Josiah after all the things Erinn had suggested. Every time she even *thought* of their whispered conversation on the train she felt her cheeks go a deeper shade of crimson as a fresh wash of perspiration broke out on her already damp skin.

What if Josiah had heard? His eyes had been open! She'd seen that undeniably revealing gaze from beneath the brim of his tan hat. What if he actually believed she was considering the sorts of things Erinn had suggested? And the worst, most horrifying part of it all— she *was* considering them! Just the thought of giving herself freely, wholly, to Josiah made her feel light-headed and wonderful and scandalous and altogether in need of spending several hours at confession.

Bowing her head over her ham sandwich, Moira carefully crossed her breast in fervent hope that she might be spared the fires of hell for all her many sins on this ill-begotten journey. She had run away from her guardian; that was bad enough. She had spirited off another man's wife and was taking her to a place where she could annul the marriage or petition for divorce! She was merrily spending poor Seamus Sullivan's money from his stolen pouch. Every waking minute and most of her sleeping ones she was lusting after a man she shouldn't even look at twice.

How could the good Lord forgive her? She had broken nearly every one of the Ten Commandments—she was sure of that, if she only had time to remember what they were. Stealing, yes. Failing to honor her guardian, yes. Adultery, not yet, but . . .

"Eat!" Erinn elbowed Moira in the ribs.

Quickly coming out of her prayer, Moira focused on her sandwich. She stared at the thick slice of ham. Her stomach was a knot.

"The whistle will blow soon, and you'll not have taken a bite," Erinn chided her. "Faith, you're going to fade away before we reach St. Louis, Moira."

"I'm not hungry. It's simply far too . . . too hot." Moira couldn't help glancing at Josiah. He was seated at the far end of the counter with some of the male passengers, chuckling between sips of lemonade.

My, but he looked handsome. What it was that made Josiah stand out among the others, Moira couldn't quite understand. Most of the men were dressed like him. A few—most likely doctors, lawyers, and such—wore suits of pale linen with double-breasted frock coats and checked or striped trousers. Their wing-collared shirts sported knotted ties stuck with gold pins. They had leather ankle boots and bowler hats, and they looked as uncomfortable in the heat as pigs without a mudhole.

Josiah and the rest of the men wore homespun cotton shirts in shades of pale gray, brown, or cream. They made no pretense in the heat, but rolled their sleeves up to the elbow and unbuttoned their shirts partway. Denim or broadcloth britches in various stages of fading, patching, and unraveling were cinched up with leather belts and holsters. Chaps had been discarded, but the silver spurs on their worn, dusty leather boots were a sure sign that these were hard-riding, working men.

Josiah was one of these men, himself in a white chambray shirt, a black vest, and jeans. So why should the sight of him take Moira's breath right out of her chest? Because he *wasn't* the same, that was why. He was taller and broader of chest than the others. His arms were roped with the solid cords of muscle that he had earned at his labor in the copper mines. His skin was the buckskin brown of New Mexico's mesas. Hatless in the lunchroom, he looked younger than he had on the train. His dark blond hair was thick and straight, and a hank of it fell across his forehead.

How many of those men around the counter had brown eyes? More than half at least, in various shades from muddy tan to mottled hazel. But to Moira, Josiah's eyes seemed deeper than the other men's, lustrous and chocolate-rich like a patch of prized velvet in the crazy quilt she had stitched for Erinn's wedding. They were deep-set and penetrating, eyes that could haunt a woman and put the fear of the devil in a man. His gaze darted from one man to another as each spoke, and to Moira it was clear that Josiah was the most alert and intelligent of the lot.

When he laughed, his eyes crinkled at the corners, and she knew that one day those lines would become permanent. Would she still know Josiah when his face had been seamed and molded by the hands of time? Would she ever see him when his golden hair had turned to pale silver and his face wore the memory of his laughter?

"Do you want to take it with you, then?" Erinn's voice cut into Moira's thoughts.

"What?" Did she want to take Josiah with her? Yes, she did. Of course she did!

"Your sandwich. Everyone's packing up. Do you want to take it on the train?"

Moira stared down at the unfamiliar square of uneaten bread and ham. "I told you, I'm not hungry."

"We won't be stopping again until late this evening. And they say Raton is miles and miles up in the mountains. You'll have an appetite in that fresh air, so you will."

"I *said* I didn't want the sandwich, Erinn." Sliding off the high counter chair, Moira joined the other passengers who were filing out onto the depot platform.

"Well, you don't have to shout at me!"

Moira turned to retort, but the train whistle sounded just in time to cover her words. God's blessings, she thought. Just when she was about to sin yet again by berating her dear sister, the locomotive took over.

In the unbearable din, Moira ducked her head and hurried up the steps onto the train. It wasn't easy to make her way among the throng of passengers arranging their belongings, but she elbowed through to the bench and sat down. Maybe she could go to sleep, she thought as she sank against the hard, worn wood. Sleep would certainly block out all the confusing mess of the day.

Shutting her eyes, she felt Erinn settle next to her on their bench. She put out her hand, and her sister's smaller hand settled into it. Why had Erinn said such things about Josiah? Moira wondered as she let the darkness soothe her tired eyes. Sure Erinn had always been a bold mischief-maker, talking before she thought and doing naughty things just for the fun of it all. Where Moira had been the good child, obedient and devout, Erinn had been a scamp of a girl, always searching for the next pot of mischief she could leap into with both feet.

But *this*? This wasn't like Erinn, was it? Moira squeezed her sister's hand. Erinn had sounded like one of those painted ladies of the evening in Las Vegas, so she had. Moira could barely fathom that her sister had been married to one of the finest, richest men in the Peñasco Valley, and yet she was throwing that marriage away— dismissing the very notion of marriage itself, in fact. To think that Erinn would actually bed a man who wasn't her husband! Oh, it was a mortal sin. Making matters worse in Moira's eyes was the man Erinn had set her sights on: Josiah Chee.

The train started up with its hiss of steam, cloud of coal dust, and bone-jarring lurches, but this time the chaos served only to force Moira's eyes open as she held on to the side of the bench. Instantly she looked across the small space to Josiah's seat. It was empty.

"Where's Josiah?" she gasped, sitting upright.

"How should I know?" Erinn was clutching Moira for dear life as the train threw them back and forth. "The devil bless this train! Look at my dress—covered with soot again. By japers, I don't think I'll ever come clean after this dreadful journey."

"*Where's Josiah*, Erinn?" Moira repeated over the clatter of the wheels on the track.

"Back in Springer if he's smart. He was still sitting at the counter when we walked out with the rest of the passengers. I told you he had no good reason for following us all the way to St. Louis. And with this infernal train jangling our bones and shaking our teeth from their roots, it's no wonder he would want to mount a horse and head south."

"Do you think he really did leave us?" Moira felt clammy all of a sudden, despite the stifling heat inside the metal train car. Once there had been a time when she had willingly ridden away from Josiah. But now that she had been with him again for these few hours, she suddenly couldn't bear the thought of losing him.

"Oh, Moira, don't worry about Josiah," Erinn was saying as she brushed the coal dust from her sleeve. "He'll make his way back into God's pocket just fine without your fretting him along."

Shutting her mouth, Moira tried to make herself believe she didn't care. So Josiah wasn't on the train. What difference did it make? She had plans enough without a dark-eyed man to foul them up. There was this long trip to St. Louis with Erinn in tow, then another long trip alone back home to Fianna. Innis was waiting for her, and dear silly Scully with his paintings. They needed looking after, didn't they?

Blinking back tears, she suddenly knew losing Josiah for good was more than she could stand. She jumped out of her seat and shoved the window wide open. Amid exclamations of dismay from the other passengers who were being peppered with chunks of hot coal, she propped her hands on the sill and stuck her head out into the sooty air. She could just make out the Springer depot far down the track, and on it stood a lone man. He was tall and well built, and he wore a tan hat.

"Josiah!" she shouted. "I didn't mean what I said about you! Truly, I didn't!"

"Better watch it there. You might fall out." A man's bare arm, sinewed and brown, slid just under her breasts and drew her back against the solid, warm plane of a male chest. "I wouldn't want to lose you *this* way."

Moira twisted her head around as Josiah's other long arm reached around her to shut the window. "Now, what were you saying?"

She swallowed. "Josiah! Oh, I thought you were out there. There was a man in a tan hat. I didn't see you on the train."

"Here I am."

"But you weren't—"

"I was in the car behind this one visiting with some of the men. We were discussing ranching. They tell me sheep are thriving this year in spite of the drought."

"Sheep . . ."

His arm still around her, he settled onto his bench, taking her with him. He knew holding her like this put a stamp of claim on her he might not have earned. But he had heard what she'd been shouting out the window. That was enough for now.

"Sheep need a lot less water than cattle do, you know," he said, deciding he'd better come up with some conversation to cover the way her body made him feel. "They can forage farther from wells and springs, and they'll eat forbs that the cows won't touch. Everyone who's savvy about the business agrees that sheep are the way to build a ranch these days."

"Oh." Moira knew Josiah was saying something about sheep, those chuckleheaded villains of the range, but all she could think about was the feel of his hand molded around her waist. His warm fingers pressed into the rise of her hip, and she could sense the back of his arm just above the curve of her buttocks. If she'd had a bustle, she would have felt nothing. For once, she thanked the good Lord she was too poor to be in style.

"Transhumance is what they call it," Josiah was saying as he settled into the conversation. "My father's Mexican ancestors have been practicing it for years, only without giving it such a fancy name. See, a good sheepman grazes his flocks in the mountains during the summer. The grass is green, and the streams are flowing with melted snow. When winter comes on, he takes them down into the valleys where it's warmer and there's plenty of ungrazed land."

"Oh," Moira repeated again. What on *earth* was he talking about? It was all she could do to concentrate. His hand had slid up to her shoulder, and his fingertip was drawing little circles on her arm. Though they had a whole bench to themselves, he was sitting so close she could feel his long thigh straight and hard against hers. It was almost as if by some fairy magic the fabric of her dress had vanished clean away. She was quite sure the damp heat on her skin came directly from his and that they were touching flesh to flesh.

In spite of her dismay at having revealed her feelings about Josiah by yelling them out the window, Moira was all too aware that every nerve in her body was jangling. Not only did she know each tendon and plane of muscle in Josiah's leg, but she felt as though she could smell the very starch in his shirt, the dust that coated his boots, the trace of lemon on his breath. She couldn't keep her eyes off his mouth as he spoke. The way his lips moved to form words mesmerized her. She studied his teeth, white and strong, and she watched his tongue, thinking of the way it had played so boldly with hers.

Oh, she was certain the shee had taken hold of her heart and were toying with it! But if it was fairy magic that had overcome her, it must have been a good little leprechaun who had led her to this cache of gold. Moira had never felt so wonderful, so completely enthralled, as she did at this moment, with Josiah's arm tightly around her and his words dripping down her spine like warm honey.

Somehow wanting to share the glory she felt, Moira glanced at Erinn, seated across the aisle. Her sister was making a sustained effort to attract Josiah's attention. She hung on every word he was saying, her great luminous eyes batting with feigned interest. While he spoke, Erinn dusted at her dress, her pale hands brushing the upper swell of her bosom in a decidedly seductive manner. When she took a comb from her saddlebag and began to draw it through one long golden curl after another, Moira had had enough. She made a move to get up.

"We've always run a common breed of sheep on our place," Josiah said, tightening his grip on her shoulder and forcing her to remain next to him on the bench. "Churros, we call them."

He had waited too long for the chance to be this close to Moira, he decided. Now that he knew he meant more to her than just an irritation, he wasn't about to let anything, especially her little sister, get in his way. He relaxed his hand but still kept her close. He felt good—better than he'd felt in a long time. He had Moira with him and, for the first time since he'd laid eyes on her back at Grady's ranch, he felt confident that one day he would make her his. The more he thought about it, the more he knew he wanted her to understand his dreams for the future.

"Churros are a hardy and tough bunch," he told her. "Navajos have tended them for generations, but my Apache grandfather and others of the Indeh thought as poorly of sheep as you do, Moira. It's true that churros don't give the best wool, not what factories back east are looking for. When I stake my claim on some land, I plan to bring in some other strains and breed them with the local churros to see what I get, or I might just run my imports pure. Merinos might do just fine in the valley. They're Spanish and they've got a heavy fleece that makes high-quality, fine-grade wool. The men in the other car tell me that shepherds over in France are working to breed sheep that will be bigger and sturdier than anything we've ever grown around here. I think I could put my sheep in the valley and make more off them than any cattleman ever dreamed about."

"Valley?" Moira asked. "Which valley?"

Josiah rubbed the back of his neck. Might as well tell her now and get it over with. "I'm thinking of staking a claim to some waterfronts up the Peñasco from Innis Grady's place."

"The Peñasco!" She sat up straight. "You can't run sheep in *our* valley! If you must import the nasty pests, put them on the Pecos or the Rio Grande."

"The Pecos is pretty much claimed out, Moira. Besides, the Peñasco valley belonged to my people for many generations before the White Eye ranchers settled on it."

Heat prickled down Moira's back at his words. "I'll have you remember your own dear mother is a White Eye, so she is, and I'm sure she's proud of her fine Irish blood. Your Mexican and Apache ancestors weren't able to keep their hands on the land along the Peñasco, and now it's ours to do with as we please. And we don't want sheep!"

"We would if we were smart. Sheep might make the difference between our land thriving and our ranches growing—or not."

" 'We'? Who are you speaking of here?"

"I'll have you remember my mother is a White Eye, so she is, and I'm sure she's proud of her fine Irish blood."

"Don't throw my words back at me!"

"But don't you see, Moira," he said, turning on the bench and taking her shoulders in his hands, "that if the land belongs to the Irish, then by right I can claim part of it for myself? If it belongs to the Mexicans, it's mine. If it's Apache land, it's mine, too. I've seen the Peñasco Valley, and I know what I can do there. It's not greed that pulls me, Moira. I feel the land calling, crying out. I told you once, one night in the little room at Fianna, that I know what I'm supposed to do in my life. I've got to save the land."

"By running *sheep*?" Deciding she'd had enough of his talk, Moira again tried to slide out of Josiah's embrace. This time he gripped her so hard that she could barely breathe. She glanced at him in confusion.

"Moira, listen to me," he whispered, his words barely audible over the rattle of the train's wheels on the track. "A few minutes ago you shouted out the window that you didn't mean what you said to your sister about me. I want to believe that. When you look into my eyes, I want you to see past the Mexican and the Apache and even the Irish in them. I'm all of those and none of them. I'm an *American*."

She searched his brown eyes, trying to understand. It was strange to think of blending with other races and nationalities to become something altogether different. She had never imagined herself anything but Irish through and through.

"This is a new land, Moira," Josiah insisted. "People can't cling to their old prejudices. Already the English are marrying Scots. Germans are marrying Swedes. Italians are marrying the French. My Apache grandfather took a Mexican wife, and my father took an Irish bride. We're mixing together, don't you see? Like the sheep I plan to breed, we'll come out stronger, hardier, better people for our mingling. Innis Grady's dreams of building an untainted Irish civilization here won't work. His own mother proved that."

"But she's . . . she's an outcast, Josiah. For what she did, she's been forced to live away from us. She's lost her roots, her traditions. She no longer has her Irish family to hold her close. Sure she has nothing dear to call her own."

He smiled and shook his head. "My mother is the happiest woman I've ever known. She has a home, six healthy children, a claim to rich, fertile land, a church, and best of all, a man who loves her more than life itself. What's so bad about that, Moira?"

Swallowing, Moira gazed into those brown eyes and knew she didn't have an answer. The life he had just described was all she had ever wanted. It was what she wanted now. With *him*.

"I'll tell you what's so bad about it," Erinn piped up from her position on the bench across the aisle. "A home, children, land, and the church are nothing but bondage to a woman. And I've never known a man who could convince me otherwise with his loving. Sure Moira and I watched our own guardian slave her way toward an early death. If childbirth hadn't taken her when it did, Deirdre would have gone soon enough anyway, so she would. Tell him, Moira."

"Deirdre *was* very worn, as we remember her."

"Aye, and not happy," Erinn said. "She had come all the way from the green pastures of county Cork to a poor desert land filled with thorns, weeds, and wild Indians. Scully was the only child she was ever able to bear. She told us Innis had married her out of love, but when he was drunk he beat her. So she buried herself in religion. Then, in a holy fit on her deathbed, she made Moira swear to tend that devil Innis for the rest of her life. Not every man hits his wife, that I know, but the whole killeen of them do expect a woman to scrape and bow and serve them till their dying day, Seamus Sullivan included."

"Deirdre wasn't like that, Erinn," Moira said softly. "She truly loved God, just as she truly loved Innis in spite of all his faults. Her kind arms reached out to us when we were orphaned. She loved you, Erinn."

"Blather!" Erinn snorted.

Moira gazed at her sister, wishing she could erase the lines of bitterness and anger that crisscrossed her brow. "Oh, Erinn," she murmured, starting up from the bench.

Josiah's hand tightened on her arm. "Stay with me," he said under his breath.

She glanced at him, but his face was impassive, as if he hadn't spoken. "Erinn, I think you're going to be a lot happier in St. Louis," Josiah said, adjusting his big shoulders against the back of the hard bench. "I hear a woman doesn't have to work so hard back east, especially if she can find a rich man to set her up in the lap of luxury."

Erinn arched one one blond eyebrow, apparently considering whether or not to take his words as an insult. Finally a slow smile spread across her full lips. "I don't suppose I would object to that," she said. "Being rich, I mean. Deirdre used to settle in the rocker by our bed and tell us stories about the days when she was a young girl in Ireland, before she was wed to Innis and carted off to the end of the earth. I always liked to hear her talk about the fine big farm she grew up on. A grand stone castle the house was, wasn't it, Moira?"

Moira nodded absently. Josiah had started stroking her arm again. She tried to concentrate on Erinn's prattle.

Something about lovely, swishy silk dresses and embroidered slippers. Grand parties. A house within the ruined walls of a great castle beside a river.

Moira remembered the stories. They had seemed like something out of fairyland. At the time she had half wondered if Deirdre was making them up. Erinn, it was true, had loved the tales, lapped them up like warm milk, and played at being a rich young Irishwoman herself. But Moira had always dismissed the accounts as soon as she went to sleep. She preferred the Peñasco Valley with its rushing green river, its tall golden grasses, its prickly pear and cholla, its distant brown hills, and its sweet wildflowers to any old crumbling Irish castle.

Settling against Josiah, she allowed herself to soak in the warmth of his body. In spite of the heat, she relished the damp fabric of his shirt pressed against her arm. She drank in the softness of his breath brushing over her hair and cheek. Just to make sure she wouldn't forget this moment in days to come, to make certain it was all she perceived it to be, she pressed her thigh against his. He pressed back. He was talking to Erinn as if nothing were happening between them. Moira could hear him asking questions about Ireland and repeating brief comments that his own mother had made. All the while his leg was rock hard against hers.

At their sweet shared secret, she shivered and relaxed her shoulder against his chest. Perhaps this was all she would ever have of him, these stolen moments that lit a fire deep down inside her. Perhaps it was enough. Then again, every time they touched, she wanted more. She ached for another kiss, but when and where could they ever be alone on this crowded train?

Passengers were everywhere—salesmen with their rat-catcher suits, heavy samples cases, and hair smelling of Macassar oil; punchers looking for fun in the big city; rich ranchers smoking foul-smelling cigars; ailing patients traveling to hospitals; mothers with fretting babes; children dancing up and down the aisles; news butchers peddling tinned beef, coffee, towels, soap, and whatnot from their little carts; and the conductor checking every nook and cranny for things out of place.

This melee was enough to make a person's head swim. Moira didn't know when she'd ever been around so many people, and the heat in the car was suffocating. Certainly there would never be a moment for her to spend alone with Josiah. Faith, she shouldn't care! The man wasn't hers to kiss and dally with as the painted ladies did. Moira lifted her eyes and gazed at his mouth. That wonderful mouth.

His words had made such sense to her! Why couldn't people blend together in this new land, marrying the one they loved despite tradition and heritage? What was so wrong with Josiah wanting to own a bit of ground that was his people's rightful land anyway? And even sheep . . . By japers there were sheep in Ireland, so there were. It might not be so bad to have a lovely woolen shawl to wear in wintertime. It might not be so terrible to cook up a tasty mutton stew. . . .

Moira felt her head loll back on Josiah's arm. She knew it wasn't proper of her to go to sleep. Not in the middle of Erinn's conversation. Not with things so unresolved. Not with Josiah so boldly clasping her to him in full view of all the passengers. But it was so warm in the rhythmically swaying train, and he smelled so good, and the sound of his voice seeped through her mind . . . and his finger stroked her arm with a promise of things to come. . . .

# Chapter
## 9

Moira, Josiah, and Erinn ate dinner late that first evening of their train journey to St. Louis at the fancy depot restaurant in Raton. The Harvey House, it was called, after its famous proprietor, Fred Harvey, who had opened elegant dining rooms all along the Atchison, Topeka, and Santa Fe line. Lovely young women served a meal fit for a king—oysters, roast sirloin, ice cream, and huge slices of apple pie. The waitresses wore tidy black and white uniforms, and their movements were as regulated as if they were soldiers endowed with feminine grace. For a passing moment, Moira thought she might like to be a Harvey Girl herself, but then the train whistle blew, and everyone hurried across the platform and back into the crowded car

Knowing this was the last she would see of the New Mexico Territory for a long time, Moira gazed wistfully out the train window as the engine chugged slowly up and up over Raton Pass, across the trestle bridge, and through the tunnel. For all her bold claims of being one hundred percent Irish born and bred, Moira couldn't deny that New Mexico was her home, the beloved land that had nurtured and cherished her. She vowed to return.

The evening ritual on the train presented a whole new set of challenges for its passengers. With the Atchison, Topeka, and Santa Fe Railroad engaged in stiff competition with the Missouri Pacific and the Rock Island lines, stock in the railway had dropped to almost nothing. And with its stock worthless, the railway could hardly afford to outfit its cars in the luxurious style of the palatial Pullmans the eastern railways boasted of—the velvet upholstered seats, white linens, and brocade draperies that Moira had heard so much about.

Instead Moira and Erinn spent the evening and the following days in quarters hardly better than those of their immigrant parents who had traveled west in railway cars called zulus, though no one was sure why. A common cookstove had been installed in the front end of Moira's car, and primitive plumbing was built into the back. Down the middle of the car hung a row of Pintsch gas lamps that swung with the movement of the train.

Their car had been designated as sleeping quarters for the single women and married families on board the train, so that night after dinner Moira and Erinn pulled down the bed that hung by chains from the ceiling. There were no changing screens, no mattresses, and no linens, so they were forced to sleep in their dresses on the hard wooden platform suspended in midair. That in itself was enough to give Moira the jitters as she climbed up into the swaying nest and tried to settle herself next to Erinn. But with the still-lit gas lamps undulating back and forth and causing her to dwell on her parents' awful death by fire, she was almost too distressed to sleep. If there was one thing Moira truly feared, it was the thought of burning to death.

Josiah joined the other single men in the adjacent car, and during the night the train descended from nearly eight thousand feet in the Sangre de Cristo Mountains toward the Great Plains of the Midwest.

The following days were a whirlwind of new sights for Moira as the engine chugged across the southeast corner of Colorado, through Trinidad and then past La Junta, the site of Bent's Fort on the old Santa Fe Trail. The rails followed the Arkansas River into Kansas, and the train stopped in Dodge City and Topeka before swinging north toward Kansas City.

In Kansas City the wayfarers left the Atchison, Topeka, and Santa Fe line in order to take a train on the Missouri Pacific Railway that would transport them to St. Louis. As the locomotive rolled across Missouri, Erinn wanted to get off and visit every city and town they passed.

"Oh, it's a wonder!" she kept exclaiming as the train rattled over rolling green hills and dipped into verdant valleys. "Missouri is grand indeed! One of the United States of America, Moira. It's just as I pictured it! No— even better! Isn't it lush here? Faith, it's practically a jungle!"

No matter how Erinn pleaded and wheedled, Moira refused to allow her younger sister to set foot off the depot platforms in the towns along the track. This bold state of Missouri was clearly a modern, audacious, and cocksure place, and not at all to be trusted.

But she had to agree with Erinn that she'd never seen anything quite so lush as the thickly wooded hills dense with oak, maple, and hickory. As it was still cool in this part of the country, and wetter than New Mexico had ever thought of being, the wild dogwoods hadn't quite finished blooming. Along the myriad streambeds, they blossomed in such glorious shades of white and pink that Moira knew Scully would love to capture them with his oil paints. Innis would appreciate the state, too. Sure there was enough water in Missouri to fill the dry rivers in New Mexico and have plenty more besides.

Farms and homesteads nestled against the hillsides, their cozy log cabins hemmed in with zigzagging split-rail fences that reminded Moira of the stitches she had used to join the patches of Erinn's crazy quilt. It was a wonder to her how many of these little farms flourished so close together. The land in the New Mexico Territory certainly couldn't support such a dense human population and so much livestock crammed into one spot. Yet everything in Missouri seemed to be thriving—the cattle, the pigs, the goats, the chickens, even the dogs.

And, oh, the towns! Sure they must have been touched by the fairies. Never had Moira seen so many mercantiles with so many varieties of goods displayed behind their plate-glass windows. Never had she seen such fine carriages, such lovely homes, such beautiful churches. God must be very pleased indeed, she thought, for there was a white clapboard church with spires and bells on nearly every street corner. Never mind that many of them were Protestant churches and of a slightly different persuasion than her beloved Catholic faith. She knew the angels would be smiling as people streamed inside to worship the good Lord of a Sunday morning.

Erinn gave not a moment's heed to the churches. She was wild for the ladies' dresses. She kept jabbing Moira in the arm and pulling her to the train window to see this gown or that coat or the other pair of shoes. She vowed to have as many dresses as she pleased one day, in as many colors as the rainbow. Moira tried to remind her that their destination was a convent in Florissant, but Erinn hardly listened. She was bent on having for herself a grand bustle that poufed out behind her in yards and yards of silk. She wanted to change her hair, too, from the simple pinned coil she had always worn to one of those outlandish modern fashions they were seeing everywhere.

"I'll pile it right up on top," Erinn told Moira as the train whistled its way through the center of the city of St. Louis, a sprawling giant on the west bank of the Mississippi River. "I'm going to cut the front right off, so I am. I'll buy a curling iron, and I'll give myself a fringe the likes of which you've never seen. Then we'll go shopping, shall we, Moira?"

Moira was staring out the window, her heart beating faster than the train's wheels as they rolled over the last of the track into Union Depot. Never, never, never had she imagined such a place as this St. Louis! The streets were wide and grand and lined with gaslights. Telephone wires were strung from pole to pole like a wondrous gossamer spiderweb. Not a single open sewer could be seen anywhere. Rising high overhead, almost blocking out the sky, huge houses of commerce and finance mingled with the spires of churches. Horse-drawn streetcars ran on rails up and down the city streets. And as the train approached the Mississippi River, Moira couldn't help but catch Erinn's arm and squeeze it tightly.

"Steamboats!" she whispered. "Erinn, can you see them?"

Unimpressed with a mode of transportation that the railway had put on its last legs, Erinn merely nodded. "Dangling earrings," she went on, "with delicate silverwork. That's what I want. Did you see those on the lady we passed just a bit back there?"

Moira couldn't bear to hear another word. She turned to Josiah, who was looking at the approaching bustle of the riverway.

"Steamboats, Josiah!" she said.

He smiled. "Would you like to ride on one, Moira?"

"Oh, my . . . Well, of course. But we haven't the money for it. Erinn's pouch is growing lighter by the day, so it is, and if I can't keep her out of the mercantiles in St. Louis, we won't even make it to Florissant."

Chuckling, Josiah took her hand and drew her across onto his bench, determined to share this moment of discovery with her. The past days of travel had been hell. Moira had been close enough for him to touch, and yet he had been forced to keep his distance. He knew she couldn't have borne the shame if he had courted her openly the way he wanted to.

Moira was always conscious of the other passengers. Not only was she concerned about what they might think of her, but—as she typically did—she spent much of her time making the rounds of the car. She rocked fussy babies to give their mothers a rest; she played quiet games with restless children to calm them; she took over the duties of a tired wife whose husband had a bad leg and was traveling to a hospital to have it amputated.

Everyone loved Moira. And Moira had done her level best to please them all—everyone but Josiah. He had found himself alone with Erinn more times than he cared to count. Moira's younger sister evidently had decided to make a play for his attentions, and it was all he could do to keep her at a distance.

Once on a depot platform in Dodge City he had practically had to pry Erinn off him when their train stopped for a late evening meal and Moira vanished. The little blonde had pretended to be scared of a gunslinger walking past, and she'd thrown her arms around Josiah's neck. The next thing he knew, she was kissing him as she tried to push him into the shadows of the station overhang.

How he'd gotten out of that one, he could barely remember. He supposed he had heaven to thank. It was sure going to be a relief to drop Erinn off at that convent and finally have Moira all to himself.

The train came to a stop with a hiss of steam, a squeal of brakes, and a final, ear-piercing whistle. *St. Louis.*

As Josiah helped the two young women gather their belongings, he wondered what on earth he was doing in a city like this. Chasing Moira O'Casey, of course. Again he had to wonder if she was worth it. He knew he didn't belong in a city any more than one of those newfangled telephones belonged on a ranch. The two just didn't mesh. Come to think of it, he wasn't all that sure he could even abide life in the rolling hill country of Missouri. He needed space, vast stretches of empty land, a big blue sky cupped like a bowl from one horizon to the other. If Missouri's hills made him feel closed in, he couldn't imagine how he was going to swallow what lay in wait just outside the train.

Following Moira and Erinn, he made his way down the long, familiar aisle and out onto the depot platform. The moment he lifted his head, his ears were abused with a crazy medley of sounds—streetcars clanging, wagon wheels rattling over cobblestones, horses neighing, dogs barking, steamboats whooing, trains whistling, policemen shouting as they tried to direct the flow of traffic, stevedores hollering and cursing at each other while they loaded the ships, vendors crying out their wares.

"I'll be damned," he said under his breath as he settled his hat on his head. He glanced at Moira. His thoughts of turning tail and climbing back on the first train headed west evaporated at the sight of her pale but determined face. She had clutched her old saddlebag to her chest and was chewing on her bottom lip as her blue eyes darted back and forth. Moira, he knew, would not set foot out of Missouri until she'd taken care of her precious little sister.

"I wonder how we can find transport to Florissant," she said, almost to herself. "Perhaps another train."

"Oh, let's don't go there yet," Erinn whined. "We've only just gotten to the city, so we have, and I'd like to see the sights."

Moira turned a stern eye on her sister. "You'll be going into the novitiate, Erinn O'Casey Sullivan, if it's the last thing you do. We didn't come all this long way to this dreadful place to go shopping! Now follow me, and we'll find ourselves another train."

"Oh, Moira, don't be such a googeen!"

"What?" Moira faced Erinn, her face determined. "Sure you're not going to be contrary about this now, are you?"

"Aye, if you mean to lock me up with the nuns, I am. Moira, can't you see the glory of where we are and what we've done? We've escaped! We're here in a free city where we can do anything we like. Anything at all!" She swung around to Josiah. "Faith, *you* want to explore a bit, don't you, Mister Chee?"

"If I had my druthers I'd be riding a horse up the Peñasco Valley right now."

Erinn rolled her eyes. "Moira, please listen to me. When I first thought of coming to St. Louis to find the novitiate, it seemed a grand and elegant plan, so it did. But now that I'm here, now that I've had a taste of the city, I can't bear to be locked up with a flock of righteous crawthumpers."

Josiah had been waiting for this moment, almost certain it was going to come. He had sensed from the beginning that Erinn would never be content to live in a convent. She was too impulsive and not the least bit religious.

"Erinn," Moira threatened, narrowing her eyes, "you will do exactly as we planned, so you will, and no wavering from it. Bad enough I ran away from Innis and left him and poor Scully to fend for themselves. Worse, I helped you escape from your rightful husband whom God and Innis gave you. But I'll not add to my carn of sins by failing to put you with the holy sisters where you belong."

"Oh, Moira!" Erinn began, but Moira was already marching off toward the ticket window. "Moira, please . . ."

Josiah grinned as he took Erinn's elbow and propelled her along behind her sister. Moira might be good-hearted to a fault, but she was able to stiffen her back when the situation called for it.

"To Florissant, Missouri," she was saying to the elderly agent when they joined her, "the novitiate of the Order of the Sacred Heart."

"Don't know a dern thing about no sacred heart around these parts, ma'am, but I do know ain't no gettin' to Florissant by train. Yu'uns bettah take a streetcar from the station; the Union Depot here's at Twelfth and Poplar. Them streetcars is goin' evah whichaways. Once yu'uns done clum on, you gon' be stuck, so make sure you pick the right one." He gave Moira a nod, as if that explained everything.

"The streetcar?" she asked, glancing warily at the rattling metal conveyances. "Aye, we'll try to board one, so we will. But faith, where should we go from Twelfth? And we don't have the strength for much of a trek, do you twig me?"

"Lawsy mercy, yu'uns must be fahunahs. Where you hail from?"

"We've just come in from the New Mexico Territory, so we have."

"You got a quair way of talkin', sho' nuff. I reckon you must be Spaniards, then?"

Josiah saw Moira's shoulders stiffen. "We're Irish. At least my sister and I are."

"Now, don't git yoah nose outta joint, ma'am. We got all kinds here in the city, and we don't much cotton to folks keepin' to theirselves. We got Spaniards, French, Rebels, Yankees, Britishers, Hollanders, Germans, Irelanders, Negroes, and even a few Injuns. You want to git along here in St. Louie, you bettah fergit where yoah pappy hailed from. You in the United States of America now."

"Yes, sir." Moira swallowed. "I'm sorry."

"Aw, now. You look sad as a fallen cake. Listen up— yu'uns gon' be fine here in St. Louie. Hop on a streetcar and take Twelfth to Market. Then ride westbound on Market. When yu'uns get to Jefferson Avenue, get off and take the northbound a fur piece. Pret' soon you'll hit Florissant Road and yu'uns be on your own from there. Might ketch a wagon or a carriage. Traffic's not too heavy into Florissant this time of day, but you might find yo'selves a ride. 'Course if yu'uns wait a spell you'll ketch more of a flow 'round the shank of the evenin' when folks is heading back to Florissant from their jobs in St. Louie."

"I see. Twelfth to Market to Jefferson to Florissant."

"That's raht. If you misremember what I done tol' you, jest ask someone. Folks 'round heah be happy to help yu'uns find the way."

"Thank you very much, then. Sure you've been most kind."

Moira turned to Josiah with an uncertain smile, and he knew exactly what she was thinking. She'd never been in a town that had more than one street, let alone a multitude of intersecting avenues, lanes, and roads.

"We'll get there," Josiah reassured her, though he wasn't too sure himself about the notion of climbing onto one of those streetcars.

"If the agent recommends that we wait a bit," Erinn put in, "why don't we go shopping, Moira? It wouldn't hurt to spend some of the afternoon looking at the stores."

"Erinn—"

"Sure you'll lock me up with the voteens!" she exploded without warning. "Then you and Josiah can parade off doing whatever you like. What's so righteous about that, Moira? The pair of you enjoying the city alone together and then riding back on the train all by yourselves as though you were man and wife."

"Whisht, Erinn!" Flushing crimson, Moira grabbed her sister's arm and swung her away from the interested ticket agent. "I'll have none of your slack jaw."

Laughing as easily as she had angered, Erinn gave Moira a quick kiss. "Oh, come on, then. Let's see the city, shall we? We'll practice riding the streetcars up and down, and then when it's time to go to Florissant, we'll know our way on them."

Josiah could sense Moira weakening. Why she loved that sister of hers so much, he couldn't figure, but it was certain that Erinn could get whatever she wanted out of Moira. It wasn't going to be as easy as he had hoped to settle her in the novitiate.

"Well," Moira said, wavering, "perhaps it would be wise to wait a bit until the traffic builds up. As the ticket agent said, we might have trouble finding a ride out of the city at this hour."

"Oh, Moira!" Erinn whirled around twice, her skirts flying up to her ankles.

Josiah grunted and lifted both girls' saddlebags over his shoulder. So Erinn had won this round. How long would it be before Moira was able to put her sister's needs to rest and come into his arms? As he followed them along the muddy street, he began to wonder if that day would ever arrive. What if Erinn worked her wiles and persuaded Moira to stay with her in St. Louis, a plan he felt certain was at the forefront of Erinn's thoughts? Or what if they did finally manage to stash Erinn away somewhere and then Moira wanted nothing to do with him?

It was a definite possibility, he thought as he watched them picking their way among the puddles. The Moira he knew and desired wasn't likely to cast her scruples to the wind simply because she was finally alone with Josiah Chee. She had kept distant from him through the whole train trip, even though he had seen the look of desire on her face every time their eyes met. But hungry as she might be for him, he couldn't be sure she would want what he planned to give her—his body, but not his soul.

The days on the train had given him time to think. He realized he had no future to offer Moira. Though he had more than enough money to keep her in comfort, most of it was tied up in his copper mining interests in Butte. With the rest, he planned to buy equipment for the land he would claim. But he didn't own any land yet, not even a handful of dirt. He didn't have a house to take her to, and Moira needed a home. He didn't have a waterfront to put his name on, nor did he know where he could get one. Even if he did buy a section or more, he was certain to have trouble with the cattle owners in the valley— especially one Innis Grady. Most important, Josiah knew he wanted to run sheep. And to Moira O'Casey, sheep were God's pestilence upon the earth.

How could he expect her to leave her home at Fianna when he had nothing to promise her but a pocketful of dreams she didn't even share? It hadn't taken Josiah long to put the notion of a permanent life with Moira out of his mind. But even if he couldn't have her forever, he wanted her now. Whatever it took, he intended to make her his.

"There's a streetcar that's going to Market!" she was exclaiming from the corner. "See the sign, Josiah?"

He saw it all right, but he sure didn't like the thought of trying to board that rattletrap. The vehicle was much smaller than a railway car, and it ran on wheels so tiny they didn't look as if they could support the car's weighty steel and canvas, let alone the jostling crowd of passengers trying to stuff themselves into every available inch of space. The sides of the streetcar were open to the air with narrow vertical window bars on which people hung like so many monkeys. The sloped roof had a rounded apex, and there was a platform in front on which stood the harried man who was both driver and ticket taker. He held the reins to a pair of horses that presumably were supposed to march along the beaten center path between the two rails.

"Come on, Josiah!" Moira called, beckoning to him from the line of people climbing into the streetcar.

He took off his hat and scratched the back of his neck. He might be a sheepman, but he knew horses. Western breeds took a strong man to keep them on the trail, and they didn't take kindly to being hitched up to much of anything. The trail of manure along the path between the iron rails testified to the fact that the city horses kept on track most of the time. But he sure didn't like the idea of what might happen if one of them took a notion to buck or shy at something.

"Josiah, you'll miss it, so you will! We'll never find you again if you don't come now!" Moira was waving to him from the top step of the streetcar.

Her concern pleased him, but all the same, Josiah merely ambled over, not a bit eager to board. Sure enough, as he set foot on the first step, the horses started up with a jerk, and the car sailed down the rails faster than he'd thought possible.

He joined Moira and Erinn somewhere deep amid the throng of people and grabbed a leather strap that hung down from the ceiling. If he had thought the train was crowded, this streetcar felt like the inside of a tin of oysters, and it smelled about as good, too. The streetcar swayed and rocked; it hit a pebble and jolted sideways. Moira lost her balance and threw her arms around his waist—and Josiah decided he didn't mind these city contraptions so much after all.

They made it to Market Street, a distance any western man gladly would have walked. The street was well named, Josiah decided. All up and down it were enough mercantiles to keep a household in supplies till kingdom come. Erinn went wild. Spending Seamus's money, she bought herself a ready-made dress with a bustle so big she could have served tea on it, a pair of kid gloves, some slip-on shoes that didn't look as if she could get from here to there without them falling off her feet, and a pair of dangly earrings that made her squeal every time she thought of them.

She insisted on buying Moira one of those ready-made dresses, too. Josiah didn't much like the notion of standing around in a ladies' store, so while they were trying on clothes, he went outside to lean against the building and smoke a cheroot. The one good thing about the city, he decided, was that he didn't need to give much thought to John Fisher, the mine owner who had shot him back in Butte. The Cornishman was probably still lurking around in New Mexico somewhere, trying to sniff him out. But even if Fisher was on Josiah's trail, he could never track him in this populated terrain.

It was getting on to late afternoon, and Josiah realized
the sky looked like rain—an unfamiliar sight for a man
who'd been living through a siege of drought. Big gray
clouds rolled up and over the tops of the buildings. The
heat turned muggy, and the air became as thick as butter.
Mosquitoes and flies began to swarm. Josiah had just
tossed his smoke to the sidewalk when he felt someone
brush up against his side.

He turned, his blacksnake already in his hand. Erinn's
blond hair was the first thing he saw. She slipped her
damp little hands up his arms and gave a slight tug.

"Josiah," she whispered, her voice urgent, "I must talk
with you now!"

"Where's Moira?"

"She's inside the store trying on dresses." She was
blinking up at him, and he knew the black clouds brew-
ing overhead weren't the only storm in sight. "Josiah, I
must beg a boon of you. Please don't refuse me!"

"Hey . . ." He made to brush her hands away, but she
only held on to him more tightly. "Listen here, Erinn,
I've hauled you this far, and I've done the best I could
to keep an eye on you and your sister. I don't know what
more you want from me."

"It's clear you think well of Moira for the care she
gave you when you were ill," she whispered, "but I beg
you to turn your eyes on me now! Don't leave me here
in the city alone, Josiah. Don't take me off to the nuns
where I'll wither away. I need your help!"

"What do you want from me?"

"Stay here in St. Louis, Josiah. With me. I'll be everything you've ever wanted in a woman, so I will. We can
find a place to live, and you can get yourself a job
making more money than any rancher ever thought to
see. Sure I'll work, too, and keep us in fine style. There's
plenty of employment here for women, in eating houses,
mercantiles, saloons—"

"Saloons!" Josiah took off his hat. "Listen here, Erinn,
you better not set foot in one of those places unless you

want to lose your reputation as a good Irishwoman."

She let out a breath and lifted herself up against him, her breasts grazing his arm. "Josiah, how long will it take you to see that I don't care about such blarney as that? I've already lived the life of a woman of good repute, and it didn't suit me. I want my freedom. I want passion! I want to know the world in and out, up and down. If you'll come with me, we'll find it together, so we will."

"But Moira—"

"She won't stay here! Sure she thinks Fianna is God's gift. You saw how Innis treated her, but she doesn't mind him, really. I think perhaps they even have an arrangement, you know?"

He frowned. "What kind of arrangement?"

"I lived with Innis Grady long enough to know that the man won't give away something for nothing, Josiah. He's kept Moira there at Fianna, in food and clothing. Sure he's the sort of man to want more out of her than just her cooking and cleaning. You saw that he treats her as if he owns her, slapping her about and such. I'm certain he beds her now and again. And Scully has plans of his own for Moira. She told me he's asked to marry her, and I think she'll agree to it. She dotes on the boy—you know that. The best thing for Moira is to send her back to Fianna where she belongs and where she's truly happy."

Josiah swallowed, but his mouth felt as dry as an old boot.

"But I have no one!" Erinn went on. "I can't start my new life here in this big city all alone, Josiah. But with you I could do anything! I could make a future for myself, and so could you. And you'll have me as you please." After glancing through the store window, she slipped her arms around him and pressed her bosom against his chest. He tried to push her back without offending her, but she clung to him like a slug on a rock.

"Sure I've seen how you look at me," she gushed while he took her shoulders and tried politely to untangle himself. "You know I have what it takes to make a man happy, so I do. And I'm no crawthumper like Moira. I won't hold back in bed with you. I'll give you everything you want and more. We'll have fun! We'll be free! When you're ready to go your own way, I'll send you off with a kiss, so I will. I won't tie you down or latch on to you like a wife. Only stay with me, Josiah. Please let me touch you—"

"Erinn?" Moira stepped out of the mercantile, a bundle cradled in her arms. "Erinn! What are you—"

"Moira, did you choose something?" Erinn swung away from Josiah and took her sister's arm. "I hope you picked the pink one! Did you? The one with the fine lace?"

Moira's heart was beating in her throat as Erinn hurried her toward the corner where the streetcars were loading and unloading. She tried to glance behind at Josiah, but he was somewhere in the shadows. It hardly mattered. She had clearly seen him holding Erinn, his hands tight on her shoulders, his arms pressing her so close to him that her peacock-proud diddies were smashed against his shirtfront!

Her stomach churned, and she tried to blink back the sudden tears that filled her eyes. Raindrops, fat and heavy, splattered the sidewalk and made big damp spots on her package. She bit her lower lip, fighting to swallow the rock in her throat. So Erinn had won Josiah after all.

Well, hadn't Moira spent much of the journey trying to avoid him? She'd done her very best to assure Josiah that he meant nothing to her. Why shouldn't he respond to Erinn's beauty? Men had always been fools over her, and now Josiah was the latest in the long line. Erinn was planning an annulment of her marriage with Seamus, so what was to keep them apart? Nothing. Especially not a dull crawthumper of an older sister.

"Or did you choose the yellow?" Erinn chattered. "I thought it was splendid, Moira. Did you buy the dress with the green polka-dots or that lavender with the red stripes. Heavenly! So much better than that dull, boring blue thing you tried on first. Which one did you pick, then?"

"The blue," Moira whispered, her spirits sinking lower than ever. Of course she had picked the blue dress. It was serviceable and neat. It didn't have so many elegant shingerleens that might get caught in the coffee grinder or dangle into a pot of stew.

"Well," Erinn went on undaunted, "I'm sure Innis will think it grand when you get back to Fianna. It's just the right dress for a good day in your little kitchen, so it is."

"Aye." Moira could hardly bring herself to climb onto the streetcar that was headed north on Jefferson Avenue. She felt Josiah move up behind her, his big body close against hers in the tight space. She wished she could just shrink up altogether like a pair of new wool socks in boiling water.

"We'll go to Florissant," Erinn was saying to him, her eyes bright as burning coals. "We'll speak to the nuns about my annulment from that sherral Seamus Sullivan. Perhaps they'll even put us all up for the night."

Josiah didn't respond, but from the corner of her eye, Moira could see Erinn slip her arms around his waist as comfortably as if they'd been courting for a year. Turning away, Moira stared out at the rain puddling the ground. It was coming in sheets now. Lightning flickered across the sky, turning the buildings into great towering ghosts. Thunder boomed through the city, fairly shaking the ground that the little streetcar rolled over. The horses skittered, and the car bounced off and on the rails, splashing mud on passengers unlucky enough to have taken places near its open sides.

Stopping and starting at every intersection, the streetcar gradually discharged its riders into the rain all along

the way. At the end of Jefferson Avenue, the fine road-
way dwindled into a rutted track. The few remaining
travelers dashed through the darkness toward waiting
conveyances. Moira, Erinn, and Josiah made for the
paltry shelter of a small tree.

"This is Florissant Road," a rotund little man shouted
at them as he climbed down from the streetcar and
started across the street toward a small black-hooded
carriage. "Come with me, if you like. I'll take you
where you want to go!"

"Thank you kindly!" Erinn cried, beckoning to the
others.

Splashing through puddles and pouring rain that
soaked her to the skin, Moira followed Errin and
Josiah into the covered carriage. They piled in on top of
each other, Erinn and Josiah tumbling onto the backseat,
Moira and the stranger squeezing into the front beside
the driver.

"Where are you headed?" the man called out over the
drum of rain on the canvas roof. It was so dark in the
carriage that Moira could barely make out his features
as he spoke.

"We'd appreciate your help, so we would," Erinn
spoke up as the carriage started down the road. "We've
come all the way from the New Mexico Territory to
Florissant to speak with the nuns in the Order of the
Sacred Heart."

"Well, there are a few nuns at St. Ferdinand's Church,
but the school and convent founded by Mother Rose
Philippine Duchesne have moved to St. Charles. The
Sisters of Loretto have taken over the ministries. What
was it that brought you all this way, may I inquire?"

"I've come to have my marriage annulled from a devil
of a fellow, a Mister Seamus Sullivan," Erinn said. "I
thought the nuns could help me."

"I see. Then you'll be wanting to remain at St.
Ferdinand's for a time while your case is sorted through.
And your companions?"

"I'm Erinn's sister," Moira answered softly. "Moira O'Casey."

"And you, sir?" He glanced over his shoulder at Josiah. "Will you and your wife be staying at St. Ferdinand's with Missus Sullivan, then, Mister O'Casey?"

"My name's Josiah Chee. I'm looking out for the ladies. And no, I'll be taking Moira back to the Territory. Tomorrow."

"But . . ." The stranger hesitated. "But you can't take Miss O'Casey back to New Mexico, sir. It wouldn't be right, the two of you traveling together *alone*."

There was a long silence in the carriage. Moira wanted to sink into the seat, imagining what this kind man must think of the three of them. "I'm sure I . . . we . . . that neither of us—" she began.

"We're engaged to be married," Josiah said suddenly. "Moira and me. It'll be okay for us to go together."

"Engaged? Well, then, you must speak your vows before God ere you set out again. It wouldn't be seemly for you to travel alone otherwise." He relaxed against the back of the seat, and Moira heard the breath leave his chest in a sigh. "I'll speak to the nuns about caring for you during your reconsideration of your marriage annulment, my dear Missus Sullivan. And I'll take the matter of the other two of you into my own hands."

"*Your* hands?" Josiah asked.

"Certainly. Oh, did I fail to introduce myself?" He gave a light chuckle. "Do forgive me. I'm Father Murphy, the parish priest at St. Ferdinand's here in Florissant. I'll be more than happy to take care of *everything*."

# Chapter
## 10

Moira hardly noticed the church and its adjoining convent as she hurried out of the rain, up the steps, and into St. Ferdinand's. Father Murphy was greeted at the door by a buxom nun who wore a black habit and a white wimple that set off her squarish bulldog face. While the nun helped him shed his heavy raincoat, the priest began speaking with her in a low but urgent voice. Moira did her best to eavesdrop as she stood in the vestibule and tried to wring some of the rainwater from the hem of her skirt.

But when Josiah stalked into the church, her mouth went as dry as a New Mexico riverbed. He dumped the wet saddlebags on the stone floor, then planted his feet in a stance that said he meant business. He hooked his thumbs in his pockets and glared at the priest. A tower of fury and determination, Josiah was a picture of the indomitable man Moira had glimpsed only briefly. His brown eyes had turned almost black, and his jaw was clenched so tight the sinews quivered. Beneath his wet shirt, the muscles in his arms tightened and contracted.

"They'll be leaving tomorrow, Sister Theresa," the priest was saying, "bright and early, I'm quite sure, so we'll want to take care of this matter tonight. We'll have a special marriage ceremony if you can prepare the altar for us, Sister. And will you be so good as to call the other nuns—"

"Now just a minute here," Josiah butted in. "I never said Moira and I were planning to get married anytime soon. It's sort of a . . . a notion, that's all."

"Young man, are you a Christian?" the priest demanded with a bluntness that matched Josiah's consternation.

"A Christian? Well, sure." Josiah took a step back and pulled off his tan hat. "My mother brought me up to follow the Good Book."

"Ah, but are you a true believer in the teachings and the divinity of the Lord Jesus Christ?"

"Yes, but—"

"Then you must understand that to travel alone with this young woman would be the vilest of sins, sir. If you have any decency, if you have any honor, you will marry her before you set one foot outside this church!" As if that settled the matter, Father Murphy turned to the waiting nun. "Take the young women to a private chamber, Sister Theresa, will you please? They'll want to bathe and eat, I'm certain. Missus Sullivan has come to us on a misguided mission to obtain an annulment of her marriage to the good husband God has given her."

Sister Theresa gasped. "Oh, my!"

"And Miss O'Casey must be readied for her wedding. Do tend to them, Sister, for God's sake."

"Yes, Father Murphy. Of course."

Before Moira could get a word in edgewise, the nun grabbed her arm and hauled her through a side door. As she marched the sisters down the hall, she made a sound that reminded Moira of the train engine that had brought them from New Mexico.

"My desire to have my marriage annulled is *not* misguided," Erinn protested when the sister threw open the door to a small room and practically shoved them in. "Seamus Sullivan is a cruel man. And ugly! He's got a nose the size of a potato, so he has!"

Sister Theresa regarded her with a look that made Erinn clamp her mouth shut. "I shall return with hot water from the kitchen and dry garments from our supply of clothing for the needy. There will be soup and bread as well. Until then, good evening."

She shut the door and set off down the hall, her heels clomp-a-clomping on the wooden floor. Erinn flopped onto the narrow cot and covered her eyes with her hands. For once in her life, Moira elected not to sink down beside her little sister and console her. Erinn lifted her head in surprise, her eyes pained.

"Moira . . . they're not going to let me leave this wretched place, are they? They're planning to keep me here until I change my mind!"

Moira shrugged and turned to the window to watch the rain streaming down the glass pane. "I don't know," she said finally. "Maybe you'll decide to go back home to Seamus after all."

"Oh, no. I'll never do that. Not ever."

"Why? Because you've already set your heart on Josiah Chee?" Moira couldn't stop the jealous-sounding words.

"The saints preserve us," Erinn moaned, shaking her head as it hung in her hands. "Josiah and I made a plan to live together in St. Louis. We want to work at jobs and have ourselves a fine life. An elegant, grand life. But now that spalpeen of a priest has put his foot into it and made *three-na-haila* of it!"

"So Josiah means to marry you?" Moira asked, hardly able to speak. But she already knew the answer. She had seen Josiah's face when he confronted the priest. It was clear that the *last* thing he wanted was to marry Moira. He was in love with Erinn.

"There will be no marriage," Erinn muttered, clearly lost in her own misery. "An arrangement for the benefit of both of us. But he had to go and blabber that nonsense about marrying you, just so you wouldn't feel ashamed in front of a stranger! Who would have guessed that the man would turn out to be a priest? And a bold Turk at that."

Moira laid one hand on the windowpane as if somehow by touching it she could slip through into a world beyond this one. She could hardly believe how this muddle had turned out. Her plan to help Erinn was nothing but a waste, a sham. She had left Innis and Scully, left her home, only to realize that she hardly knew her own sister.

"Erinn, you wouldn't just live with Josiah, would you?" she asked. "You would share his bed, too."

Erinn stood and began pacing. "Of course I would sleep with him, Moira. Have you been so blind as to miss the way he's been looking at me all this time?"

"But, Erinn—"

"Moira, I'm not the little girl I was back at Fianna. Through all the years of my childhood, the only things I had to offer were my wit and my beauty. I was the cooleen only because of my charms. Being pretty and delightful is all I know, Moira! But you've got your cooking and cleaning and mending and such—things a man needs to make a proper home. I never learned my lessons well because I didn't like them. I still don't. I'll get by as I always have, Moira, on my beauty."

"Oh, Erinn, you can learn to cook and wash."

"Listen, Moira," the younger woman said, coming across the room and taking her sister's hands, "I don't *want* to. I've discovered something new for myself. Men will do anything for a woman they want to bed, Moira. She can go where she wants and be who she wants. Sleeping with a man is the easiest thing in the world— and I like it, so I do! Why shouldn't I follow the simplest path? Tell me that?"

Moira tried her best to read the depths of her sister's eyes. And then she realized there was nothing—nothing at all—beneath that frank, dull stare. "How can you say you like it? You plainly told me that you and Seamus weren't a match in bed, Erinn."

"Oh, Moira!" Shaking her head, she gave a tinkling little laugh. "You're such a child. Sure Seamus was a great beast of a man in bed—and rather good when I come to reflect upon him. But you don't think I was content with only his ways? Not when other men were casting sheep's eyes at me? Sure it was the grandest time of my life. These were wonderful men, Moira—nothing like the dull galoots at Fianna. Seamus knows gentlemen from Roswell and Albuquerque, and even Santa Fe! But there was one—sure as I live I don't know what possessed me to return that devil's affections—a puncher just in off the trail. Oh, but he was such a fine man and he treated me so elegantly, Moira, you just can't imagine. It was a wonder, the best time in my whole life—until along came Seamus to catch us in the act."

"Erinn!" Moira gripped the edge of the windowsill.

"So of course I can't go back to him, don't you see? He was so scalded he tried to flail the skin off me. I set my ten commandments on his chest, so I did," she said, holding up her fingers to show the long nails that had raked her husband's flesh, "and sure the scars will last the rest of his life. And then I hotfooted it off for Fianna before the man could kill me. And he would, too, Moira!"

"But, Erinn, you committed—" She caught her words as a pair of nuns swung open the door and marched into the room bearing a heavy tub of steaming water. As they set it on the floor, another entered carrying a bundle of poor, patched clothing. While she laid the clothes across the bed, a fourth nun came in with a tray of soup and a half loaf of crusty brown bread.

"You're to be in the nave for your wedding in half an hour, Miss O'Casey," Sister Theresa announced.

"But I'm not going to marry Josiah Chee. Neither of us—"

"Mister Chee is the one who sent me to tell you. He'll be waiting there with Father Murphy."

When the sisters had shut the door, Erinn swept the pile of old clothes onto the floor. "That's what I think of those voteens and their blatherumskite!" she snarled. "Come on, Moira, let's climb out the window and be on our way. I'll show you what I mean about the good side of life. We'll go and set the world aflame, so we will. You don't need Fianna or that worthless Innis Grady. You were meant for grander things than a rusty cook pot and a steamy little kitchen."

Erinn hitched up her skirts and climbed onto the bed. Moira watched her working at the window latch. Her golden head was lifted sharply, and there was an animal quality about her that Moira had never seen before—the flared nostrils, the bared teeth, the fiery eyes. Even her fingernails looked like scrabbling claws.

What had become of the little child Moira had cared for and loved so deeply? Where were the silly pranks, the innocent laughter? Sure Erinn had been forced to live a difficult life in some ways. But this wayward path was something she had chosen on her own.

Moira knew she could let her sister go, allow her to climb out into the night to face a future of her own making. Perhaps it would be for the best, though Moira couldn't imagine what good might come of Erinn's willful hopping from bed to bed. Sure she'd be a painted lady before the month was out, forced to sell her body in order to feed her mouth.

Moira could go with her, of course, continuing on as the duped protector she had been for so long now. The notion of never returning to Fianna was becoming a temptation. Though Moira didn't like the city and would never feel at home there, during the train ride she had seen other opportunities. Perhaps she could persuade Erinn to sign on with her as a Harvey Girl in one of the railway restaurants. They could make a wholesome living at that. Or maybe Moira could find employment somewhere in St. Louis for a few years while she went to school to study something. Perhaps she could be a teacher. Perhaps, with Fianna behind her, the world *would* open its arms to her. She could make a new life, free of Innis Grady and his cruel ways.

Moira had always longed for a measure of freedom, it was true. She had thought the suffragettes were bold and brave to stand up for voting rights, and she wouldn't have minded joining them. It would feel wonderful, too, to have the liberty of her own pay, her own transportation, her own clothes, and possessions she had dreamed of but never really thought to claim.

As Erinn pounded on the locked window, Moira studied the willful child who had been coddled and nursed by everyone into her own undoing. Perhaps these nuns and good Father Murphy were just the ones to set Erinn on the right path. They certainly wouldn't stand for her nonsense and lies. Perhaps the best way Moira could love Erinn was to let her go.

With a sigh, she sat on the bed and watched Erinn twist the welded latch and hammer on the glass. The truth of the matter was, Moira had to acknowledge, freedom sounded lovely, and making her own path would be an adventure. But what she really wanted more than anything else was a home.

She loved cooking in her kitchen, no matter what Erinn thought of it. She loved the feel of soapsuds up to her elbows, the smell of starch tickling her nose, the snap of laundry on the line. She was proud of her white sheets, her quilts, her cakes, and her stews. She loved the rich, damp earth in her garden as she dug out carrots and pinched off beans. Moira knew that more than anything, she wanted a home—and Fianna was where she belonged.

While Erinn unlaced her boot, apparently planning to knock out the pane of glass, Moira carefully stripped off her wet dress. She stepped into the tub of hot water and ran the dripping cloth over herself until every trace of the long, grimy train trip had vanished. Then she leaned over and dunked her head underwater. With a good rubbing of the soap the sisters had provided, she was able to scrub away weeks of soot and dust. Erinn had just smashed out the window when Moira emerged from the bath and began to towel herself off.

"All right, I've done it!" Erinn cried in triumph as glass tinkled around her feet. "Let's get out of here, Moira, before those blazing nuns—"

"What in the name of all the saints have you done to our window, young lady?" Sister Theresa shouted, barging into the room. "Are you destroying the house of God now?"

Erinn clamped her mouth shut and stared at the shards of glass with the first sign of remorse Moira had seen in weeks. A thrill of victory flooding through her heart, Moira pulled on the worn undergarments the sisters had provided, then unwrapped her new blue dress.

"You'll have to keep a close watch on her, Sister Theresa," Moira said as she buttoned the dress up to her throat. "Erinn has a strong head on her shoulders, and she'll do whatever she can to have her way, so she will."

"Moira!" Erinn gasped.

"I'm ready now to speak to the father," Moira continued while brushing out her wet hair and coiling it into a neat bun at the nape of her neck. "Will you show me the way to the nave?"

"Moira, you can't mean to leave me here!" Erinn cried. "You're not going to go off without me, are you?"

"You'll be well cared for here at St. Ferdinand's, Erinn. I can't think of a better place for you than God's house."

"Oh, Moira!" Weeping hysterically, Erinn threw herself at Moira, her knees sinking to the floor at her sister's feet, her arms wrapped around her thighs. "Oh, Moira, don't leave me! I need you, so I do. I can't live without you! You're the only family I have. You're the only one in all the world who loves me. Oh, Moira, Moira, don't go, I beg you! I shall die here all alone in this frightening, terrible place with no one to care for me! I'll waste away, so I will! Please, Moira, don't abandon me!"

Moira laid her hand on Erinn's head and stroked her damp golden hair. How easy it would be to kneel beside her and comfort her as she always had. And the things Erinn said were true: she did need Moira; she needed love and tending. How cruel it would be to abandon her sister here in this huge foreign city among total strangers. . . .

"I'm leaving you here *because* I love you, Erinn," Moira said, swallowing the knot of guilt. "I'll write to you, so I will. Be good, now."

Pulling out of her sister's arms, Moira left Erinn weeping on the floor. But when Sister Theresa shut the door, Moira could hear the tears turn to screeches as a bevy of nuns scrambled to haul Erinn into the bathtub.

"Let me go, you cruel crawthumpers!" she screamed. "The devil take the lot of you! Cats of a kind you are, in your boring black duggins! Just take your hands off me or I'll lay my ten commandments on your faces!"

Moira lifted her skirts and ran down the hall until she could no longer hear her sister's howling. As she burst into the church's nave, Josiah caught her in his arms.

"Moira!" He took a step back in the surprise of seeing her so suddenly, but he didn't release her. "Moira! You look . . . beautiful."

Like an angel, Josiah thought as he stroked his hands down her arms and held her away from him just far enough to take a good look. The blue dress fit her better than anything he'd ever seen her wear—skimming over her shoulders and swelling out at her bosom. It had a pretty belt that cinched in her narrow waist, and it flared out around her hips and lifted into a draped bustle over her bottom.

"You smell like flowers . . . roses," he murmured, adrift in the sweet scent of her pale skin and the perfume that wafted up from her damp hair. The color of her new dress seemed to deepen the blue in her eyes as she stared at him, and he knew he'd never been so swallowed up by a woman in all his life.

"We'll begin now, Mister Chee, Miss O'Casey," Father Murphy said, coming up behind them. "Please follow me to the altar."

Moira started at the sound of the little priest. For a moment—just long enough to make her heartbeat falter and slow to a deadly thudding—she had been captured in Josiah's words, in his arms, in his deep, earnest voice. But now she set her hands on his chest and gave the mightiest shove of her life.

"Stand back from me, sherral," she snapped at him. "I won't listen to your sweet lies any longer."

"Moira—"

"Erinn told me everything the pair of you planned to do." Crossing her arms over her stomach as if that might protect her from the physical presence of the man, she turned to the priest. "I won't play a game of deceit here, Father Murphy. I respect your office and the holiness of this place, so I do, and I won't defile them, but Mister Chee is merely my guardian's brother. He and I have no relationship, nor did we ever plan to marry. He came to protect my sister and me on the journey, and he fell in love with Erinn—"

"No, I didn't."

"Enough, Josiah," Moira retorted. "She told me everything. That you were planning to live together in St. Louis and make yourselves a grand new life."

"Moira, it's not true. Erinn invented all that. She asked me to stay with her, but I never agreed to it. I don't have any feelings for your little sister. It's you I want, Moira."

"Blarney!" All the same, she gulped in a bubble of air at the intensity in his expression. "You're no better than she is, with all your blatherumskite. Trying to force me into things, the both of you. I won't have it, Josiah. I'm through with being pushed about and talked into doing what I know isn't right or Christian."

"You know how I feel about you, Moira, and you know it's right. As much as you want to deny it, there's never been anything more right in your life than you and me and what we want with each other."

Flushing in betrayal of her hostile words, Moira nevertheless stiffened her back. "All I want is for you to let me go in peace." She turned to the priest. "Father Murphy, I'm choosing to leave my sister here in your good hands. Erinn needs more help than I can give her. I beg your forgiveness for this trouble, so I do, and I trust you to pray for us all."

"Of course, my dear," he said solemnly.

"As to the future, I'll return to my home and my guardian on my own. Mister Chee may do as he pleases."

Father Murphy nodded in silence as he studied the floor. Finally he lifted his head. "We'll tend to your sister, Miss O'Casey. But as for the other matter . . . Mister Chee told me what he pleases to do is to marry you, and the sooner the better."

Moira glanced at Josiah. He took off his hat and regarded her evenly, his eyes a dark mahogany in the shadows of the church. "I do want to marry you, Moira. If you'll have me."

"Can you mean that?"

"Marry me, Moira."

"But I . . . No, don't be a googeen. There's Fianna and Innis, Scully . . . and the sheep, and I think—"

"Don't think."

"But there's no future in it."

"There's *now*. That's something. Moira, do it. Do what *you* want to do for once in your life."

"It wouldn't be right, Josiah, not with everything so unsettled."

"The padre's here and ready to marry us. The nuns are waiting at the altar. God's up there watching. Sounds right to me."

Moira sucked in her bottom lip and stared at Josiah. She couldn't believe she was actually considering this—actually thinking of taking another heedless, foolish step into a future she hadn't planned.

"I don't trust you, Josiah," she whispered finally.

At her verbal thrust, he felt a physical pain sharper than any he'd ever known. "Moira . . ."

"I'm not sure of you. Erinn said things about you . . . Innis did, too. And my own brain tells me that we're not a match. I can't be certain of you, Josiah."

"Have I ever hurt you? Have I ever betrayed you? I promised to take care of you, and I did. When you needed me, I protected you from Innis. Just so you could keep your love for Erinn pure, I protected you from the truth about her. For God's sake, Moira, I even protected you from myself! Every day on that train, every night, it was all I could do to hold myself back. You don't know what that took out of me. But I did it because I swore I'd never hurt you; I'd always watch over you. I want what's best for you, girl, I always have. And what's best for you is me."

Moira's eyes darted to Father Murphy, who had been listening to Josiah. He looked at her and lifted his eyebrows. "A convincing argument," he said. "I've certainly heard worse reasons for making a marriage. Come with me, my dear, and we'll speak a moment in private. Excuse us, Mister Chee."

Taking her elbow, the priest drew her into a pew at the back of the church. As he settled beside her, he lifted both her hands and clasped them between his. "If you don't want to marry this man, I won't urge it on you. From what he tells me, you've been through a great deal with your sister in the past weeks."

Moira nodded, but she found she couldn't say anything.

"Your young man tells me what a fine woman you are, good to a fault. He doesn't believe that you'll ever marry without some prodding—and he does mean to marry

you. As the good Lord has told us in the Scriptures, a
woman and man should leave their parents and cleave
together. Unless we're called into celibacy, we're to wed
and bear children. This is God's will for us, my dear."

How could she argue with what she had been taught
all her life in church? Yet marrying Josiah seemed so
irrational. "I hardly know him, Father."

"Perhaps so. But he cares for you—of that I'm certain.
When he came into the church tonight and protested my
plan to wed the pair of you, he was only trying to protect your wishes. He told me as we talked later that he
has never courted you properly, nor has he asked your
guardian for your hand. But Mister Chee wants the very
best for you. And he swears he'll protect you whether
you decide to stay in Missouri or return to the Territory.
My heart tells me he's a good man."

Moira felt so swayed by the priest's words that she
couldn't even bring to her lips the greatest obstacle of
all—her vow to Deirdre to stay with Innis. "There are
other problems, Father," she tried. "The future—"

"The future is in God's hands. As the Good Book
says, 'Who knows what the morrow may bring?' Your
young man is also concerned about what may lie ahead
for the two of you. But I assured him that with a bond
of trust and commitment between them, two people can
weather anything. Other marriages have survived worse
than a wayward sister, an angry guardian, and a bit of
uncertainty." He patted her hands, then laid them in her
lap. "Now then, you must make your decision, my dear.
I see that Mister Chee has already gone to the altar. If
you wish to join him there, then I'll see you wed. If
not, slip out the door behind us, and my prayers will
go with you."

Moira nodded as the priest rose and padded his way
down the aisle toward the altar. She could see Josiah
in the light of the rows of candles burning in a soft
glow. He was holding his hat as he talked to the nuns
who had clustered around him. Towering over them, he

was a picture of strength, his broad shoulders encased in the damp fabric of his white shirt. The dim light made his hair shine like burnished gold as it spilled over his forehead and down his neck.

She heard his voice inside her head, the melodic tones washing through her like echoes in a deep canyon. *It's you I want, Moira,* he had told her. *There's never been anything more right in your life than you and me and what we want with each other. . . . I do want to marry you, Moira. If you'll have me. . . I want what's best for you, girl, I always have. And what's best for you is me.*

Forcing down the bubbles of fear, the knots of uncertainty, Moira slid out of the pew and began walking down the aisle. She could feel her feet touching the floor, but they seemed to make no sound, as though she were floating toward him. One by one the nuns looked up, stopped talking, turned to face her. Then Josiah lifted his head. Holding his hat tightly in his hands, he watched her come toward him. Slowly . . . drifting . . . barely breathing . . . she moved closer and closer. Her face felt hot, her mouth dry . . . was it the heat of the candles?

Rain drummed on the roof and spattered against the windows. A crash of thunder rumbled through the church and shook the floor. She clasped her hands, digging her fingers into the thin bones and pressing her palms together so tightly they ached. And then Josiah was smiling, an almost shy grin, taking her elbow, turning her to face the priest.

"Josiah Chee," she heard a voice intone, "wilt thou take Moira O'Casey, here present, for thy lawful wife, according to the rite of our holy Mother, the Church?"

"I will." It was Josiah's voice, and she saw his lips move. Those lips.

"Moira O'Casey, wilt thou take Josiah Chee, here present, for thy lawful husband, according to the rite of our holy Mother, the Church?"

She couldn't speak. Her breath felt as light and fleeting as a feather in her breast. Josiah turned to her, his brown eyes beckoning.

"I will," she whispered.

*Be unto them, O Lord, a tower of strength from the face of the enemy.* With the priest's final words drifting around inside her head, Moira felt Josiah slip his arm around her shoulders and draw her against his side. He felt warm and strong, his fingers cupping the fabric of her sleeve, as she listened to him saying his good-byes to Father Murphy and the nuns. Then he was walking up the aisle—she somehow moving along with him, though her feet seemed to have disappeared from her body—and through the front door out into the rain.

"Here's my hat," he said, settling the crown of his tan Stetson on her head. "It'll keep the rain off."

Mute, she nodded and kept moving, her feet still taking steps she couldn't quite feel. Along both sides of the street, small houses of French design jumbled for room, their deep, dry porches inviting her to take shelter. Here and there a light shone in a window. A dog curled up on a doorstep. A wagon rolled past.

"Figure we'll check into a hotel here in Florissant. What do you say? There's bound to be something along the main street."

Moira lifted her eyes. "A hotel? Oh, no."

"Why not?" He slowed his steps. What else could they do on a night like this? He wanted nothing more than to get her out of this rain and into a warm room with a big, soft bed and a lamp that would light the curves of her body. What they had waited for so long had finally happened, and he didn't want anything to block the way. He ached to hold her in his arms and kiss her lips the way he'd been imagining.

"Well, it wouldn't be . . . right." Her big blue eyes were looking up at him with the innocence of a new-born babe.

Surely she couldn't object to him now, Josiah thought. Erinn had told him that Moira already knew the ways of a man with a woman—Innis had seen to that.

"We're married, Moira," he said.

"Aye, but I want to get as far away from here as possible. Sure I'm likely to go off and rescue Erinn, so I am. I swear I can still hear her screaming."

"All right. We'll find a livery and try to get a carriage back to St. Louis."

"To the Union Depot. I want to take the first train to New Mexico."

"Tonight?" Josiah stopped on the muddy road and looked down at her. Sopping wet, she was trembling as if it were a winter night instead of the middle of summer.

She nodded. "Faith, you can't mean to stay here in Missouri, Josiah."

"Well, just for one night I thought it would be all right."

Moira swallowed. He lifted a hand and ran his fingertips over the curve of her brow. She closed her eyes, feeling the raindrops dampen her shoulders. If they went to a hotel, or anywhere private, he would want to bed her. Of course he would . . . and why shouldn't he? She was his now, for better or for worse. There was no denying she desired him, too. In fact, it was probably fleshly ardor more than anything else that had carried her down that aisle.

But now she felt so shy, almost fearful of him. Oh, he was pulling her against him, pressing her to his hard wet body. She was afraid to open her eyes and see the passion in his face. His hands were moving up her back, kneading the tight muscles along her spine, sliding over her shoulders and up her neck.

"Moira," he whispered.

She blinked. His mouth was so close, only a breath away.

"Moira, why did you marry me?" he asked.

The answer reared up inside her like a wild stallion. "Because . . . because I . . ." She tried to hold back the truth. She couldn't let him know that what had won her over in the end was the sight of him standing there at the front of the church, his great shoulders gilded with candlelight, his hair glinting, his mouth forming words she couldn't hear. Lust, pure and simple. That was why she'd married him. And now . . . now that it was done, she felt ashamed.

"Moira, answer me," he was saying, and her eyes followed the sensual movement of his lips.

"I thought . . . I thought you could take me back home safely."

"To Innis?"

His hands had slid into her wet hair, and his thumbs rested under her jaw, tilting her head upward so that she was forced to look into his face. The desire in his eyes was bare, raw, so hungry it sent a coil of tingles sliding down into her stomach and settling in the nest between her thighs. She ran her tongue over her lower lip, trying to moisten the parched feeling. His gaze dropped to her mouth. One hand left her hair and pressed against her waist so that his belt buckle pushed into the soft flesh of her belly.

"Do you want to go back to Innis Grady?" he repeated. "I know about you and him. Erinn told me he had his way with you."

Moira sucked in a breath. "Oh, she's wicked, so she is! Never did Innis so much as look my way for more than a hot meal or a sock that needed darning." She felt suddenly sick inside. "That Erinn! I can't believe she would tell such a sinful, treacherous lie."

"Moira . . ."

Bowing her head, she stared through the blur of rain and tears on her eyelashes. "Yes, I can believe it," she whispered, finally admitting the truth about her sister. "Erinn *would* say such a thing to get what she wanted. And she wanted you."

"Her lie didn't stop me from going after what *I* wanted. What I wanted—what I've wanted from the very start— is you." He lifted her chin, his brown eyes caressing her mouth even as his hand slipped lower into the folds of fabric in her bustle. "Do you want me, Moira?"

In spite of the gathers in her new skirt, she could feel him pushing against her. His lean thighs grazed hers. His whip pressed into her hip. And at the apex of her legs, hard and demanding on the soft cushion of flesh that hid her pulsing secrets, she could feel his arousal. His denim jeans and the layers of her petticoats did nothing to blunt the ridge that had settled into place. He shifted slightly, and a thousand stars shot upward through her, skittering to the tips of her breasts where they sparked and tingled.

"Moira, just say the words," he murmured.

She could barely breathe. His mouth hovered so close to hers she could feel the tips of his whiskers on her lower lip. Inside her skin, her body was dancing. Her breasts swelled and budded. A dampness seeped through the tender petals of her flesh. Her eyelids drifted low, and her blood seemed to sink to her knees.

"I want you, Josiah Chee," she heard herself say, though her voice was husky and low. "If I don't have you tonight, I'll die of the wanting."

His mouth crushed hers. Their lips pressed together, bruising, wetting, sliding. His tongue tore into her mouth, meeting hers, and then began to drive . . . thrusting deep . . . tormenting her . . . playing out a promise of things to come. . . .

# Chapter
## 11

How Moira got from a rainy street in Florissant to the porch of the Lafayette Hotel on Laclede's Landing in St. Louis was somewhat foggy to her. She recalled Josiah hailing a farmer on his way to market. She knew they had spent almost an hour bumping along in the drizzle. She was vaguely aware that she had been awake more than half the night—settling Erinn, getting married, and dealing with an assortment of other strange occurrences—and that now the faintest pink hues were beginning to tinge the eastern sky. The rest of the journey's details had been lost.

What she recalled with great clarity was Josiah lifting her into the back of the covered cart and making a place for her among baskets of cherries, strawberries, tomatoes, radishes, and spring peas. She knew he had wrapped a single blanket around them. His arm had slipped behind her shoulders, and in no time the heat from their bodies had made their wet clothing begin to steam. Nestled in a misty, warm nest among the fruit and vegetables, they had ridden along in silence for a while, watching the stars through the open canvas at the end of the cart, listening to the downpour taper off into a gentle patter, absorbing the sweet, ripe scents that drifted around them.

And then, as though it were the natural order of the evening, Josiah had kissed her. He didn't say a single word—no preamble, no small talk, just that wonderful, thrilling first kiss. Oh, and then the kissing went on forever. Moira lost herself, swimming in the swirling dream of his mouth, his lips pressing and sliding against hers, his tongue dancing and teasing and tantalizing her. How could she do anything but drift away in his embrace? For so long now she had dreamed of a moment like this, when nothing, no one, could come between them.

Always before, she had been practical, level-headed, sensible. Everything in her life had been scheduled and orderly. Washday, ironing day, baking day, gathering eggs in the morning, mending in the evening, milk in the cup before the tea was poured, a pinch of salt, prayers before bed. A place for everything and everything in its place. Then, quite suddenly, none of that mattered.

There was only Josiah, his muscled arm pressing her closer, closer against his chest; his lips taking possession of her; his breath hot and his skin damp. She forgot all about propriety and manners. Her demure, caretaking, subservient demeanor evaporated. Instead she tangled her fingers in Josiah's thick hair and pulled his mouth harder against hers. Bold as a strap, she ran her hands over his shoulders and down the front of his shirt while they kissed. She molded her palms on the ridges of sinew that stretched over his chest, and she stroked her fingertips across the flat circles of his nipples.

"I've never wanted anything or anyone the way I want you, Moira," he had murmured against her ear, but she had only nodded because his hand was sliding around her waist and up the fabric of her new dress. Words were lost in a breathless gasp as his palm cupped one of her breasts, lifted and weighed it, curved around it.

She thought she might cry aloud from the sheer ecstasy of his touch. Immobilized, her whole body centered on his caresses. She felt his fingertips search out, find, circle the crests of her breasts. As his tongue stroked hers, his hands played over her bosom until her nipples blossomed and pebbled into sweet, aching points of need.

"Laclede's Landing," the farmer called out, and Josiah barely had time to draw away from her before the wagon came to a stop in front of a large three-story hotel. "How's the Lafayette Hotel sound to yu'uns? It's not the fanciest we got 'round these parts, but it's raht dry and clean."

"Fine," Josiah answered, thinking that anything but a swamp would do at this point. He forced his breath to steady, but his body refused to obey. He was wound up and on fire, and it was all he could do to make himself climb out of the wagon and casually lift Moira down as though they were just a pair of ordinary travelers.

He didn't feel the least bit ordinary as he walked her under the cover of the hotel's porch and then returned to give the farmer a few coins for his trouble. Memories of the way she had responded to his kisses made him feel about ten feet tall and powerful enough to take on the world. When he turned back to the hotel, he thought he might swell up and explode from the sheer need that drove him toward her.

In the past he had thought of Moira as an angel. There was no doubt in his mind about that now. She was as good, kind, and gentle as he could ever have wanted. But when he saw her standing on the porch he was sure he'd been right about what lay beneath the righteous exterior of Miss O'Casey. Under all that sweetness waited the unexplored Missus Chee—married woman, simmering with arousal, and just waiting to be stroked into the height of passion.

In the golden lamplight her auburn hair had turned a flaming red. The combination of rain and their blanket had loosened her bun and twirled the wispy tendrils around her face into a hundred soft curls. Like a glowing halo, her hair framed her head, spilled down onto her shoulders, fell across her brow, and tumbled over her ears.

Her blue eyes were locked on his body as he took the three steps onto the porch. There was no mistaking the hunger in them, desire that crackled like a flame. She was thinking about what lay ahead for them. She was imagining the way he would touch her. He could see those images in her eyes as she watched him walk across the wooden floor toward her.

"You're very wet," she said.

Unconscious of the effect her actions had on him, she ran her tongue over her lower lip and then took in a deep breath. Her bosom lifted and fell. He couldn't keep his eyes off it.

"Let's get inside." He picked up her bag and took her elbow. It felt small and warm in his palm. Shouldering open the glass door, he walked her across the lobby to the long front desk. "We'd like a room," he told the sleepy clerk.

"At this hour? Why, it's almost morning, sir."

"We've just gotten into town. We need a room." He wanted to add, "*Now*, before I do something I might regret." Instead he silently signed the hotel register and counted out a few bills from his pouch.

*Mr. and Mrs. Josiah Chee*. Moira read the names he had written. His hand was strong and bold, and the ink black. It was as if he had penned the inscription in such a way that no one could argue with the fact of it: they were married.

She tried to make herself breathe evenly as they walked across the carpeted floor to the wide staircase and began to ascend. The wooden stairs creaked. The scent of the gas lamps drifted through the air. A steamboat blew its whistle just outside the hotel. She tightened her fingers on his arm and felt his muscle tense.

He looked at her. "I'm a lucky man, Moira."

She glanced away, shy suddenly. "Sure I'm the lucky one, so I am. You're a fine man, Josiah Chee."

"And you're the most beautiful woman I've ever seen."

At the first landing they stepped into a hall dimly lit by globed gas lamps. Rows of doors stood on either wall. Behind them, Moira knew, people slept the early-morning drugging sleep that made eyes puffy and mouths dry. Unconscious, they would not know that she and Josiah were as wide awake as if it were a Fourth of July afternoon.

He stopped at a door, checked the room number, fitted his key to the lock. The latch turned with a click. She watched him take hold of the knob and saw his fingers, long and strong, cup it the way they had cupped her. A shiver ran down her thighs.

Stepping into the dark room, she could make out only a single object—the huge brass bed. Josiah crossed to a bedside table and turned up a lamp. As its light coated the other furnishings in the room, she sucked in a breath of pleasure. An Oriental carpet! A deep maroon with intricate patterns, the huge rug made her think of someplace exotic and rich. Velvet chairs flanked the single tall window that looked out over the Mississippi River. Between the chairs sat a marble-topped table crowned with a lush green fern in a porcelain basket.

In one corner stood a fretwork changing screen with lace inserts. Moira studied it as she stood just inside the door. From his place by the bed Josiah sensed her uneasy musings and wondered how he could reassure her that he intended to give her nothing but pleasure. He wanted this to be the most special night of her life, and of his. But as he pondered it, he wondered if he really knew what a gentle, sensitive woman like Moira would need or want from a man. Oh, he'd had some experience with ladies, but nothing serious or meaningful. The women Josiah had known in the mining camp were loose and coarse.

With them a man wasn't expected to concern himself with niceties.

He watched Moira standing there staring at the changing screen, her hands clasped in a knot of uncertainty. As she chewed on her bottom lip, her breath came in quick gasps like that of a rabbit caught in a trap.

"I'll unpack your bag if you want to wash up . . . or . . ." he began.

"Oh . . ." Her blue eyes were as bright as sapphires.

He bent over the old saddlebag, wondering if she was ever going to move from that spot. Wouldn't she just peel out of that new dress and hop into bed the way he'd dreamed? For weeks now he had pictured her all stretched out across a white sheet, her auburn hair spread around on the pillow, her long legs and hips turned invitingly, full breasts standing up at attention, and her naked body just waiting to be pleasured.

Glancing at Moira from the bedside, Josiah had to admit that despite his imaginings, she wasn't the type to sashay around in the buff for anybody—especially a man she wasn't sure she trusted. So how was he supposed to let her know how he felt and how much he wanted her? Grab her and tear her clothes off? That was an exciting thought, but Moira might let out a screech and run for cover.

Kneeling beside the dresser, he pulled a pair of denim trousers and a man's shirt from her bag and stuffed them in a drawer. Whose were those? he wondered. He tugged out a couple of wool stockings, a camisole, a faded green skirt. There was a comb down at the bottom of the bag, a bar of soap, too, and a wrinkled cotton towel.

He set those last few items on the dresser top and ventured another glance over his shoulder. She had moved from the door to the window, where she stood looking down at the river. A shaft of pink light crossed her face. Admitting that he didn't know the first thing about seducing a woman, he gave up his daydream and decided to just take care of her. She looked so worn out she'd probably drop over in a dead faint.

"Are you tired?" he asked, rising and starting toward her.

Moira was instantly aware of his movements. "I should be, but my nerves are jangling like those steamboat bells." She could hear him coming across the room. Her fingers tightened on the curtain she was holding. What would he do? Grab her? Tear her clothes off? It might not be so bad, she thought. On the other hand . . .

He stopped just behind her. She could hear his breath coming deep and ragged. Though she couldn't see him, she could feel his presence as plainly as if he were inside her own skin. He was there, big and strong, wanting to touch her as badly as she wanted to touch him. She stared out the window, seeing nothing, hearing nothing, feeling nothing but the sure sensation of the man behind her, wanting nothing but to feel him stir up and then ease the ache inside her.

Then his lips touched the back of her neck.

"Josiah," she murmured with utter relief. His mouth, hot and damp, trailed up to her hairline, then slid back down to the collar of her dress. "Oh, yes . . ." She reached behind her, and her fingertips touched his thigh, rock-hard and hot.

His hand slid around her stomach, moving her backward until she was pressed firmly against his length. She could feel his legs touch hers, his chest settle along her back. His lips kissed a line of sparks around the side of her neck and up to her ear. When his tongue touched the tip of her earlobe, a thousand stars sprinkled down her spine and clustered between her thighs. He took her earlobe between his teeth and gently tugged. Then he traced the outer shell of her ear with his tongue. She thought she would melt into a puddle on the floor.

"Remember when you would come into my room back at Fianna?" he whispered, forming the words against her ear so that his breath stirred shivers inside her. "I'd watch you working over me—putting on medicine and bandaging my stomach—and I'd imagine what it would be like to run my fingers into your hair and feel its weight."

As he spoke, he loosened the pins that held her bun and let the coil of her hair slip down her back. "Your hair is like a cloud at sunset, Moira."

"You're a poet, so you are," she murmured. "With your words and your hands."

He smiled, aware that in spite of his doubts he had stumbled on the key that would unlock this woman and open her to him. The secret had been in his hands all the time—touch her, feel her, gentle her into response the way he had from the beginning. A marriage ceremony and a brass bed didn't give him license to turn into a rampaging stud stallion, nor did it transform her into a randy vixen. This was Moira—*his* Moira—shy, tender, a little afraid of life. He had promised to take care of her, and now more than ever she would need that.

"After you left my room at Fianna and went next door," he whispered into her hair, "I used to picture you unbuttoning your dress."

She could hear him behind her, not breathing, waiting, on the edge. Slowly she lifted her hands. "Like this?" she asked, easing the buttons from their holes down the front of her blue dress.

"I would tell myself it was nothing—just a woman getting ready for bed. But all the same, I couldn't keep from wondering about the way you would touch your clothes, and how you'd take them off."

She dropped the curtain to cover the window, then turned in his arms. As his eyes devoured her, she unbuckled her belt and let it fall to the floor. The front of her dress slid open, and her breasts expanded to fill the soft gathers of her camisole.

"This is how," she whispered, brazenly meeting his hungry eyes.

"As long as I live, I'll never get tired of watching."

Awed at her own power over him and emboldened by his undisguised desire, she shrugged her dress from her shoulders and let it slide to the floor at her ankles. When she looked down at herself, she could see that her nipples had beaded up, making the cotton fabric over them jut out in high, sharp points.

Josiah lifted a hand and touched the tip of her breast. She caught her breath. "And I'll never grow tired of this," she whispered. "You can't imagine how it feels."

He rolled her taut nipple and felt it tighten even more beneath his fingers until it was as round and hard as a river pebble. Her hands gripped his arms, slid up to his shoulders, tangled in his hair. Heavy-lidded, her eyes glazed over, and her head lolled against her shoulder. She pulled him closer, instinctively needing the thrust of his body against hers.

"I can imagine," he said, tugging the camisole from her corset, "because there are parts of me that feel the same way."

She lifted her head. "Here?" she murmured, boldly sliding her hand down the front of his britches. At the feel of the hardened ridge, her instincts told her to draw back, to keep away from such foreign territory. But she refused to listen. "If you can make me feel so wonderful with only a touch, Josiah, then I'll do the same for you."

"Moira," he murmured, unable to hold himself back as she ran her palm up and down his body, setting him aflame and shattering the fragile hold he had on his urges. "Oh, Moira, let me see you."

He tore the camisole over her head and devoured the sight of her breasts falling full and heavy over the upper edge of her corset. Rosy-tipped, they beckoned him, and he couldn't resist lowering his head to take first one nipple and then the other like a bead of candy between his lips. She shuddered in his arms, and her hands began to knead him harder and more urgently.

"Josiah!" She felt as though she might explode. Her body was a melting candle, hot and sweet and liquid. Her thighs ached, and her hips twisted out of control against his pelvis. She jerked his shirt from his britches and unbuttoned it with trembling fingers. The moment she caught sight of his brown chest, her mouth fell on him, her lips covering his flesh and her tongue lapping at his nipples.

He groaned. The bed seemed a million miles away. He swept her up in his arms and strode across the distance as her mouth worked a sweet torture on his skin. As they fell across the sheet, she began to flick apart the hooks on her corset. He hovered over her, hindering her fingers by licking at them, and teasing her nipples, her breasts, her neck with his tongue.

"Now you," she commanded, feeling as brazen as a whipster beneath him. "It's your turn to come out of some of those clothes, so it is."

When he refused to stop tormenting her breasts, she took over the job of disrobing him, her fingers desperate on the buckle of his belt, and on the brass studs that buttoned his britches. And then, just when she thought that the stroke of his mouth on her breasts would transform her into a great pulsing fiery ball before she evaporated altogether, his jeans fell open.

"Oh!" The surprise of her discovery took her breath away, and the feel of him so urgent and hungry thrilled and frightened her almost into paralysis. Stiffening, she pulled her hands away and tucked them under her bottom.

He lifted his head from her breasts and saw the undisguised shock in her eyes. "Moira?" he whispered.

She couldn't speak, didn't even know what to say. Here they were, tearing at each other, exposing parts of their bodies that were meant to be private. In church she'd been taught to respect the privacy of others. The flesh was the stronghold of sin . . . wasn't it? Oh, but she ached to touch him again, to fully know a part of him so strong, so powerful, so unbearably male that it made her weak. But this great throbbing secret was his own personal possession. What right did she have to . . .

He took her hand and cupped it around him. Then he closed her fingers and taught her his pleasure. "Touch me, Moira," he murmured. "I want you to. This is the way you can give me the same pleasure that I give you."

Closing her eyes, she gently stroked him, a mixture of emotions tumbling through her body. She felt awed, frightened, thrilled, and more than a little wicked. That was it—that sense of wickedness—that made her rise up on the bed and drape her breasts on his chest as though she were a strap without a moral bone in her body.

As she massaged him, she watched her nipples kiss the hard flesh of his torso. A sheen of perspiration appeared on his body, and his breath came in ragged gasps. Their thighs tangled together. Their feet played. His hands grabbed for her undergarments, the last barrier between them, and she felt them slide down her legs.

As she lay naked against him, his big hands cupped her buttocks, taking the soft cheeks and working them, kneading them. She kissed his mouth and ran her tongue over his lips. "This is the greatest ecstasy I have ever known in all my life," she whispered.

He smiled. "Just wait, my love. There's much more to come." He turned her gently onto the bed so that her breasts tipped up at the ceiling. As she continued caressing him, heightening his pleasure until he throbbed and ached for release, he slid his hand down her stomach and into the soft nest between her thighs.

"Josiah?" she murmured.

"Trust me, Moira." He could feel her relax just a measure, and he slipped his fingers into her moist petals. She gasped, but he covered her mouth with a kiss as his fingertips began a magic dance. Oh, but she was ready for him—hungry and needing him. Yet he knew that if she had never been touched by a man, there would be pain before her final pleasure. He dreaded that moment, and he postponed it by caressing her until she writhed beneath him.

"Josiah, what are you doing to me? I feel as if I've been swept away by a shee. Oh, please . . . please . . ." Her head tossed on the pillow as she clutched him, her teeth nipping at his shoulders and pushing her hips into his hand.

"Do you want me, Moira? Inside you?"

"Will it take away the aching?"

"Not at first. Moira, there's pain for a woman the first time a man opens her to his love. Do you know that?"

Her blue eyes were wild. She shook her head. "No, I've never been told anything. But I don't care. I want it, Josiah. I want you, all of you, even if there's pain."

"I swore I'd never hurt you."

"It's hurting me more to be this way with you and not have it all! Please, Josiah, I'm trembling all over, so I am. I feel hot and cold at the same time. Stars keep shooting over my head and down into my eyes. And I ache like I've never ached before. Oh, please, for the love of heaven, don't torment me any longer."

Her words cut the final cords of his restraint. He bent over her, suckling her breasts until she cried out, caressing her until her hips writhed and her body pushed against his fingers, grinding and crushing in her need. Then he drew his hand away and slid his own magic down into her damp nest. At the unbearable sensation of her warm silken treasure, he tossed his head back and hurtled through a realm of pleasure he'd never known. He caught her hips in his palms and thrust into her, butting against the barrier of her maidenhood.

"My love," he uttered, "forgive me," and he tore through her delicate flesh and into the sweetness of her depths.

Jagged pain like white lightning ripped through Moira's body. She gasped, cried out, moaned. Her things tightened up like steel, and her fingers dug into his back.

Tortured by her anguish, Josiah covered her mouth with gentle, healing kisses. He lay on top of her and inside her, not moving, absorbing her pain, willing it away. A tear trickled from the corner of her eye and ran down her temple toward her hair. He caught it with his lips.

"I'm sorry," he whispered.

She shook her head, unable to speak. Oh, it was horrible after all! She should have known such sinful lust could lead to nothing good. Now she must pay for all those long hours of silent lasciviousness when she'd gazed at him in carnal desire. She had been sentenced to suffer the consequences of allowing him to fondle her and tempt her into things she had always known were wrong. The wages of sin were death, so the Good Book said, and at this moment Moira wanted nothing more than to die. Quickly.

Their eyes met, and she saw hunger mingled with compassion. "Moira," he whispered, "I'll touch you for hours if that's what it takes to bring you back to where you were."

No, she would never know again that unbearable driving need, she was certain of it. Pain raked through her. Her body throbbed. Worse, now she finally understood about sin and its consequences. She couldn't let herself be taken back to that place of heedless pleasure.

"I'll just lie here," she said, aware she must now play the role of the dutiful wife she had become when she'd agreed to their hasty wedding earlier that night. "Do whatever you need to do to take care of things for yourself, Josiah. I won't mind."

Torn between an urge to chuckle at her innocence and a desire to growl out his anger at the situation, he studied her damp body. She'd just lie there, would she? Let him take care of things for himself? Was that what she thought this was all about?

"Moira," he said, his mouth against her ear and his body beginning a slow dance on hers, "you be sure not to move a muscle, now. After all, it might be a sin to let yourself get carried away."

She nodded. "Aye, it would."

He moved. A quiet ripple ran through her body. He slipped slightly out of her, then deep inside again. A shiver trembled down her thighs. He touched the tip of her nipple with his tongue. Something began to thud in her damp crevice. He ran his hand down the side of her breast, then up and over, then around. His fingertips caught the pink crest that had gone soft and senseless. Stroking over it, he began to roll and tug, arousing that sweet ache she had learned to crave. Her hips swayed into him and began to undulate.

"I can't help but move," she announced in an anguished whisper. "It's beyond my control, Josiah."

He studied her with a feigned solemnity. "Are you sure?"

She nodded, uncomfortably aware of a swift throbbing flame that was being stoked into a roaring fire by the delicious caresses of his body against hers. Glancing down at herself, she saw that her nipples had budded again; her breasts were gathered up in his hands, and his fingers were plucking and kneading their tips until they fairly hammered with pleasure.

"You wouldn't want to sin, now, Moira," he went on, baiting her. "I mean, the good Lord couldn't have had any particular purpose in mind when he gave you all these jangling nerves, and all these tender secret places, and this magical craving between us. It must have been an accident, I reckon. Or maybe a mistake."

"Aye," she managed. He rocked on top of her, and her body continued to belie her convictions. Her hips pushed against him in her unbidden desire to know more fully the sweet penetrating strokes. His neck hovered near her mouth, and she couldn't resist touching it with the tip of her tongue, dampening a line up it to his ear, taking his earlobe into her mouth. Her nipples thrummed with pleasure. Her hips began to dance. Her feet locked around his, slid up his thighs, dug into his hard buttocks.

"No," she contradicted herself. "God doesn't make mistakes."

"The way you feel, Moira . . . it's part of the big design. Give yourself to it."

With rhythmic abandon, he drove into her again and again. Their bodies began to move as one. The bed swayed. The sheets tangled. Pillows fell to the floor. Swept up in the roar of vibrations running rampant through her, Moira forgot all about pain. She forgot about the hotel and the people waking up next door. The brass headboard bumped against the wall. Her gasping cries of ecstasy played tag around the room.

She rolled on top of Josiah and let him toy with her breasts while she rode him. Then he mounted her again, this time drumming his passion into her with such intensity that she thought she would scream aloud in need of release. She dug her fingers into his muscles as her head arched backward on the bed. And her body erupted. Spangles of light showered her; a roaring river rushed through her head, deafening her. Wave upon cresting wave shot down her thighs, up to her breasts, out to her very fingertips.

Just as she thought she might die, Josiah tensed and exploded inside her in a great rocking, shuddering release. His arms crushed the breath from her chest. His hips pounded hers into the mattress. They pumped and swayed and rode the waning waves until finally they lay drenched and exhausted in each other's arms.

As his breath began to steady, Josiah rolled to his side and cradled her against his chest. "Oh, Moira. I never knew it could be this . . . that you were such a . . . that I'd ever feel so . . . so incredible."

She couldn't help smiling. "Sure it was more of a surprise to me than it was to you."

He laughed and snuggled her closer. "Marrying you was the craziest thing I've ever done. And the best. I'm looking forward to every minute of every day of every year to come."

His words sobered her a little. "Whisht," she said, touching his lips with her fingertip. "Don't speak of the future. We don't know what it holds for us, Josiah."

"I do." He hitched up onto one elbow and gazed down at her as she lay on the white sheet, her auburn hair spread all around and her long legs turned to expose one creamy hip. "The future holds you and me—together."

She shut her eyes. "But where? How?"

"I'm taking you back to New Mexico, Moira," he said. "I'm going to set us up there."

She couldn't bear to hear the rest of it . . . not now. Looking up at him, she ran her palm over his chest. "Let's get some rest, Josiah. I'm so sleepy."

"I know you're tired, but I'm asking you to hear me out, Moira. I'm a man who knows what he wants— always have been. I paint a picture in my mind of the way things should be. Then I set out to make them happen, and I don't rest until everything's in place."

"You're like Scully, then, with his paintings and his foolish dreams."

"My dreams aren't foolish, Moira. They're a man's dreams. I follow them until they're within reach. Then I capture them. The picture I've painted of my future is going to come to life."

She studied his brown eyes and knew she shouldn't ask the question that danced on the tip of her tongue.

"You want to know how I've painted the future in my mind, Moira?" he asked, taking over the job. "Do you want to see my dream as clearly as I see it?"

Turning her head to the window, she focused on the shaft of bright morning sunlight streaming between the curtains. "Oh, Josiah . . ."

He took her shoulders, unwilling to let her elude him. "Here it is, Moira. It's a ranch. It's acres and acres of good fertile land, the land of my ancestors. It's a house with a long shady front porch. It's a rushing green river lined with cottonwoods. It's apple, plum, peach, and cherry trees planted in neat straight rows. It's cattle grazing in the valley. It's sheep on the hills, Moira. Flocks of woolly white sheep."

Before she could pull away from him, he drew her against his chest. "It's you and me, Moira, smack-dab in the middle of that picture. You and me living together, laughing and crying together, loving together. You and me growing old together. It's us, Moira, that's my dream."

She tried to blink back the tears that filled her eyes. How could she tell him that his dream—his wonderful, beautiful, beckoning dream—might be as elusive as a leprechaun's pot of gold? A black cloud still hung over their rainbow. That cloud was a man whose greatest skill lay in the crushing of hopes and dreams. And his name was Innis Grady.

# Chapter
## 12

In St. Louis, Missouri, lying in the arms of Josiah Chee, something happened to Moira. Perhaps it happened because she was so very far away from Fianna, from Innis Grady, and from the bondage they represented. Perhaps it happened because she had placed Erinn in Father Murphy's hands and felt free of that responsibility. Or perhaps it was a result of the hours of lovemaking she enjoyed in the Lafayette Hotel overlooking the Mississippi River. Whatever caused this change, the result was clear: Moira felt like the boldest, cheekiest whipster who had ever lived. And she loved it!

All through breakfast in the hotel dining room, Moira and Josiah chuckled over the thinly disguised stares of the other patrons. "Sure they heard us romping in our room this morning," she whispered to him. "Faith, what must they all think of us!"

"They're jealous," Josiah announced with confidence.

Moira took a swig of fresh orange juice and then grinned at her husband. "And well they should be."

Josiah had never seen Moira looking so alive, so vibrant. She fairly glowed. Her blue eyes sparkled like

Pecos diamonds; her skin was flushed and pink; her hair shone like a new copper penny. And she was purring like a cat in a creamery. Every time she laughed, she tossed back her head, and her breasts went tight against the front of her dress. It was all he could do to get his breakfast down before dancing her up the stairs and into bed again.

The morning vanished in a mist of sweet passion as they explored each other's bodies by the light of day. Moira put everything out of her mind but this braw man whose smile lit up her life and whose loving touched places inside her she hadn't even known were there. Josiah couldn't see beyond the playful vixen he'd somehow managed to lure into his arms. Once Moira got over the shock of what they were doing—and made up her mind that God approved of such fleshly activities between a man and his wife—she fairly threw herself into the pursuit of hedonistic pleasure. Josiah thought he'd died and gone to heaven.

They finally rolled out of bed sometime in the early afternoon. While strolling along the streets of St. Louis, they stopped at one of the many vending carts and bought a lunch of hot frankfurters tucked into long, white buns. These strange concoctions were all the rage in the city, and Moira thought they tasted wonderful even though she had to eat them with her bare hands.

After lunch Josiah suggested a baseball game. Though Moira had never seen baseball, or any other organized sport save sack races and greased-hog-catching contests on the Fourth of July, she thought it might be fun.

Indeed it was. Never had Moira seen so many people crowded into one place. Never had she imagined such a roar of cheering as she heard when the St. Louis Browns trotted onto the baseball field. What mighty power, speed, and finesse they displayed in their battle against the Cincinnati Red Stockings!

Moira thrilled to the sight of the strong athletes racing around the bases or taking a stance at bat. She lost every ounce of her decorum as she joined the other spectators in hurling reprimands at the umpire and exhorting the Browns to triumph over their foes in this magical arena called a baseball diamond. The whack of the ball striking wood sent a shiver of pleasure down her spine. At the sight of the same ball soaring through the air and over the fence, she leapt to her feet, cheering, jumping up and down, throwing her arms around Josiah's neck.

"A home run!" men shouted, clapping one another on the back. Ball players leapt into each other's arms. Whatever a home run was, Moira felt certain it was the most exciting thing on earth.

When her attention wandered away from the playing field, she found a hundred other things to interest her. All sorts of food could be purchased from vendors—hot popcorn, lemonade, peanuts, and St. Louis's famous Anheuser-Busch beer. Ladies clad in a rainbow of gorgeous dresses held parasols over their heads to keep the sun off their pale faces. Men in genteel sporting attire laughed, joshed, shouted, jeered, and cheered until Moira began to wonder if they'd reverted to childhood.

The children themselves, when not running up and down the aisles and stepping on people's toes, spent their time begging their parents for baseball cards. Curious about the attraction of the little pictures, Josiah bought himself a package of Sweet Caporal cigarettes. During a slow point in the game, he and Moira examined the photographs, each showing a player posed in a studio while pretending to catch or bat a ball dangling from a string.

When the last baseball had been pitched and the final bat had been swung, the Browns marched proudly off the field, having triumphed over the Red Stockings in a dazzling victory. Elated, Moira and Josiah shouldered their way through the crowd and out into the street.

"You would do well at that game," Moira commented as they boarded a streetcar headed toward the riverfront. "Sure you're a grand big whacker of a man with strong arms and legs, and there's no doubt you could knock one of those little balls into a home run on your first try."

Josiah laughed. "Maybe I could play baseball," he said, "but I've got other things to do with my time than slug a baseball over a fence."

It had occurred to him during the game how odd it was that there in Missouri, while men were eating popcorn at baseball games, in the Territory other men were engaged in bloody shoot-outs. While these eastern fellows hopped on streetcars and read their newspapers, western men rode mustangs and fought Indians and outlaws to protect their land claims. The two worlds, as different as night and day, were connected only by the slender silver line of the railroad.

"Ah, well, and besides that," Moira was saying, "you'd have to earn a living at a regular job in between all that baseballing."

"Not these days. A good player can earn upwards of two thousand dollars a season at baseball, Moira."

"Two thousand dollars!" she exclaimed. "And you want to raise *sheep*?"

He chuckled, but in a moment the reality of her question sobered him. "Yes, Moira, I do want to raise sheep. It's something we've got to talk over."

She turned away from him to study the riverfront with its array of paddle-wheel boats, trains, streetcars, and wagons. "Not now, Josiah. If I start to think about it, I'll lose the joy of this day." She looked back, her blue eyes pleading. "Don't take it away from me, please. In the years to come, I think . . . I think the memory of today may be my only pleasure."

"Don't say that, Moira." He put his arm around her shoulders and pulled her against him. "We've barely had a taste of the pleasures the future holds for us."

"Is that a church?" she asked suddenly. She pointed to the tall spire of a building just ahead. "Oh, Josiah, I want to go inside. You can't imagine how much it would mean to me."

"Let's go," he agreed, choosing to ignore the fact that they had been in church getting married the night before. Oh, well, he thought, going to church two days in a row probably wouldn't kill him.

The cathedral on the waterfront was more than fifty years old, a towering building with a huge front portico supported by four white pillars. A marker out front stated that the sanctuary bell had been cast in 1772, over a hundred years before. Josiah bowed his head as he and Moira entered the church. She said she wished she could go to confession, and he thought it might not hurt him too much either, since he hadn't talked about his setbacks to a priest for years.

On the other hand, Josiah knew, he had acted mostly according to upright principles all his life, so he wouldn't have much to talk about. Moira managed to find a priest, and she seemed to spend forever with him. Josiah sat on a pew at the front of the church until she finally slipped to his side. They knelt together in silent prayer for a moment before rising and making their way up the aisle.

"I'm washed in the blood," Josiah announced in a jaunty voice as they walked down the steps into the late afternoon sunshine. "My sins were scarlet, but now they're as white as snow."

She glanced at him, and he could see at once that her mood had altered. "I told the priest everything I'd done," she said in a low voice, aware that her fear of losing the day's joy had been justified.

Josiah's grin faded. "So, what did he say?"

"He told me I'm to stay with you."

"Well, how come you look as if you just bit into a raw persimmon? Moira, that's good news! If the priest says our marriage is all right, then it must be."

"He didn't say it was right that I married you. He said I must honor my vows." She caught his hands. "Oh, Josiah, I feel as wicked as Erinn! When we were at the convent in Florissant, she told me all about the way she acted—doing everything for her own pleasure and thinking nothing of others. She abandoned poor Seamus who had always been faithful to her and had given her everything she ever needed. Out of lust for a cowpuncher, she betrayed Seamus! She let her own fleshly desires carry her into sin. Don't you see, Josiah? I've done the very same thing!"

He frowned. "You're planning to bed down with some cowboy?"

"No!" She couldn't help but laugh over his confusion. "It's Innis, so it is. *He's* the man I've betrayed. The moment our parents died in that fire, God rest their souls, Innis and his wife took Erinn and me in. Deirdre loved me as if I were her own daughter, so she did. Though she passed on, too, Innis continued to keep me safe, housed, fed, and clothed. He gave me honest labor for my hands. Josiah, if Innis hadn't taken me as his ward, I might have become one of those painted ladies we saw in Las Vegas, forced to sell myself in order to stay alive. Can't you see what I owe him?"

Josiah pondered her question, trying to see his way to a solution. "It was good of Innis to take you into his home and look out for you while you were growing up, Moira. I'll grant him that. But you paid him back for everything by taking care of him and Scully. The way I see it, you gave him as much as he gave you, fair and square. You don't owe the man the rest of your life just because he did you a good turn when you were a young girl."

"But I promised to stay with him and take care of him! I made Deirdre a vow on her deathbed, and now I've broken it out of my own low fleshly desires."

"What you and I have isn't *low*, Moira." He felt angry now. "You're a full-grown woman. You're every bit entitled to marriage and what goes along with it."

"Maybe you're right, but all the same, Innis will never release me from my promise, Josiah," she said with conviction. "You don't know him."

"You're not married to Innis Grady. If you swore you'd take care of him and his kid, you did it out of the loyalty a child feels to a parent. But you're an adult now, and you chose to marry me for better or worse. That was your decision as a woman."

Moira looked at the sidewalk, her vision blurred by the tears that had swum into her eyes. How could she make him understand? It wasn't just that she felt a sense of loyalty to Innis. She felt undeniably certain that her marriage to Josiah was doomed, and had been from the start.

"It's not only Innis," she admitted as she lifted her eyes to his face. "We don't belong together, you and I. I've always been obedient, loyal, a good woman. I hold with the things I was taught—my Irish roots, my Catholic faith, my duties in life. But you . . . you're a renegade, Josiah. You've rebelled against the traditions I hold most dear. You want to steal lands your Irish kinsmen claim as their own. You want to plow up the soil, like those awful nesters who are fencing in the range to build their precious farms. Worst of all, you want to raise sheep!"

Josiah studied Moira's face, a picture of intensity, her eyes as stormy as a gale over the mountains and her cheeks flushed with passion. How tempting it was to defy her with his words, to refute everything she said with cold fact and undeniable logic. But detached analysis was a man's way of solving problems.

Moira was a woman—intuitive, sensitive, ardent. Josiah knew by now that all the talking in the world wouldn't persuade her to change her mind about something. She was a creature of emotion and feeling. How she got along with people carried more weight than all the carefully constructed arguments in the world. Her convictions were as deeply embedded as sand in a block of concrete.

He would have to show her.

"All right," he said, aware that he was playing with fire. "I'll take you back to Innis."

"You will?" She swallowed at the unexpectedness of his answer.

"Sure. Let's go." As he spoke, he was already striding on ahead of her toward a waiting streetcar.

Just the sight of Josiah sent a wash of doubt flowing through Moira. His broad shoulders reflected the last of the sunlight. His Stetson put him a good foot above the head of everyone else on the crowded street. The whip at his side showed him for what he was—a man intent on his purpose in life. And, oh, those tight buttocks beneath the fabric of his britches stirred a wicked flame to life inside Moira.

"Come on," he beckoned from the corner. "Got to catch a train for Kansas City."

"Well . . . well, what about Erinn?" she asked, grasping for something to slow him down as she hurried after him. "I can't just go off without making certain she's all right."

"Erinn's in the hands of Sister Theresa and Father Murphy. What could be safer?" He stepped up onto the streetcar and bent to catch her elbow. Before she could protest, he had swung her up beside him. "I've had enough of the city anyway. It's time I headed back to New Mexico and put my claim on some property."

She studied his face as the streetcar rattled toward their hotel. Was he serious? Could he actually mean to take her back to Fianna and let her go just like that? But that was what she had asked for; she had pled her case so well, she must have convinced him she was right.

And she *was* right. Every time she had tried to picture herself living with Josiah in some sheepherder's havverick on land he had stolen from the Irish, tending a flock of woollies, and cooking mutton for dinner, she felt ill. She couldn't do it!

Oh, this wild trek to Missouri had been a mistake from the very first. She had been swept into doing things she knew she couldn't live with. And now she would have to pay the price.

As they collected their baggage from the hotel where they had spent so many hours in heedless, ardent ecstasy, Moira tried to fill the emptiness in her heart with a picture of herself at Fianna. It would be as it always had been—her little kitchen, her laundry line stretched out in the sun, her garden and quilt rack and churn. Innis and Scully.

Oh, dear Lord!

More than one ugly fact kept Josiah from looking forward to his return to the Territory. Not only was he reluctant to encounter Innis Grady and face him down over Moira's future, but he strongly suspected that another enemy awaited him: John Fisher.

In St. Louis it would have been an easy matter for Josiah to lose himself forever. He knew he could stay in touch with his partner, Paddy Connor, in Butte to keep abreast of his claims and the progress at his mines. But once he crossed back into the New Mexico Territory, where cities were more scattered and folk didn't hold the law in such high regard, he'd be easier to track down.

He turned the butt of his whip in his palm as he lay stretched out on the hard bench beneath Moira's platform bed on the train that first night. She had scoffed at his *látigo*, and maybe rightly so. It was a sheepman's weapon—a deterrent, not an annihilator. With a whip, a man could fend off danger, but not eliminate it. And Josiah knew his enemy was out to kill him.

All the same, he would return to the Territory and face the inevitable. One of these days the Cornishman who coveted Josiah's mines would step out of the darkness. They would face each other in a final battle—and only one of them would come out alive. Josiah had decided it would be him.

No threat would keep him from pursuing his dream of owning land in the New Mexico Territory and raising sheep there. Not an angry Cornish copper king who claimed a mine for which Josiah held the legal papers.

Not a bullying Irish cattleman who claimed the woman Josiah had put his stamp on. Not even a mule-stubborn, hidebound female who wooed him with her body, yet fended him off with her words.

He lifted a leg and put his foot on the underside of the bed that hung over him. "You asleep, Moira?" he whispered loudly, giving the bed a little shake.

Her head appeared over the edge. "Not with you kicking my grug, I'm not."

"Quiet!" someone muttered from a bed on the other side of the car.

The gaslights down the center of the car had been turned out, but the moonlight lit the interior enough so that Josiah could make out Moira's hair, a tumble of auburn curls around her head and shoulders. He pictured her breasts pressing into the hard wood of that bed, and without intending it, he began to feel aroused.

"I think we'll take the trail from Las Vegas to the Peñasco by way of Roswell," he said, making conversation, "instead of through White Oaks."

"Why?"

"Easier traveling. Better road."

"Say, will you folks please tone it down?" someone in a bed at the end of the car asked. "The wife and I, we're trying to get some sleep here."

"Sorry," Moira whispered.

Josiah could see her scowling at him over the edge of the bed. She held a finger to her lips before disappearing again into the shadows. He lay there awhile, thinking about the way they'd spent the night before—rolling around on that soft hotel bed. That was before Moira had taken it into her head to start feeling guilty and having doubts about everything.

Lord, why couldn't she just take him at face value? He knew they belonged together. He knew she wanted him as badly as he wanted her. She was probably up in that bed right now dreaming about the way she had ridden him, her hips sliding up and down as her pleasure heightened to its peak. She had as much as admitted that she'd married him because she was feeling lickerish and rutty. In Josiah's book, lust was as good a reason as any for a man and wife to stay together.

Smiling at his thoughts, he jiggled her bed again with his foot. In a moment, her head popped over the side. "What?" she mouthed, frowning at him.

"I'm cold," he said.

She rolled her eyes. It was a steamy hot night, practically boiling in the stuffy railcar—so hot, in fact, that Josiah had stripped off his shirt and was lying there half naked and looking more tempting than he ever had. Moira ran her eyes over his dark, smooth chest and studied the way his stomach narrowed into the waist of his denim jeans. When she looked back at his face, she saw that slow, sulky smile he sometimes wore when he wanted to tease her.

"Lonely, too," he added. "I'm sure sad and lonely down here all by myself."

"Whisht!" Moira swung her arm down to try to shut him up.

He caught her hand and kissed her fingertips. "I reckon I'd feel a lot better if I could just talk to someone."

"You're full of blarney, so you are." Moira knew what Josiah really wanted: to climb up into the bed and hold her in his arms.

She wanted him, too, but they had hardly spoken since buying their tickets at the depot and boarding the late evening train for Kansas City. Their car was crowded, dirty, and hot, leaving neither of them in a pleasant mood. A sick baby had wailed for what seemed like hours. The train's dinner fare had consisted of soggy cucumber-and-tomato sandwiches and lukewarm beer sold from the cart of a news butcher who looked as if he hadn't washed his hands in months. Finally the conductor had banished all the single men from the family car and gone down the aisle turning out the lamps.

Moira had lowered her bed on its chain supports, and without so much as a good-night, she had climbed up onto the hard platform to try to get some sleep. Instead she had tossed and turned, thinking about Josiah down below her on the wooden bench. How could they have come to this? That morning they had made passionate love for hours. Tonight they weren't even looking at each other.

Was this the mess they had already made of their marriage? Now she studied his massive body as he lay sprawled across the seat beneath her bed. His brown eyes were depthless, but she knew he was gazing up at her, wanting her. With his arms cocked behind his head and his bare chest gleaming in the moonlight, the man was a sore temptation. Just the notion of running her hands through his dark gold hair sent a shiver of longing into the pit of her stomach.

"If you want to talk," she whispered finally, giving in to him against her better judgment, "you'd better come up here. You've already got the other passengers chittering at you."

Grinning, he rolled into a sitting position and gave a mighty stretch. From overhead she watched the muscles in his arms bulge and jump and felt her heart leap in response. He took hold of the swaying chain ladder and swung himself up until they were face to face.

"Evenin', ma'am," he said, giving her a wink.

She scooted against the metal side of the railroad car to make a place for him. At first she didn't think he would even fit in the tiny space. But he managed to slide down the edge of the platform and wedge himself against her, their bodies touching lengthwise.

"Now go to sleep," she instructed him, shutting her eyes by way of example.

For a moment she thought he really was going to obey. In the darkness, she could hear his slow breathing, and feel the muscles in his thighs relax against her legs. Then his hand covered her breast.

Her eyes flew open. "Josiah!"

"Whisht, Moira," he reprimanded her, laying a finger on her lips. His voice held a teasing Irish brogue. "Sure you don't want to wake everyone up and set them to having a great cugger-mugger over what the pair of us are doing up here in the dark, do you now, my sweet thuckeen?"

"Braddach man!" She shook her head as his palm smoothed over the fabric of her new blue dress, cupping the globe of her bosom, kneading it slightly until her nipple began to stand upright. All the while she lay unmoving in the shadows and struggled to make reason lift its sensible head in the midst of her confusion.

It wasn't right for him to lie there and play with her, was it? Not when they'd had such a falling-out over their future plans. Not when propriety demanded that they keep their distance. Not when they were surrounded by others—men, women, even little children.

His mouth found hers and began to stroke her lips. She caught her breath. Against the soft mound at the base of her stomach, she could feel the growing evidence of his desire. But here in a crowded, stuffy railway car? Oh, no, it certainly wasn't the time or the place for such behavior.

"Josiah," she whispered, and his tongue slipped into her mouth, meeting hers, stroking in a deep, delicious caress. She could feel his hand on her hip, sliding up and down over the smooth curve, then around behind to the rise of her rear. He pulled her closer against him and began to unbutton her bodice.

"Now, Josiah," she managed between the dizzying kisses that had begun to sweep away her reason. "You really mustn't. . . ."

His hand slipped inside her chemise, and his finger found the sensitive tip of her breast. While she lay paralyzed with dismay and delight, he began to stimulate her nipple into an aching peak. He tormented the tender cherry until she felt a rush of sweet honey flow into

her depths and begin to throb between her thighs. All
thoughts of the barriers to their intimacy fled before
her onrushing desire. Suddenly the future didn't matter.
Neither did the past.

"Moira, touch me," he said, his mouth moving against
her ear.

"Here?" she asked, meaning the railcar.

"No, here." And he settled her hand on his rock-hard
arousal.

The first touch banished her awareness of the passengers who snoozed nearby, unaware of the clandes-
tine activity occurring a few feet away. Shivering with
wicked delight at their secret play, Moira found herself
unable to keep from stroking his length and returning his
deep, satisfying kisses. In spite of the cramped space, he
had managed to unbutton her bodice all the way to her
waist, and he took both her breasts in his hands to lift
and titillate them.

"Erinn told me I have a nice pair of diddies," Moira
said into his ear.

He grinned and ran his thumbs over their throbbing
tips. "The only pair of diddies I ever want to hold."

At his avowal of loyalty, she found herself unable to
keep from sliding her hand down inside the waistband
of his britches. He held his breath, poised, waiting, until
her fingers found him and began to stroke with an even,
measured rhythm.

They lay in the darkness, fondling, playing, tantalizing for what seemed to Moira like half the night.
Their previous adventure had been bold and ravenous,
but this was a sweet, slow torture that she found even
more exciting. She couldn't imagine how it would end.
Certainly in the midst of a crowded railcar they couldn't
fling their clothes off the platform bed to lie naked and
amorous, crying out at each burst of passion.

But end it must. Moira knew she was quickly climbing
to that peak where Josiah was leading her with his tender, drugging caresses. She could feel her body hovering

on the brink, her breath so shallow she could no longer hear it beneath the chug of the train engine, her fingers trembling as she plied Josiah's body, her mouth wet and bruised from his kisses, her breasts tumescent, throbbing at the very apex of stimulation.

When she thought she would slip over the edge without him, she suddenly realized that he had unbuttoned his jeans. Though he didn't pull them down and expose himself, all the same he emerged free into her hands. At the same time, he slipped her skirt up her thighs and tugged her smallclothes down to her knees.

"Do you want me, Moira?" he said softly. "Here?"

She could barely make herself nod, for his fingers had found her moist depths, and he was playing sweet music with her secret pearl. Just when she knew she was gone and she began to stiffen with the first paroxysmal waves sweeping through her body, he moved against her, barely parting her thighs and sliding deep into her. It took only a stroke, a silken thrust, and the cords that bound their control were severed in one blinding moment.

In utter silence they came together down the crest of the mountain they had climbed, sliding, rolling, undulating in blessed release. Moira sank her mouth against Josiah's neck to keep from crying aloud. He gripped her buttocks as the life essence pulsated from him. Their legs tangled, and the hard bed swayed with more than the rock of the train on its track.

"I want you, Moira," he breathed as the last of his surge shuddered her depths. "I want you now, and I'll want you tomorrow. I made up my mind a long time ago that if I ever had you like this, I wouldn't let go. No matter what stood in my way."

She eased her bare breasts against the warmth of his chest and ran her tongue up the side of his neck. "Did you dream of me a long time ago, Josiah?"

"You were my angel from the minute I looked up out of that death cart and saw your face for the first time. Moira, I'm going to make us a life, one we can both live with. I swear that to you right now, here on this miserable train. I'm going to build us a future."

She ached to believe him. Even as his hands drifted over her damp skin, she thought he might be right. Perhaps there was hope for them, even in the face of every obstacle. Oh, she wanted his promises to be true. She longed to spend the rest of her life with Josiah Chee, this man in her arms.

But even as he kissed her forehead and settled her cheek on his shoulder, she could feel the rhythmic, forward propulsion of the train. It took them onward, onward to New Mexico, to sheep and cattle wars, to her Irish kin and his Apache ancestors' lands, to strife and struggle and enemies with shotguns aimed high, and finally, to Innis Grady.

In Kansas City, Moira and Josiah boarded the same train that had taken them from Las Vegas to Missouri. They even found the exact bench where Moira had sat with her sister a few days before. She wanted to worry about Erinn, as she always had, but Josiah wouldn't let her. Erinn was fine, he assured her again and again. She was locked up in a convent. What could go wrong?

The trip across Kansas was long, flat, and unbearably hot. But the sweet cool nights were filled with secret passion. Moira had never imagined that a hard wooden bed could be the scene of such ecstasies. But it was, and every time she made love with Josiah, their commitment to each other solidified. It was as though their physical union was a picture, a reinforcement, of the spiritual bonding that was occurring during the long daylight hours when they sat on the bench together talking, teasing, and eventually sharing dreams.

By the time they stepped off the train in Las Vegas, Josiah had convinced Moira that their impulsive marriage might actually work. He bought a new wagon, which he hitched to the horses he had stabled at the livery there. Then they set off down the rutted road along the Gallinas River and then the Pecos, and with every mile he strove to paint a picture she could cling to.

"I'll build you a house on my claim," he told her as they rattled down the last stretch of the interminable plain between Fort Sumner and Roswell.

"A sheepherder's havverick?" she returned, expressing the fear she had turned over and over in her mind.

He frowned at the notion. "I wouldn't put you in some rough-and-tumble shack, Moira. I'll build our house out of adobe brick. There's enough forest up in the Sacramentos that I could build a log house if you want one. Or maybe even stone."

A stone house! Moira couldn't imagine such luxury. The very idea of a home of her own nestled like a sweet, precious treasure in the center of her heart. Innis Grady's Fianna was the most she had ever hoped for, but to think of actually owning her own house with a tidy kitchen and pots and pans that she'd purchased for herself! Oh, it was beyond dreaming.

"I'll buy you a stove, too," he said, adding kindling to the fire. "A great big black steel range, nickel trimmed." He glanced at her and saw that she was practically adrift in the wonder of his vision. So he heaped more logs on the flame. "I reckon a six-hole range would do best. You'll need one of those nickel-plated teapot shelves, too."

"Sure you don't have the money for a wonder like that! Such a stove would cost upwards of thirty dollars, so it would."

"You might be surprised at the amount of cash I can lay my hands on, Moira. When you married me, you got yourself a sonsy gentleman, so you did."

She laughed, certain he must be teasing again. "And where will my elegant daltheen take me when we get to the grand city of Roswell today? To the opera house, or perhaps the theater?"

Josiah studied the distant cluster of ramshackle adobe houses and frame stores on the road ahead. Then he gave the reins a shake before lifting his head to meet Moira's blue eyes. "I'm not taking you into Roswell, Moira," he said. "I'm driving down the banks of the Berrendo to a little settlement of sheepmen. Mexican shepherds, Moira. I want you to meet my parents."

# Chapter

## 13

The last thing on earth Moira wanted to do was meet the willful strap of a woman she had heard gossiped about all her life—the heathenish whipster who had forsaken her own son to run away with a man she hardly knew; the clarsha who had traded life on a fine, thriving cattle ranch for the arms of a half-breed sheepherder; the reckless, impulsive traitor to the Irish community— Josiah's mother.

Moira most certainly never expected to have to demean herself by speaking to the sheepherder himself—the wretched Apache-Mexican spalpeen who had stolen a fine Irishwoman from her home and family, only to set her slaving for him while he roamed about with his devilish woollies—Josiah's father.

Every time there had been a gathering of the Irish who lived along the Peñasco and Pecos rivers, the subject of Sheena Grady and Gabriel Chee was whispered back and forth among the women. During the span of Moira's life, the woman's reputation had gradually sunk lower and lower until now it lay at the very bottom of the scum bucket.

At first Sheena Grady had been "that poor widow" whose husband had died of a fever and left her with a half-grown boy, the fine young Innis Grady. Then the scandal hit, and she became "that innocent colleen" swept into marriage as soon as she was widowed. When it was learned whom she had wed and why, Sheena became "that irreverent whipster" who had been carried off in a heat of passion over some sherral who had no respect for her dead husband or for Irish tradition. When years passed and Sheena Chee never returned to her home and her son at Fianna, she was labeled "that wild and wicked clart" who was used by mothers as an example of the depths to which a daughter might fall if she ever departed from the Irish ways.

As Josiah's new wagon bumped along the winding Berrendo River road beneath the benevolent shade of the black walnut and cottonwood trees that grew at the water's edge, Moira tried to steel herself for what lay ahead. She must summon every grace her own mother had taught her. It would never do to exclaim in dismay over Missus Chee's miserable state—the tumbledown adobe house she must be forced to call a home, the poverty-stricken sheepherder she had wed in a foolish passion, the killeen of little lice it was said she had bred with the man she called husband.

Of course, one of those lice was Josiah. Moira shouldn't forget that.

She ventured a glance at him and wondered how he would react to seeing his mother again after such a time. His face had relaxed into an easy smile, and he was whistling a tune she didn't recognize. Of course, Moira must never betray her horror to Josiah. He must never be allowed to hear the terrible things that were spoken about his mother. He surely loved her, after all, as did any good son.

And how much better was Moira than Sheena Chee anyway? Why, she had practically followed in the woman's footsteps, so she had—marrying a poor landless shepherd she hardly knew, carried away into a hasty wedding out of a fit of unholy lustful desire, abandoning the prudent and sacred ways she had been taught.

Moira was ready to sink into the wagon seat for shame when Josiah sat up straight and began to wave. "Mother!"

In the distance a small woman with deep copper hair straightened from a basket of laundry she was hanging on a line. She shaded her eyes with her hand and gazed in silence for a moment. Then her arms shot into the air, palms extended and fingers spread wide in a gesture of utter exaltation. "Josiah! Oh, praise be to God, it's you! Boys, Gabriel, Josiah's home!"

Wiping her hands on her white apron, the woman trotted down the dusty driveway toward a gate in the fence that surrounded her house and land. Moira gaped at the sight of the neat buckskin-tan adobe home graced with white window frames, a blue door, and a shiny tin roof. Startling crimson geraniums sprang from boxes on the windowsills. Creamy lace curtains hung just inside gleaming glass panes. A rosebush laden with heavy pink blooms climbed up one side of the shady *portal,* while a fragrant honeysuckle vine twined up the other.

"God save you, Josiah!" his mother cried as he threw the brake on the wagon and leapt down into her arms. "Oh, I feared we'd lost you, so I did! But you're no frainey, now, are you? Your wounds are healed? Innis wrote that you were well and that you'd gone off in search of the little slip who'd run away from Fianna—"

Her green eyes suddenly darted to Moira, and she clamped her mouth shut. Josiah kissed his mother's forehead and turned her toward the wagon. "Mama, this is the little slip I went after. Moira, I'd like you to meet my mother, Missus Sheena Chee."

Moira swallowed and held out a hand. "God save you, Missus Chee."

"God save you kindly, my dear." As their hands met and shook, Moira felt a strength mingled with gentleness in the woman's small work-toughened palm.

Josiah's mother was beautiful. Her green eyes fairly glowed with kindness, and though her skin was ruddy from the sun, she had neither a wrinkle on her face nor a white hair to mingle in the pouf of cinnamon tresses swept into a knot on her head. The only sign of her age was the settling of her body through the years—full breasts heavy over a waist not as small as it must have been once, hips that had spread with the burden of childbearing. All the same, the woman was delicate and sprightly, and her smile warmed the hardened corners of Moira's heart.

"Mama, I want to tell you—" Josiah began, but his words were cut off by shouts of greeting from a band of strapping young men tearing down the same path Sheena had taken moments ago.

"Josiah! God save you! Welcome home!" the boys called in various tones from bass to tenor. The four of them made a matched set in descending heights, waving muscular arms as their long legs ate up the distance between the house and the wagon.

Moira stared wide-eyed at the brawny youths whose stature and physique mirrored their brother's. Ranging in age from about ten to eighteen, they wore homespun shirts and denim trousers, straw Stetsons, and suspenders. Each carried a whip exactly like Josiah's.

As they arrived at the wagon, they clapped their brother on the back while he ruffled their hair and gave them each a special greeting. Laughing and blurting out snippets of news, they were the merriest bunch of young strock'aras Moira had ever seen. She felt sure Josiah must have forgotten her altogether, but when she made a move to climb down from the wagon, he turned and caught her around the waist.

"Moira, I want you to meet my brothers," he said swinging her to the ground and keeping his arm tightly around her. "Oldest to youngest, there's Peter, John, Paul, and Mark. Each named for a saint—though you won't believe it when you get to know them."

"Pleased to meet you, I'm sure." She held out her hand to each of them and received in return a firm handshake. "And I'm Moira O'Cas—" Catching herself, she turned to Josiah.

"Mama . . . boys," he said, giving her a squeeze that almost pushed the breath right out of her chest, "I trust you'll welcome Moira Chee. We were married two weeks ago."

At the announcement, an explosion of whooping and cheers mingled with laughter surrounded Moira and Josiah as his brothers swarmed them. Having grown up with only one sister, Moira hardly knew what to make of the wild slapping and wrestling that was going on among the throng of husky boys. She was certain she'd be clobbered senseless in a moment, but then a hand on her arm pulled her out of the melee.

"Moira," Sheena Chee said, holding her at a distance but regarding her with eyes as warm and green as new leaves. "Welcome to our family."

The heat that started up in Moira's cheeks had nothing to do with the late evening sunshine. She felt ashamed. Ashamed and penitent. "Missus Chee, I—"

"Oh, you'll call me Sheena, so you will," the older woman admonished with a gentle smile. "And you must know that any woman bold and beautiful enough to win the heart of my Josiah must be special indeed. The good Lord saw fit to give me six fine sons, and I love them every one. But I'll be more than glad to welcome a lovely colleen into my home, if you'll have me."

What could Moira do but wrap her arms around the woman and hold her tight? Her own mother had never been so kind, so loving. Tears sprang to Moira's eyes, and she bit her lower lip to keep them back as she thought of all the abuse this gentle woman had taken at the hands of others.

"Now, look you, here comes my husband," Sheena said, giving Moira's hand a squeeze. "Sure he'll be in kinks at having lost his first son to marriage."

Moira stiffened as she peered around the woman's shoulder. Sure enough, down the path strode a man as tall and strong as any giant that ever walked through a storybook. Fear quaked Moira's heart at the sight of him. Now she understood where Josiah had gotten his height and weight, and the power of his build. But where the son's hair was light, the father's might have been spun from the blackest corner of midnight. Josiah's skin was a sun-burnished tan, but his father's flesh was a deep, natural bronze. Eyes dark and flashing above sharp, high cheekbones and a strong nose were trained on the knot of young men still laughing and joking by the wagon.

Oh, if this man was anything like Sheena's first husband, Innis's father, was rumored to have been, cruel and unrestrained in his wrath . . . Moira gulped at the sudden knot in her throat. Josiah's mother had as much as stated that her husband would be furious to find that his oldest son had married without his father's approval. What would he do to Josiah? And to Moira?

"José!" the man barked as he neared the wagon. "Is it you?"

"Papa?" Josiah emerged from among his brothers and stared at the man striding down the path. Then with a boyish leap, Josiah tore through the gate and hurled himself into his father's strong arms. Laughter rang down the valley as father and son slapped each other on the back and turned around in circles of joy.

"José, *hijo,* I thought you would die in those mines you were digging. And when the army sent a message that you were lying in the hospital at Fort Stanton with a bellyful of buckshot, again I was sure we had lost you. But you come back to us! See, your mother cries over you now. And who is this? The señorita you went to find for Innis Grady?"

Josiah's father was approaching with a scowl that sent the fear of God into Moira's stomach. All she could think about was the man's Apache blood and the warlike heritage of his ancestors. His black hair hung down to his shoulders, and he wore a band of twisted red cloth around his forehead. His great shoulders and chest filled his tan shirt to its seams. His long legs and thick thighs stretched the fabric of his britches, and he wore beaded leather moccasins.

"Papa," Josiah was saying as Moira considered how far she might get if she took off at a dead run, "I want you to meet my half brother's ward. This is Moira."

"Moira." Gabriel Chee studied her, his dark eyes unwavering. "The name is strange."

"Sure in the Irish tongue, Moira only means Mary," Sheena put in.

"Ah, María!" With a smile as wide and winning as you please, he grabbed her hand and pumped it three times. "Welcome to our house, our casita. You don't run away from here, María. If you do, we have five big boys to catch you!"

He laughed, and the others joined in, but all Moira could think about was the announcement Josiah still had to make. Even as she pondered it, she could hear him clear his throat.

"Papa, Moira was the one who took care of me at Innis Grady's house," he said.

"*Muy bien*! Thank you very much. And now we take care of you here at our house."

"Papa," Josiah cut in as his father grabbed Moira's arm and started toward the gate with her. "Papa, I want to tell you something."

Gabriel Chee swung around. "José, you water your horse. We talk later, *hijo*."

"No, Papa." Josiah walked toward his father. "I want to tell you now the news I have."

"*Sí*, tell your big news, my boy, and then we can get out of this heat."

"Moira and I . . . well, we got married back in Missouri," Josiah stated. "She's my wife."

There was a silence so long Moira thought she could hear her own heartbeat. Gabriel Chee's hand on her arm tightened until the blood stopped in her veins. So this was the moment she had been dreading. She shut her eyes, waiting for the explosion of anger.

"Married?" Gabriel demanded. "Without telling us?"

"We were far away in Missouri," Josiah returned.

"Well, then . . . we must have the fiesta *after* the wedding!" With a loud laugh, he jerked Moira nearly off her feet and turned her again to the path. "So my oldest boy follows in his papa's footsteps. A quick marriage! Come on, José, let your brothers tend the wagon, while you tell me the story of this surprise you made for your mama and me."

Moira felt smaller and more delicate than she ever had as she was escorted down the driveway between the brawny father and his massive son. They practically swung her up the steps onto the *portal*, and then swept her inside the cool, clean house.

"You left María's sister at a *convento*?" Gabriel asked with a laugh. "So—no more trouble from her!"

Josiah had to chuckle as he seated Moira in one of the chairs that flanked the beehive fireplace in the home's small parlor. He could see his mother eagerly listening to the tale, and he knew that she must be recalling her own swift and passionate union with his father. He settled on a wooden bench and stretched his legs out in front of him.

"Erinn will be happy," he said, "once she gets used to it."

"So you lock one sister up with the nuns," his father said, "and you marry the other, José? Is this the way I taught you to solve problems?"

Josiah laughed. "No, no, Papa. You don't understand. I married Moira because . . . because . . ." Suddenly he didn't know how to finish. Why *had* he married the pale, silent woman who sat across the room from him? Because he'd been wanting to bed her from the moment he laid eyes on her? Once, his raging desire had seemed like reason enough to take any measure necessary to accomplish his goal. He took off his hat and set it on his knee. "Well, I married Moira because . . . because . . ."

"Because you love her." Sheena Chee smiled like a gentle cherub. "It was so with your father and me. At first . . . oh, my, all we could think about was how crazy we were for each other. We met in Roswell, just by accident. The accidents that angels plan."

"I had gone to town to buy salve for my flock. The screwworms were bad that year. So many of my lambs were dying, and I felt very discouraged." Gabriel went to his wife's side and took her hands as they sat together on the bench. "Sheena was settling the estate of her first husband. There came a great hailstorm that day. Stones the size of peaches."

"I thought I could run across the street from the bank to the hotel." Sheena glanced at her husband, a flush of youth spreading across her cheeks. "It wasn't very far, really."

"Not far, but great rocks were coming down out of the sky. Still, she goes, lifting her skirts and dashing around the puddles."

"He was watching me from the porch of his grandfather's house, so he was. Señor Baca was the old man's name. Have you ever heard of him, Moira?"

She shook her head, mesmerized by the easy way this man and woman had with each other. Never in all her days had she seen a husband look at his wife with such tender affection. His dark eyes were soft with the memory they were spinning. His gaze lingered on her lips as she spoke.

"Señor Baca was a wonderful man. I had known Gabriel's grandfather from the days when my first husband was alive, though I'd never met Gabriel himself. Señora Baca was famous thereabouts for her tortillas. The hotel owner in Roswell bought them daily to serve to his customers, and people knocked on her door to buy fresh hot tortillas every time they were in town. Everyone called her Abuela, which means Grandma in Spanish. Sure Innis loved to eat those tortillas, so he did, though he won't admit to it now."

Gabriel Chee chuckled. "She talks about my *abuela*'s tortillas so I will forget to tell you the rest of the story— how Sheena ran out into the middle of the hailstorm and got her head broken by a great stone of ice. I watched her fall face down into a puddle. Her green dress flew halfway up her legs, and her parcels spilled across the mud."

"He remembers the color of my dress," Sheena noted with a proud smile.

"I rushed out into the hail and picked her up, but she didn't move even her eyes. I was afraid she was dead. Blood everywhere from the cut on her head."

"I didn't wake up for two days."

"We kept her at my *abuelo*'s house. There was no doctor in Roswell, then, and we decided she could not be moved. We sent a message to her boy, but of course it took long for the news to reach him and long for him to travel to her. In that time, while she lay in my grandmother's bed, I lost my heart to Sheena Grady."

"Gabriel was the kindest man I had ever met. So different from"—she glanced at Moira—"from other men I had known."

"At first Sheena thought my blood must be filled with war. My father was an Apache warrior, you know, María. Very brave. He fought at the side of Victorio, and he was killed in a battle with White Eye soldiers. But my mother was not of the Indeh. My father had captured her in a raid on a village in Mexico before the Bacas moved to Roswell. He had planned to keep her as a slave, as was the Apache way, but he fell in love with her instead. Oh, she was a beauty, Luz Baca. Her name means 'light.' "

"Gabriel's mother died not long after her husband was killed. Gabriel was very young, and so he was pulled back and forth between his two sets of grandparents like a shuttle on a loom. At first there was much anger and hatred between the Bacas and the Chees. Indians and Mexicans had been warring for many years. How could they hope to get along? But the little boy, Gabriel, he brought peace to the two families."

"Peace!" Josiah exclaimed with a laugh. "Papa, I always heard that you were such trouble neither family could control you, and *that's* why they sent you back and forth between them."

"Are you telling bad stories about your father to your new bride, José?" Gabriel gave Moira a wink. "Anyway, there was finally peace between my two families, and I learned much from both about the ways of the Mexicans and the ways of the Apaches. I took the best. From my Indian roots, I took my strength and cunning, my bravery—"

"Your stubbornness," Sheena cut in.

"*Sí*. How can I deny that? My Apache grandfather taught me to track and hunt and to live off the land during winter and harsh, dry summer. My Mexican grandfather taught me to love the sheep and care for them and their pastures. He taught me how to build a strong house and a fence that would keep the coyotes away. From him I learned to use the *látigo* and to fight the screwworm. But it was from both my families that I learned to respect and honor my wife."

"It was like a fever the way I felt for Gabriel," Sheena said, speaking to her husband more than to anyone else. "During those long years at Fianna, I had become nothing but a shell. I was so empty, so dry. Gabriel filled me with love and kindness. He made me want to *live*. I cared not a stim for what my Irish kinsmen thought of my actions. When Gabriel told me he wanted to make me his wife, I went to him without a second thought. And so we have been together twenty-four years now."

She beamed as she settled back against her husband's chest. Moira felt confused and lost. This was not the story she'd been told. Sheena Chee was nothing like the wanton strap everyone had portrayed her as. Certainly her husband was not the wicked half-breed savage gossiping tongues had made him out to be.

"And Innis?" Moira asked.

"Oh, Innis was furious," Sheena interrupted. "His father hadn't been dead a year, and suddenly I was married again without even telling him. Certainly without consulting him. Innis is not one to cross when he's angry. He's so like his father in that, drinking to blunt the rage, but heightening it instead. Innis will strike out before he thinks. He can be . . . cruel."

Moira saw the searching look in Sheena's eyes. *Has my oldest son ever hurt you?* she seemed to be asking. *Have you felt the harsh pain of his anger?*

"Innis is still angry that you remarried," Moira said boldly, habit making her defend her guardian. "He feels betrayed by you."

Sheena heaved a sigh that lifted her breasts and made her face grow soft. "Aye, so he does. Innis has nursed his anger for more than twenty years now, Moira. He can't forgive. He won't forget. He has become harder and more distant with each passing day. At first I tried to talk with him, tried to make peace. He was married himself for a time, and I did my best to win Deirdre's heart. But I believe Innis poisoned her against me until it seemed she quite despised me by the time she died, God rest her soul. I don't know why my grandson cares for me at all."

"Scully is more like you than he's like his father," Moira said without hesitation. "He's a gentle person, so he is. He doesn't have a cruel bone in his body. I don't believe Scully has the ability to hate."

Sheena smiled. "Then there's hope for us. Innis, I fear, will one day be destroyed by his own hatred and anger. I've given my oldest son to God, so I have, for it's impossible to win him back to my heart. Perhaps—if I were to give up my life as it is now—he would forgive me. But, Moira, you must understand that I won't do that. Not even for my firstborn. Why should I forsake a man who loves me with a depth I never dreamed possible? Why should I abandon five sons who aren't consumed with the black side of life? No, I'll go on as I have. I'll pray for Innis, but I'll trust his future to heaven. And I'll have faith that the love and peace in our family will flow out to other generations through Josiah, Peter, John, Paul, Mark . . . young Scully . . . and you, my daughter."

Moira gazed at the couple through mist-filled eyes and wondered if her own marriage could ever become as whole and fulfilling as this one. She could see Josiah seated across the room, his eyes on the distant mountains that rose beyond the window in a rolling purple border between earth and sky. Even now she felt a warm surge of desire for the man. But she wondered at the depth of their feelings for each other.

"So you've been truly happy all these years?" she asked Sheena, not quite able to accept the woman's avowals of contentment. "With your husband and sons . . . and your sheep?"

"Happy? Sure Gabriel and I have had a hundred thousand problems!" Sheena laughed.

"More," Gabriel added. "Shall I tell you how it goes? Her people hate me. Those Irish cannot see beyond their shamrocks and their whiskey. On the other hand, my father's people hate all White Eyes. As you know, Apaches have raided and killed until the earth is soaked with the blood of Germans, Spanish, English . . . and Irish. White Eyes hate Apaches, too. Geronimo and his warriors are hunted down, and those not murdered are rounded up like coyotes. Who can say which group started the hating?"

Moira wanted to respond, but she had no answers. She herself was caught in the endless cycle of prejudice and hatred passed on from father to son, mother to daughter.

"Mexicans hate Apaches, too," Gabriel Chee went on, "for taking their land and their women. Apaches hate

Mexicans for stealing their land and making war on them. Is that all? No! White Eyes hate White Eyes. They shoot each other. They steal land, cattle, horses, and women from each other. What is the answer, María? Do you have it?"

"No," she said honestly.

"My grandfather Baca told me a secret one day while we were guarding our flock in the Capitans. He said there is no peace, no joy, no love, except within a man's own family. If a person wants peace at all, he has to build it there . . . at home." Gabriel turned to his son. "You hear me? You understand what I'm saying, José?"

Drawn from his reverie, Josiah turned toward his father. "I hear you, Papa. I have plans for my future. Mine and Moira's. But peace seems a long way off."

There was a strained silence in the room before Sheena nudged her husband. "You should tell him, Gabriel. Tell him now, even on this day of celebration."

"No, Sheena. We'll plan a fiesta and make a few days of joy together, all our family, before we talk about such things."

Moira could see Josiah's back straighten, his hand go instinctively to the *látigo* at his side. "What is it?" he demanded. "I'm not a child to be protected from the truth, Papa. Tell me what's going on."

His golden brow furrowing, Gabriel Chee stood and went to the window that faced the mountains. "A letter came from Paddy Connor. Your partner writes that the lawmen in Butte are still searching for the one who shot you." He paused, then let out a breath. "But there is more. A man was in Roswell asking for you."

"What did he look like?" Josiah stood up. "Did he come out here? Did he bother you, Mama?"

"No, no." Sheena twisted her hands on her lap. "We don't know anything more. Maybe it's not important. Nathan Jaffa just happened to mention it one day while I was in his store. He told me a fellow had been around

Roswell the week before asking people if they knew of an Irishman named Josiah Chee."

"An *Irishman*?" Josiah stuffed his hat on his head. "That's him, then. The fellow who peppered me."

"How do you know?" Gabriel Chee demanded.

"Because it's the Irish in me he hates. His name's John Fisher, and he's a Cornishman."

"Ah, how could I forget those friendly Cornishmen?" Gabriel asked. "We have more to add to our list now, María. The Irish hate the Cornish, and the Cornish hate the Irish."

Moira knew his words were true. She had heard such tales at every Irish gathering. At the Comstock Lode in Nevada, it was said fully one-third of the miners were either Cornish or Irish. Their feuding began long ago, far across the Atlantic Ocean in their motherlands. At Cripple Creek the same story held true. Grass Valley was hardly different, though at one time the Irish and Cornish had united against mine owners. And in Butte, Montana, Moira had heard, the Irish totally dominated the miners' union.

"This man would shoot you only because you're Irish, Josiah?" Moira asked.

His face had grown impassive and cold, his brown eyes as hard as oak. "That and other things."

"What, then? Sure you haven't hurt him—you with only your whip about you."

Josiah had unleashed his *látigo* and now held it loosely but ready in his hand. "I'm riding for Roswell," he said, unwilling to answer her for fear that too much knowledge could only bring her harm. "Do you remember the packet of papers I gave you back at Fianna, Moira?"

"It's still in my saddlebag where I put it that night, so it is. Do you want it?"

"Keep it. If anything happens to me, those mines are yours."

"Josiah!" Alarm coursing through her, Moira jumped to her feet as he started for the door. "You won't be riding off at this late hour, will you, now?"

"I've got to talk to Nathan Jaffa. I'll be back."

"When?" she called, but he had already stepped out the door.

"Papa, look after Moira," he called from the yard. Moira ran to the door, but she'd already lost him.

She swung around to face his parents. Sheena was as white as one of Moira's newly laundered sheets. Gabriel had turned to the window, his expression stony. "Won't you go after him, Mister Chee?" she asked. "Sure he needs company if there's an enemy hunting him down!"

"My son is a man now. If he asks me, I go. If not, I stay here and guard my wife and sons." He turned to her. "This is a dangerous land, María. Here in our village we have faced many troubles. A few years ago, before the big war in Lincoln Town, the Horrell gang rode down the Berrendo Valley. They murdered a White Eye named Joe Haskins only because he had a Mexican wife. Later they killed five Mexican freighters on the road just west of Roswell. Even after that famous battle in Lincoln, our village continued to suffer at the hands of outlaw gangs who roam around looking for trouble. Once, the men who live on the Berrendo decided they had had enough. Their plan was to take revenge on the first Americano to come this way."

"It was Captain Joseph Lea," Sheena put in quietly. "He's the man who built Roswell into a respectable town. Such a peaceable, good person he is. He happened to be riding along the Berrendo Valley, and some of the men from our village stopped him. They were going to kill him, I think, but Gabriel put himself between the captain and the men. Gabriel stayed there, guarding the peace until Captain Lea had ridden safely away from the danger."

"We might have killed the man who has brought Roswell from a collection of five or six men to a town of more than four hundred people. Thanks to Captain Lea, we now have mercantiles, and we talk of building a courthouse and a jail. We make plans for irrigation that will give us richer farmlands and pasturelands. We hope for a railroad. We dream of the future. And yet we fear for our lives at the hands of our enemies."

"Gabriel is afraid to leave me alone," Sheena continued. "When he's out with the flocks, one of the boys stays with me here in the village. And when we move the sheep to higher ground in the summer, we all go together. Our family has a small cabin there, so we do, where it's safe for us."

At Fianna, Moira had never had to live in such fear, though she understood there was still some danger from Indians and outlaw gunmen who might pass through. Now her alarm for Josiah's safety swelled until it formed a painful knot in her stomach.

"I'll go after him," she said. "If you won't stand at his side, then I will."

"No." Gabriel Chee shook his head and pointed at the bench. "Sit down, María."

Moira was ready to argue when young Mark Chee strode into the room. "Peter and John have ridden to Roswell with Josiah," he announced. "They've left Paul and me in charge with Papa."

"There now," Sheena said to Moira. "These sons of mine are tighter than burrs on a wool sock. Sure Josiah will be fine, so he will. He's the best man with his whip, and Peter and John will be at his side if there's any trouble."

Moira reluctantly sank onto the bench. She felt trapped, and it made her angry. She hardly knew these people, and yet Josiah had abandoned her to them. What was she supposed to do while he was gone? And what would she do when—if—he returned?

"I should go to Fianna," she said suddenly. "Innis will be wondering what's become of me after all this time. He'll be needing my help in the house."

"Nonsense!" Sheena Chee chuckled as she rose. "Innis Grady can look after himself, so he can. You stay here

with us, Moira. We'll feed you well and give you a soft
bed at night. Until Josiah comes back you can spend your
days with me. We'll bake our boys some hot bread, and
we'll wash that mountain of dirty clothes that's been
growing since last laundry day. How does that sound to
you, my daughter?"

"Well enough," Moira said, unable to generate much
enthusiasm for chores she had formerly relished.

"Grand, then! And most important, you can help me
with my biggest job."

"What's that?"

"Caring for the sheep, of course!"

# Chapter
## 14

Moira decided that she had finally sunk to the lowest possible point in her whole life. Once she had been the proud manager of a fine Irish household with her own kitchen, laundry supplies, sewing basket, and thriving garden. But in a rash, misguided moment she had thrown it all away.

She had traveled hundreds of miles from home. She had wrongly helped her sister escape from a faithful husband, then abandoned her. She had married a man out of pure, heedless passion. She herself had been abandoned. And now she had been assigned to look after a flock of damnable woollies!

Early spring shearing was already complete on the Chee farm, and lambing was well under way. The morning after Moira's arrival, Gabriel and his sons set off to ride pasture and to check on the newborn lambs. Sheena and Moira were left to labor at home. If Moira had clung to a faint hope that she wouldn't actually have to work with any sheep herself, that notion was quickly demolished. After putting away the breakfast dishes, Josiah's mother led her out to the sheds.

"If a ewe has twins," Sheena told Moira, "sometimes she'll claim only one lamb. The other will be left to die if Gabriel can't find it. Our ewes lamb out on the range, you see, though when we had smaller flocks we could herd them into corrals and sheds for lambing."

"How many sheep do you have?" Moira asked as Sheena lifted the heavy wooden bar that held the shed door shut against predators.

"Oh, near onto a thousand, I'd say. It's hard to tell without fences, but of course we can't build any enclosures or we'd have a devil of a clamper with the cattlemen, so we would. Things are bad enough with them as it is." She pulled open the rough-hewn door and stepped into the square of sunlight that fell across the shed floor. "Gabriel and the boys herd the sheep nearest the house so they can come home in the evening, but we have some hired hands, too. They care for our sheep farther out toward the mountains. Then at shearing and lambing time, we put on many more men."

Moira followed Sheena into the dusky, hay-scented interior of the shed. When she felt a soft bump against her legs, she almost cried out with surprise. But as her eyes adjusted to the dim light, she saw a tiny, spindly-legged lamb gazing up at her with soulful, trusting brown eyes.

"Oh, my . . ." She instinctively bent to stroke the creature's head. When her fingers touched the soft white wool, the lamb bounded away, legs springing into the air as if they were connected to its body by only a loose thread.

Sheena laughed. "Sure sheep are about the slowest-brained animals on God's green earth, but they can be a pleasure, too—and they bring us a good living. Here now, we've a killeen of these little ones to feed, and full ewes waiting to be milked. Listen to them bleat!"

Amid a deafening cacophony of *baa-aaa*s, Moira was handed a milking stool and put to work emptying the udders of several ewes whose lambs had died but who would not accept abandoned lambs of other sheep. When they had filled a number of pails with warm, creamy milk, she and Sheena poured nippled bottles full of the nourishing liquid and set to work feeding the hungry lambs.

Moira knew she should protest that such labor was beneath a cattleman's daughter, but there was no time to argue. The lambs were ravenous, and Moira felt a sense of satisfaction spread through her as she watched them suckle the bottles dry. The lambs were really not so different from any other stock. A little smelly, so they were, and totally dependent, but essential to their owners' livelihood all the same.

In fact, Moira found herself almost enchanted with the bouncy white lambs, whose ears flopped as their long tails swung in crazy arcs. It was almost with regret that she joined Sheena at the door of the shed.

"They'll be marked soon," the older woman told Moira. "The men will cut off their tails, crop their ears, castrate, and brand them—the poor little dears. As soon as we can wean them, we'll set them out to pasture, so we will, and they can forage on the short grass and the weeds."

Bolstered by Sheena's openness, Moira couldn't refrain from asking the question that had been bothering her all morning. "How can you have fallen to working sheep? Sure your first husband was a bold cattleman, and he would turn over in his grave if he knew that you'd turned to herding flocks of woollies."

Sheena slipped her hands into her apron pockets as she walked toward her house. "A good woman supports the work of her husband, Moira, no matter what it is." A soft smile feathered the corners of her mouth. "I hear myself in your hostile words, so I do. When Gabriel and I first were wed, I wouldn't touch his sheep. I called them the devil's own flock, and I vowed I'd never lay a hand on them. But it wasn't long before I realized that if I wanted food on my table and clothes on my sons' backs, I had better put all that nonsense aside."

"Nonsense?"

"Most of what they say about sheep is pure blarney, Moira. Oh, sheep can destroy a bann, that much is true, if their shepherd lets them. They'll eat every blade of vegetation to its roots and leave nothing but barren dust behind them. But so will cattle, and indeed, they are doing just that right here in Lincoln County, if you'll look about you. Any creature will strip a patch of ground if that's all it has to eat. Sure it's not only the drought and the harsh winters that are killing the land, Moira. It's the men who own it. The range is a living thing. It must have the chance to breathe and come back to its health once the animals have grazed it."

"That's why you move your flocks after the lambing," Moira finished, remembering Josiah's words to her on the train. "You pasture them in the mountains during the summer and in the valleys during the winter."

"Ah, you'll make Josiah a fine wife, so you will!" Sheena put her arm around Moira's shoulders and gave her a squeeze. "Already you understand better than I did."

As they walked into the house, Moira was thinking about Fianna, about the cattle that had stripped the pasture bare, about the range that was dying. Her own father's legacy to her was dying, too. Innis Grady was seeing to that. She remembered Josiah's fevered dream. . . .

*In a strong marriage, the husband and wife both profit. And that's how it should be with the land. I've got to go back to that. . . . I'm going to rebuild the dream. That's why my life was spared. I'll make that marriage, and it's going to bear fruit. One day my fathers' lands— the Sacramentos, mountains of the Holy Sacrament—will be rich with fruit trees and fields of cotton and alfalfa. Sturdy cattle will cover the hillsides, and sheep heavy with wool . . .*

Suddenly everything he said made sense. And Moira began to want Josiah, her husband, with an ache that defied reason. As she walked into the house to continue the day's chores, she began to open her mind to his vision. She plunged her hands into a great bowl of white flour and saw Josiah's apple trees white with blossom. Kneading sticky dough in the wooden trough, she pictured mountain pastures dotted with cattle. Sliding greased pans of bread into the hot oven, she imagined a field thick with hay. She saw the hay cut and ripening on the steaming earth. She saw it baled and stored in huge airy barns. As she laid strips of dough to form a lattice across her cherry pies, she imagined orchards heavy with fruit—not only apples but cherries, peaches, and apricots as well.

As lunchtime neared, Moira found herself turning more and more often to the kitchen window. Where was Josiah? Was he safe? Sheena seemed at ease about her son's absence as she cut great hunks of mutton and peeled a killeen of potatoes for the stewpot.

Moira tried to calm herself. She filled a large tin pan with flour, formed a depression in its center, and poured it full of sourdough starter. She dissolved a teaspoon of soda in some lukewarm water and put it into the sourdough along with a little salt and lard. As she worked the loose flour into the central batter, she stared out the window at the deserted road.

"Shall I grease your oven, then?" Sheena asked from the stove where she was stirring the stew.

Moira glanced away from the window, startled by the sound of a human voice. It was almost as if she had drifted away from the kitchen and the dusty scene outside it. She had slipped into the kitchen of a stone home half buried on a gentle mountainside. Roses grew at the front door. Cattle and sheep grazed on the slopes. Blossoming orchards spread to one side of the house, and fields of alfalfa lay on the other. A bubbling brook flowed past a kitchen garden ripe with tomatoes, beans, peas, potatoes, squash, even lettuce.

"Moira? Do you want your oven greased, my girl?"

"What? Oh, thank you kindly." Embarrassed, Moira began to pinch off egg-sized hunks of dough and roll them into balls.

"You've slipped into the land of the shee, have you?" Sheena asked as she dropped a spoonful of bacon grease into the large Dutch oven that hung over the fire. "Are you at ease with your marriage to Josiah, Moira? You wedded quickly, and I gather from your speech and your actions that you're a strong, sensible woman unused to rash decisions."

Unwilling to respond immediately, Moira carried the balls of dough to the Dutch oven and began to place them inside, rolling each biscuit in the hot grease so it wouldn't stick while cooking. When she had set the oven on the hearth to give the biscuits a chance to rise, she finally brought herself to answer Sheena. "I'm happy with my marriage to Josiah," she said softly. "Your son is a good man, and I'm beginning to see hope for our future together."

"Then why do your eyes so often fill with tears as you stare out that window?"

Moira checked on her pies and bread, still unsure how to answer this blunt yet kindly woman. Finally she straightened and faced Sheena. "I'm worried about Josiah's safety. His wounds were bad . . . so bad he almost died of them. But in truth, it's not Josiah who makes me unhappy so much as it is everything else."

"Innis?"

"Aye, and Scully. The boy wants looking after. He's scattered, if you twig me. He fancies himself an artist, but Innis can't abide his paintings. Scully needs me there at Fianna. And though your eldest son is a grown man, he needs me, too. Sure he's hopeless with the housekeeping."

"Housekeeping!" Sheena laughed. "If Innis can't do better than to live like a hog in a wallow, I say let him, then. He'll soon learn to care for himself—or fetch another wife from Roswell."

"No one will have him. Or the other way round."
Moira gave Sheena's stew a stir. "Anyway, the most
important thing is that when Innis's wife was dying
after the stillbirth of her second child, God rest them
both, I gave her a promise. I swore to Deirdre that I'd
stay on at Fianna and care for Innis and Scully. Scully
has even toyed with the notion of marrying me!"

"Oh, for heaven's sake. Well, you're in a pickle, so
you are, and it's not my place to sort you out. But I
would think a woman's vows to her husband hold greater
power than any other."

"That's what Josiah said."

Sheena smiled broadly. "He's learned his lessons well,
that boy of mine. Come now, check your biscuits and
see if they've risen. We don't have much time before
our boys will be in from the pasture."

As Moira lifted the lid of the Dutch oven to gaze at
her puffy white biscuits, she slipped away to Fianna.
"Innis," she heard herself saying, "you're a grown man
who can look after himself. I'm a married woman now,
and my first loyalty's to my husband. More than that, I
love him, so I do. Yes . . . I love Josiah."

But Josiah didn't come home that day or the next.
Moira was fit to be tied, though Sheena and Gabriel
went about their chores with stoic faces and never openly
discussed the absence of their three sons. In the long
hours that passed, Moira found Sheena to be more than
a mother-in-law. She became a boon companion, a true
friend. Together they slipped into a comfortable routine,
feeding the lambs every two hours, then baking, cleaning, churning, washing, and mending.

But it was the spinning that gave Moira the greatest
pleasure. Oh, she loved the spinning!

"We'll spin this wool in the grease," Sheena announced
the third morning of Moira's stay after they'd come in
from feeding the lambs. "That means the fleece hasn't
been washed, so it still has all its lanolin. It'll be easier

for you to work with that way. And afterward we'll knit some fine, waterproof sweaters for our boys."

Moira wasn't sure how it had happened, but she'd come to think of Sheena's husband and sons as her boys, too. The picture of knitting warm, thick sweaters for them to wear in the pastures during the winter swelled and comforted her heavy heart.

"The centers are the cleanest parts of the fleeces," Sheena was saying as she unrolled three large rugs of shorn wool. "Now take up your cards. I always use number threes with their widely spaced teeth, for we've rough, coarse wool out here in the Territory."

Moira felt the sense of peace that spread from Sheena across the room as the two women placed wool on their cards and began stroking the wooden paddles back and forth to rid the fleece of dirt and burrs. The carding seemed to go on for hours, and Moira began to think she would fall asleep, so soothing was the task. Sheena taught her how to shake the wool from the cards, then roll it between her palms to form a long bundle of fibers that she called a rolag.

"Now you shall learn to spin, my young shepherd's wife," Sheena announced when they had carded a great mound of fleece between them. She took Moira to her spinning wheel and taught her all its secrets—the tightening of the tension screw, the clockwise turning of the wheel, the treadling.

At first Moira practiced without wool, but soon Sheena laid several rolags side by side on her student's lap. She showed Moira how to tie a leader of wool to the bobbin, pass it through the flier hooks, draw it through the orifice, and then push the wheel to start it spinning. Moira learned to treadle slowly, joining the leader to the rolag and then drawing out the fibers of wool as she spun. It seemed no time before the spindle began to fill with yarn.

"But it's all different thicknesses, and the twist goes tight and then loose again!" Moira declared on examining the disappointing results of her labor.

"Practice, my dear. You'll have the feel of it soon enough." Sheena was silent for a while as she churned, but finally she spoke her mind. "Carding and spinning are in your blood, Moira. You know as well as I do that the Irish on the old sod have been shepherds for centuries. It was only when our tribe came across the seas and here to the Territory that we began to shun sheep in favor of cattle. Our dislike of woollies is newly learned, and we would do well to remember the ways of our fathers."

"Aye, Sheena." Moira had to acknowledge that the older woman spoke the truth. When she bent back to her spinning, Moira felt herself again drifting away to that stone house in the mountains. Now there was not only an orchard outside and sheep and cattle on the hills, but inside there was a fine spinning wheel and a pair of number three cards and a great mound of white wool for spinning in the grease. And that wool would be knitted into sweaters—grand warm waterproof sweaters for Moira's own boys . . . Josiah . . . and the little ones to come.

Mark Chee had just bitten into one of Moira's fluffy sourdough biscuits at lunch that day when he leapt to his feet. Mouth full of biscuit, he could only point out the window in great excitement.

"It's the boys!" Paul filled in for his brother.

Moira was on her feet in an instant. Dashing across the room, she threw open the front door. Josiah? Where was he? Just as her heart jumped into her throat, she spotted his horse behind the other two. Seeing her, he lifted his hat and began to wave it, his face breaking into a warm smile.

"Moira!" he called.

Shedding all propriety, she flew across the yard, scattering chickens before her as she ran. "Josiah!"

He reined in his horse and swung down just as she slammed into him. "Whoa, now!" Catching her up in his arms, he held her tightly against his chest, crushing her breasts and leaving her feet dancing in midair.

"Oh, Josiah, I was so afraid that man had shot you again!" she blurted. "Every time I thought about you, I could only see you being carted up to the house at Fianna with your stomach all bandaged and bleeding, and all those horrid flies—"

"But I'm here now with you. No blood. No bandages." Surprised by her outpouring of emotion, Josiah couldn't make himself let go of her, even when he heard his parents and brothers talking in the distance about their adventures. He lowered her slowly to her feet as he relished the delicious feel of her body alive and warm against his. Looking into her blue eyes, he saw a change in them. They were deeper somehow, more alive with joy and passion.

"You won't go away again, will you, Josiah?" she pleaded. "Your mother and I—"

"Moira," he cut in, "I have to leave. There's no choice in it."

"When?" Alarm flickered like a blue flame in her eyes as her fingers dug into the sleeves of his shirt.

"Today. This afternoon."

"But why, Josiah?"

"It's that man, John Fisher. He's after me, Moira. He talked to Nathan Jaffa and several others in Roswell— Homer Clarkson, Neighbor Gayle, Pat Garrett."

"Pat Garrett!" Moira recognized the name of the former sheriff of Lincoln County, the man who had shot and killed Billy the Kid seven years before.

"Him and Sheriff John Poe, too. They both said Fisher had nosed around asking about me, the Irishman, Josiah Chee." He gave a low laugh, recalling the way Poe and Garrett had joshed him about that. In Roswell, Josiah was thought of as a Mexican—as Señor Baca's great-grandson, one of the Mexican clan along the Berrendo. Some of the boys in the village where he'd grown up had jeered at him, calling him El Indio—the

Indian. Of course in Butte he'd been lumped among the Irish, once the miners discovered his mother's heritage.

"Why would Fisher talk to Sheriff Poe?" Moira asked. "Josiah, are you in trouble with the law?"

"Not yet. But I may be when I finally track Fisher down and knock him butt over teakettle. Peter, John, and I followed his trail south along the Pecos. Sure enough, he stopped at one of the homesteads along the way. You know the Wilsons who ranch just north of Lake Van? They took him in and put him up for the night. Mister Wilson told me Fisher got drunk and started talking. Moira, he means to kill me if I don't stop him first."

"Oh, no!"

"That's why I've got to find him and settle this thing once and for all. The boys and I think he's headed for the Peñasco to talk to Innis. Sheriff Poe told him that was where I was the last time anyone heard of me."

"You're going to Fianna?" A flood of images poured through Moira's mind—Innis, Scully, loneliness. The thought of Josiah riding out alone was intolerable, especially with someone lying in wait to take his life. "Will Peter and John go with you?"

"They've already been away too long. Papa needs them here to ride pasture. Lambing is one of the most dangerous times, Moira. The problem's not only the coyotes that go after the lambs, or the lambs who get abandoned by their mothers. It's the screwworms. If those maggots get ahold of our little lambs and no one's there with smear . . ."

Moira shut her eyes. She knew what screwworms could do to a calf. Sheena had shown her the devastation they wreaked on newborn lambs whose navels were vulnerable to the flies that laid their eggs in any open wound. Screwworm flies were a shepherd's greatest pestilence, for their maggots fed on living flesh, bloating the bellies of lambs and killing them if left untreated. The only hope a rancher had against the infestation was constant vigilance and immediate treatment with a medicating smear. Losses from screwworms were often greater than losses from predators.

"Your brothers can't leave the pasture," Moira said, "but I can. I'll go with you, Josiah."

"No. I want you to stay here with my family. Papa and the boys will protect you, and you can help Mama. She's never had another woman around, and I'm sure the company will do you both some good."

Moira glanced at the little copper-haired woman whose sons towered over her while they related the adventures of their journey. "Sheena would tell me to go with you," Moira said, turning back to Josiah. "Your mother believes that a woman's place is at her husband's side."

Josiah didn't know whether to laugh or get mad. Moira was right, of course, but he hadn't expected the two women he cared about most to conspire against him. "Moira, I can't let you come with me. Fisher could be anywhere on the trail. He knows me by sight, and he'll shoot before he'll say howdy. It's too dangerous. I'll feel better knowing you're safe and sound."

"And is your contentment all that matters?" Moira crossed her arms and set her jaw.

"Well, no, but—"

"Sure I've been in kinks of worry over you these last three days since you rode away. If you go to Fianna you'll be gone at least two or three weeks, more likely a month. Will you have me stay here and turn into an old lady with wrinkles and white hair from worrying that Fisher's shot you full of holes again?"

Josiah considered the intensity of her words. Did Moira really care about him so deeply? Somehow he hadn't expected it. He had formed the definite idea that Moira was more interested in the way he touched her body than in being his partner in life.

"Besides," she said suddenly, cutting into his thoughts, "Innis needs me at Fianna. I told you that a long time ago. I should be getting back to check on him."

She studied Josiah's face and wondered if her argument would sway him. She was edging over into untruth, of course, for Innis Grady no longer had any hold on her loyalty. In fact, she had been regularly practicing her speech to him—the one about duty to a husband being more binding than an oath made in childhood. But Josiah didn't look the least bit happy. The moment she had mentioned Innis's name, his face had grown hard, and his eyes had darkened to a depthless brown.

"And," she went on, "I must check to see if a letter has come from Erinn. She'll have posted it to Fianna, of course, and I need to know how she's getting on, or if I should send for her."

Josiah shoved his hands into his pockets as he watched Moira's bright blue eyes sparking fire. He should have known it wasn't *him* she was interested in. She didn't want to ride with him because she feared for his life or because she wanted to spend time with him. It was misguided loyalty to Innis Grady that drew her. Innis and that damned Fianna. Oh, and Erinn. Moira would put her sister's happiness over anyone else's.

"Not only that," she added, "there's Scully. The poor boy might be starving to death if all he's had to eat is Innis's cooking. Scully is such a dear, and I simply must check up on him, Josiah. I'll have to go with you. There's no arguing to it."

"I guess not," he said, brushing past her on his way to the house. So Innis, Scully, and Erinn still held top place in Moira's heart. Josiah fumed over the turn of things as he climbed onto the *portal* and went into the parlor. Hadn't he followed her to Las Vegas and then protected her and her sister all the way to St. Louis? Hadn't he taken care of her all the way back to the Territory again? Maybe he'd given her the fire of his touch and the promise of a future. But obviously that wasn't enough for Moira.

What more was there? If a man couldn't win a woman's heart by offering her his protection, his fortune, and his bed, how *could* he win her? There was nothing else . . . was there?

"So you've come back to us mad enough to eat the devil with his horns on," Sheena commented as Josiah stomped into the kitchen, where she was washing the lunch dishes. "Anyone would think I'd raised you on sour milk, so they would."

Josiah grabbed a cold biscuit and tore off a hunk. He tried to chew it, but his mouth was so dry and full of bile he could hardly swallow. "If it isn't one thing it's another," he said finally.

"So you're fretting over this fellow who means to kill you. Do you think he can do the job?"

"Not if I have my say in the matter."

"That's good news." She scrubbed the stewpot for a while. "Well, then, something else must be troubling you. Some matter you *don't* have a say in. Perhaps it's your young Moira. . . . That lovely colleen was so happy to see you she fairly floated across the yard and threw herself into your arms. Is she somehow the cause of this black mood, then?"

Josiah studied the scene outside the kitchen window while he chewed on the biscuit. He could see Moira talking to Peter while he unsaddled Josiah's horse. She was stroking the stallion's neck, and it made him think of the way she had touched his body not long ago. My, but she was a sight in her soft green dress, the hem dancing around her ankles and the sleeves puffing out in the breeze. At something Peter said, she tossed back her head and gave a laugh that tinkled across the yard. Her auburn hair was fiery in the waning afternoon light, and the need to touch it became a palpable ache in Josiah's chest.

"It's Moira," he snapped. "I don't know what the woman wants. A few minutes ago she started out saying she wanted to travel with me to Fianna because she was worried about me. When I refused, she came out with all the *real* reasons she wanted to go: Innis needs her;

Erinn might have sent a letter saying *she* needs her; poor young Scully needs her."

"But it's *you* who need her, is it?" Sheena asked.

"I don't need her! I'm no suckling lamb who'll die without constant attention. I've lived on my own for years now. No, I don't need Moira."

"Yet you want her to need you."

"Well, she *is* my wife. She does need me whether she knows it or not. She needs my protection, and she needs me to provide for her. I'm good to her," he said, turning on his mother, "as good as Papa is to you. But she doesn't treat me the way you treat Papa. She's not loyal to me. I'm not everything to her. As soon as Innis, Scully, and Erinn cross her mind, off she goes to look after them. I don't know what more I can give the woman!"

Sheena studied her reflection in the white enamel plate she was washing. Josiah wished she would hurry up and give him the answer. He was sure she knew what he was doing wrong. His mother was a wise woman. She would know about this sort of thing.

Finally she set the plate in the rinse water and turned to him. "What has your papa given me, Josiah, that you haven't yet given to Moira?"

*Don't ask me questions*, he wanted to shout. *Tell me the answer*! But she wouldn't, of course. His mother was sage enough to let her boys figure out answers on their own.

"I married her," he said. "So I gave her that. I protected her. I've been kind to her, good to her. I've treated her the way a woman should be treated by a man. I've been gentle. I reckon the only thing I haven't done yet that Papa did for you is give her a house to live in."

Sheena's face fell, but Josiah hardly noticed. Elation welled up inside him. That was it! The answer he'd been searching for. The way to win Moira's heart was to stake a claim on some land and start building her a house.

The more he thought about it, the more certain he

became that he was right. Hadn't Moira told him all along that all she'd ever wanted was a home of her own? She wanted a kitchen, a stove, a washtub, a garden, a churn, a laundry line stretched between two trees. She wanted a man to look after, and maybe children, too. By heaven, he could take care of that!

"All right," he announced, "if a house is what she wants, a house is what she'll get. I'll take her to Fianna with me, and when I've settled things with John Fisher, I'll head up the Peñasco to start building her a home."

"So you think that's what Moira wants from you, then, Josiah?" Sheena asked, wiping a soft cotton towel over a damp bowl. "A house."

He could hear a note of doubt in his mother's voice, and he didn't like it one bit. Surely she didn't think there was something else Moira could want from him. He didn't have anything else to give.

"A house," he repeated. "She's been telling me that from the day we met. It's all she's ever wanted in life. A home of her own."

"A home of her own. Protection. Food on the table. Tenderness in the night. What more could a woman want from her husband?"

"Right." Josiah finished the last of the biscuit and waited for some kind of confirmation. But his mother merely took up a stack of plates and headed for the cupboard. "I'll be going, then," he said as he headed for the door. "I'll be taking Moira with me, and I'll build her a house."

"Let us hear from you now and again," Sheena said.

Vaguely unsatisfied, Josiah stepped out into the open air and started walking toward Moira. Behind him he could hear his mother begin to sing. At first he couldn't place the tune. But then, automatically, he began to murmur the words along with her:

*Grant, Lord, that with thy direction,*
*"Love each other," we comply,*
*Aiming with unfeigned affection*
*Thy love to exemplify.*
*Let our mutual love be glowing.*
*Thus will all men plainly see*
*That we, as on one stem growing,*
*living branches are in Thee.*

# Chapter
## 15

**M**oira could hardly believe Josiah was going to take her to Fianna. Part of her wanted to rejoice. Now they would be together all those days on the trail, and then again at Innis's house. She could help him keep watch for his enemy along the way. It was as though he was accepting her, finally, as a part of his daily life, for better or for worse.

But part of her worried about his intentions. She'd named Innis and Scully as the reasons to let her travel with him, and he'd gone along with it. What if he planned to deposit her with Innis and go off hunting for this John Fisher devil? How could she bear to stay under Innis's roof again after she'd been with Josiah as his wife? In Sheena's home Moira had had her first taste of what a real family could be like, sharing warmth, tenderness, loyalty, love. She ached to build such a family with Josiah. But would they have the chance?

As they set out on the trail that evening, planning to spend their first night in Roswell, Moira wished she felt comfortable enough to confront her husband head-on. From her seat in the wagon, she watched his broad back as he rode his horse just ahead of her down the twilit trail. The sight of his squared shoulders and thick blond hair beneath his hat stirred tiny sparks in the pit of her stomach. But was this physical yearning enough to bind them forever?

Moira knew she was beginning to want far more from Josiah than his warm flesh and magic fingers. She wanted his heart. But how could she win it? Was a marriage based on heated desire any stronger or more binding than an arranged marriage like Erinn's? Moira longed for the sort of union she had seen between Gabriel and Sheena Chee, one built on true love. She was equally aware that the Chees' was the only such marriage she had ever witnessed. As a result, she had very little idea how to build one for herself.

So far, the only thing that had kept Josiah nearby was her merest mention of Innis, Scully, or Erinn. She decided he somehow understood her concern for those she felt responsible for, and he always gave in to her. He had helped her take Erinn all the way to St. Louis, hadn't he? Now he was taking her to check up on Innis and Scully.

Perhaps he admired the fact that she concerned herself with other people's needs. Sheena certainly took care of her own precious family, and Moira knew how highly Josiah regarded his mother. Maybe his love for his wife would finally be complete if, like Sheena, she kept a constant vigil over the needs of others.

When they stopped at the hotel in Roswell, Moira asked the owner for a tub and two buckets of boiling water to be carried to their room. As she made the request, she saw the pleasure spread across Josiah's face and light the depths of his brown eyes. But when they got into the room, she began to pull all his dusty clothes, along with a bar of lye soap, from his saddle-bags. He sank down on the edge of the bed and scowled at her.

"What are you doing, Moira?" he demanded.

"The laundry, of course. Washing clothes is the work of a caring and faithful wife, which is what I am. You just got back from a three-day journey across the dusty plains, and now you've set off again without even a good hot meal or a chance to wash yourself. I'm going to launder your shirts and britches and pin them on a line across the open window. They'll dry. You'll see!"

"Laundry?"

His voice sounded grumpier than she would have expected, considering that she was doing his washing to please him and make him love her. She rolled up her sleeves and knelt beside the steaming water.

"After all, it's the least I can do for you, Josiah," she said in her softest voice. "You've been so good to me, helping me with my dear sister, Erinn, and now taking me to Fianna so I can look in on poor old Innis and my little sheela, Scully."

As she fumbled with the buckle on his saddlebag, she could see him rise from the bed and start pacing the tiny room. He didn't look the least bit happy or loving.

"One day I should like to cook you up a great pot of mutton stew, so I would," she went on. "Your mother taught me how to cook it, so she did. And she taught me to card wool and spin it. I've gotten ever so good at spinning, Josiah."

"Hmmph." From across the room, Josiah could see Moira pulling out his dirty shirts and sorting through them. First she turned them right side out by plunging her arm down one dusty sleeve and grabbing the soiled cuff. Next she smoothed each sweat-stained collar and turned it this way and that, checking for worn places she might need to mend.

It fairly turned his heart over to see her taking such care with his clothes. But he wanted some of her tenderness for himself.

"You'll be so surprised to learn that I don't hate sheep anymore," she was saying as she pulled a pair of britches from his saddlebag and settled them on the floor in a puff of alkaline dust. "I fed those adorable little lambs, and I even learned how to put the screwworm smear on their bellies. I milked your mother's ewes. I ate mutton stew. I spun wool in the grease, so I did, and it was a joy."

She turned to him with eyes as bright and blue as a summer sky, and his knees suddenly had the consistency of grits. "I've brought the skein of yarn I spun along with me," she continued, "and I'm going to begin knitting you a sweater. It'll be waterproof in the rain and so warm in winter that you'll melt like a tallow candle! You can wear it when you ride out to pasture and look after the sheep . . . our sheep."

Josiah could hardly believe what he was hearing. This was the chance he'd been waiting for. Now he could tell her what he was going to do to win her over. "Moira, I'm going to build you a house of your own," he said, crossing the room to hunker down at her side by the washtub. "Plan out the house exactly the way you want it, Moira. I'll build you a parlor. A loft, too. I'll put in a wood floor. Pine. And I'll plane it so flat you can skate on it. I'll buy glass panes for the windows. You can have your own kitchen, too. I'll buy you a brand-new stove . . . with a teakettle warmer."

"Oh, Josiah!" She flung her arms around his neck. Her strategy had worked! If he intended to build her a home, then surely he must love her, and it wouldn't be long before he would say those words she ached to hear. "Oh, I'll wash every shirt you own every day if it makes you happy. I'll bake pies and cakes for you. I'll churn your butter—"

"I'm churning right now," he whispered, sliding her up onto his lap. "Ever since I laid eyes on you again, Moira, I've been feeling all whipped up inside with wanting to touch you and hold you."

His mouth found hers, and their tongues collided in a warm thrust of bold passion. Sliding his hands into her hair, he moved his lips across her cheek and down her neck until she could hardly breathe. Beneath her bottom she could feel the evidence of his arousal, hard and already demanding satisfaction. He cupped her breasts in his palms, and a low groan rumbled deep in his chest.

As he tipped her nipples into firm, sensitive beads, she felt a delicious liquid warmth begin to throb. "I'm feeling a bit like a pat of melting butter myself, so I am," she whispered.

Chuckling, he began to unbutton his own shirt. "I'm getting into that hot water, Missus Chee. I need washing a lot worse than those britches of mine. Care to join me?"

"You could do with a bit of soap, Mister Chee. You're as dusty as an old tumbleweed." She feasted her eyes on his chest as he stripped off his shirt and started to work at the buttons of his britches. Never had the good Lord created such a chest on a man, with muscles that swelled over a massive frame and skin that was stretched as sleek and tight as saddle leather. Bending, she brushed her lips across the flat circles of his nipples, then used her tongue to dampen and heat them.

By the time he slipped her off his lap and pulled down his jeans, he was standing at full attention. Suppressing a gasp at the sight of his bold member, she watched him step into the steaming tub and slide down until only his head, chest, knees, and ready arousal emerged from the water.

"Oh, my," she murmured, almost in shock.

"Are you planning to get in—or just stand there staring at me, woman?"

Flushing as bright red as the velvet curtain in the room, Moira clapped her hands on her cheeks. Josiah laughed and flicked a handful of water at her. She gave a little squeak and jumped backward. "I—I don't think there's room for me in there," she managed.

"Is there room for me in *there*?" he asked, giving her skirt a little tug to pull her near, then sliding one hand up her leg.

Josiah hadn't known a woman could blush quite as crimson as a tomato, but Moira was giving it a good effort. Was she actually shy after all they had done together? He glanced down at himself, and felt a swell of cocky male pride. But his grand arousal wasn't something that should make Moira flush like a spinster, was it? How many times had she held and fondled him? How many times had he slipped inside her to feel the velvet stroking of her sweet body?

"Oh, my," she said again as her hands slipped up to cover her eyes, and she stood as rigid as if she were made of stone.

"Moira?" Confused, Josiah stood and stepped out of the tub, dripping like summer rain on the floor. "Moira, what's wrong, darlin'? You aren't afraid of me, are you? Not after all those nights on the train."

"The train . . . was dark."

Josiah shook his head, trying to hold back a chuckle. The curtained hotel room had been almost dark, too. So this was his wife's first sight of her naked husband—and he'd scared her half to death.

"Now see here," he said gently, taking her arm and pulling her toward him. "I'm wet enough to drown a duck, and I mean to give you a hug for thinking of washing all that laundry for me. If you don't want to get wet, too, you'd better let me help you out of these things."

With her eyes shut tight, Moira shivered as she felt his damp fingers against her neck. He worked open the buttons of her dress until it blossomed out with the release of her breasts. In moments she sensed her dress slip to her feet, and then he unclasped the hooks of her corset.

"Your sweet kissing is what swelled me right out of my britches," he whispered against her ear as he dropped the corset to the floor and slid his hands up under her camisole. "It's all your doing, don't you know? We were just sitting there talking about dirty laundry and such, and the next thing I knew, you were kissing my chest and running your tongue over my skin. Didn't you do that, Moira?"

She nodded, lost in the rapture of his hands grazing the tips of her nipples. "I couldn't help it."

"And I couldn't help what happened to me. It's the natural thing between a man and his wife."

*His wife.* Moira felt nothing like her image of a wife—dutiful, obedient, subservient. With Josiah's fingers tearing her camisole over her head and sliding her small-clothes to the floor, she felt like the wildest, freest animal of a woman who ever lived. She ran her fingers down his skin and allowed herself to look, finally, at his magnificent body.

"You *are* a grand whacker of a man," she acknowledged with frank admiration.

He laughed out loud. "And you're a bold, beautiful colleen."

He bent to kiss her breasts into sweet, throbbing peaks of arousal. Before she could catch her breath, they were in the tub, she straddling her great stallion and he kissing her until she was dancing with the need for release.

Clutching her milky bottom, he raised and lowered her atop him, all the while nipping her breasts as they swung past his face. Blue eyes locked on brown as she rode him, auburn hair atumble around her shoulders. The water in their little tub sloshed and lapped onto the floor until there was almost none left to cover them.

Just as she felt her mounted stud rear up inside her and begin to thrust with the ecstasy of his release, her own body began to shudder in sweet, undulating waves. She sank onto him, burying her mouth in his neck as she convulsed and gasped and cried aloud.

They lay curled together, she in his arms in the empty washtub. She sighed and nestled her cheek against his shoulder.

"I'll build you a hundred homes, Moira," he whispered. "A hundred thousand homes, if it will make you want me."

She smiled. "Ah, Josiah, don't you know? I'm home already."

Moira had never thought a dusty trail could feel as pleasant and comfortable as a house with four walls, a fireplace, and a good strong door. But as she and Josiah traveled by wagon from Roswell down the Pecos River to its junction with the Peñasco, she began to realize that a home wasn't so much a place as it was a person—a beloved person in whose embrace she could finally find rest, peace, security. Now she knew without a doubt that she truly loved Josiah Chee.

Oh, it might have been pure, unbridled passion that had drawn her to him at first. But now she knew the man—the whole man, every side of him both good and bad, tired and fresh, angry and joyful, sullen and lighthearted, worried and at ease. She knew him sleeping and awake. She knew him dripping with sweat and clean as rainwater. She knew him alert and distracted. She certainly knew his body, every angle, plane, and hollow of it. And she loved him. Oh, how she loved him!

But she couldn't bring herself to tell Josiah how she felt, not when he never acknowledged his own love for her. She had to admit the possibility that he didn't love her at all. Not once in all their days of travel did he mention how he felt toward her. He just talked about what a grand house he was going to build. The house, the house, the house!

So Moira resorted to the only thing she could think of to try to woo him into speaking words of affection— she took care of him. She not only washed his clothes in the Pecos but she also drew on her culinary skills to prepare meals fit for a king. After all, Josiah was the lord and ruler of her heart.

In Roswell they had purchased supplies for their journey, so Moira was able to bake her soft, fluffy sourdough biscuits in a Dutch oven. She boiled aromatic Arbuckle's coffee over the fire. And she cooked a variety of succulent dishes using the slab of dried mutton Sheena and Gabriel had sent with them.

Moira dredged mutton steaks in flour and fried them in hot lard. She added flour, salt, and water to the bubbling steak fat to produce the thick gravy Josiah called sop. Beans boiled with bacon joined steaming rice in a meal that warmed both Josiah's stomach and his heart.

One evening Moira baked up mutton and dumplings—hunks of meat with snippets of biscuit dough dropped into the sizzling pot to swim in the rich gravy. Another night she crafted a wonderful stew of mutton, canned tomatoes and corn, and wild onions she pulled from the riverbank.

When Josiah caught a mess of fish in the Pecos, she dressed and fried them to make a mouth-watering dinner. When he found a turkey's nest, they enjoyed a feast of scrambled eggs and flapjacks. Potatoes, of course, were part of every meal Moira cooked. No good Irishwoman would think of serving her man without them.

For dessert, Moira drizzled sorghum syrup over a mixture of dried peaches, apples, and apricots. She made bread pudding by soaking leftover biscuits in warm water and adding raisins and sugar. This mixture she beat back into dough, then poured it into the Dutch oven and baked it to a golden brown. One evening she gathered enough blackberries to make a pie, and Josiah declared it the best he'd ever eaten.

These were halcyon days—hot at noontime but cool by evening. Usually they rode together in the wagon, but sometimes Josiah took one of the horses and scouted ahead. One evening while she was cooking, Moira heard the crack of a pistol, and she ran to the riverbank—only to find Josiah practicing with his whip. She watched in amazement as he deftly flicked the swelling green buds from the tips of a prickly-pear cactus. He set up a row of empty cans on a rock ledge and, like a puncher with a six-shooter, knocked all of them off in rapid succession.

When the clatter stirred the ire of a nearby rattle-snake, Josiah whirled and whipped the buzztail to a quick oblivion. Moira was still holding her breath when the end of the *látigo* gently wrapped itself around her waist three times. How such a deadly weapon could suddenly turn sensual she never quite understood, but it hardly mattered. Josiah pulled her into his arms, and when his mouth covered hers, all peril vanished save the thrilling danger of his fiery touch.

At Josiah's insistence, Moira used the long hours in the wagon to plan the house of her dreams. There would be a central room built of smooth round river stones. A fine fireplace with a mantel would warm the area in which they would place both the dining table and the settee. On either side of the main room would nestle rooms of adobe brick—thick-walled and heated with corner beehive fireplaces. Attached to the back by a dogtrot, the kitchen would run the full width of the house. It would be a grand room with a stove and a fireplace, a long kitchen table, cupboards galore, and windows on every side.

Talking about the house took up a good bit of their traveling time, since neither was willing to raise other deeper issues. Moira didn't even want to think about Innis and his reaction to the announcement that she had married Josiah. For his own part, Josiah couldn't bring himself to discuss with Moira his plans for their future.

He felt pretty sure she wouldn't be happy if she found out he'd spent part of his time in Roswell studying survey maps and filing claims on two homestead sites along the Peñasco River, one in her name and one in his. Across the river, the claim faced the land Moira had inherited from her father, and if she was willing to add her acreage to this new land, it would give them the largest ranch in the area. There would be more than enough room for sheep, cattle, orchards, alfalfa, and maybe, at the lower elevations, even cotton.

But Josiah had no doubt that Moira would be reluctant to reclaim her legacy from Innis Grady, to whom she had entrusted it for thirteen years. She felt guilty enough that she had disobeyed her guardian by marrying without his consent. To take away land Innis had considered his own for more than a decade would be unthinkable to Moira. She would be equally unhappy to learn that Josiah's claim included a stretch of the stream that Innis had been freely drawing from, even though he didn't own the rights. Now that section of the river belonged to Josiah, and he intended to keep it the way a river ought to be kept—free of brush and weeds, shaded here and there by cottonwoods, and used sparingly for irrigation. He had planned to build Moira a home of her own there.

As Josiah drove the wagon up the Peñasco toward his half brother's land, he thought of all the things he hadn't told the woman sitting at his side. She knew almost nothing about her husband's life in Butte, Montana. Nor was she aware that John Fisher, the man who threatened to kill Josiah, would not let the presence of a woman stop him from exacting his revenge. Though she was blissfully ignorant of the danger she might face should her husband be unable to protect her, Moira's life was in peril. Torn between wanting to keep her near and knowing she would be safer with Sheena and Gabriel or even with Innis, Josiah guarded her night and day.

As brave a man as he was, Josiah found himself shunning every notion of talking over these issues with Moira. She was a woman who valued peace and stability, and she would be unhappy over the uncertainty of a future as the wife of a hunted man. More significant, she never intentionally hurt anyone, and Josiah was concerned that she might reject him if she knew he wanted her to take her legacy away from Innis. He didn't want that. He couldn't stand the thought of losing her just when they were beginning to build something that might last.

The fear of losing Moira also kept him from telling her the biggest secret inside him: he loved her. He didn't love her the way a headstrong boy loves a pretty young gal. It went way beyond wanting to hold her sweet body, though he couldn't deny that was part of it. No, the way Josiah felt about Moira was so deep and so fierce it went beyond words. He would do anything for her. He'd be anything. He'd go anywhere. He would lay down his life for her. And if that kind of love scared the hell out of him, he figured, think what it would do to her!

So he flicked the reins and drove the wagon up through the gate of Innis Grady's homesite. Would there ever be a day, he wondered, when he could relax in his love for Moira? He glanced at her beside him and saw the tension in her face. She was so complicated—her loyalties spread around among all the many people she cared about, and her caring nature keeping her abustle over the daily tasks of life. If he could just come right out and spill the beans, if he could just tell her he loved her and that he would do anything to make their marriage the best it could be, maybe things would work out. Maybe all those secrets he'd been keeping could finally be told. Maybe she wouldn't run off after all.

"Moira," he began. At the thought of what he was about to say, his palms went wet on the reins. He swallowed, and he could feel his Adam's apple travel the entire length of his throat. He took off his hat and raked one hand through his hair before setting it back on his head. "Moira, we're almost to the house, now, and there's something I'd like to talk over with you."

"Aye," she said, turning to him with a rush of breath. "I'm sure you've been thinking about Innis, as I have. I want to tell you that I don't think we should let on to Innis about the marriage we made. I've been stewing on it for days now, and I'm certain he won't like the notion a bit."

Josiah closed his mouth and stared at her. Her blue eyes almost overflowing with tears, she gave him a tremulous smile. "Innis is a civil man," she said without much conviction, "but you saw how he gets when he's angry. And I'm certain he'll be angry as a hornet if he ever finds out what I've done. Sure he would accuse you of wanting to steal my father's legacy from him, even though I know you would never do such a thing. Would you?"

Blank-faced, Josiah shook his head. He mentally lopped off the extra acreage he had hoped for. While he was readjusting his dream, Moira continued talking.

"Innis would go quite insane with rage if he thought the house we've been talking about would be built along the Peñasco somewhere—especially anywhere near Fianna. You don't intend to build on the Peñasco . . . do you?"

"Are you scared of Innis Grady, Moira?" he demanded, turning to face her. "Is that why you don't want to tell him about us?"

"He'll kill you, Josiah," she answered with quiet conviction. "He owns enough pistols and rifles to arm Fort Stanton. He drinks so much he could drain the Pecos every day of his life. And when he's drunk he's as strong and wicked as the devil, so he is. I know he's your own blood kin, but he won't let that stop him."

"I would never let him hurt you, Moira. You know that."

"I'm not worried about myself! Sure I've lived with the sherral thirteen long years. I've survived his rages and his beatings. It's you I fear for. Josiah, you must believe me. Innis *will* kill you if he finds out you've married me."

"He would kill me for marrying his ward?"

"It's not the loss of me he'd be angry about. It's the *land*, do you twig me? All Innis has ever had is his land and his cattle. His wife died, and his son has turned out to be a sweet sheela who wants to paint pictures more than he wants to ride the range. Innis has put his whole life into his cattle, so he has. If you threaten that, Josiah, he'll destroy you."

Josiah frowned at the sight of the crumbling adobe house with its withered flower beds and dry yard. Did Moira think so little of him as a man that she honestly believed Innis Grady could kill him? Didn't she know he could defend himself?

"There's Scully!" she whispered, and grabbed Josiah's arm. "Oh, promise me, promise me now! Swear you won't tell Innis about us. We'll stay here just long enough to learn about John Fisher and then we can leave. But promise me you'll not mention our marriage!"

Josiah turned to her. The tears that had been threatening had spilled down her cheeks and were dropping onto her bosom. "All right," he said. "It's against my will, though. You're my wife in God's eyes, and I don't hold my half brother in nearly as high regard. I'm not afraid of Innis, and I'd never let him harm you. I'll keep our marriage a secret for now, but one day, Moira, he'll have to find out about us."

"One day. After we've gone safely away from him." Blowing her nose in a white handkerchief, she gave a great sniffle of anguish. It was all Josiah could do to keep from putting his arm around her and drawing her into the haven of his strength. But in the distance Scully was shouting and waving with excitement, his red head bobbing up and down like a scrawny chicken's.

"Moira! God save you, Moira! Papa, it's Moira and Josiah! They've come back, so they have!"

Josiah reined in the horses and set the wagon brake. Moira was on her feet in an instant and jumping down into Scully's arms. "God save you kindly, dear Scully," she said, giving him a quick peck on the cheek.

"About time you stopped your roving about, you wicked whipster!" Innis roared as he stalked out of the house toward the wagon. "What have you done with your sister? Stashed her with the nuns? Don't you know she's a married woman?"

"We know Erinn's living at a convent in Missouri," Scully confided, as Moira stepped quickly behind Josiah for protection against the steaming locomotive headed her way. "Last week the mail hack brought a letter from her. I had to grab it from Papa and hide it in my studio to keep him from tearing into it."

"A letter from Erinn!" Moira cried.

"And *you*!" Innis stopped in front of Josiah. He was all a picture in red—flaming hair, crimson nose, bloodshot eyes, union underwear beneath his suspenders. "What are you doing on my land?"

Behind him, Moira could feel Josiah's tension. His shoulders squared, he rested his hand lightly on the butt of his blacksnake. "I've come to ask about a fellow I understand is looking for me. A Cornishman by the name of John Fisher."

"Sure I thought you'd come to bring my long-lost ward back home again." Innis lifted the bottle of whiskey in his hand and took a long swig. "Get your skinny grug into the house, Moira, and cook us some dinner. We haven't had a decent meal since you ran away, the devil take your soul."

"Aye, Innis." Before Josiah could grab her, Moira bowed her head and fled to the kitchen.

"And as for you, half-breed, get your stinkin' feet off my land and don't come back." Innis drew his gun and leveled it at Josiah.

It took Josiah about half a second to realize that the drunkard's wobbly aim probably wouldn't hit the side of a barn. "Shut down your bluster, old man," he scoffed. "Pull that trigger and you'll probably shoot your foot off."

Keeping one eye on Innis, Josiah walked across the *portal* and into the house. In the weeks Moira had been gone, Innis had turned the parlor into a sty unfit for a pig. Empty whiskey bottles lay scattered and smashed on the floor. Plates of half-eaten food, maggot-ridden and putrid, were strewn about. The place smelled like the backside of hell.

Josiah stalked through the house and out the back door, then followed the dogtrot into the kitchen. Moira, as he had already suspected, was crumpled in a corner, sobbing. This kitchen had been her glory, her pride in life. Now calling it a cesspit would have been a compliment.

"Hey there, girl," he said, kneeling beside her and drawing her into his arms. "Now then—"

"Get away from her!" Innis's voice exploded through the kitchen like a thunderbolt. A shot rang out, and the water bucket by the door sprang a leak. "Get your damned hide back on your horse and head out, Chee! If I catch you laying a finger on Moira again, I'll bore a hole in you big enough to drive a wagon through."

"I'll be damned—"

"Out!" Innis screamed. A second blast from his pistol sent Josiah diving across Moira. The bullet ricocheted off the kettle and buried itself in a wall.

"Josiah, go!" Moira sobbed, grabbing him and pushing with all her strength. "For the love of God, please go!"

"Do what she says, unless you want me to send you hoppin' over coals in hell!" Innis growled.

Again he lifted the six-shooter and aimed at Josiah. Before he could squeeze the trigger, Josiah grabbed his whip and in the same motion snapped the gun from Innis's hand. It clattered to the floor and spun in dizzy circles toward the wall.

"Let's go, Moira," he ordered, taking her arm and lifting her to her feet. "I've had enough of this jackass."

"You'll be leavin' her here!" Innis shouted as he grasped his wrist with his other hand. "She's mine, so she is!"

"No. She's mine." Josiah marched Moira out of the kitchen as Innis stormed out behind them.

The moment they were in the open air, Moira stopped and brushed Josiah's hand from her arm. "Wait just a minute here," she said hotly. "I don't *belong* to you, Josiah. Not like that! And you, Innis, I don't belong to you either. I belong to myself, so I do, and I'll do with myself exactly what I like."

"Oh, she's back to her ballyraggin' now," Innis snarled. "I'll have to knock that blatherumskite out of you, Miss O'Casey."

"Try it and I'll take one of those guns of yours and shoot you full of lead. And *I* won't miss!" Moira scrubbed a fist across her damp cheek, then crossed her arms and stared first at one man and then at the other. "You'll kindly put your whip away now, Mister Chee."

Frowning, Josiah slung the *látigo* over one shoulder. "What do you want, then, Moira?"

"I want peace. I want the world put back in order." She glanced into the ravaged kitchen. "I'll give you a week of my time, Innis. I'll set your house straight, and if you like, I'll teach one of your punchers to cook for you. In return, you'll let Josiah stay here at Fianna while he goes about his business of finding this John Fisher sherral. You won't shout at him or try to larrup him—and you *won't* shoot him."

"And after one week's time?" Innis shouted. "What do you think you'll be doin' then, you little clart? Traipsing off to St. Louie to visit your wayward little sister?"

Moira swallowed. She glanced at Josiah, but he said nothing. Turning back to Innis, she narrowed her eyes. "I'll do exactly as I please, Innis Grady. And I don't think I'll be terribly pleased to stay here at Fianna with a fat, red-faced drunkard who ballyrags and larrups me until I'm bleeding. I've seen better things, so I have. I've learned that there's more to this world than Fianna and a man who treats me like a burr on his bottom. Now you get your grug into the house and start sweeping!"

She grabbed a broom from beside the door and shoved it into his hand. Then she turned and stomped into the kitchen, leaving the two men open-mouthed and speechless behind her.

# Chapter
## 16

Moira had just hung a pot of water on the fire when Josiah walked into the kitchen. "What the hell was that all about?"

"It was the truth, every word of it," she answered, keeping her eyes on the pot. "As much as we've shared, and as good as the days have been between us, Josiah, I won't trade one slave driver for another."

"Moira, I never meant—"

"I know you didn't mean what you said. You were hot and angry after Innis shot at you." She turned to him, once again holding back tears she hadn't expected. "You've always treated me better than Innis has, but you've never convinced me that I mean more to you than I do to him."

"I married you. Innis never did that."

"Aye, you did, but what for? To warm your bed? To cook your meals? To wash your shirts?"

"I've told you I'd build you a home."

"Sure Innis has given me a home these thirteen years."

"You'd throw that gift in my face?"

"Never. I want a home of my own more than almost anything, and I bless you for offering me such a treasure. But between a husband and wife there ought to be more than houses and more than chores. More even than bedding down together at night."

He took off his hat. "What ought there to be between a husband and wife, Moira?"

"There ought to be . . ." She grabbed her apron from its hook and slipped it over her head. She smoothed down her hair, then stuffed her hands in her apron pockets. "There ought to be . . . Well, there ought to be something more."

"Like what?" His heart was beating so loud he was sure she could hear it across the room.

"Something that makes the wife certain her husband values her more than an old workhorse. Something that makes her feel she's more to him than a painted lady he could pay to please him."

Josiah figured the time was right to tell Moira exactly how he felt about her. "I'd sort of thought we might be talking this over someplace more private," he said, walking toward her. "Someplace besides the middle of Innis Grady's wreck of a kitchen. Someplace that smelled better than the bottom of an old slop bucket." By now he was so close he could see her hands trembling as she touched the lace on her apron bib. "But I reckon a man ought to tell his wife how much she means to him no matter where they are. Moira, I—"

"Mister Chee, I thought I'd better—" Scully came to a skidding halt in the kitchen doorway. "I thought I'd better . . . that is . . ."

Josiah dropped his hands from Moira's shoulders. "What is it, Scully?"

"Sure I didn't mean to intrude."

"Josiah was comforting me after the spat with your father," Moira cut in, stepping away and hurrying to study the roiling water in her pot on the fire. "What do you have to tell us, young Scully?"

"When you were outside just before, Josiah mentioned a fellow . . . a John Fisher."

"What about him?" Josiah demanded. "Has he been here?"

"Aye, not long ago. I thought you should know he came looking for you. Papa wouldn't invite him into the house, him being a Cornishman and all, but he did ask a lot of questions about you. Had you been here at Fianna? Were you injured? Did you get well?" Scully lifted one red eyebrow. "Papa and I didn't know you'd been shot, Josiah. We thought you'd been in a mining accident, so we did."

"It amounted to about the same thing. So Fisher left after he'd talked to you?"

"Aye, but I doubt if he's gone far. Papa told him you'd ridden off to look for Moira and Erinn and that you'd be bringing Moira back to us soon. Fisher said he'd be waiting for you."

"Josiah!" Moira gasped, abandoning the hot water and rushing to his side. "That man could be lurking about even now. Scully, run and fetch Josiah one of your papa's guns."

"No, Scully." Josiah's voice stopped the youth. "I've never carried a gun, and I won't start now, Moira. I'm a shepherd, and this *látigo* is all I need to protect myself. Now, Scully, which way do you think this Fisher rode?"

"West, I'd say, up the Peñasco. He told Papa he'd bide his time in the mountains where there was plenty of game to keep his belly full."

"That suits me fine, then." Josiah slipped his arm around Moira's shoulders. "I need to head up the Peñasco anyway to look over a few things. While I'm at it, I'll see if I can find Fisher and settle matters with him."

"You won't go alone!" Moira cried.

"I won't take you with me."

"I could go," Scully put in. "I've learned to ride pretty

well since you've been away. At least I can keep my grug on a horse."

"I'd like you to stay here and keep an eye on Moira, Scully." Josiah clapped one hand on the young man's shoulder. "Innis is looking for trouble, and I don't want to come back and find her with a split lip. Do you catch my drift?"

"I twig you. Sure I'll look after Moira, but I've never been much at standing up to my father. I've found the quickest way to cool his wrath is to take to my heels."

Josiah smiled. "Well, when you take to your heels, grab one of Moira's hands and take her with you."

Scully gave a returning chuckle. Then he looked at Moira with eyes that begged for approval. "Will you come to my studio? I'll show you Erinn's letter, and you can have a peek at my newest painting. Since I've been out of the house more, I've changed my style a bit, so I have. I'd like to show you what I've done."

Moira gave a reluctant shrug. "I'd like to see your work, Scully, but I was just talking to—"

"It's okay," Josiah interrupted. "You go on and take a gander at that painting. I need to ride out anyway."

Moira's face darkened. "But, Josiah, you were just going to—"

"Knowing I haven't told you what needs to be said between us will give me a good reason to come back alive, Moira." He wrapped his hand around the whip that curled over his shoulder. "And I mean to come back alive."

"Come on, then," Scully said, taking her hand and pulling her toward the door. "I'm working in oils now, not just pencil, and the colors I ordered from the Prang Company in New York will fairly make you drool. I've a green lusher than the grass of Ireland, and a blue brighter than the New Mexico sky."

"Josiah?" Moira called, staring at him over her shoulder as Scully dragged her out of the kitchen.

"I'll be back," he promised.

\*   \*   \*

But he didn't come back for more than a week. Moira's worries were far more intense than when he'd left her with his family to go search for Fisher the first time. On that venture he'd had his two brothers with him. And he'd been better rested . . . and more recently loved.

Moira read Erinn's letter and was gratified to learn that she was still living at St. Ferdinand's with the nuns. That was the good news. The bad news went on and on—the food tasted terrible, the beds were as hard as boards, the clothes she'd been given were nothing but rags, and the hours spent at prayer were interminable. Father Murphy had agreed to work on Erinn's annulment, but he was always preaching at her about the sin of abandoning a good husband.

Moira would have been tempted to ride out to rescue her sister had not one small section of the letter caught her attention: "Once a week we all go to the Maryville College of the Sacred Heart to clean and suchlike," Erinn had written. "It's my duty to dust and polish in the library. Nasty work. I do like the books, though, and I get to talk to the librarian, who knows more than any man I ever met. He thinks I'm smart."

The notion of Erinn falling in love with a college man—a librarian, at that—piqued Moira's interest. What sort of husband could be more secure, more stable, than that? If Erinn continued to live with the nuns until she got her annulment, then married the librarian, all would be well.

Comforting herself with the idea that she had truly been of help to her sister, Moira tried to put a good face on everything else. She scrubbed down the kitchen with lye soap and vinegar. She mopped the floors in the main house and drew water from the well to revive the dying kitchen garden. She churned butter and collected a supply of fresh eggs. She mended, washed, and, despite the heat, ironed stacks of laundry. When she wasn't working, she chatted with Scully.

The young man had indeed transformed his art, moving away from unsuccessful efforts to capture on canvas imaginary Rubenesque ladies in filmy white Greco-Roman garb. In fact, people were altogether absent from these new, bolder paintings of Scully's. Instead, the sprawling landscape of the New Mexico Territory stretched out in all its raw, magnificent splendor. Moira could hardly contain her surprise at the skill with which the young man had captured the Sacramento Mountains in shades of lavender, periwinkle, and navy. Aspen trees nearly glinted with gold and bronze. Rivers undulated in olive green and frothy white.

Moira's favorite painting was a winter landscape with snow that ranged in shades from white to cobalt and made her shiver at the very sight of it. The small home in one corner of the painting looked nothing like the house at Fianna that Scully had grown up in. Though the building was also adobe, there was warmth to the brown stucco that the Grady household had never known. Snow was piled high on Scully's painted house, but golden lamplight shone in the windows, and *ristras* of glowing red chiles hung by the front door.

As she lay in her bed one night thinking about Scully's little house, Moira felt the tears begin to well. Poor Scully never had known the joy of a loving mother. He'd lived his whole life being shouted at and belittled by his father. Still he painted his dreams of beautiful women and warm, loving homes. These were his escape. Where would Moira escape to if Josiah never came back for her?

Once upon a time the kitchen at Fianna had seemed to be enough, but now she needed more. The married woman inside her ached for the solid warmth of a man at her side in bed. She longed to talk to someone more responsive than the kitchen cat. She had grown used to laughter, shared dreams, companionship. Oh, what if Josiah were dead? How could she bear the loss of him?

She wouldn't. She couldn't stand it any longer. Tomorrow morning she would take one of the horses from the barn and ride up the Peñasco in search of her husband. Scully could come, too. They'd tell Innis they were going to look for a new landscape scene for Scully to paint, which was partly true, for the boy did need a change of perspective.

Settling against her pillow, Moira tried to take comfort in her plan. She had just shut her eyes when a tapping on the window sent her bolt upright.

"Who's there?"

"Moira?"

She flew across the room and tore back the curtain. "Josiah! Oh, thank God!"

Opening the window, she grabbed his face and gave him a kiss that nearly took his breath away. "Hey!" He laughed, swinging one booted foot over the sill and working his big shoulders through the window frame. "If I'd known that kiss was waiting for me, I'd have come back sooner."

"You great spalpeen, you knew how worried I've been!" She was fairly dancing with delight at seeing him as big as life, healthy as a horse, and smelling all of leather and the grand outdoors. "Sure it's been more than a week since you left. Innis is crowing that you were killed and never coming home, and he's been threatening to show me the back of his hand for giving him such slack jaw all these days."

"Moira, I missed you." Josiah caught her arms and pulled her against him. Oh, but she felt good. Her body was so warm and soft in the billowing white nightdress. He raked his gaze over her hair, then slipped his hands into the thick, rumpled mass of spun auburn silk. "I missed your hair."

She stared up at him with blue eyes glowing. "I missed the smell of you."

A grin tilted the corners of his mouth. "I've hardly been off my horse for a week."

"And you've brought the scent of green grass and blue sky and warm sun with you."

"*Our* green grass." He ran his hand down her back, comforting himself with the feel of her smooth flesh and the tiny pearls of her spine. "Moira, I've got to tell you now, while the future's still so real to me. I staked a claim on some land. It borders on the Peñasco, and it's smack-dab in the middle of Grady and O'Casey range. I know you won't be happy about that, but I had to hope I could win you over. I started building us a house, Moira. I hired some fellows who were camped along the river— sheepshearers out of work for the season. They were looking for some way to make a little cash, so they were glad to be paid to gather river rocks and help me lay the foundation in. It's good land, Moira, and it once belonged to my father's people."

"Kiss me, Josiah Chee, before I go mad with wanting you!" She took his chambray shirt in her fingers and pulled his chest against hers.

It didn't take Josiah long to abandon the big speech he'd been planning and claim Moira's lips with his own. She melted into him, her breasts full and peaked, and her thighs sliding against his. His hands found her hair, her neck, her hips, her shoulders. The hem of her nightgown wrinkled up to her knees, then fell to her ankles again.

"The river runs right past the front door," he whispered as his fingers feathered the downy skin of her neck.

"Shhh." She took off his hat and dropped it on the floor, then slid her hands into his thick tawny hair.

"Two aspens shade the kitchen porch."

"Mmm."

His hands formed around her breasts, and his thumbs teased their crests. "There's a little valley just right for a kitchen garden."

"Ohhh, yes." She shivered as his thigh nudged apart her legs and his pelvis settled against the small mound at the base of her stomach. "How lovely."

He chuckled and began to unbutton her gown. She returned the favor by freeing him of his shirt. When at last they stood naked in the moonlit room, he drank in the sight of her silvered body with his eyes.

"Moira," he whispered, "with every stone I dug from the riverbed, I repeated the words I've been wanting to tell you. With every shovelful of dirt I took out of the ground, with every tree I cut and every path I cleared, I said them: I love you, Moira. I love you."

She soaked in his voice like a fresh biscuit poured over with sweet golden honey. "Say it again."

"I love you. You're not a workhorse; you're not a painted lady. You're my wife. By every star in the sky, I swear to you, Moira, I love you."

Smiling, she drifted against him. "I don't care if you put me in a sinkhole to live . . . I love you, Josiah. I love you with all my heart."

It wasn't long before the bed drew them, and the soft mattress knew the sweet crush of ardent bodies, and the crystalline moonlight bathed tangled limbs and dewy breasts, and the gasping cries of ecstasy mingled with the chirp of crickets, the hoot of an owl, and the whisper of wind against an open curtain.

"It's all as it was before, here at Fianna," Moira murmured as she lay in Josiah's arms. "Only worse."

"Has Innis hit you?" Josiah's body stiffened with tension.

"No, I won't let him near enough. His drinking is so bad he often blacks out and can't remember a thing when he wakes up. He's hardly ever out on the range these days, and the punchers who've come around the house have told me he's going to lose everything if he doesn't take control. He takes all his anger out on Scully and me, or he drowns it in whiskey. Sure I've stood up to him more than I ever did before. That part is different—better, I suppose. Still, I think his rage is only building inside him until one day he's going to explode like a freight wagon full of dynamite."

"Is Scully looking out for you?"

"He tries, poor thing. But he's no good with his father. Innis bullies him so, you know. All the same, Scully would defend his father even in the face of the ugly truth, just as I once did. The boy has never known anything but Innis, and he doesn't have the spine to stand up to him."

"Is the house back in shape?"

"Aye, but it doesn't feel as it used to." She turned her hips and slipped her bare leg over his thigh. "It's not the house that has changed. It's me. I'm not the same as I was before you came. I want to be with you, Josiah."

He stroked a strand of her hair between his fingers. "When I used to lie in the room next door dreaming about you, I thought if I ever had you I'd never let you go." Then he turned and cupped one shoulder with his hand. "But, Moira, I need to ask you to stay on here at Fianna a little while longer."

"Here? But why? Oh, I'm so unhappy without you!"

"It's dangerous up there. I'd worry about you more in the mountains than I would leaving you here with Innis."

"Why?"

"I never saw Fisher, but I sensed he was watching me, waiting for a time when I wasn't alert. My hired hands were around all the time, and I kept my eyes open. But I know if I let my guard down once, Fisher will be ready for me. Moira, let me go back alone and work on our house. I'll feel better bringing you into a room with four walls and a roof. While I'm gone, you can prepare the things we'll need when we move in—quilts and sheets, that sort of thing. Send a letter to Jaffa and Prager's store in Roswell with a list. The mail hack can bring back whatever you order. Buy everything you want to turn the house into a home—food supplies, dishes, pots and pans, a churn, fabric, lamps."

"How will we ever pay for all that? The good Lord

knows I'm not stingy, but all the same I won't go in debt up to my ears. Even if we manage to buy some sheep and cattle and to plant some crops, we'll hardly make a fortune our first year, especially with summer already here and the drought parching every growing thing. I won't owe my soul to Jaffa and Prager. We must be frugal."

Josiah kissed her cheek. "Moira, you're a good woman. We will keep an eye on our pocketbook, I swear, but as my wife you should know where we stand with our money. Why do you think John Fisher is after me?"

She studied the square of his jaw and the small muscle that flickered there every time he mentioned his enemy. "You said he was Cornish, and you're Irish. I supposed it was trouble over that."

"That plays a part. But there's more. When I got to Montana, I was just like all the other miners there, looking to make a few dollars and hoping to strike it rich. I joined the miners' union in Butte. It was dominated by Irishmen. As a group, we fought the mine owners for higher wages and steady work, and we won. Eventually I joined another organization, the Ancient Order of Hibernians, which is only for Irishmen. Through all this I earned the trust and confidence of my fellow Irish miners. When times got tough, I was the man they sold their claims to."

"You bought other men's claims?"

He nodded. "When prices rose, I developed the claims I owned. Every piece of modern, newly developed equipment I could afford, I bought and put to work. I increased both efficiency and safety that way. Men wanted to come to work for me. It wasn't long before most of my claims started to make a lot of money. A whole lot. Every time prices went down, I bought up more claims. I joined my claims together and formed larger working mines. Finally I went into partnership with another fellow there in Butte, an Irishman named Paddy Connor. We worked well together, sharing equipment and making our mines pay out."

"And John Fisher? Where does he fit in?"

"He was another copper king in Butte, like Paddy and me, but his claims started to play out. He hadn't bought well, and he didn't know how to manage his business through the tough times. He came to see me one day, arguing that I'd jumped a couple of his claims. Fact is, I'd done business with two of his countrymen that he'd tried to cheat. I showed him the papers that gave me legal title, but that didn't convince him. When Paddy saw how mad Fisher was, he decided to hightail it for the sheriff."

"Was that when Fisher shot you?"

Josiah nodded, a rueful expression on his face. "Fisher and I had been talking in my office, and I didn't expect trouble. I didn't even have my whip handy—a mistake I haven't repeated. He was on his way out the door when all at once he grabbed Paddy's gun from the rack and shot me in the gut. Then he took off."

"He ran away like a coward?"

"Fisher's no brave gunslinger, Moira. He knew he'd done me wrong. My men fetched the doctor, and he patched me up. As soon as I thought I could travel, I told Paddy I wanted to go home. He arranged to have me sent down to the hospital at Fort Stanton."

"And then you came to Fianna." Moira ran her hand over his scarred stomach, thinking of the pain and agony he had endured at the hand of the Cornishman. "Oh, Josiah . . ."

"Anyway, I don't give Fisher that much heed. He's like a fly buzzing around my head. I just have to stay alert. But until I settle all this, I don't want him getting near you, Moira. In the meantime, you just spend all you need to outfit our house."

"You're certain you have enough money from all these mining ventures to pay our bill with Jaffa and Prager?"

Josiah laughed. "Enough to fill ten houses and a mansion, too."

"Blarney!"

"It's the truth, Moira, and if a mansion's what you want, it's what I'll build you."

"I don't want a mansion, Josiah. I told you I'd live in a sinkhole if that's all you could afford. All I want from you is your love."

This time he kissed her lips. "You have it."

"Then I'll order a few things for our house, and I'll trust you to mend your fences with John Fisher so that we can live safely and in peace."

Josiah settled her against him and studied the moon through the window. He'd made the situation sound simpler than it really was. He didn't want to alarm Moira by telling her just how much money was at stake in the two mines Fisher claimed, or just how angry and vengeful his enemy really was. Fisher might be a yellowbelly, but he'd shown himself willing to kill.

"You can knit me that sweater," Josiah told his wife. He ran his hand through Moira's hair and studied the fiery silk strands that slid between his fingers. "I'm going to need a warm sweater this winter. Up there on the river it's going to be colder than frog legs."

"The Peñasco River," she said in a whisper.

"I know it's not what you'd choose for us, Moira." He tilted her chin so that she couldn't hide the honesty in her eyes. "Our land snuggles right up to the Peñasco, across from your father's place and bordering on Innis's. It might be troubled land, but it's your home country, too. I've got a legal claim to it, Moira, and a blood right."

"So you do," she had to acknowledge. "All the same, the Peñasco is not a good place to try to put down roots."

"I think it's the smartest choice I've ever made. It'll be fertile land, Moira, when it's managed right. If I could turn a profit from copper mines, I know I can work land that my family has called home for generations."

"It's not you I'm doubting, Josiah. It's Innis."

He shut his eyes and trailed his fingers over the rise of her breast. "Let Innis challenge me, Moira," he said. "I'll take him on. I'm not afraid."

She felt the familiar glow of desire begin to stir within her, but she knew that before she could lose herself in his loving, she must say what had to be said. "I'm afraid, Josiah," she whispered as his hand slid down her thigh. "I'm so afraid I'll lose you."

"You won't lose me, Moira," he returned. "I'll always be yours. Trust me."

Josiah slipped away before dawn. Though Moira was exhausted from a whole night of lovemaking, talking, and lovemaking again, she kept his visit a secret from Innis and Scully and carried out her tasks with her usual vigor. In spite of this pretense of enthusiasm, the only thing that kept her spirits up was the knowledge that she and Josiah soon would be together.

Before he had ridden away, they had made a plan to meet in three days at the edge of Innis's land. A small, abandoned squatter's cabin on the bank of the Peñasco would be the site of their rendezvous. Moira would slip away that afternoon on one of Innis's horses. She and Josiah would meet for a few sweet hours together—a time to discuss events, prepare for the days ahead, and renew their love.

But three days seemed like an eternity that first morning when Moira sat down to breakfast. Innis, claiming he had a throbbing headache, quickly turned his black mood on his son.

"You'll ride to the north pasture today, Scully," he ordered as Moira set a plate of eggs before him, "and check on the roundup."

"But, Papa, I've just blocked in the background for my new painting of Sierra Blanca. It's a storm scene, and I've got the gray tones—"

"Shut your smush, boy, and do as I say!" Innis shoved back his plate. Bits of scrambled egg tumbled across the table. "Blast your soul, all I ever hear from you is blather about your blazing pictures! What's wrong with you, Scully? Are you a sheela, then? A sweet molly who takes no interest in men's work?"

Scully's face paled to the shade of one of his blank canvases. "No, Papa, of course not."

"All you ever do is sit about on your grug dabbling in paint. That's a woman's idleness, boy! Don't you know that?"

"To be sure, Papa, there's been a killeen of honorable men who've painted landscapes and such. Leonardo da Vinci, Michelangelo, Titian, Rubens—"

"Enough!" Innis roared, hammering the table so that the plates jumped and clattered. "I'm starting to think you'd rather be a fond colleen than a man! You don't like riding or tending to the cattle. You won't even wear your boots or your hat! You show not a whit of interest in manly things—drinkin' and shootin' and such."

"Oh, Papa, I've not time for—"

"What about women?" Innis grabbed Moira's arm and jerked her out of her chair. "Have you failed to notice there's another sort of creature in this world, Scully? I'm starting to think you'd rather play with your paintbrushes than with a woman's diddies! Take a look at Moira now, boy. Have you never noticed these grand teats of hers?"

When Innis made a grab for one of Moira's breasts, she screeched and wrenched her arm from his grasp. "The devil take you, Innis Grady! You'll not be touching me, you grand oaf!"

"Oaf, is it?" Innis was out of his chair and lunging after Moira. "Come here, you whipster! Do you think you're too elegant for a man like me, now? Sure you've been prancing about with your nose in the air these days since you came back to Fianna. Did the sights of the big city put you into heat, you young ruddy mare?"

Innis stalked her around the table as he spoke. Moira backed away, keeping her eyes on his swiping hands.

Scully had scampered to one corner, his usual refuge.

"Ho, Scully! Shall your old papa show you how a man takes care of himself?" Innis glanced at his son, and in that split second Moira grabbed a knife off the table. "Come on, boy. Watch how a man treats a woman in heat. I'll take her to the ground and rip into her with my proddy horn. See if that don't get your rut up. See if that don't make you want to act like a man, eh?"

"Innis Grady, for shame!" Moira clutched the knife behind her back. "Such talk will send you straight to hell, so it will. Now calm yourself and sit down. Your eggs are getting cold, and the coffee's fair turned to ice. Sure you've a splitting headache, and you're not well. A taste of breakfast will put you right, and then you can sit on the front porch and rest in your chair."

Innis stopped stalking her and paused to stare at his spilled breakfast. "I feel as if someone buried an ax in my damned forehead."

"Oh, you poor frainey," she said, softening her voice. This was the way it had always been between them—his rage followed by her gentle soothing. But never before had Innis threatened to touch Moira's body. And never had she felt the need for a weapon. She kept her fingers tightly around the handle of the knife as she spoke calming lies. "Sit yourself down, Innis, and take a bite of that dry toast. Why then, it'll calm your stomach. Sure I'll go put the coffee back on the fire, and in ten minutes I'll bring you a nice hot cup."

"Ahhh, God." He slumped into his chair and laid his cheek on the table. "I need . . . need a woman. Need a doctor. Need a drink. Moira, fetch my whiskey, will you? Be a dear."

Still breathing hard, she glanced at Scully. He turned to the cupboard and grabbed a bottle. Almost on tiptoe, he set the whiskey before his father. Moira poured the amber liquor into an empty coffee mug and placed it just in front of Innis's eyes.

"Now then," she said. "Here's your drink, Innis."

When he didn't respond, she bent to stare into his face. Eyelids shut, he gave a deep snore. His mouth opened, and a rivulet of drool ran down his cheek to puddle on the table. She pushed the mug against his nose in a gesture of contempt.

"May the peace of the devil himself be upon you," Moira softly cursed him. "And if you ever threaten to defile me again, Innis Grady, I swear by heaven I'll kill you."

# Chapter
## 17

Moira set the coffee pot back on the stove, then sank onto a chair and covered her face with her hands. The table knife swung heavily in her apron pocket.

"Moira?" Scully entered the kitchen and hurried to her side. Crouching at her feet, he lowered her hands and took them between his own. "Moira, you're crying!"

"And why not?" She lifted her head. "Did you hear the things your father threatened?"

"Papa would never hurt you, Moira. Not really. He isn't well these days. He's been worse ever since you ran away with Erinn. There are days I fear he'll die of his sickness."

"It's not an illness that's taken hold of your father, Scully. It's the blazing whiskey."

"He drinks only to blunt the pain of his sorrows. The drought is killing Fianna, Moira. You should see the cattle, all ridgy with their ribs sticking out and their skin hanging on them. Half the punchers have quit and gone off to seek better work. Who can blame them? There aren't enough cattle here to keep anyone busy. After the terrible winter, the spring roundup was a disaster. The

291

summer isn't proving any better. Papa will be lucky to have any stock at all by autumn."

"I know Innis has trouble, Scully, but—"

"It's not only the farm. Papa's lonely, so he is. In the evenings I hear him singing all alone on the porch. He won't go to any of the dances in the Irish community. He won't court any of the women. He won't even befriend the punchers. But I know he's lonely. He wouldn't have come after you the way he did if he weren't in need of a woman's company."

"Oh, Scully!" Moira gave a mirthless laugh at the absurdity. "What Innis wanted from me was not my company. He meant to use me ill, so he did."

"Then marry me!" Scully squeezed her hands and bent his head over them to gently plant his lips on her fingers. "Oh, Moira, I spoke my feelings to you once before. Sure I'm no bold cattleman like my father. But I do love you! I'll take care of you as best I can. We'll go away to Paris, so we will, and there I'll study art and learn to paint better."

Moira laid her hand on the bristle of red hair. "Dear Scully, you're a kind young lad to think of me so. But I'll not wed you now or ever."

"No?" Scully looked up, his green eyes watery with emotion. "And why not? Do you think I'm a sheela, too?"

"Of course I don't. I know you're a fine man, and a bold, elegant gent. I care for you, too, so I do. And I admire you. You've the wit and brains to match any scholar alive. You've talent pouring through your veins. And you're pleasant to look at besides, with your bright hair and your kind green eyes."

"Then marry me, Moira! I've adored you from the moment you came to live at Fianna, so I have. Your beauty and charm fair dazzle me! I paint the color of your hair into the sunsets over the mountains. I hear your laughter ringing in my ears. The scent of your skin lulls me to sleep at night—"

"Scully!"

"No, Moira, don't back away from me." He tried to grab her shoulders, but she jumped up from the chair. "Moira, I'll make you a good husband, so I will."

"No, Scully!" Moira backed into the kitchen wall as he came toward her. He fumbled for her hands and finally managed to locate her wrists. Taking them, he pulled her against him. She wanted to smile, gazing down at him from her greater height and feeling the sweaty tremor in his thin fingers. But this was no laughing matter.

"Moira, say you'll be my wife." He stared up at her, moonstruck. "Say you'll come away with me to Paris." Before she could push him away, he stood on tiptoe and pressed his mouth against hers. "There! Don't you feel it? The passion?"

Moira took a deep breath and detached her wrists from Scully's hands. "No, Scully, I don't feel it. But it's not because of any lack in you. You're a dear boy, and I shall always think fondly of you. But there's no passion between us."

"Yes, there is! My heart is beating like a drum. My blood pulses through my veins like floodwaters. Oh, Moira, I must hold you. I must." He grabbed her and planted another dry kiss on her mouth.

"Scully, stop it now!" She wiped her lips with the back of her hand. "Don't do that again. It's isn't right."

"Why not?"

"Because . . . because . . ."

"Why, Moira?"

"Because I'm married, that's why." She stomped over to the fire and grabbed a potholder. Scully stood in utter silence. She lifted the coffee pot lid and stared into the blackened depths. "I'm married, so I am."

"But who's your husband?"

"Josiah Chee." She turned and faced the youth. "It's Josiah I love with a passion, Scully. And it's with him I would go anywhere."

For a moment she thought his face would crumple.

Breathing heavily, he gulped twice. Then he knotted his hands into fists and ran from the kitchen.

Moira rode the bay mare up the Peñasco River toward the border of Fianna. For surviving the last three days she had only the good Lord to thank. Innis's dark mood grew blacker by the hour, it seemed. Moira felt sure that her presence only stirred him to further anger. Somehow she was a reminder of things he had lost—his youth, his wife, his lands. He drank his whiskey morning, noon, and night, and when he wasn't raving drunk, he was either passed out in his chair on the porch or galloping off on his horse.

Moira considered taking his whiskey away, pouring it out on the ground, smashing the bottles. But then where would his anger be focused? On her, of course. Things were bad enough as it was.

If she wasn't hiding from Innis, she was fretting over his son. Scully hadn't spoken two words to her since the morning he had proposed marriage. When he was about the house, he sulked and pouted, his head hanging low and his eyes downcast. Most of the time he lingered in his room, and Moira could hear him muttering while he painted.

As she rode her horse up a gentle hill toward the log cabin, Moira had only one plan in mind—to convince Josiah that she mustn't remain at Fianna a day longer. But how could she make him understand without telling him everything? She knew he would be murderous at the thought of Innis threatening to defile her. As much as Moira had come to despise her guardian, she didn't want to see him in a showdown with Josiah. If only she could leave in peace, just slip away and start her new life in her new home.

"Moira! God save you!" Josiah stood waving to her beside the cabin's front door. He wore a broad, radiant grin that instantly warmed the edges of her troubled heart. His blond hair lifted and scattered in the soft breeze, and his chambray shirt flattened against his chest.

"God save you kindly!" She tried to put on a bright voice. How wonderful he looked, clean-shaven and handsome. His shirt was tucked into denim jeans fastened with a silver-buckled belt. His long legs and booted feet carried him toward her through the tall yellow grass.

She reined in the bay and slipped down into Josiah's waiting arms. "I've missed you, Moira," he whispered against her cheek. "Thought about you day and night."

"I've worried myself almost sick over you. Has there been any sign of Fisher?"

"I think he's vanished. Gave up on me, I guess."

"Saints be praised!" She stood on tiptoe and kissed his cheek. "Josiah, don't ask me to go back to the house at Fianna. From now on, I want to live with you."

He held her a little distance away and looked into her blue eyes. There was something written in them he couldn't read, something that reminded him of a frightened rabbit on the run, scared for its life. Moira seemed smaller to him, more fragile in his embrace. There was a delicate, faded, almost translucent quality to her that sent a pang of fear into his chest.

"Moira, what has Innis done to you?"

"Nothing." She lowered her eyes, and her lashes fluttered for a moment. "Sure he's been drinking and ballyragging me as always. But he hasn't laid a harmful finger on me, I swear it."

"Scully?"

"The silly boy still fancies himself in love." Her blue eyes scanned his face. "I finally had to tell him I was married to you."

"Does Innis know?"

"Not yet, but I don't want to be around when he finds out. Oh, Josiah, let's talk about something else. Let's talk about our plans. How is the house coming along? Did you build the walls yet? Or the roof?"

Josiah ran the side of his finger down her neck. He

knew Moira would never lie to him. There was too much honesty in her for that. But she had always protected those she loved from the harsh realities of life. Was there more she hadn't told him?

"Come sit with me under that cottonwood by the river," he said. "I'll tell you everything."

From the distance she saw that he had laid out a blanket for them in the shade. The river gurgled past in softly undulating curves fringed with green grass and yellow-flowered blueweed. When they had settled themselves, he slipped off his whip and laid it to one side. Then he lifted a bottle of wine from the chilly river and took a round loaf of bread from his saddlebag.

"I'm not much good at cooking, but last night I baked this bread in our fireplace."

"Our fireplace!" She couldn't help but laugh in delight.

"It's as wide as a man is tall and it's almost high enough to walk inside. Our house will be so warm this winter the heat would wither a fence post. I've built a chimney high enough to keep sparks off the roof."

"What else?" she asked, sipping wine from her tin cup. It was so wonderful to think of a bright future without Innis Grady and his drunken rages, without John Fisher and his lurking threat, without Scully and his sulking. "Tell me everything. Tell me about the whole house from floorboards to roof shingles."

Josiah pulled Moira onto his lap and wrapped his arms around her. "You feel like heaven to me, woman. Just the sound of your voice lifts me higher than a hawk on a pine tree."

"I dream of falling asleep in your arms. I imagine what it will be like to wake up every morning with you beside me in our own bed." She ran her hand down his arm, marveling at the corded muscle and the coarse golden hair that matted it. "I've been embroidering pillowcases for us. One for you and one for me. I like to dream of your head lying on the pillowcase, your hair brushed across the white cotton. I've ordered things for our home. I sent off to Jaffa and Prager for a churn, a bird roaster, a spice chest, a sifter, a small coffee mill, a washtub for the laundry—"

"I've hung up a clothes line for you, right behind the kitchen."

"The kitchen! Have you built it already?"

"The main part of the house is basically ready, all but the bedrooms, and they're halfway up. It's going a lot faster than I expected. Men keep coming over the mountains from Alamogordo because they heard I have work for them and I pay well. One of my hired hands, a good carpenter, is starting to build the furniture. He's made a big dresser for your dishes, and now he's putting together a pie safe. I built you a kitchen table out of pine. It's strong and solid, though the top is a little rough."

"Scrubbing will smooth it. Oh, Josiah!" She threw her arms around his neck and kissed his mouth. As their lips met, a shiver of desire thawed inside her and slipped down to the base of her stomach. His hands rounded her shoulders and found her hair, her neck, the curve of her jaw.

"Can you come up with me now and move into the house, Moira?" he whispered, already fighting the desire to lie with her across the blanket. "It's not completely finished, but I want you—"

"Oh, yes, I'll come. Of course I'll come." She threaded her fingers through his hair and trailed kisses across his mouth. As though drawn to know her fully, he curved his palms around her breasts, lifting and molding them. The desire that had begun to bud inside her heated into a pulsing flame. She splayed her fingers across his back, kneading his hard muscles. "Are there people hereabouts?" she whispered. "Could you love me now, Josiah?"

"I prayed you'd want me." He stroked his thumbs over her cheeks. "I've already built us a bed at the house."

"I can't wait." She drifted for a moment in the pleasure of his hands on her hips. "Will you love me here in the fresh, clean air? Love me now, Josiah, while we're all alone."

"All alone except for me." The voice was accompanied by the click of a revolver. "Name's John Fisher."

Josiah lunged for his whip. Fisher's toe hooked the leather loop and kicked it out into the woods. It landed with a thud well down the hillside. Instantly Josiah sprang to his feet in a crouch, guarding Moira with the bulk of his body.

"What do you want from me, Fisher?" he growled. "Speak your piece and then get off my land."

"You know what I want, Chee. I want to string you from the nearest tree by your Irish neck."

"Not a chance."

"Oh, no?"

Moira could see the smaller man run a hand through his limp blond hair. He was short and stocky with blue eyes so pale they hardly had color. Dressed in a suit that had once been fine and natty, he was now filthy, covered with dust, twigs, and burrs.

"Last time we met," Fisher said, "I wasn't prepared for you, Chee. It was a matter of luck that your friend Paddy had left his shotgun in your office. This time I'm ready for you. Now hand over what's mine before I put a hole through your conniving heart."

"Last time we met," Josiah countered, "I wasn't armed. I'm not armed now. Only a coward would shoot an unarmed man—twice."

"I'm no coward, Chee."

"No, you're a Cornishman. Would your people be proud to claim a man who gets what he wants with the barrel of a gun? Let me arm myself, Fisher, and we'll have it out."

"A shoot-out? Do you think I'm a fool?"

"My whip against your gun. You'll have the clear advantage."

"Josiah, no!" Moira cried behind him. "You'll be killed."

"It's all right, Moira." Josiah eyed the Englishman. "My whip?"

"Get it for him, woman," Fisher barked. "Then I'll make you a widow before you can count to ten."

Moira could hear them talking as she scrambled in panic into the woods. Could she slip a gun to Josiah? She carried a rifle on her saddle, but there was no way to give it to Josiah. As skilled as he might be with his blacksnake, how could he face his enemy with nothing to protect him but a strip of braided leather?

Moira found the whip in a clump of scrub oak. She snatched it up and hurried back to the two men.

"Where've you hidden the papers?" Fisher was demanding.

"They're at my brother's house. You kill me and you can have them."

"Who'll give them to me, then?"

"My wife knows where they are." Josiah took the whip she handed him.

"I'll wait by my horse," Moira said softly.

"Stay out of range," he returned, then looked back at Fisher. "If you touch her, you'll never get the claims. On the off chance you win this little duel of ours, see that you give my wife a decent escort down the river to the house. When she's safe—and only then—she'll hand over the claims, and you can take them back to Montana. But you'd better know that Paddy Connor has copies of the documents on every mine we own. You'll have to fight him, too. Paddy sent a letter to my father's house to let me know the law is already looking into your actions and your false claims. You go up there with those papers, Fisher, and you'll have to explain how you came by them."

"No problem." Fisher sneered. "I've got papers of my own, Chee."

"Fake ones."

"Real enough to fool a sheriff. Now face up and say your prayers."

Josiah deftly settled the butt of the *látigo* in his palm and called over his enemy's shoulder. "Moira, count to three. Then it's you and me, Fisher, and may the Lord grant mercy on your soul."

At a distance behind Fisher, who was facing Josiah, Moira slid the rifle from its sling. "One," she cried. She raised the stock to her shoulder. "Two." She took aim at Fisher's shooting hand. "Three."

A pair of gun blasts shattered the silence in the clearing. Birds squawked and flapped into the air. Through a pall of black smoke, Moira ran toward the river.

"Josiah? Josiah?" Blood was bitter in her mouth where she'd bitten the inside of her cheek. Her shoulder throbbed, nearly torn from its socket by the kick of the rifle. "Josiah?"

"Moira!" Josiah was bending over the fallen Fisher. "Moira, what the hell did you do? You shot him!"

A wave of nausea washing through her stomach, Moira ran the last few breathless steps. "I couldn't let him . . . let you . . . Is he dead?"

"No, but you blasted a hole right through his leg. Must've cut across one of those big veins. Blood everywhere. He's out cold." Josiah was wrapping his shirt around Fisher's left thigh in an attempt to stem the pulsing flow of crimson blood.

Moira stared in horror at the savage destruction she had caused. Dropping the rifle, she fell to her knees. "Oh, Josiah, I have killed him!"

"Not yet. Scoop some water into one of those mugs. See if you can wash him down a little. I need to wrap him up in the blanket so he won't get the shakes."

Moira hurried to the river and sloshed water into a tin cup. As she knelt on the pebbled bank, a gray object trapped in the roots of a bush caught her attention. She lifted the branches and peered at John Fisher's revolver.

As she ran back to the tree, Moira saw what she had been blind to at first. Fisher's gun hand was empty. The end of Josiah's whip was wrapped tightly around his wrist—and his revolver lay twenty feet away on the riverbank.

"Josiah, your whip was faster than Fisher's trigger?" Getting no answer, she averted her eyes and began to sponge the blood from the man's leg.

When she had cleaned up most of it, Josiah wrapped his enemy in the blanket and lifted him like a baby in his arms. As he strode toward the wagon he'd driven down from the hills, he finally looked at Moira.

"My *látigo* is all I needed," he said. "It's all I'll ever need. I told you that, Moira. Fisher and I could have worked this out without you shooting him."

Bitter tears welled up in her eyes. "But I didn't see how. I couldn't . . . didn't . . ."

"I've asked you to trust me, Moira, and I don't understand why you can't do it. You didn't trust me to take care of you on our travels. You didn't trust me to make our marriage last. And you didn't trust me to finish this thing with Fisher without bloodshed."

"Josiah." She stood helpless as he settled the man in the back of the wagon and began to hitch his horse to the harness. "Fisher had a gun. You had a whip. I was only trying to save your life!"

He tied Moira's horse to the back of the wagon. "I know. I understand. But if Fisher dies, all our dreams will come to nothing. I want to take him down to Fianna. I want you to tend him, if you will."

"But I was going to move into the house with you. And Innis will—"

"Moira." Josiah stopped her and took her shoulders. "I'm not a man of violence. I come from a line of shepherds, and I've chosen to become one myself. There's peace in that. Try to understand. I'll stop my enemy, but I won't kill him."

"I didn't intend to kill Fisher, Josiah," Moira sobbed.

"It's a mortal sin what I've done. Oh, I know that, I do! I only thought that he . . . that you—"

"I love you, Moira." Josiah gathered her in his arms. "I love you for wanting to save my life. Now, what do you say we get this failing Cornishman down the mountain and into a warm bed? You can give him a drink of your greasewood tea, how's that? Then he'll wish he really had died. That's the best revenge I could have on him."

Moira tried to smile at his gentle teasing. He brushed a kiss on her cheek before he helped her up onto the wagon seat. When he climbed up beside her, he took her hand in his and gave the reins a flick.

"I won't come between you and trouble ever again," she vowed to him. "I swear it, Josiah."

He glanced behind him at the bundle of blanket. "I expect John Fisher's the last trouble I'll see."

"All the same, I won't ever step into your path. No matter what comes your way, I'll let you handle it. Alone."

Nodding, he settled his hat lower on his brow and swung the wagon onto the rocky trail. The trail that would lead them to Fianna, home of Innis Grady.

"I'll come for you in a week," Josiah told Moira as the wagon rolled toward the adobe house at Fianna. "I've got sheep and supplies arriving tomorrow. I bought a flock from a fellow on the other side of the Sacramentos. I'll get the sheep settled and finish the house. Then I'll drive down in the wagon and load up all your things."

Halfway through the journey Moira had climbed into the back of the wagon. Now she was trying to calm the writhing man who had come fully awake and was groaning with pain. "Sure the goods I ordered should be up from Roswell by then," she called over Fisher's moans.

As much as she wanted to sound bright and hopeful, Moira felt a constricting band of dread around her heart. What if John Fisher died? Could she be arrested and hanged for his murder? What if he lived? Would he continue to challenge Josiah until ownership of the mining claims was settled?

Worse, what on earth would she tell Innis about all this mess? Laying one hand on Fisher's chest, she sat up and stared over the edge of the wagon bed at the house, now a hundred yards away. How could she explain sneaking off on one of the ranch horses, only to return with Josiah Chee and a wounded stranger?

"Do you think you'll be safe around Innis if I leave you here?" Josiah asked, studying her over his shoulder. "It worries me, to tell you the truth."

"Sure I'm able to handle Innis," Moira returned with more confidence than she felt. "It's this Fisher devil I'm not sure of."

"Send a letter to Seamus Sullivan when you're sure Fisher's not knocking on the pearly gates. Seamus will come up to Fianna. He'll take Fisher to Roswell and put him in the hands of the law."

"Seamus? Do you trust him so much, Josiah?"

He set the brake and jumped down from the board. "Seamus Sullivan is a good man, the best around these parts. I'd trust him with my life."

"What's this, now?" Innis Grady's voice rang out from the porch. "Moira? Is that you there? And it's Chee, too, so it is. Saints be praised, the half-breed is back."

"Innis, stop your blarney and give us a hand here," Moira snapped, taking the offensive. "We've an injured man, and it's time he was laid abed."

Whiskey bottle in hand, Innis staggered down from the porch and across the drive. He peered into the wagon as Josiah slung Fisher up into his arms. "John Fisher's his name," Josiah explained. "You might remember him, Innis. He tried to kill me this afternoon, so Moira shot the hell out of his leg."

"Which?" Innis looked dumbfounded at Moira. "*You* shot him?"

Moira ducked her head and followed Josiah into the house. It pained her to think that the filthy villain would be sheltered in the room where she once had tended Josiah. But there was no option.

"*You* shot him?" Innis repeated, following her into the bedroom where Josiah was unwrapping Fisher's blanket. "What were you doing with Chee anyhow? Where've you been all afternoon, strap? Tell me that, eh!"

"I went for a ride, so I did. I met Josiah upriver. Sure he took care of me all the way from here to Missouri and back again, and he wanted to know how I've been since he left Fianna. We met for a bit of a chat, that's all. So don't start filing your teeth over it."

As brave as she sounded, Moira could hardly control the tremor in her fingers as she examined the bandage on Fisher's wounded leg.

Innis snorted and took a swig from his bottle. "And what's this poor glunter done that you'd want to plug him, Moira?"

"Fisher and I had trouble back in Montana," Josiah answered for her. "He's been hunting for me ever since. You know that. He was here, and you sent him up the mountain to wait for me."

"I never—"

"Don't try to cover your butt, Grady. Fisher wouldn't have been lurking around waiting to ambush me if you hadn't told him that I was coming back to the Peñasco Valley with Moira."

"So I did tell him. What of it? It wouldn't break my heart if he'd landed you in a shallow grave. You've got your greedy eyes on Fianna, and I know it. I'm no fool. Just because we share the same mother, you think you're owed some of my land. Well, I won't part with a handful of dust, you hear? I'll kill you first!"

"Innis!" Moira rose from the bed where she'd been bandaging Fisher's leg. "You wouldn't lay a hand on Josiah."

"He'll not be casting sheep's eyes on my land, girl, or

I'll blast him to kingdom come." He grabbed her arm and jerked her against his chest. "And he'll not be wooing you, neither. Your papa's land is *mine* now, hear? I put my cattle on it, and it's mine! Chee, you keep your lusty hands off Moira. You won't get my land through her or any other way."

"I don't want your land, Grady," Josiah retorted, taking two strides across the room and knocking Innis's hand away from Moira's arm. "And you keep your hands off Moira, too. I won't kill a man for claiming my mining rights. I won't kill a man for trying to steal my land or my livestock or my horse. But you lay a rough finger on Moira, brother, and you're dead."

"What's this?" Blustering, Innis followed Josiah out of the bedroom and down the hall. "What's this . . . a threat, is it?"

Moira sank to her knees at the edge of the bed. She couldn't take this anymore! All she wanted—all she'd ever wanted—was peace. She wanted the security and solitude of a home. She wanted the stability of a man's arms around her in the night and the warmth of golden sunshine on her shoulders in the day. Her dream was so close to reality now. The home in the mountains was almost built. The wagonload of goods would arrive from Roswell in a few days' time. The sheep were on their way over the mountains. The clothesline was already stretched and waiting to be hung with fresh white sheets.

But here lay a man half dead, shot by Moira's own hand. Outside in the yard Innis and Josiah threatened and insulted each other. Across the plains the rivers were drying up, and the cattle were dying. Gabriel Chee's words haunted her with reminders of the hopeless, endless prejudice of one man against another. Apaches hated Mexicans, who hated Anglos, who hated Mexicans, who hated Apaches. Irishmen hated Cornishmen. Cattlemen hated sheepmen. Danger licked at the edges of Moira's dream, sniffing and scratching, waiting to spring.

Tears squeezing from the corners of her shut eyes, Moira folded her hands and breathed a prayer. "Dear God," she whispered. "Oh, dear God, when will we all be free of this hell of our own making?"

"The devil take him!" Innis shouted as he swung down the hallway in a drunken rage. "The devil take his soul!"

Moira set down the spoon with which she'd been stirring John Fisher's stew to cool it. A week had gone by, and her spirits had lifted with the realization that the Cornishman would live and that Josiah soon would return for her.

"May he roast in hell!" Innis hollered. "Eternal damnation to him!"

"Now what?" Moira sighed.

"He's sloshed again," Fisher said. "Full of piss and vinegar."

Moira stood up and went to the door of the spare room. "Now then, what's troubling you, Innis?"

"It's Chee! That spawn of the devil has built a fence! A *fence!* Barbed wire, it is, and three rows high." Innis leaned against the wall and swallowed a mouthful of whiskey. "The bastard has stolen my land, so he has, and fenced it!"

A sick chill curled through Moira's stomach. "A fence on Fianna?"

"Up by the old log house, so it is. Straight as you please from the river and out a good two miles."

"But the log house is on the property line of Fianna, isn't it, Innis? Sure you don't claim the upper part of the river, do you?"

"The hell I don't! I've grazed my cattle all along the Peñasco Valley for more than twenty years."

"But the stream frontage—"

"It's mine! Maybe I don't hold legal title to the waterfront up toward the mountains. Maybe I haven't registered a claim on the land itself. Why should I? I own the Peñasco River! This valley is mine by right of occupation. And Chee—damn him to hell—has built fences on my land!"

Moira clutched her stomach. How could Josiah have put up a fence? Nesters built fences. Dry farmers built fences. Fences were the scourge of the land! The range was intended to be open pasture, freely grazed by those who claimed it. All her life Moira had been taught to revere the highest principle of the cattleman: *no fences*.

"And here's the best part of it all," Innis roared. "Do you know what's roaming loose across my land now? Shearing the grass to its roots, trampling the dirt, fouling the range? *Sheep!* Chee's fenced off the land with barbed wire, and he's brought in a killeen of damned woollies!"

"Dear God, what will you do, Innis?" Moira whispered.

"What will I do? What have I already done, you mean? I've sent my men after him, so I have. I've given them orders to cut the fences, tear down the posts, burn them to ashes. Then I've told my men to tie Josiah Chee to a tree so that he can watch them club his flock of woollies until there's not a sheep alive."

"Club them? Oh, Innis—"

"Shoot 'em, burn 'em, stampede 'em off a cliff, cut their throats. I don't care, as long as I never lay eyes on 'em again. And after that, my boys'll be bringing my dear brother to me here at Fianna, so they will."

Moira laid a hand on her hammering heart. "Josiah? But why, Innis?"

"So I can kill him, that's why."

In the spare room, John Fisher began to laugh.

# Chapter
## 18

The first thing Moira did after she had collected her wits was to send a message to Seamus Sullivan by way of one of the punchers. She explained her action to Innis by assuring him that Seamus would take John Fisher off their hands. It was best to be rid of him if trouble was at hand.

But in the letter to Seamus, Moira asked the Irishman to bring the sheriff when he came. Not only did Fisher need to be taken into custody for attempted murder, she wrote, but there was bad feeling between Innis and Josiah. Trouble that she feared would explode into violence.

The days following the news that sheep had come to the Peñasco Valley were torture for Moira. Though the week of waiting for Josiah had passed, he didn't show himself at Fianna. Moira ached to ride west to the mountains in search of him. She wanted to warn him, protect him if she could. But Innis saw to it that she was kept in the house at Fianna. He ordered one of the punchers to watch her at all times—ostensibly to guard her from danger, but in reality to keep her a prisoner.

And a prisoner she was. Day and night she paced the hallways of the house, wringing her hands and hating her helplessness. By the end of the second week, there still had been no sign of Josiah. Nor had there been word from any of the punchers who had been sent to cut the fences and kill the sheep.

Days passed. Finally the punchers returned. They had met a formidable army of men assembled by Josiah to protect his sheep. Mostly Mexicans they were, once regarded as shiftless vagrants on the land. These were men who had taken a job here and there to keep themselves alive, men never considered fit for the difficult, skilled labor of a puncher. But Josiah Chee had hired the lot of them, and he'd trained them into a dauntless force that had held off the attackers for days—with nothing but whips as their weapons.

To be sure, the punchers had managed to cut down a great line of fencing. They'd shot two of Chee's sheepherders, and they thought they might have killed one of them. They'd poisoned a small number of sheep. All the same, the rest of the sheep were still there—nearly a thousand of them, they reckoned—and still grazing. The shepherds were still at their posts, still keeping watch. Most of the fences were still there, still strung along for miles. And Josiah Chee was still at large. Still very much alive.

Moira went about her tasks with a fervor that bordered on obsession. She baked pies until the pie safe was over-flowing. She washed and ironed every scrap of linen in the house. She scrubbed floors until the wood was so smooth and slippery Innis could barely stay upright.

Brought back to life by his own hatred, Innis curtailed his drinking. But the personality that emerged in the sober man was even angrier, more vengeful, more evil. Scully slunk around his father like a scared cat, coming out of his room only at mealtime. Yet whenever Moira tried to talk with the boy about the situation, Scully defended his father as though Innis were a great hero engaged in a battle of monumental proportions.

As the days slipped by without word from Josiah, John Fisher grew healthier. Seamus didn't arrive to take him away, nor did the sheriff appear. For that matter, the expected load of household goods from Roswell had not come either. This last was a relief to Moira, for she had no idea how to explain to Innis the presence of a wagonload of dishes, churns, kettles, and washtubs.

Fisher got better, just well enough to start causing trouble. More than once Moira caught him hobbling about as he dug through chests and cupboards in search of the packet of mine claims Josiah had given her to safeguard. If Innis hadn't despised the man so much for his Cornish blood, Moira didn't know how she would have controlled him. As it was, Innis finally resorted to tying Fisher to his bed during the day and leaving him guarded at night while they awaited the arrival of Seamus Sullivan.

Another week passed. Reports filtered in that more sheep had been slaughtered. More fences cut. Josiah himself had been shot at and possibly wounded, but not caught.

Moira fell on her knees every night in prayer, begging for peace, pleading for the safety of the man she loved. At night she slept restlessly, dreaming of trouble. A spinning wheel laced her nightmares together, its soft whirring ever present. She saw sheep, the soft springy-legged lambs she had tended with Sheena Chee. And then they lay slaughtered, their throats slit and their white fleece damp with blood. She saw Innis, his green eyes burning like a cat's. Over and over to the rhythm of the spinning wheel, his open hand swung at her, coming toward her face, toward her mouth. But the crack that sounded with the blow was always the snap of a whip. Josiah's whip. He hung from a tree, his body swaying and spinning in the wind, and Innis stood beneath him, lashing his back with the *látigo*, and laughing. But it was John Fisher's laugh. John Fisher holding high the packet of papers. John Fisher slipping into Moira's room in the dead of night after the guard had gone to sleep. John Fisher, clapping his hand over Moira's mouth, falling on top of her, his body heavy and . . .

"Moira!" The guttural sound tore through her tortured brain.

Rising from the depths of her nightmare, she fought the hand that squeezed her mouth, fingers that cut into her cheeks. She lashed out at the body, huge and solid, that pinned her to the bed.

"Moira . . . Moira, it's me." Now the voice was hushed, almost inaudible.

Heart racing, she tried to focus, tried to see through the darkness. She couldn't speak, but she ceased fighting. The hand on her mouth relaxed, slipped away, was replaced by the soft warmth of a kiss.

"I love you, Moira."

"Josiah? . . . You're alive." Unable to stop the tears of relief, she flung her arms around him as he crushed her against his chest. "Dear Lord, I thought it was . . . Fisher . . . Innis . . . I don't know. Oh, Josiah!"

"Has he touched you? Has Innis hurt you, Moira?"

She slid her fingers into his hair, wanting to feel its familiar warmth, wanting to be sure of him. "Innis has been so busy trying to kill you, he hasn't even noticed me," she whispered, her mouth moving over the familiar plane of his cheek. Then her eyes fell on the open window Josiah had climbed through, and she stiffened, suddenly remembering. "Sure you must leave, Josiah! There's a guard lurking outside somewhere—"

"Tied up and gagged. He won't bother us."

"But Innis means to see you dead, Josiah. He's stopped his drinking, so he has. He's turned all his hatred and anger on you. You don't know what terrible things he's threatened!"

"Moira," Josiah whispered, tilting her chin so that he could look into blue eyes silvered by moonlight. "Moira, don't cry, now. Please don't cry. I'm here with you. I'm

safe. I knew a time like this would come. I expected it
and planned for it from the very start. Innis won't let go
of his old ways easily, but I'll hold out until he does."

"Until he does what?"

"One of these days Innis will accept that his way of
tending the land is outdated. He overstocked, overgrazed.
Thanks to his mismanagement, rainstorms cut arroyos
and lowered the water table. Moira, the native grasses
are dying back here on Fianna. Yarrow and fleabane are
taking over. Sagebrush, turpentine weed, greasewood,
too. You've seen them sprouting up, and so has he. The
man's not blind. Innis has to change his ways. And I'm
going to show him how."

"You think he'll let you live so long?" Moira cried.
"Every night I tried to make you seem real to me again,
Josiah. I tried to see your face, each angle and hollow
of it. This rough stubble on your chin, the firm skin
across your cheekbones. I tried to remember your eyes,
the brown and gold threads, the long lashes. I yearned
to touch your hair, to slip my fingers through it. But
you weren't here. I couldn't conjure you up from thin
air, Josiah. One day Innis is going to kill you, and then
I'll never have you back—not even for these brief trysts
in the night!"

Torn apart inside by her anguish, Josiah laid a gentling
finger on her lips. "Rest with me now," he said softly.
"We'll talk, and you'll see that everything's going to be
okay." He laid Moira against him, wrapping his arms
around her shoulders, cradling her head in the curve of
his neck.

She tried to calm down, but the shivering fear inside
her wouldn't leave her in peace. "Why did you build
fences, Josiah?" she asked. "God's land isn't meant to
be fenced."

"This land is in dispute, Moira. Legally Innis owns
nothing but the rights to a single stretch of waterfront
along the Peñasco. He doesn't even have title to Fianna
itself."

"Sure you can't be right about such a thing!"

"Innis never bothered to file a claim on the land. That's not so unusual. Most of the big cattle barons in the Territory haven't. John Chisum didn't, and he managed to hold two hundred miles up and down the Pecos. But that's exactly why he had so much trouble with the small ranchers and the nesters. They filed on the land. They had legal title." Josiah dipped his nose in the clean scent of Moira's auburn hair, and for a moment he drifted in the womanliness of her—that indescribable combination of strength mingled with softness, of will mingled with gentleness.

"*Our* land," he went on, "is ours. Nobody can dispute our right to it and win. It's just like my copper mines in Butte. I own the papers on them. John Fisher can't claim what he doesn't legally possess. He knows that, and it's partly why he's so angry. Innis is the same way. To safeguard my property from him, I had to build a fence, Moira. A fence is something a man can see. It's a sign that says, 'This is mine. Stay off.' I needed that. Especially with the sheep."

"Innis will never let your flocks live."

"Innis doesn't have any choice in the matter. I've got good men out there guarding my sheep. I've trained them to protect the livestock. I'm paying them better than they've ever been paid. In the long run, money is what makes a man loyal to his boss. I've got money, and plenty of it. But Innis is as broke as a hind-tit calf. Most of his punchers have already deserted him, and there's not much bluff left in the rest. I'm not afraid. I wish I could take the fear away from you."

"Oh, Josiah, hold me." She shut her eyes as his hands slipped up her back and into her hair. His body was long and hard against her, and she could feel the outline of his clothing through her nightgown. His belt buckle was cold, the buttons on his shirt sharp on her soft skin. She stretched out her bare toes and touched them to his boots, to his jeans, to his spurs. "When you're this close, I can begin to hope again. When I hear you speak, I believe. But, Josiah, when you're away from me, I slip back into the old fear, the old routine of pain. Innis is so much worse now, so much angrier."

"You won't have to live with it any longer." He took a deep breath. "Moira, I've come for you. It's nearly dawn and clear enough for us to ride out. I know it's not completely safe upriver at the house, but I'm sick and tired of living without you by my side. I want you to have your own home, the way I promised. I want you to feel like my wife instead of Innis Grady's ward. I want you to know that you've got a husband who'll look out for you and keep you safe as he swore he would. Will you come with me, Moira? Will you ride tonight?"

"Josiah, of course I will! Fisher's mended enough to be nothing but trouble. And even though Seamus hasn't come for him and the goods aren't in from Roswell, I'm not needed here, and I know I can make a home for us there. Let me slip on a dress and my shoes, and we'll be off."

Streaks of sunrise had begun to purple the ceiling as he brushed his lips across hers. "I love you, Moira."

"And I love you, Josiah." With a smile of hope she was drawing out of his arms when the door burst open and lamplight flooded the room.

"So!" Innis shouted as he stalked into the bedroom, a six-shooter in one hand and an oil lamp in the other. "So this is the thanks I get for taking you in, Moira O'Casey! I catch you playing the trollop with my own brother, do I?"

"Moira?" Scully was right behind him, followed close at heel by John Fisher and two punchers.

"What did I tell you?" Fisher crowed. "I told the guard I heard someone in the room next to mine. So, it's Chee, the thief of copper mines, the thief of pastureland . . . and the thief of hearts."

Aware of Innis's gun trained at his head, Josiah sat up and rose slowly to his feet. "Move away from the bed, Moira," he said in an even voice. "It's me they want. Don't come near. Remember your promise to stay back."

With the sickening memory of her vow to let him handle his affairs, Moira slid off the bed and hurried to the wall with the open window. She could see Josiah clearly now, the pink glow of dawn lighting his hair, his pale blue shirt, his legs spread in a defiant stance, the leather whip in his hand. Facing him only a few feet away stood Innis. Beside the Irishman, John Fisher held a second gun, a pistol aimed at Josiah's heart. Enemies united by hatred. Scully, ashen, shivering, and empty-handed, stood at the other side of his father. The two punchers—Fisher's guard and Moira's guard—brought up the rear.

"So explain yourself, brother of mine," Innis snarled. "What were you doing in bed with my ward? Trying to steal her away from me, too?"

"How could I steal her, Grady? Moira doesn't belong to you. For that matter, she doesn't belong to me either."

"How's that? From the looks of it, you've had your way with her."

"She may have shared my bed, but she's not my slave."

"What is she, then, your little tart?"

"She's his wife," Scully put in, shooting Moira the first hateful expression she'd ever seen in his green eyes. "Moira and Josiah got married in St. Louis, so they did. Moira told me. They've been husband and wife for a long time now."

"Husband and wife! Husband and wife, is it?" Innis's face went red. "By herrings, I'll hear that one from the harlot's own mouth. Moira, is it true, then? Have you gone and wedded this half-breed bastard and given him free claim to your father's lands? To half of my holdings?"

"Aye, Innis." Moira stepped forward. Her carefully rehearsed speech forgotten, she nonetheless lifted her chin and looked him square in the eye. "I married your brother. And gladly. But not so he could have the land. Josiah has never asked for one clod of dirt from my father's legacy. Though I know he would like to have it and would care for it a thousand times better than you ever did, he wouldn't demand it of me. That's why I'll freely give it to him. Every acre!"

"I'll be damned if you will!" Innis exploded.

But Moira shouted him down. "Josiah wants me for myself, not for my land and my labor. He loves me for who I am. And I've given myself to him, so I have. I dealt fairly with you, Innis, as I promised your wife I would, God rest her soul. But you're a man able to look after himself now. And Scully's grown, too. You don't need me. Nor does Josiah, for that matter. But it's him I want to spend my days with, so it is. It's him I love. It's him I'll stand by against you, Innis. I release myself from my vow."

"You release yourself, do you?" Innis shouted. "I'll release you! I'll release you from your blazing soul, then!"

He turned the gun on her and pulled the trigger. The room shattered into a thousand fragments of light, a howling whirlwind of sound. Thunder. Lightning. Pain ripped through her body. Blood spattered across her vision. She slumped against the curtain. Her legs wouldn't hold her. They crumpled beneath her. She slid to the floor.

Through a crimson halo she saw Josiah, like an angel moving so slowly she could study every ripple of his muscles, the gathered steel of his shoulders as he drew his arm back. His whip coiled, released, snapped across Innis's chest, lashed around his arm. The smoking six-shooter clattered to the floor, spun beneath a table. The oil lamp flew through the air. Smashed into John Fisher. Exploded. Set his hair aflame. Dropped dots of fire across his shoulders. His flapping arms became blazing wings.

The whip curled back again, lashed across the faces of the two punchers. Like demons frozen, they screamed. Moira couldn't hear the sound for the roaring in her ears. They covered their faces with their hands, stumbled to the floor. Fisher tumbled beside them, a hellish devil, his clothes in flames.

The whip snapped again, cutting Innis to the floor. He fell, rolled. The whip slashed through his shirt, laid his chest open to the bone. Flame caught the hem of his nightshirt. He reached for his gun. Reached under the table. The whip sliced through his back, a snake of blood. His fingers closed on the weapon, gripped the handle, curled around the trigger.

Moira opened her mouth, trying to scream. No sound, only the slow-moving scene. She remembered her parents' death by fire. Her greatest fear. She tried to reach for Josiah. Her arms wouldn't move. Couldn't. Limp, her hands lay on the floor in puddles of blood.

The whip flashed through the flames that engulfed John Fisher, that crept up the tablecloth. Up Innis's nightshirt. The whip's deadly tip flipped three times around Innis's neck. He rolled, aimed the gun. Squeezed the trigger.

Josiah fell across Innis. Again Moira tried to scream. No sound. But Josiah was moving again. Their bodies licked by fire, he and Innis wrestled across the floor, legs locked, the whip tangling them together like spiders in a thick black web. Blood flew in a scarlet arc, a bright rainbow of dots across the whitewashed wall.

Scully danced around them, his nightshirt flapping at his thighs. Red hair the color of fire bobbed down, then up. Then Scully was gone, running on white legs through the hall. Still Josiah and Innis tumbled amid the flames. The bed whooshed in a grand inferno. Quilts, pillows, once-white sheets, all blazing. Smoke billowed, black and choking.

All at once the gun flew through the air like a white-hot kernel of popcorn. It landed beside Moira. Fired a bullet randomly. Came to rest one inch from her leg. Innis and Josiah scrambled toward it, hands reaching, fingers outstretched.

Moira stared through the red fog, wanting to seize the gun herself. Unable to move. Unable to hear, to speak, to breathe. This was what it was like to die.

Scully scampered back into the room. He pitched a bucket of water on John Fisher. He pitched another on the bed. Too little, too late. He danced toward his father again, arms waving, white feet flying.

Breath wouldn't come into Moira's chest. She sucked at it with all her might. It wouldn't come. Smoke clogged her throat. Her head fell back against the curtain, weighting her down. The gun rested beside her leg, untouched. The two men, tangled in leather, writhed across the wooden floor. Now Innis was closer. Now Josiah. Moira prayed.

But Innis won. His fingers grabbed the flame-blue barrel. Jerked it toward him. Josiah reached for the handle, touched the trigger. Oh, God, the trigger!

But Innis hammered Josiah's hand into the floor. Laced his own finger through the trigger guard. Josiah twisted, buckled. The gun exploded between them.

The report of the gun was the only sound Moira heard. She slumped against the wall, unable to breathe. Smoke wrapped itself around her head, slid its fingers through her hair. Flames crept across the floor to lick at her hem.

# Chapter
## 19

White sheets, white as the soul of a sinner saved, drifted in the blue New Mexico sky. Or were they clouds? White clouds, silvered by sunshine, hovering over green mountains. Rolling mountains that drifted just over the horizon. The horizon of a wagon's side, worn wood and white bird droppings.

Moira jolted awake. Drifted asleep again. Awakened. The white moon shone overhead. Too bright. Stars were sprinkled over the sky like sugar across a black tablecloth. Sweep it up, Moira. Such a mess. Don't spill the sugar, the ants might get it. Take in the laundry, Moira. The sheets have been dry for hours.

A cool cloth on her forehead. On her eyes. A dark hand. A pale hand. Whiskey running down her throat. Bitter. Smoke drifting into her nose. No, not smoke. Dust. Trail dust. Warm grass. Sweet clover. Someone looking down at her. Who was it? The sheriff. In from Roswell. No, it was Seamus Sullivan. Up from the Pecos. Or was it Scully? Green eyes frightened, watery.

Oh, pain. Knives of pain turning and twisting. A great weight sitting on Moira's chest. Take it off. Too many covers on top. Too many quilts. Hot. Cold. Take them off. Put them on. Can't breathe.

Night. Day. Where was Josiah? Dead. Their cabin wrapped in red flames. Bloody flames. Sparks like stars rising into the black sky. Stars. Spilled sugar. Sweep it up. Put it away. Don't think about it. Don't think about him.

Awake again. Moira was lifted off the jolting wagon by warm arms. Whose arms? Josiah! Oh, he wasn't dead! Or was he? That halo hung around his head. His golden hair. A golden halo. Tears shone in his eyes. Slipped down his cheeks. His face was pale, too pale. Not Josiah after all. An angel.

"No, I don't want to live." Moira's own voice. "I could . . . *could* . . . but I don't want to. Not without Josiah."

A hard table. Bright lights. A man was looking down at her. A doctor? No, a demon. Shining a light into her eyes. Pulling back her eyelids. Opening her mouth. Putting something over her face. Something that made it hard for her to breathe. A mask. A stench. A horrible, clawing, scrabbling blackness.

"Moira?" Sheena Chee's voice came from somewhere in the soft, fluffy pillows in Moira's mind. "Moira? Can you hear me? Can you see me at all, alanna?"

Moira opened her eyes. Sheena was dabbing the corners of her eyes with a white handkerchief. Her red hair had sprung out around her head, unkempt and wiry. Her hands looked small; they were trembling.

"I'm so sorry about the lambs," Moira said.

Sheena's head snapped up, her eyes blinking back tears. "Moira!"

"Sure you mustn't weep, Sheena. Innis cut their throats in a rage against . . . against Josiah, not you. It wasn't you he hated. It was Josiah. Josiah and Innis just couldn't . . . couldn't . . ."

Confused, Moira looked around. She was in Sheena's house. The house on the Berrendo River, near Roswell. There was the oak dresser. The hooked rug. The oil lamp.

*Oil lamp.* "Saints in heaven!" Moira gasped. "John Fisher's on fire! Put out the flames!"

"There now," Sheena whispered, laying a cool hand on Moira's cheek. "It's been two weeks since the fire at Fianna. John Fisher was laid to rest long ago."

Moira stared at Sheena. Two weeks. "Fisher died?"

"Him and one of the punchers. Burned up in the room." Sheena picked at the lace on her sleeve. "The house is gone. Not the walls of course. They're adobe. But the floors, the roof."

"Fianna?" Moira tried to imagine Fianna without a house. How could that be? "Where will Innis and Scully live?"

Sheena touched the corner of her handkerchief to her eye. She sniffled, and her chin quivered. "My son is dead."

"Josiah?" Moira sat up. A pain tore through her lungs. "Josiah?"

"No, Innis." Sheena rose and eased Moira back onto the bed. She tucked the quilts around her. "Innis is dead."

"May he rest in peace." Moira said the words instinctively. But she couldn't imagine Innis dead. He had always been full of life, full of bluster, blarney, fury, willpower. "Was he burned?" Moira asked.

Sheena shook her head. "Shot."

Moira remembered the blast of the gun between the two men. "Where's Josiah?"

Sheena squeezed her eyes shut. For a moment she couldn't speak. Tears rolled down her cheeks, and suddenly she looked old. An old woman, burdened and scarred. "Josiah," she whispered, "is in jail."

"Jail! But why? Where?"

"In Roswell. He's accused of killing Innis. He's being held for murder."

Moira stared at Sheena. *Murder.* No, that wasn't right. That was not the way it had happened. Innis had been holding the gun. Innis had had his finger on the trigger. Innis had shot himself.

"After Innis was killed," Sheena was saying, her voice thin and frail, "Josiah carried you out of the house. Scully and the other puncher crawled out, too. Everything was in flames. Scully battled the fire as hard as he could. He lost his eyebrows and part of his hair in his efforts. It wasn't an hour before Seamus Sullivan rode up with the sheriff. Scully told them how Fisher and the puncher had burned up and how Josiah had shot Innis—"

"No! Josiah didn't shoot Innis!" Moira sat up again, this time ignoring the pain in her chest. "They fought for the gun. Innis had it. It went off between them. Innis shot himself, Sheena!"

She shook her head. "No, Scully says—"

"Scully's lying! Josiah didn't shoot Innis. I was there, only inches away. I saw Innis take the gun. I saw his finger on the trigger just before the gun went off."

Sheena swallowed. "Are you sure, Moira?"

"I would swear to it with my life."

"But you'd been shot through the chest. You had a bullet in your lung. Scully said you weren't even conscious."

"*I* was shot?" Moira lifted a hand and touched her chest. As her fingers found the smooth bandage she recalled the moment when Innis turned the six-shooter on her. "Innis shot me," she whispered. "Now I remember."

"Oh, God! Innis shot you?" Sheena buried her face in her hands. Sobs racked her small body, shaking her shoulders. "Oh, God!"

"Sheena?" Gabriel strode into the room and gathered his wife in his arms. "*Mi amor,*" he whispered. "*Mi amorcita.*"

"I'm sorry," Moira said, reaching for the kindly woman. "Oh, Sheena, I'm sorry."

Gabriel lifted his wife from the chair and led her out into another room where her other sons waited anxiously, their faces pale and drawn. When Gabriel returned, he sat down by Moira and took her hand.

"A woman loves her children," he said, "no matter what sins they commit. My wife's pain is as great as yours."

"I'm sorry," Moira repeated, devastated that she had inadvertently wounded Sheena. "I suddenly remembered everything, and I blurted it out without thinking. But, Gabriel, you must go to the sheriff! You must tell him the truth about Josiah. He didn't kill Innis. He didn't even have the gun. Please, go! Please—"

"María, this is not so simply resolved." Gabriel took off his hat and wiped the back of his hand across his forehead. "Josiah is in jail, accused of the murder of his brother. Men say Josiah married you to steal your land from Innis, and when Innis challenged him, he paid for it with his life. The trial before Judge Lovell is set for next week. Scully is the primary witness."

"But I told you—"

"You're Josiah's wife! Of course you would defend him, María. That's what the justice will say."

"And Scully is Innis's son. Of course he would defend his father."

Gabriel shrugged. "You'll both speak, I'm sure. But your account will hold no weight. You'd been shot through the chest, María. Your lung had collapsed. When Josiah carried you from the house, you were unconscious. When Seamus and the sheriff arrived, you were still unconscious. You were unconscious all the way to Fort Stanton in the wagon, all through your operation, and all the way here to the Berrendo settlement. You've been unconscious for two weeks, María. And you expect the judge to believe you saw and can remember every detail of what happened in that smoke-filled room?"

Moira shut her eyes. Her chest ached. "I did see it. I know Josiah didn't kill Innis."

Gabriel let out a sigh. "I'll send Peter for the sheriff. You can tell him what you witnessed. You can try to save Josiah from the hangman's noose. But in the court, María, the justice's eyes will be on Scully Grady."

The small frame-sided clapboard hotel in Roswell housed Scully Grady and the injured puncher, the two sworn witnesses to the death of Innis Grady, John Fisher, and Scrub Williams, the other cowpuncher. Sheena had invited her grandson to stay at her house, but he refused to come. Instead, Scully holed up in the hotel and painted pictures.

But Seamus Sullivan came. One afternoon two days before Josiah's trial he rode his horse into the yard of the Chee homestead. Moira could see him through the window of her bedroom where she lay crocheting the edging for a pillowcase.

"Moira," Sheena said, pushing open the door. "Mister Sullivan's here asking to see you. Shall I send him in?"

"I'll come out," Moira answered. "Will you help me walk, Sheena?"

The older woman smiled, a sad smile that touched Moira's heart. "Sure I'll help you, my love. Come with me now. But don't wear yourself out. Remember, you're still a frainey."

Together the two made their way out of the bedroom and into the living area. As they entered, Seamus stood, a towering black-haired man holding his hat clumsily in his big hands.

"God save you, Missus Chee," he said in greeting.

"God save you kindly, Mister Sullivan." She settled on the cushioned bench and drew her shawl tightly around her shoulders.

"How are you getting on?" he asked.

"Finely and poorly. And you?"

"About the same." He sat down and began to turn the

brim of his hat. "I'm glad to see you up and about."

"I'll mend." Moira cleared her throat. "Mister Sullivan—"

"Missus Chee—" he said at the same time. "Uh, pardon me."

Moira looked out the window. The hills were crowned with great black clouds, the surprising blessing of promised rain. Taking a deep breath, she turned back to Seamus. "I wrote you a letter to come after John Fisher," she said. "And also to bring the sheriff so that he could tend to the troubles at Fianna."

"I'm sorry we were too late."

"So be it." Moira studied her hands for a moment. "There was a third reason I sent for you, Mister Sullivan. It concerns my sister."

Seamus pulled an envelope from his pocket. "I have a letter here from Erinn. It's addressed to you. The post office had it in Roswell, and when I went in to collect my mail . . . well, they gave it to me. They supposed that Erinn and I were . . . that we were still together. I've brought it for you."

Standing, he quickly stuffed it in Moira's hands, then sat down again and stared at the empty fireplace. Moira turned the letter over in her hands.

"Erinn." Moira sighed, studying the bold hand that had penned her name in slashing letters across the white envelope. "Seamus, it's Erinn we must speak of."

He lifted his blue eyes. "Aye."

"I wish to beg your forgiveness for helping her to run away from you. She told me things. Lies, they were. I know that now, but I didn't at the time. I didn't understand. I was blinded by her. She persuaded me to help her, and I did. I loved her so. I do yet. But there's a wickedness in Erinn that only God can mend. It was through her I was led to sin against you. Seamus Sullivan, I plead for your forgiveness."

He slumped in the seat and hung his head. For a moment he could say nothing. Then he spoke in a low voice. "Sure I never thought to see myself a broken man, Moira. I thought myself as strong and bold as this new country. But Erinn made me a vow, and she violated it." He lifted his eyes to Moira's face. "I received word from the Church a few days ago. The marriage has been annulled. It's as though we were never wed."

"I'm so sorry, Seamus," Moira whispered. "So sorry!"

"Sure I don't blame you. Put that out of your head. You have my forgiveness for your small part in it. And I'll go on. I have my work, my land. I'll make myself a good life. But not with a wife by my side. That part of me is dead."

Lowering her head, Moira slit open the letter from Erinn. She read in silence, expecting to hear that her sister had run off and married the librarian. Instead Erinn had written about Seamus, about the annulment and her relief to be done with it all. She wrote, too, about the nuns and Father Murphy, but her words were tinged with gratitude and affection rather than anger. And then, at the end, she had penned a message that rocked Moira to the core.

"I'm leaving St. Ferdinand's in a week's time," Erinn wrote. "I'm going to enter the university in St. Louis, where I'll study to become a doctor. Yes, I know it seems odd, almost unthinkable. Selfish Erinn, a healer? Impossible. But I want to learn, Moira. I want to be challenged. The most difficult field I could think of was medicine, so I chose it. I want to grow beyond my petty, greedy little self. Do you think I may have heard too many sermons?"

Moira had to smile. Not too many, she thought. But perhaps nearly enough. "Erinn means to go to the university," she told Seamus. "She wants to become a doctor."

He shook his head, then gave a rueful smile. "That I would like to see." He put on his hat and stood up. "I've visited Josiah, Moira. He's well, but he worries about you."

"Oh, please go to him again. Tell him . . . tell him I miss him. Tell him I'm thinking of him, praying for him. Tell him I'll go to court and speak for him. I'll tell the truth."

Seamus stopped her. "Moira, there's nothing you can do. The puncher was blinded by Josiah's whip. He didn't see who pulled the trigger. You're Josiah's wife, and just as blind to what happened there in the house. No, the whole burden of proof is in Scully's hands."

"But Scully has always defended his father! Scully is blind to Innis's faults, don't you see? It never mattered what Innis did—how hard he beat us, how viciously he abused us. Scully always stood up for him."

"And he'll stand up for his father in court. You must accept that."

"Why should Scully's word hold more weight than mine?"

"Because you're the defendant's wife. And because you're . . . well, you're a woman. Scully Grady is a man."

Moira gritted her teeth at the harsh truth in Seamus's words. "But if Scully testifies against him, Josiah will hang! Scully heard the arguments between his father and Josiah. He'll repeat Innis's accusations. Scully wanted to marry me himself, so he'll tell Justice Lovell that Josiah wedded me in order to claim my father's land. Innis accused Josiah of coveting Fianna by right of their mother, Sheena. Scully will testify that Josiah killed Innis to get Fianna. Josiah has no hope, Seamus!"

The tall man gazed at Moira, his blue eyes gentle. "Then you must let him go. Just as I've learned to let go of my wife, you must learn to free your heart of your husband. Turn away, Moira. Turn away. There's no hope for Josiah. None at all."

Seamus Sullivan's predictions came true. Moira sat in the courtroom with Sheena, Gabriel, and their four sons, all of them equally helpless to save the life of the man they loved—husband, son, brother. The rest of the room was filled with the curious—Irish ranchers, their wives, friends of the Chee family. The sweating, straining throng leaned forward to hear every word of the testimony by which the jury would decide Josiah's fate.

Josiah waited in a chair, his strong wrists shackled by handcuffs, as the prosecuting attorney called men forward one by one to speak against the defendant. The surviving cowpuncher told how Josiah had crept up on him in the night, beaten, gagged, and bound him so he could slip inside the house at Fianna to murder Innis Grady.

Other punchers testified that Josiah intended to be king of the Peñasco Valley at any cost. They called him a renegade, a thief who had stolen land that didn't belong to him, a cold-blooded killer who had hired a band of Mexican roughnecks who were as bloodthirsty as he was. They said Josiah had armed his men with lethal weapons and had trained them to be killers. They told how Josiah was bringing sheep onto the land.

*Sheep*! The Irishmen in the crowd gasped and began to grumble.

Josiah had stalked Innis Grady to his death, the punchers said. Innis owned land Josiah wanted. Innis was the only barrier to Josiah's dreams. So Josiah had calmly burned down Innis's house and shot him to death.

As if that wasn't enough to tie the noose around Josiah's neck, men from Roswell—shopkeepers and saloon owners—stood to recollect the visit of John Fisher. Yes, they admitted, Fisher had visited them asking after Josiah Chee. Fisher stated that Chee stole a packet of mining claim titles from him. These claims were worth hundreds of thousands of dollars. Fisher had called Josiah a thief, a liar, a demon who would stop at nothing to get what he wanted.

But the worst moment Moira experienced was when Scully took the stand. How many years had she known

Renegade Flame                          331

and loved the boy? She could recall a thousand meals
she'd fed him, a thousand times she'd ruffled that springy
red hair, a thousand times she'd listened to his dreams of
becoming a famous painter.

He was wearing a shirt she'd sewn for him. She'd polished those boots. She'd mended his britches, shortened
them and then lengthened them again as he grew. She
had held Scully's hand on his way to school during the
few weeks a year he'd been able to attend. She'd slipped
into his room and rocked him to ease away his nightmares after his mother died. Together they had hunted
for turkey eggs, climbed trees, teased Erinn. Moira had
helped Scully gather chunks of coal from the fire so
he could draw his first sketches. She'd saved her own
butter money to buy his first set of watercolors. She had
praised his portraits of sausage-fingered women without
batting an eye.

She had loved Scully. She still did.

"Aye," he told the attorney, "Josiah Chee and my
father had harsh words from the very beginning. We
took Josiah in when he was wounded and nearly dead,
so we did. He was my father's half brother, but he . . .
he argued with my father all the same."

"Did you ever see him strike your father, Innis
Grady?"

"Aye, that first time he was living with us at Fianna.
He and my father got into a bit of a scuffle, so they did.
The next thing we knew, Josiah pulled out that whip of
his and lashed Papa's hand with it."

*To keep him from striking me!* Moira wanted to scream.
*Scully, tell the truth! Oh, please, boy, tell the truth.*

"So you saw Josiah actually beat your father. Did you
ever hear him threaten your father with words?"

"Aye, that I did. Josiah said Moira didn't belong to
Papa, even though she was his ward. Legally, too. Josiah
told Papa if he ever touched Moira, he'd kill him."

A collective gasp ran through the courtroom. Moira
buried her face in her hands. *Tell it the right way,*

*Scully*, she pleaded silently. *For God's sake, tell the whole truth!*

"So you saw Josiah whip your father, Mister Grady," the lawyer said, "and you heard him threaten to kill your father. Now tell me exactly what happened on the morning of your father's death."

Scully squared his shoulders. "I was asleep when Papa came into my room and kicked . . . kicked me . . . and told me to get up or he'd . . . he'd beat my brains out." Scully gulped and went on. "He said Josiah Chee was down in Moira's room, and he was . . . was with her . . . in bed . . . even though I'd asked her to marry me."

Moira looked at Scully, and he returned the gaze. His green eyes went hard and cold. "Moira should have married me. I needed her, so I did. She was . . ." He sagged, and the ice in his gaze melted. "She was always good to me. She protected me from . . . from trouble. She looked out for me."

"So you and your father went downstairs."

"Sure Papa grabbed his six-shooter and said he'd kill that half-breed son of a—" Scully sucked in breath. His eyes darted to his grandmother. "Papa thought Josiah meant to take Fianna away from him. From me."

"And then you went downstairs to Missus Chee's room and found them together. What happened then, Mister Grady?"

Scully tore his eyes from his grandmother and looked at the attorney. "Papa and Josiah began to fight. Josiah started whipping him. The oil lamp crashed onto John Fisher, and he caught fire. Then Papa fell down and Josiah kept whipping him until his skin was cut down to the bone and the whole room was in flames and . . ." Scully bent over and hid his face on his knees, covering his head with his hands.

The attorney tapped his tablet with one hand. "And then, Mister Grady? Did Josiah take the six-shooter from your fallen father and kill him with it?"

Scully sobbed. Unable to speak, he huddled farther into himself.

Moira gripped the chair in front of her. *No, Scully! Be strong, boy! Tell the truth.*

Slowly Scully stood, leaning on the rail, his shoulders bent. He sniffled, pulled a handkerchief from his pocket and rubbed his nose. "J-Josiah," he wept, "Josiah—"

"Now then, young fella," the judge said softly, "tell your tale."

Scully lifted his head. He looked at Moira and straightened his shoulders. "Josiah shot and killed my father, Innis Grady."

When the prosecution rested, Moira knew Josiah's only hope rested with her. The defense attorney called her to the witness stand, and Gabriel Chee helped her across the floor. As she told what she remembered of that fateful night, she looked at Josiah, seeing him fully for the first time since he had climbed through the window into her room. How he had changed! Thinner, drawn with concern, his face had lost the bronzed glow of health. His eyes were so dark, so deepset, she thought they looked like pools of hunger, of aching need. His broad shoulders were forced into a slump by the tight manacles on his wrists.

After her testimony, the prosecution chose to cross-examine her.

"Josiah didn't kill Innis," she reiterated, her eyes ablaze. "I swear it! I was there the whole time, so I was. I saw everything that happened. Sure I lay wounded only inches from the gun, sir. Innis grabbed it and killed himself in their struggle! He was trying to shoot Josiah. I saw it all with my own two eyes, so I did."

"Missus Chee, I have sworn statements here from everyone who was on the scene, and I have a letter from the doctor at Fort Stanton, too. You'd been shot. You couldn't speak, couldn't move, couldn't hear. You were unconscious, ma'am. You couldn't have seen a thing."

"But I did!"

"Please, Missus Chee. Allow me to continue."

Moira clasped her hands. "Aye," she whispered, feeling manacled herself. "Forgive me."

"Moving on, then. Did you ever receive from Mister Chee an envelope of papers for safekeeping?"

Moira nodded. "The mine claims. But they belong to Josiah. Just ask Paddy Connor, his partner in Butte. The claims are all legal."

"That's for the jury to decide, Missus Chee. Do you have the papers with you now?"

Moira blanched. "They were at the house at Fianna. I suppose they . . . they must have burned."

Impassive, the squire made a mark on his tablet. "Thank you, then. No more questions, your honor."

"But—" Moira's eyes flew to Josiah as the sheriff took her arm and helped her down from the witness stand. Before she could say anything, she was seated beside the Chee family, being gently warned by the sheriff that if she spoke out of turn again, she'd have to be removed from the courtroom.

Then the judge rose. "The court will recess for lunch," he said, slamming the wooden gavel on his table. "The prosecution has requested to place a rebuttal witness on the stand. When we reconvene, we will hear again from the son of the deceased, Scully Grady."

Moira's empty stomach churned as she watched Scully walk across the courtroom and step onto the witness stand. The prosecuting attorney questioned the youth about Moira's presence in the room the night of Innis's death—a clear attempt to prove that she had lied about witnessing the incident.

"Papa shot Moira," Scully said. He rubbed a finger in the corner of one red-rimmed eye. "He had killed her, I thought. She was unarmed, standing there in her nightgown, ballyragging him as usual—and he turned the gun on her and shot her in the chest."

"You saw her fall?"

"Aye. And there was . . . blood . . . all over her white gown."

"Did Missus Chee ever call out or move again during the remainder of the incident?"

"No." Scully sniffled. "She just lay there, so she did . . . bleeding. Before Papa could shoot her again, Josiah whipped the gun away. But Papa fell on it. He tried to . . . to kill Josiah."

"Please focus on the role of Moira Chee—"

"She was lying beside the curtain. They fought, rolled across the floor, and got tangled up in the whip. Everything was in flames. I ran for a bucket of water. When I got back, they were both crawling across the floor after the gun. It lay right beside Moira's leg. She was . . ."

Scully looked up. His eyes met Moira's. She caught her breath. *Yes! Yes, tell them, Scully! Tell how it really was!*

"Moira was watching Papa and Josiah, so she was," he said firmly. "She couldn't speak or move, but her eyes were wide open."

"What?" the attorney cut in. "Now, wait a minute! That's not what—"

"No, Moira saw it all." Scully looked at her and gave a weak grin. Then he turned back to the lawyer and squared his shoulders. "Josiah grabbed the gun, but Papa pounded his hand away and took it himself. The gun got buried between the two of them. It was my father, Innis Grady, who pulled the trigger. And it was him who took the bullet. He meant to kill Moira. He meant to kill Josiah, too. But in the end, he killed himself."

Scully pointed across the room as he spoke to the gathered crowd. "Josiah Chee is as good a man as can be found in the Peñasco Valley. He's honest, loyal, and kind. Maybe he does run sheep, and maybe he plans to fence in the range, but he's a fair man. Moira says he means to bring the land back to life. I believe he will."

For a moment these last revelations silenced the courtroom. Then the prosecuting attorney requested permission of the court to treat Scully as a hostile witness for the purpose of impeaching his testimony. Judge Lovell denied the lawyer's request to try to attack Scully's credibility. When the defense attorney took the floor, he moved to dismiss the case based on the failure of the prosecution to prove beyond a reasonable doubt that Josiah Chee had murdered Innis Grady.

The judge nodded and said, "Based on the testimony before this court, I have no alternative but to direct a verdict of acquittal in favor of the defendant. Mister Chee, you're free to go."

Gabriel Chee let out a loud whoop. A second later, the place erupted in hollers of joy from the Chee brothers, a thunder of clapping from the watching men, and a burst of tears from Sheena Chee and her friends.

For the second time in her life, Moira was rendered speechless. Scully, beaming from ear to ear, looked for all the world like a grown-up man ready to start living his own life. He made his way to Josiah, and Moira heard the breathless exchange.

"I'm offering you Fianna in trade for a one-way ticket to New York, and then to Paris, where I'll study art," Scully said. "If all the other grand Irishmen in this room can follow their elegant rainbows to the pot of gold, then I can too, by japers. Is it a deal, Mister Chee?"

Josiah gazed at the boy, the first flush of color in his cheeks. "It's a deal, Scully lad," he returned. "And I'll buy the biggest painting at your first exhibition."

In the next moment the sheriff unlocked Josiah's shackles. His brothers slapped him on the back. His mother slipped her arms around his waist. His father clasped him in a bear hug. Yet his brown eyes were on Moira. Like the angel he had seemed to be on the night of the terrible fire, he came slowly toward her, slowly moving through the crowd, slowly reaching out to her.

She couldn't stand. Couldn't move. Couldn't hear. Couldn't speak. But she could see him, his hands stretched toward her, his face filled with an aching love, his whole body straining to reach her.

"Josiah," she said.

"Oh, my love." He caught her shoulders; his fingers slid into her hair. She rose into the warm circle of his arms. Closing her eyes, she laid her head on his shoulder and drifted in the sweet stroke of his lips across her ear.

"Take me home," she whispered.

"A home of our own. A stone house with a grand fireplace and two bedrooms. A kitchen with three cupboards. A pine table. A stove with a teapot warmer."

"Orchards," she continued, "laden with apples, cherries, apricots. Fields of sweet green alfalfa. Cattle grazing on the hillsides. And sheep. Thousands of glorious woollies."

He laughed. "Mutton stew for dinner. A spinning wheel humming beside the fire. And warm wool sweaters in the winter for all our sons and daughters."

"A fine long clothesline," Moira finished, her Irish eyes smiling, "stretched from a pecan tree to a cottonwood. And sheets dancing in the mountain breeze . . . spotless white sheets . . . shining as bright as all our tomorrows."

# AUTHOR'S NOTE

I owe my deepest thanks to the following: Lynn Koenig, for her assistance in my research of the Peñasco Valley and the sheep and cattle ranchers there; Sandra Brown of Southwest Baptist University's Estep Library, for information on whips; Kim White of Hagerman, for her guided tour of a settler family's homestead and school and for the loan of research materials regarding the Peñasco Valley; Sylvia Johnson, for the trip up the Peñasco Valley and for her information on household implements and furnishings of the 1880s; Nita Harrell, for the adventure on the Berrendo River; and Andy Bennett, for assistance with legal clarifications.

These and many other excellent sources provided information for the historical background of *Renegade Flame*:

Atherton, Lewis. *The Cattle Kings.* Indiana Univ. Press, 1961.

Frantz, Joe B. and Julian Ernest Choate, Jr. *The American Cowboy: The Myth and the Reality.* Univ. of Oklahoma Press, 1955.

Hinkle, James F. *Early Days of a Cowboy on the Pecos.* The Stagecoach Press, 1965.

Monaghan, Jay, ed. *The Book of the American West.* Messner, Inc., 1963.

Morgan, David W. *Whips and Whipmaking.* Cornell Maritime Press, 1972.

Schmitt, Martin and Dee Brown. *The Settlers' West.* Bonanza Books.

White, Richard. *"It's Your Misfortune and None of My Own": A History of the American West.* Univ. of Oklahoma Press, 1991.

Williams, Ernestine Chesser. *Echoes Break the Silence.*
————. *Treasures of History.*

*If you enjoyed this book, take advantage of this special offer. Subscribe now and get a*

# FREE
## *Historical Romance*

*No Obligation ( a $4.50 value )*

Each month the editors of True Value select the four *very best* novels from America's leading publishers of romantic fiction. Preview them in your home *Free* for 10 days. With the first four books you receive, we'll send you a FREE book as our introductory gift. No Obligation!

If for any reason you decide not to keep them, just return them and owe nothing. If you like them as much as we think you will, you'll pay just $4.00 each and save at *least* $.50 each off the cover price. (Your savings are *guaranteed* to be at least $2.00 each month.) There is NO postage and handling – or other hidden charges. There are no minimum number of books to buy and you may cancel at any time.

### *Send in the Coupon Below*

To get your FREE historical romance fill out the coupon below and mail it today. As soon as we receive it we'll send you your FREE Book along with your first month's selections.